DARING

A novel by

O. S. ADAM

Every copy sold provides another donation for the
incredible charity that is 'Robbie's Rehab' - this amazing
community, a charity and service that helps children with
brain tumours, can be found online and on facebook -
www.facebook.com/robbiesrally

About Robbie's Rehab
- a charity and service that helps children with brain tumours

Robbie Keville said goodbye to his mummy, Kate, when she died suddenly after a recurrence of breast cancer. He was just 6. Then and there he decided to become a doctor. Possessing a good mind, there was no doubt that he would realise his ambition one day. However, two years later, Robbie himself was diagnosed with cancer: a malignant brain tumour.

Through the months and years of painful surgery, radiotherapy and chemotherapy, Robbie never lost his sense of wanting to help those like him and his mummy. A great favourite of the NHS staff at Southampton and Basingstoke hospitals, Robbie was asked to star in a video on paediatric radiotherapy. When the children's cancer ward schoolroom was refurbished, it was Robbie who was asked to cut the ribbon at the grand opening.

The charity was his idea. His doctors told Robbie's family where the money was needed and Robbie's Rehab was formed. Now the service runs out of Southampton Hospital providing outpatient and at-home rehabilitation to children with brain tumours from 12 allied hospitals in the South of England.

Robbie saw the early fundraising and had a wonderful time designing logos and coming up with ideas of 'Robbie's' events. There have been more than 60 such events and these along with many other activities have raised, at the time of writing, £675,000 for the children who now receive the treatment they need. It is free at the point of delivery - just like the NHS itself.

Robbie's family were very happy that Robbie managed to attend the first ever event and wave the chequered flag at the crazy car race that was Robbie's Rally. However, despite the best efforts of dedicated NHS staff, Robbie died in 2016 aged 10.

I was fortunate enough to go to school with Robbie's elder brother and sister, who are, by all accounts, the most remarkable individuals. I am honoured to be allowed to play a small part in their fundraising efforts.

For the hero that is my mother, who not only gave me life
but, twenty-four years later, saved it.
None of this would exist without you.

PROLOGUE

Cleo had known from the outset that this was going to be the biggest trial of her life so far. She could not afford to lose this case. After all, she had a lot riding on its outcome.

In the middle of the room, almost silent save for the din of the evening traffic outside and the soft regular breathing of the defendant sat behind her - who seemed determined, despite her endless cajoling, to slouch - Cleo contemplated the deal she had made with the prosecution the night before. The prosecution, on this occasion, was being represented by a lawyer who had beaten her at seven of the last eight trials that they had been pitted against one another. He could not beat her again, she thought scratching at her palm.

Momentarily oblivious to her surroundings, having succumbed to the constricting panic of losing, Cleo considered whether the deal was good enough. Would Chief Crown Prosecutor Claudius May honour it? Of course he would. He always had before. But one dilemma still troubled her - she had yet to convince him of the defendant's innocence and, although not something she would openly admit to, his opinion mattered more than any jury's.

The witness sat at the stand by the window. Hunched. Quiet. His pointed nose, copper hair and crossed, glassy eyes stared furiously back into Cleo's own determinedly steady gaze. She knew she had him, and if she had him, she would have Claudius.

Cleo felt like she could breathe for the first time, as she stepped up to stand before the witness, all prior panic gone. It was as though a weight had been lifted from her shoulders. Her vision was clear. Her case was strong. She would win.

'Will the record reflect that the witness has identified the defendant?' Cleo allowed herself a small smile - the witness shouldn't have been able to do that. 'The truth remains, Monsieur Renard, that you killed Henrietta. You killed her and then blamed it on Mr Blackstone.' Hearing his name the defendant cocked his head and turned his big, drooping hazel eyes on Cleo who had turned back to look at him. His long tongue brushed lazily across his lips.

Cleo returned her attention to the assembled jury and Monsieur Renard, 'But you hadn't planned on me finding out about Mrs Cheep, and you certainly hadn't—'

Before she could finish, the door at the back of the room burst open, scattering the carefully assembled spectators who had filled the rear two rows of the courthouse. A loud wailing emanated from its rusted hinges. Cleo turned to the intruder, red faced and furious. Her shoulders fell as she recognised the short, rounded frame of Burt Whittle.

His face, already heavily lined and dominated by a twisted grey-white beard, wrinkled further as he rubbed it with a spotted hand. His expression was balanced between fatigue and distress, but Cleo did not notice this at first. Around her the room had descended into utter chaos. Blackstone, clearly no longer content to leave his fate in the hands of the jury, had broken free from his poorly constructed restraints and, capitalising on Cleo's momentary distraction, had made a bolt for the open door. Three soldiers, in pillar-box-red uniforms, who had been silently observing from the front benches with painted frowns, hurtled backwards as he trampled over them.

Sulking, Cleo returned to her chair and crossed her arms tightly. She would not look at Burt until he had apologised. Instead she spoke over her shoulder, 'Mr Whittle, you're interrupting the trial. Perverting the course of justice and, to top it off, it appears you've let the defendant get away.'

'Does the prosecution not have to be present for a trial?'

'The prosecution is late,' Cleo pouted, 'as always.'

Cleo had considered Claudius' absence to be a small advantage during her cross-examination of Monsieur Renard. Claudius usually dazzled the jury - and her - unfairly, but she was sure this time she had worked out a watertight case. Discovered the truth behind the crime and unequivocally identified the culprit.

'Cleo, I need to talk to you,' Burt continued. His gruff voice, broken by too many cigarettes, caught in the back of his throat.

'Not here,' Cleo hissed scowling at Monsieur Renard who was still perched by the window.

'Cleopatra! I need a few minutes.'

Cleo turned and stared hard at Burt. He rarely demanded anything of her which made his request all the more unsettling. She continued to stare until, after closer inspection, she noticed that his flabby eyelids were red and blotchy. Not wanting to be held responsible for his apparent distress, she took him gently by the hand and led him from the room.

Holding her small, soft hand tightly, Burt followed the young lawyer out into the corridor and down the hallway. He listened as she hummed a melancholy tune, the noise of which was the only sound to fill the terraced house. It was not the first time Burt had witnessed one of her "trials." He had found himself a witness, a juror, a judge and even a defendant when the last Quality Street chocolate had disappeared two Christmases previously. Monsieur Renard, the weaselling one-eyed stuffed Fox from a second hand shop in Truro had been the witness in that case. Vaguely, wanting a distraction, Burt wondered if now that the Fox had been found guilty of murdering Cleo's favourite velveteen chicken, if there was cause for an appeal? Mis-trial? Re-trial? He didn't know. Tonight, the only thing he was certain of, was that he would have to step up now and learn some things about the law. She would need him to. The trouble was, Burt hadn't learned a lot in school and hadn't learnt much more after. Besides fishing, a subject which he knew a great deal about, he was no academic. This fact however did not make him a fool. Instead, he had been bestowed with the types of skills not recognised by college exam boards. He possessed the unquantifiable virtues that came from the soul, or perhaps formed it. Where Claudius was concerned, Burt's principles were secure and his heart was as golden as they came.

Unusually, Cleo had been prosecuting the case of the stolen chocolate herself, instead of her father, who had presided as Judge on that occasion - a judge who with a wink to his little girl had sided with her every argument. Claudius May had been a friend of Burt's since the day they had met at his wife's funeral. Burt had known the late Mrs May since she was a child not much older than Cleo was now and knowing the woman chosen to be Cleo's mother, how well she would have suited the role, how much she would have enjoyed it, how much Cleo had needed her, made her absence harder to stomach every time he held the hand of the motherless child humming innocently before him.

Despite this, Burt thought Claudius had done alright with the lass. He had never missed a birthday, despite all the missed bedtimes. And had, rather successfully, navigated a life of unintended duality from the moment he had left the woman who had born the child, to the loss of the woman he had loved. He had played both mother and father. Parent and friend. The feared chief crown prosecutor of London South and staunch defender of the courthouse in Cleo's bedroom.

They remained in silence, save Cleo's soft humming, until they had arrived at the kitchen. Blackstone wagged a frantic hello. The large St Bernard looked longingly from

Burt to his empty food bowl and back again. Burt was not sure how long the dog had been kept waiting for his dinner.

'You know what date it is?' Cleo piped, dragging the closest kitchen chair up alongside the counter.

Burt did not answer. He merely stared into the drooped gaze of Blackstone, searching for words he could not find.

Cleo bustled on seemingly unaware. 'December 17th,' she stated, climbing onto the chair. The tins, hidden high above her head in the top cupboard, rustled as she searched for the right one. 'So… Dad got us these,' she beamed, holding a tin of Quality Street chocolates. Thrusting the purple tin into Burt's open hands she carried on speaking, 'Well you can open them. So then whatever you've been crying about, we can forget over a strawberry cream.'

Burt looked at Cleo, meeting her wide-eyed, hopeful stare, and set to work opening the chocolate box. The tin let out a satisfying pop as the lid gave way and, encouraged by his cooperation, Cleo grabbed the box back.

Spilling the jewelled contents onto the kitchen table, she began rummaging through the pile. 'Also, where's Marta?' Cleo asked. Having found what she had been looking for, she held a shining scarlet-wrapped chocolate out to Burt, 'May the best of your past be the worst of your future.'

Accepting the gift, Burt almost fell onto the kitchen table, his legs had gone weak beneath him. Marta, the kindly Spanish neighbour who had routinely watched over Cleo when her father hadn't been able to make it home, another concerned party trying to ease the strain of Claudius's own brand of single-parenting, had phoned

6

Burt a few hours before. He had excused her as soon as he had arrived. Her services would no longer be required tonight.

In fact, Burt realised, starting to drown in the crushing truth of what had transpired, Marta would never again be called upon to wait for Claudius to return from work. She would no longer prepare dinner while Cleo played in her makeshift courthouse. No longer see the child's glee, no matter the hour, at being embraced in her father's arms when he had finally made it home. Claudius May would not be late home ever again. No, he would not be late, he would simply never come home at all.

THIRTEEN AND A HALF YEARS
LATER

ONE

He was alone, silently moving across a checkered marble floor, a single chess piece, long forgotten, skirting the memory of a once loved game. The air was frozen, his breath a broken stream of mist that marked his path. The silken soles of his naked feet were cold as he crept through the cloying darkness. Bitterly cold. He shivered. Looking up, high walls adorned with art surrounded him. Canvases hung too high to see. Instead, he could only make out the bottoms of the heavy, gilded frames. Intricately carved. Expensive.

He looked forward again. He was in the next room. A new room. Still marble. Still cold. He was still silent, his view now partially obscured, hidden behind a solid wooden object. The pained wail of a chair falling made him jump and he hugged closer to the wooden object. Dissolving into a shadowed sanctuary. A desk. The awareness that he was an unwelcome spectator saturated his body. Two men stood over a third before him. They didn't know he was there, watching them with potent horror. The third was kneeling now. Something about his movement was strangely comforting. Familiar.

A knife gleamed in the darkness, its blade capturing the moon outside. He wanted to scream, he opened his mouth. He thought better of it. A voice broke the silence. His voice? No. A foreign voice. Unfamiliar. Something about a cat? Gato? Gloves? Ratones? Mice? Two pale eyes floated toward him. He knew those eyes. Whose eyes were those eyes? But they were alien to him now. Unburnished. Life extinguished. The once comforting familiarity turned to sickness.

Rain started to pour from above. He shivered in his now sodden clothes. *It never rained here?* His subconscious gave way a little. The image dissipated, the rain turned to petals. He was surrounded by a mass of soft white petals. The mass was growing exponentially. He was drowning in them.

Adrenaline.

His subconscious collapsed.

He woke up.

* * *

Raphael rubbed his face as he sat up. The realities of his situation slowly returned as he stretched out his arms, his muscles welcoming their release. He had been sweating heavily and his makeshift bunk, that had been

10

supporting his back against the ever shifting desert terrain, was wet through. Squinting in the darkness he checked his watch. Four green numbers glowed faintly in the gloom. One hour to go. Raphael inhaled deeply before rising from the bunk. Flushing his lungs with cool air, briefly enjoying the refreshment soon to be lost to the heat of the approaching day.

His legs were stiff from six weeks of reconnaissance work. His days having been marked by innumerable hikes, climbing up and down the never ending, sheer-sided sand dunes, and his calves protested in vain as he bent to retie his boots. He fought the remnants of the dream that had stirred him and that was still, despite his now conscious mind, clawing at his brain.

The desert had remorselessly assaulted his body, but he knew the unparalleled importance of keeping a clear head, the requisite duty of compartmentalising everything and anything distracting, unnecessary or even, something he had taken a while to perfect, emotive. The dream, the strangely familiar dead eyes, the absent cat, the flowers were nothing new to Raphael. The same dream, or nightmare, had haunted him since he was seventeen and he would, as he had always done, banish it once more to the coming day. Stubbornly ignoring the knowledge sure within him, that the dreams were getting worse.

After brushing off his ballistic helmet, a moulded piece of fawn-coloured plastic that was once again layered with a film of desert dust, Raphael fastened it back on his head. He cursed the fine grains of sand that, despite his brushing, still found their way into his eyes. The helmet was snug and the pressure on his temples provided a subtle promise of safety, creating a barrier between him and the world outside. He had seen the kit fail enough times to be certain of its limitations, but that wasn't how you thought once deployed. Trust in the kit. Trust in your men. Trust in your training. Trust in the plan. Forget the rest - there was no room for inconvenient truths or moral dilemmas. The sand was harder to ignore, it had weaselled its way into every corner of his clothing, equipment and most annoyingly made attempts to rub sores upon his heels and Raphael knew it would not be long before it succeeded in breaking even his experienced skin.

The quiet hiss of shifting sand alerted Raphael to the approaching figures. Two members of his unit had just returned from the radio station that they had set up nine hours before and they had come to deliver the verdict from Control. The mission was a go. Despite the bone-piercing chill, which the unit had come to expect nightly, Simmons was sweating as he relayed the message on to Raphael. He was the newest member of their team and this had been his first desert deployment. He had excelled throughout training, as had all the others in their day, but no amount of determination, nor tape, could prevent his young, fresh skin from the biting of the sand, which, on mixing with his sweat had ravaged his feet, leaving red, weeping sores from ankle to toe.

The message delivered, Raphael watched as Simmons limped away in search of Alec. Alec had promised to help him the best he could with his sores before the day's excursion. Alec had once tried to help Raphael, many years ago in a similar way. Despite this, Raphael felt nothing for the pathetically limping soldier. He had dealt with it. Simmons would too.

Alec was a first class soldier who had passed SAS selection alongside Raphael with distinction. He was unfailingly brave, possessed the necessary mental detachment they all had and yet somehow acquitted himself with a rare concern for his comrades, his ability to perform his duty had not eclipsed his empathy. Of course defensively they all had each others' backs, the safety of every man their primary concern, but blisters and emotions were their own individual responsibilities, yet Alec knew how to help with those too. Raphael had often said he was more loyal than any dog and having shared more than just their careers they were, by any man's estimation, brothers.

By the time the inky sky was bleached pink and a thin fiery line of sun scored the horizon, the ancillary unit which had been located twelve miles north of Raphael's position, had reached the base. Wordlessly, the soldiers exchanged greetings, fixed visors to their helmets and loaded into two roofless *RWMIK* Land Rovers and a new Jackal 2 4x4. The armoured vehicles, fitted with roll bar cages painted to match the terrain and primed with .50 caliber heavy machine guns, would transport them to their next - and all being well - final destination.

From his newly assigned position in the back of the Land Rover that would be travelling in the middle of the convoy, Alec watched Raphael inspect the base of the dune. His eyes carefully scanned for any unnatural disturbance, signals that the dune had been inhabited by anything other than the restless wind or a wandering gazelle. In less than a few hours, the shifting sands, encouraged by the desert breeze, would have covered the vehicle tracks from this morning and there would be no indication that a covert SAS unit had called the spot home

13

for the previous three days. They had repeated the same process several times throughout the last six weeks, relocating in order to remain undetected as they zeroed in on their target.

Whispers concerning a group of terrorist insurgents hiding amongst the bombed-out remains of a small, rural village, lost deep within the Syrian Desert, had been circulating within the intelligence community for months. Sentences stolen from intercepted phone calls and assurances teased from other, more questionable, sources had first found their way along the corridors of Langley and then behind the doors of the SIS building at Vauxhall Cross. Only then had the two units begun what had become the last six weeks of reconnaissance, trying to confirm the validity of these mutterings and doing their best to turn murmurs to verified intelligence.

Checked, confirmed and with the consent given, they were finally on their way to detain the suspected terrorists.

With action imminent, there was a palpable buzz, a frisson of adrenaline and testosterone in the atmosphere, which fuelled Raphael as he leapt into the Jackal 2 that would be leading the procession to Zone D. Here the troops would disembark to complete the final assault on foot. The broken remains of what had once been village houses, still lay scattered, the result of a previous war's air assault, and the mounds of rubble had left the ground too fractured for the narrower tires of the Land Rovers. No one had commented on why they had been given the RWMIKs - the inadequacy of available resources had become another fact to be compartmentalised, forgotten as the village had been by those who'd destroyed it.

They were not far from Zone D, having navigated their way to an old dirt road, long abandoned and expectedly deserted, when Raphael was thrown violently forward in his seat. His upper body slammed into the exposed metal dashboard, sending shooting pains up his forearms. An eruption of flames, all noise and heat roared behind him, tearing the orderly convoy apart. The agonising sound of splintering metal ripped through the desert air, destroying the previous stillness that, just moments before, had been punctuated only by the rumble of the vehicles.

Looking back through gaps in the Jackal's exterior caged structure, past the dazed rear gunman, Raphael saw the cascading fragments of a now deconstructed Land Rover that had been thrown up in the explosion. Each hulking piece landed loudly, shooting plumes of burning sand into the ever-lightening sky.

His ears ringing painfully and his heart pounding as if trying to claw its way out of his chest, Raphael tried to comprehend the satanic vision before him. His own vehicle had just passed where the ill-fated Land Rover had suddenly exploded and now lay aflame in a mangled heap. He must have narrowly missed the concealed mine or IED, at most by a few feet. The landscape had been difficult to navigate, but the route was supposed to have been clear.

Raphael was now experiencing the suffocating, twisted alertness that accompanied cheating death. The ringing in his ears subsided, to be replaced by a wasplike humming. Out of the corner of his vision he saw the armoured reddish body of an Arabian Fattail scorpian scuttle furiously out from underneath a fragment of rock laying beside the road. It felt like time itself had slowed. Everything was suddenly in focus, raw and crisp. He could see every grain of sand blowing about the wreckage and feel each tiny bead of sweat that ran down his neck, back and arms. Yet his muscles felt heavy, his body unobligingly binding him to his seat.

Raphael had begun preparing for this one final appointment with God, his moment of death, a long time ago. In fact, on more than one occasion, Raphael had even willed it into being. *To everything there is a season, and a time to every purpose under heaven: a time to be born, and a time to die; a time to plant, and a time to pluck up that which is planted. Ecclesiastes 3,* he thought.

Half Italian on his mother's side, Raphael had been both raised a Catholic at home and on his mother's insistence, educated at a strict Catholic school. His brother Luciano, two years his senior and a short-tempered incendiary of a character, had felt stifled by the hours of scripture required daily in their youth. Much to Luciano's confusion and later deep annoyance, Raphael had always found a sort of quiet solace in religion as a child. Seen through his youthful optimism, the idea that a greater power had a plan for him, as promised to all his followers, had bestowed an indefinable meaning on his young life. But best of all, it had afforded him an extra half an hour each night with his mother, basking in her clean perfumed embrace and her loving praise every time he had recited anything remotely biblical. At one point, Raphael had even considered entering the church himself. He was not that child anymore though, not in his own or he felt, in his mother's eyes and in the years since, he had strayed a long way from the dutiful little boy who had prayed earnestly each night, kneeling in his silken pyjamas beside his mother. Nevertheless, some of the words had still stayed with him and always came to him, however unwelcome, as if carried on the invisible wings of some baleful phantom, in moments where death was lurking near.

The two other armoured vehicles in the SAS convoy skidded to a halt around the burning wreckage of the Land Rover. Having regained control of his muscles, Raphael leapt free from his seat in the Jackal. Time was moving fast now, too fast. Which vehicle had Alec been in?

'Where was Alec? Alec? Where was he? Which vehicle?' he shouted to Walker who was checking the ground around the wreckage for additional, hidden explosives. Walker shook his head apologetically. Raphael scanned the scene before him.

'Help...Help!' a strangled call cried from the far side of the wreckage.

Raphael ran towards the voice, ignoring the protests of Walker, whose team hadn't completed their ground search. Skirting the debris, Raphael spotted Alec and the image of the man's body, having been flung about twelve feet from the Land Rover when it had exploded, hit him like a punch in the gut. Miraculously the soldier was still alive, although the same could not be said about Simmons and the other two bodies whom Raphael had just passed.

Albeit alive, Alec was fading fast, his words slurred and his eyes rolling as he struggled to remain conscious. His face was blackened from the blast, but thankfully his helmet appeared, on first inspection, to have protected him from cracking his skull. As Raphael scanned down his body, searching for injury, he noticed the deep oozing gash on Alec's right leg. Even with all his experience and training, the sight produced a swell of nausea. Looking at the spread and colour of the stained sand around Alec's limp body, Raphael surmised that he must have already lost at least three or four pints of blood. He shouted for a medic whilst fastening a make-shift tourniquet around Alec's bloodied leg. His voice clear, actions professional and controlled, as if cut free from him and now somehow operating separate from the panic he felt choking in his chest.

'Medic!' he shouted again before he started speaking directly to Alec. Crouching low near his friend's pallid face, Raphael heard himself making promises that Alec would be fine. That he would be home soon. That he would be good as new. Now acutely aware of the panic, he was not sure who between them needed the reassurance more.

Raphael felt a deep personal debt to the friend, now bleeding out before him. When his family and God had left Raphael, Alec had appeared and he had never forgotten it. Preparing a shot of morphine for his dying companion, Raphael, for the first time since boyhood, found himself praying.

TWO

'Time's up! Pens down. Please keep your eyes front, mouths shut and remain seated until we ask you to leave.' The sixty-something, heavily bearded lecturer spluttered from the front of the room. He smiled, pleased with the order that he had been perfecting for the last three hours, whilst dutifully guarding the exam room from any illicit conversation.

Wearing a tailored burgundy waistcoat and a pair of small, rounded spectacles that dangled from a delicate gold chain around his neck, the man would have looked more at home in the smoking rooms of the 1890s than at a university in the twenty-first century, mused Kitty. As it happened, she had discovered during her time at Cambridge University, that many of the older dons sported such a look. Some triumphantly rebelling against the last nearly two whole centuries of advances in fashion, others coping with the gentle sadness of forlorn curators, remaining as a withered bastion of a different time, left in a world no longer their own. She thought each endearing in their own way. Their presence certainly added to the intrigue of the golden stone edifices and neatly maintained lawns and courtyards that dominated the university campus, drawing a near constant stream of chiefly American and Chinese tourists.

Kitty reckoned around ninety percent of the visitors that she had encountered in her two and a half years of study fervently believed that the university was a secret haven of mystery and tantalising romance. An oasis caught in the past, where white knights and fair maidens could still exist. The first time Kitty had encountered such intrigue, she had scoffed and uncharitably robbed the visitors of their delusions. Only upon seeing their disappointed faces had she realised her wrongdoing. For as long as she could remember, Kitty had possessed a misanthropic tendency of needlessly shattering other people's illusions and it was something that nowadays she was striving hard to correct. Having never had any fanciful illusions of her own since childhood, she was wildly inexperienced in the ways in which people seemed to live in a near constant deluded state. She knew - or had been told often enough - that her inability to sustain illusions was more than a simple byproduct of her intelligence, it was a coping strategy, a self-taught method of protection from the dangers of escapism. It was not the illusions themselves that terrified her, it was the inevitable reality once they had vanished, the crushing comparison of truth with fantasy - and they always vanished. This and her sharp tongue had isolated Kitty her entire life. It was not that she was devoid of her own dreams and aspirations, but to Kitty, a spade was a spade and her dreams were divided sharply from her daily activities.

Letting out a deep breath, Kitty slumped back into her chair. Around her, the large room remained chiefly silent, save some unnecessarily drawn out sighs from a few of the neighbouring students seeking a sympathetic laugh and the busy shuffling of completed exam scripts.

The lecturers moved slowly up and down the neat rows of ordered desks like automations. One by one they counted in each of the students' offerings, carefully thumbing the pages to ensure a complete collection. Waiting for hers to be taken, Kitty stretched out her arms. Arching her back a little, her elbows clicked uncomfortably. Placing her near spent biro on the desk in front of her, she wiggled her cramping fingers. Her palms were clammy as she rubbed at a small red writing sore that had appeared on her left hand. She had just survived an intense, three hour, grammatical evaluation of her understanding of the Russian language, whilst discussing the intricacies of the Russian tsars claimed entitlements to the Byzantine throne. The question had been surprisingly topical.

The news for the last few months had been filled with regime changes, government changeovers, terrorist threats and international alliances strained to breaking point. It seemed to Kitty that nothing much in the world of international relations had changed. Eventually, everyone wanted more and eventually everything crumbled from within. It was one of these reports, a story that had whipped the global news outlets into a startling frenzy, that had ensured Kitty had not spent her third year immersed in the Lomonosov Moscow State University but rather had remained a victim of a last minute, poorly structured curriculum firmly rooted in Cambridge.

The discovery of an Anglo-American spy ring embedded deep within the Kremlin - although no evidence had ever been provided - had attached a couple of ex-Cambridge Politics graduates (sometimes recorded as History, Economics and in one article Philosophy graduates) to the list of potential suspects. In reality the listed individuals had proved to be little more than conscientious diplomats who had recently been repatriated. Their reward for their services had been a veritable barrage of tabloid slander. The news stories had circulated for weeks on end, with no tangible result other than Kitty and her classmates' visa rejections - a fact, once leaked, that had caused the journalists to descend on Cambridge like gulls to a rubbish tip. In the shadow of the university they had kept up a steady stream of speculation littered with sensational accusations.

'...agents have been feeding Russian state secrets to the British government and their American allies across the pond for more than a decade...'

'...actions of the western government's are inflammatory and dangerous...'

'... the authenticity of such claims could be disputed...'

'... timing aids Russia in increasingly aggressive position in the Middle East...'

Much to the glee of some of the Modern History devotees in Kitty's college, the atmosphere surrounding the story had all been very reminiscent of the Cold War.

But, with little else of interest going on, it was the accusation that the issue could somehow aid Russia that had hooked Kitty. However, after weeks of searching for an answer, the validity of this accusation had remained annoyingly elusive.

The Middle Eastern issue had become deeply complex throughout the last decade, if not longer, and she knew embarrassingly little about it. On top of this, trying to understand the foreign policy of a nation entrenched in secrecy, had made the proposition harder still.

Her investigations had ended about three weeks before her sojourn in the exam hall where she now sat reminiscing, at the office of one of Cambridge's most unfairly disregarded professors. Before their meeting Kitty had discerned the most popular conclusion. It was accepted that Russia was looking for an excuse to expand its influence in the oil rich region. The exact reasons for an expansion remained uncertain, but a favourite amongst the journalists and students in her college, was to sell their new air defence missile systems. This being so, by exposing the western powers for breaking countless diplomatic precedents, Russia had severely undermined the West's primarily morally-based condemnation of Russian tactics being used in defence of debatably amoral regimes in various Middle Eastern nations.

Professor Betzalel Aaron, a mild mannered, diminutive man never seen out of his walnut chinos and rumpled shirts, the sleeves of which could be seen flopping from a limited selection of patterned knitwear, had added, 'What to do about these countries, or rather, the small minorities which they occasionally export, has become a major dividing factor in these nations' foreign policies.'

From his pokey closet of an office, whose only redeeming feature was a small window with a coveted view of the River Cam, the Professor had written thesis after thesis on extremism, its origins and its future, whilst fighting a constant stream of other dons and professors looking to knock through into his small space. He believed the key to understanding the dividing opinions was rooted in their appetites for tackling extremism. 'Subsidiary to that are the issues of influence, oil money and weapons exportation,' his crinkly mouth twitched up at one end before he added, 'well… I think so anyway. But then isn't everything just a matter of perspective?'

Over the course of a few weeks, the Professor had taken time to enlighten Kitty on the origins of a handful of deep-rooted problems facing swathes of the Middle East. They had discussed the United Kingdoms's debatably ill-conceived anti-extremism initiatives and debated the re-education tactics against the militarily-enforced control initiatives favoured by other nations. The Professor ended their time together by musing, 'As is the disparate nature of human beings and their similarly complicated myriad of beliefs, backgrounds and interpretations. Public opinion is not often changed by well meaning conversation, but rather, we are moved by a shocking event which forces upon us a change of perspective. Perhaps…' he paused, before theorising further, 'if we lived a little closer to these nations, if we shared more with them or, at the opposite end of the scale, if there was another tragic terrorist attack in the UK, our nation's views on subjects like Russia's chosen form of aggressive intervention could change? It certainly did in America after 9/11.'

After their meeting, Kitty was not sure if she felt enlightened or confused. Perspective seemed to be the issue just as it had been at the heart of the debate surrounding the Russian tsars' claims to the Byzantine throne. Depending on who you were and where in the kaleidoscope of public opinion you fitted, distorted one's view of a news story and so too the rumours surrounding the rejection of her visa application.

She had settled on one final conclusion, one that she had lived with since, that she was not going to Russia any time soon. This meant that Kitty, and a handful of other unfortunates, would be spending their year like the previous two. The sole change being the addition of a new compulsory module, and so Kitty had excelled, like she did at most linguistic endeavours, in learning Spanish whilst Cambridge desperately scrambled to create a meaningful third year experience. In Kitty's opinion, they had succeeded about as much as she had succeeded, in deciding what to do about creating *meaning* this coming Christmas. In short, not one bit.

'Is it the last one, Cleopatra? Cleopatra?'

Called back from her wandering thoughts, Kitty looked up at the lecturer stooped over her exam desk. His black gown and balding head bestowed him with a vulture like appearance. Unknowingly a single tear had escaped down her cheek. She caught it quickly, fearing anyone should notice.

'Last exam, Cleopatra? Are you all done for Christmas?'

Kitty looked at the lecturer whom she recognised as the one who had passed out the exam scripts, as her mind struggled to pull forward a name for him. He had used her full name, which she seldom heard outside of the rare occasions she went to the doctors or visited her now aged guardian Burt, her stalwart supporter in spite of her disrespect and the only person she knew who remembered the man who had named her in such a fussy, ridiculous way.

It had been a long time since Kitty had heard the name spoken out loud. The sound of it still stung. She hated it now, but here it was said with such an innocence that she forced a polite smile, 'Yes, thank you sir. I'm all done.'

'Excellent. I'm Professor Michael Deanberry by the way. We've not met, but I recently had lunch with your Russian tutor and she had much to say about you. It is a pleasure to still find such keen minds in this dusty old place. I do hope we meet again. Have a smashing break.'

Kitty smiled generously, despite inwardly cringing at the "keen minds" comment. Being under no illusion that, if any one of the law schools she had applied to countless times had accepted her transfer, she would have discontinued all of her linguistic studies in a heartbeat, it felt fraudulent accepting the compliment. However she loved these random moments in life, where the positive mutterings of one private conversation, managed to weave their way back to the subject of that conversation via a different route. She felt it was the best and truest kind of compliment. It was a rare occurrence and she was not going to waste it.

'That's lovely of you to say Professor. I hope you have a great break as well,' she breathed, returning the well wishes. *I have worked bloody hard, so i'm glad it makes someone happy.*

Smiling generously once more at the professor, Kitty gathered up her belongings and made her way out of the exam room. His kind words and the attribution of a name having humanised him. She left the room re-evaluating her view as to whether he did, or did not, now resemble a vulture. *Perspective*, she smiled to herself.

The exam had been held near the Mill Lane lecture rooms and Kitty didn't have much time to make her way back up to Trinity College, where her room was located, before making the longer return journey down to the train station to catch the 18:20 to Kings Cross.

Fortunately, due to her unfortunate family - or lack thereof - circumstances, Cambridge had assigned her a college room that would remain hers throughout the holidays as well as term time. This meant that she did not require any time to empty the room of her clutter before departing for London. That and her knowledge of the little-known back alleys which criss-crossed Cambridge allowed Kitty to reach her college in good time.

Smug at having avoided most of the streets bustling with pre-Christmas shoppers, Kitty darted into the main entrance of Trinity. Making her way directly to the Porter's lodge she swapped the expected felicitations with some lingering students and the bowler hat wearing porter, then scooped up her post. Rifling through the pitifully small stack, Kitty noted some work reminders about the next term and one hand written envelope. She knew who it was from straight away. The barely legible scrawl was easily recognisable. Kitty hastily tucked it into her coat pocket to savour it for later. Grinning expectantly as she made her way across the vast expanse of the college's central court, its lawn maintained as pristinely as a putting green, she scurried off to her room.

Having bumped into various acquaintances along the way, and swapped yet more festive greetings and well wishes, Kitty was running a little behind schedule when she finally made it to her accommodation block. Flustered as she began to climb the uneven stone steps, the realities of Kitty's post-exam celebrations had begun to sink in and only now did she start to regret her choice to travel so soon after the brutal assessments.

It had been a few weeks back, before the real exhaustion of exams had taken over every aspect of Kitty's life. In a moment of weakness whilst semi-buried under a pile of tomes in her college library, Kitty had received a plea from her closest friend Jaz, begging her to come and stay at her "earliest convenience." Immune to Kitty's occasionally undomesticated manner, Jaz had been one of the two members of Kitty's inner circle of friends whilst growing up in Truro. Now studying English Literature in London, these days the young woman could often be found reeling off dramatic prose in place of the common smattering of emojis and chatty language most people used when sending a text.

Kitty smiled to herself, quelling her flustering, as she remembered the desperate call for support which, in reality, had been Jaz's way of saying, *please come and stay, I want to tell you all about my latest, most likely inappropriate, or ill-fated love affair and go for a few drinks with my friends. Which may or may not end in dancing…or something closely resembling the most likely inappropriate, or ill-fated love affair, that we had come out to discuss and move on from in the first place.*

It had been a while since the two girls had managed to spend any real time together. It had proven exceedingly difficult for Kitty to extricate herself from Cambridge and all the work that had accompanied doing a degree at such an esteemed university. It certainly hadn't been all it was cracked up to be and most definitely had not been the romantic academic adventure that the tourists naively maintained. The hours were long, the work often tedious and her social life, despite never having been deemed boundless, had suffered miserably.

Kitty panted as she burst through the door into her room. Its parched hinges protested emphatically to their sudden disturbance. Dumping the academic notifications she had just collected on her desk, the papers vanished against the heap of revision notes and practice papers that had grown to fill the far right hand end of the room creating a forest of hope and effort.

Turning her back to the desk, Kitty proceeded to shove some clothes and her toiletry bag into a soft leather holdall which she had left on her bed, pushed against the back wall of the room, in preparation for her trip. It was a preloved treasure which she had found in one of Cambridge's independent shops the year before. Kitty adored it. The bag was a deep, chocolatey brown, with paler well-worn corners. Traditional in its design, it looked like it had seen a fair few adventures. To top it off, the fastening was a rusty metal zip, that you had to wiggle at just the right angle to make work. *A perfect balance between character and practicality,* Kitty mused removing a piece of shirt that had caught in the zip.

As she turned to go, holdall in hand, Kitty stopped for a brief moment to admire the view from her window, her attention caught by the rose hue of the encroaching twilight. Peering out past the lead bars in the glass, she couldn't help but feel a rare swell of pride that she had managed, all on her own, to win a place at such a remarkable university. There was never enough time at Cambridge for one to simply appreciate the awesomeness of the buildings, the history and the famous alumni who had walked the very same steps and streets. *Then again Cambridge, you can be a bloody pain in the arse.*

Checking the envelope in her jacket and her watch one final time, Kitty saw the hands tick worryingly past six o'clock. With due haste she locked her door and raced off for the station.

THREE

The train left on time at 18:20 and, with no changes, would arrive into Kings Cross Station forty-nine minutes later. Kitty had managed to find an empty window seat in the last carriage and had wiled away most of the time silently staring out into the countryside. She watched the modern apartment buildings and drab blocks of the Clifton Road Industrial Estate that surrounded the station melt into a tapestry of fields and leafless copses. The trees stood like watchman along the hilltops, their boughs silhouetted against the dusky sky.

About thirty minutes into the journey, her mind finally slowing after the madness of her exam and hasty departure, Kitty remembered the letter tucked in her coat pocket. Retrieving it, she gently stuck her thumb under the top flap and prized it open. Pulling out the card inside she giggled. As predicted, it was from Freddie.

The card was a cheery sky blue and on the front was decorated with a cartoon-style picture of two hamburgers. Drawn with quirky, smiling faces, the burgers were positioned above the words, "IF YOU'RE A BURGER, I'M A BURGER." Kitty smiled to herself. It was a play on the famous quote from *The Notebook* by Nicholas Sparks which usually went, "If you're a bird, I'm a bird."

The renowned love story by Sparks had unexpectedly touched Kitty six summers earlier whilst on holiday with Freddie and his family for the first time in a villa south of Cannes. Summer trips to the wondrous wisteria laced idyll had, happily for Kitty, become somewhat of an annual tradition in the years after. And it had been there, surrounded by strangers who would become the closest thing she had to family, whilst eating pizza and playing risk on the terrace, that the topic of love had sprung up.

Freddie's mother Anne had - as she'd confided in Kitty years later - been under no illusions that her son harboured deeper aspirations than friendship for the girl who had joined them for their annual summer holiday. She recognised that Kitty's feral nature her son saw as raffish, and her tendency to avoid commitment or self-revelation he found alluring. Anne was also all too aware, thanks to the other mothers in her Thursday morning knit-and-natter group - or as Anne privately called it, stitch-and-bitch - that he was not the only young man at Penair Secondary School captivated by the "stray cat" as they had named her. A girl whose rare smile could melt away a person's worries yet, as they always added uncharitably, whose emotional baggage could no doubt sink a considerable size

32

ship. They had no proof of the latter statement, but as she was an orphan and a patient of the redoubtable Miss M, they had entertained little doubt.

Anne had refused at first when Freddie wanted to bring along his new fancy. In truth, although now ashamed at the memory, she had refused her son on three separate occasions, trying in vain at each to convince him to invite someone "more suitable." It was only after multiple nonchalant suggestions of other possibilities - as the coffee morning regulars had unanimously agreed that nonchalant suggestion was the most effective way of dealing with teenage sons caught in the throes of puberty - followed by a series of arguments, that Freddie, bristling with teenage self-consciousness, had admitted why he wanted Kitty to come. It was then he had told Anne about the party he had not been invited too, the one Kitty had, and the fact that she had taken him to Perranporth Beach instead of attending.

Freddie had apparently, Kitty found out much later when Anne had told her sherry-induced confession, allowed his mother to think - rather mortifyingly - a little more of that day than was actually true.

The truth had been that puberty had been cruel to Freddie. His cheeks and back had been dominated by acne and his body lanky, where his bones had grown fast but his muscles had not had the opportunity to catch up in strength nor coordination. He had been shy and routinely left out. Kitty had gone to Perranporth Beach that day because, despite all this, he was refreshingly free from the damage these things often caused in one's self-confidence. He stayed kind and loyal and on the whole defiantly upbeat, and she had wanted to find out how he managed it. Her own trials had left her as pot-marked inside as his skin showed on the outside.

Despite some initial awkwardness on the holiday, Anne had come to care deeply for Truro's resident stray. So deeply in fact, that Anne had tried to educate Kitty in the possible benefits of having a boyfriend. She had done this by gifting her a copy of *The Notebook* one afternoon by the pool.

Kitty, who had approached the text with initial trepidation, had soon been swept away by the bond of Allie and Noah and their tale. Despairingly for Anne - confirmed in the sherry-fuelled confession - the novel had kindled some degree of openness in the girl, but despite her years of unsubtle hints, Kitty had never considered Freddie a suitable substitute for the fictional Noah.

By seventeen, Freddie's muscles had developed impressively and his acne had become a distant memory. Able to use his new physical advantage, he became a key member of the school's football team and with his now carefully mussed, beach-blonde hair and Kitty-encouraged confidence he had enjoyed, or perhaps endured, a string of girlfriends. *Not all of them particularly nice girls,* Kitty thought momentarily pulled back into the present. But girlfriends and their parties none-the-less, back to back for the final two years of school.

Despite the dramatic change, Kitty had always felt that somehow Freddie was, in his way, waiting for them to get together. After the day they had spent at Perranporth Beach, eating sandy ice creams, swapping insecurities and sheltering from the rain, their entire school year group had believed them to be a couple. As it turned out this had included Freddie who, by all accounts, had been delighted.

The shock exhibited by the majority of students that someone would want to date the awkward, spot-riddled, bean-pole boy had infuriated Kitty to such an extent that she had allowed the misunderstanding to continue long into the school term. The charade had been made easier by the visible annoyance it caused to those whom Kitty had disregarded long ago as not caring for her one snip. Eventually Kitty had told Freddie that she didn't want a boyfriend. She had settled on telling him one evening after school that she didn't want it to ever risk spoiling their friendship. This approach had been meant to protect his feelings from being hurt, and his new found confidence from being knocked, but Kitty had always felt uncomfortable about not being honest and an opportunity to correct this had never presented itself.

Aside from this one awkward moment, the two had remained very close and perhaps Freddie had actually been the kindest boyfriend-not-real-boyfriend Kitty had ever had. For Will had turned out to be a complete arsehole solely focused on sex - which he did not get and Tom, from nearby Truro School, who made up for his intellectual failings with physical prowess also, despite a surprisingly sweet and coordinated fling, proved himself to be a poor fit. With sexual attraction unable to fill the absence of understanding, Kitty's habitual bursting of illusions had led her to extricate herself from this relationship as well. Both, like Freddie, had been found lacking something she still found herself unable to pinpoint.

Pushing thoughts of Tom and Will and teenage antics from her mind, Kitty looked inside the card and picked her way through Freddie's messy scrawl. He was now based down in Southampton, finishing off his marine engineering degree. The card was really an invitation for Kitty to come and stay over the holidays. Since leaving school Kitty had been rather elusive. She spent as little time as possible in Truro, not wishing to pass her time in the place which had taken her so many years to escape. A not inconsiderable part of her feared each time she saw the *Welcome to Cornwall* sign, that she may never escape again.

On the rare occasions Kitty did return she had developed a strict routine to counter the fear. First she would deliver flowers to Freddie's mother on arrival. One cup of tea and multiple refusals for refills and custard cream biscuits later, she would head down to the beach to see Burt, the fisherman friend of her would-be-but-then-not-to-be mother, who had stood as her guardian. They would feast on crisp sandwiches, for Kitty was now old enough to refuse the mackerel he used to offer, grapes - his nod to health, which would have pleased his wife had she still been with them - and ginger beer.

Burt harboured a tender affection for stray animals of all kinds. He rescued fallen birds if he stumbled across them. Owned six abandoned budgies. Two hens who couldn't or wouldn't lay. He even had made space in his small home for two scruffy apricot mongrels and a fat, three-legged Jack Russel called Roger, a dog who had contributed little else to his life than fouling in Burt's living room, mauling his post and releasing bad odours whenever, it seemed, he had polite company. Despite this, these creatures pleased Burt. They needed him and there was nothing Burt liked more than to feel required. Kitty had loved them as a child, until she had found herself another creature in his ever growing menagerie.

After lunch, Burt would drive Kitty to the grey stone bungalow Miss M, the school counsellor who had badgered Kitty her entire teenage life, was now inhabiting in nearby Feock. Here Kitty and Miss M would sit in her conservatory. The glass panes were tinged green where the outside had pushed in through the cracks in the frame. It was furnished sparsely with two cushioned rocking chairs and an upturned whicker basket in place of a table, upon which, without fail, there would be a sandalwood diffuser, a half devoured box of Foxes Golden Crunch Creams and yet more tea - chamomile this time. The two would rock in near silence, all the while looking out over Loe Beach. Kitty had little to say to the figure who had, in her own way, helped raise her. She didn't even know why she continued to see her. Worn down by her life's trials, Miss M had always been a woman of few words, and in turn had little to say to the strident young Cleopatra.

After a couple of hours, Kitty would make her excuses and Burt, or Freddie once he got his car, would return Kitty to the train station, ignoring the fact that Kitty had made a conscious effort, yet again, to avoid the small fisherman's cottage where she had been dragged the day her father hadn't come home.

Still so sweet, Kitty mused, forcing herself to focus on the fact Freddie had sent a card and ignore the invitation it had contained, as she fought her way through the packed platform at King's Cross station.

After battling her way to the exit on Euston Road, Kitty scoured the crowds for Jaz. Spotting her leaning casually against a lamppost about twenty paces away, Kitty admired how much her friend suited city life. Wearing a pair of ultra-tight, black skinny jeans tucked in to over-the-knee suede boots, Jaz had finished her ensemble with a beautifully furry, cream-coloured coat which contrasted with the long dark tresses that cascaded down her back. Rushing over to her, Kitty dropped her bag loudly at Jaz's feet. Jaz, who had not seen Kitty approach, squealed with delight.

'Kitty-Kat! You made it. Gosh I've missed you. How are you? How's everything? Merry Christmas! Oh, so much to say!' she squeezed Kitty hard, acknowledging silently the unspoken date. The real reason they both knew she had insisted her friend be with her today.

'Merry Christmas, Jaz-ma-taz!' Kitty teased.

Jaz pouted at her, 'Tell me. Are you happy? Are you well? How's Cambridge… still a yawn? Have you found a rich Russian oligarch yet to sweep you off your feet?'

'Umm… how about mostly yes? Healthy as a horse. Mostly yes again and absolutely not and not planning on it either!'

'Ok well if you're going to be your usual private self then I'll begin with my news.' Jaz scooped up Kitty's bag and grabbing her arm headed for the tube.

The girls talked and gossiped the whole way to Jaz's student house, apologising profusely as they clumsily bumped into passing harried commuters. Jaz spoke about new things she had read, the friends Kitty was going to meet tonight and, expectedly, her many love life disasters that had befallen her this semester.

Jaz had always been a romantic risk-taker. She had been when she had lived in Truro till she was fifteen, and had continued this when her family had relocated to Holloway so her father could accept a better accountancy job in London. It was this risk taking that Kitty loved most

38

about her. She was not afraid of rejection and offered her love freely and without strings. Whenever Kitty was with Jaz she reminded herself of the importance of taking a little risk. *Better to have loved and lost*, was Jaz's mantra for life. Which Kitty, until recently would have ended, *than to have never been loved at all.* The addition of the "been" would rile Jaz and even Kitty had to admit these days it sounded a little self-pitying. Which was why, on joining Cambridge, she had made a conscious effort to take risks and find love. Her lack of action was simply due to the fact that no one had met the entry criteria yet. At least, that is what Kitty told herself.

It was not until they had made it into Jaz's bedroom that, after placing Kitty on a swivelling desk chair, Jaz started to divulge what she really wanted to talk about.

'So I do have some news for you, Kitten. There's this dream of a man. He's everything I need,' she swooned.

'Fictional?' Kitty mocked, for she knew all too well that Jaz was prone to fantastical ideals. Noah from *The Notebook* may have wriggled his way into Kitty's private thoughts, but every male hero Jaz ever seemed to read about took up permanent residence in hers.

'No! And being honest he's not quite Mr Darcy, but I still think he's wonderful.'

'Does he have a name?'

'Yes he does,' Jaz arched her eyebrow, knowing she was being teased.

'Please may you tell me the name of this gorgeous man wonderful Jazmin?' Kitty crooned mockingly.

'Yes I can, it's Beto. Well Alberto, but we all call him just Beto.'

'How did you meet "just" Beto?' Kitty flashed an angelic grin.

Jaz frowned again before continuing, 'This sounds super cheesy and clichéd. But screw it, you won't judge. He's Italian, obviously. Deep dark eyes, black hair. Full on, Kit.'

'You've got it bad, Miss Taylor!'

Jaz ignored Kitty, 'He works at the bar, where we're going tonight...' she paused, assessing Kitty's reaction.

'Oh, I'll get to spend *loads* of time with you then this evening?' Kitty teased, folding her arms in mock annoyance.

'Oh no you will! We'll have a proper catch up honestly —'

'I'm joking. I'm flattered you're going to introduce me to Beto,' Kitty soothed Jaz's worrying. She had met many of Jaz's friends over the years and more or less always had a good time. On the whole, Jaz surrounded herself with supportive, friendly and often spirited individuals - something that Kitty, in her younger years, had envied. However, now an evening spent with Jaz's friends was, Kitty told herself making a mental note, another opportunity to implement her approach to trusting and risking.

'So talk to me, how did you meet?' Kitty pushed, knowing Jaz was bursting to tell her.

'In a park. He was sitting on a bench and I was on a run. I know, hilarious, before you say anything. Me running! But I've actually taken a real liking to exercise. It's not like the shitty school group activities and public humiliation that I seemed to remember it being.'

In her youth Jaz, like Freddie, had been a bit of an uncoordinated bean.

'And he was just sitting there,' she continued, 'I feel like… I mean I know if I'm being honest I massively manufactured the situation. I'd been full on researching Austen for my dissertation and was so after a hanky dropping, man picks it up sort of moment. So I tripped over, well… stumbled and pretended to have hurt my ankle…' she finished lamely, flushing a light crimson.

'You didn't!' Kitty's mouth fell open before she collapsed into fits of laughter.

'Well I did actually!' Jaz countered ignoring Kitty's howls, 'It's the twenty first century and firstly I didn't have a handkerchief and secondly wasn't going to wait around for him to make the first move. He probably hadn't noticed me and besides, it's archaic. Not to mention a little sexist to expect the man to always have to take control. I'm a strong independent women and I fancied the pants of him… I'd already run past him three times.'

'Touché, Miss Taylor. Damn straight. So then what did he do?'

'Well initially, he was for sure a little shocked. Embarrassingly, I think he may have even stifled a laugh. God!' she put her hand to her forehead, 'But he then leapt up like the gentlemen he is and dusted me off. He walked with me for a bit and I quizzed him. He works in an über fancy bar making cocktails, sort of old fashioned, but arty vibe in Soho and his dream is to one day own his own bar, slash club, slash restaurant. I told him I was a student and we just really got along.'

'That's so cool. I mean bizarre, but really nicely done, Jaz.'

'Yeah, I mean I've only see him a few times, but he's kind and smart. I hope this one actually goes somewhere. He's from Tuscany too. How cool's that?'

'Very,' Kitty agreed.

The girls continued to chatter and change. By nine they had made it to a cosy boutique Italian restaurant just around the corner from the bar where Beto worked on Upper St James Street, overlooking the immaculately maintained Golden Square. He had messaged Jaz a couple of times on the way to dinner and was clearly keen to see her. Kitty thought Jaz's telling anticipatory blushes each time her phone buzzed rather endearing.

At the restaurant Kitty met a collection of students who were also studying English with Jaz. After introductions had been completed, the whole table ordered bowls filled with buttery ribbons of fresh egg pasta. Kitty's portion was festooned with fresh tomatoes, a star shaped helping of buffalo mozzarella and a delicate sprinkling of black pepper. She then proceeded to request the waiter cover the serving in lashings of parmesan cheese much to the man's disapproval.

'Dio mio. It is not, how you say, the Italian way,' he quipped, smiling but only half joking, whilst he grated the hard cheese until it covered every inch of the dish and even made a neat little mound of shavings on the top. Kitty hadn't needed such a large serving, but her, *on principle this is what I asked for and I'm paying so I don't care about the "Italian way"* trait had gotten the better of her.

'You can take the girl out of Truro, but you can't...' Jaz quipped to a sing-song of laughter from around the table as the others chorused, '...take Truro out of the girl!'

Kitty ignored the jibes from Jaz's friends, a few claiming that they possessed a higher, more cultured status by opting for no parmesan when the waiter offered. They continued to laugh and tease and by the time they all had gotten around to actually eating, the group had made such a fuss that they had garnered more than a few reproving glares from the neighbouring tables. Embarrassed by the level of attention she was getting and feeling overwhelmed by a desire to distance herself from their jollity, Kitty looked away from the group. Only then did she notice a man in the corner of the restaurant looking at her. The trace of a smile pulled at the corners of his mouth.

FOUR

Kitty had first noticed the man and his companion when she had entered the restaurant. It was quickly apparent that the restaurant was no student hotspot and Kitty was silently relieved that she had been given no real say in the matter of who was paying. Thankfully, Jaz's father had given the girls some money as a Christmas treat. Mr Taylor had done well for himself since leaving Cornwall and enjoyed on occasion spoiling Jaz in a way he had not been able to as a younger man. She was also grateful that she had given in to Jaz's style ideas concerning her outfit. Sporting a little black dress, with a fitted velvet bodice and full length delicate lace sleeves, that they had borrowed off Emma, one of Jaz's well-heeled room-mates, Kitty looked right at home in the upmarket establishment, a rare feeling of belonging she was greatly enjoying.

The restaurant was fancy and beautifully furnished. From her seat, Kitty could just make out the faint geometric pattern that spotted the dark, subtly expensive wallpaper which covered the far wall. Old fashioned lanterns dangled at various heights all the way along it, each twinkling atmospherically in the otherwise dim lighting. Two of the other walls, including the one they had come in on, were clad with polished rosewood panels and the fourth wall was dominated by a row of opaque, warmly lit glass windows with thick ebony frames. They reminded Kitty of the voguish interior design magazine photographs of upmarket New York warehouse renovations that Anne had once collected whilst redecorating her living room. Kitty had never worked out how Anne seemed to claim inspiration from these images and yet, quite happily, end up with something much more akin to an image from a Laura Ashley magazine. She had told Anne this of course - it hadn't gone down well.

The seating arrangements in the restaurant had received the same specific attention as the decor. Dark tables varying in size and length dotted the space. Each one was embellished with multiple copper tea lights and surrounded by studded, curved low-backed leather chairs. Down the right-hand-side of the interior, the tables had been arranged in alcoves. Here the wall side seating, instead of chairs, consisted of luxuriously plum cushioned benches, and it was in one of these low-lit alcoves that she had noticed the now amused man and his rather serious looking companion.

The man was noticeable because, oddly, he was wearing an army uniform. It was the type seen on television during the news, a forest-green coloured checkerboard outfit. Kitty thought the unmistakable camouflage a very unusual sight. She was confident that uniformed soldiers did not often frequent extortionate pasta restaurants in the heart of London.

Meeting the soldier's gaze, Kitty felt strangely excited by the slight upturn of his mouth. She frowned, an action which only seemed to amuse him more. The light was too low to make out much else about him, but she could tell the soldier's friend seemed agitated. He was suited and wore a crisp white shirt fastened at the wrist. A pair of shiny gold cufflinks poked out, catching the light as he gesticulated wildly. Noticing the soldier laughing, the man gestured angrily and rose from the table. The soldier looked up at him. He was still sporting a rather mischievous smile and only managed, a little too late, to drop his cheekbones and feign some semblance of remorse. He said something, perhaps trying to make amends, but his companion for the evening had already thrown a dark wool coat over his suit and stalked out of the restaurant. His shiny leather shoes tapped loudly as he strode passed Kitty's table.

The soldier reclined back into the cushions behind him and ran his hands through his hair. It was a lovely deep mahogany shade, Kitty thought as she watched his fingers weaving through it. *Unusual to be so long for an army officer,* she noted. Lost in her musings, Kitty blushed deeply when she noticed that he had caught her staring.

Looking away, Kitty tried to pretend as though she had not just been seen gawking like a little girl. She

46

ferociously twisted some pasta onto her fork, but before it made it into her waiting mouth, it fell off half landing in her lap. *For fuck's sake.* She did not care to look to see if he had seen that.

If she had, she would have seen a now full set of delighted white teeth.

From her left, Jaz was giving her a questioning glare, 'You alright, Kit?'

'Yeah, just overloaded the fork. Ignore me, I'm just tired…bloody Cambridge…' Kitty tried to laugh off her friend's suspicious eyes.

Jaz was about to ask something else, but thankfully for Kitty, her phone vibrated again in her pocket. Looking down, mildly apologetically, Jaz checked to see if the message was from Beto. Her face clearly disappointed when it was not.

The group talked and ate for the next couple of hours. Kitty did not look back in the soldier's direction at any point throughout the remainder of the dinner, nor as they made their way to the cocktail bar where Beto worked.

'Hey, what's the time?' Kitty asked the girl - *Sophie or Sarah?* - who had been seated on her right at the restaurant. After the mortifying gawping and pasta spilling incident she had remained uncharacteristically distracted for the rest of the meal and most of Sophie-or-Sarah's conversation had gone in one ear and out the other. Kitty kicked herself, she felt rude. She was meant to be engaging this evening.

'Eleven,' the girl replied, having to raise her voice a little. The music was reaching peak volume as they neared the bar.

'Thanks,' Kitty mouthed.

The bar was as Jaz had described. A sophisticated blend of a vintage gentlemen's club and an Andy Warhol exhibition at the Tate Modern. There was an oval-shaped, double-sided bar in the centre of the room with a huge colourful display of bottles at its core. The place was at capacity. At its fullest, the area directly around the bar was three people deep and the barmen were having to work diligently to satisfy the thirsty customers and also keep the magic going with their juggling and bottle flipping. People were dancing at their tables and in the designated space off to the left of the bar where a peroxide DJ was playing a live set for the revellers from behind her booth. The place was a sea of gyrating bodies.

Jaz and her friends seemed thrilled, even intoxicated by the sensual self-indulgence. Kitty felt a rather uncomfortable claustrophobia. She liked going out, but when a bar was completely packed and the music so loud that you couldn't talk anymore, the evening activities became a little too much about the alcohol for her liking. Kitty had experienced, and been responsible for, her fair share of embarrassing drunken antics and, on this particular occasion, did not wish to add to the list. She was of course looking to take a little more risk in life, but that was in trusting people, not chancing a stomach pump. For this reason, Kitty was particularly relieved when Jaz grabbed her arm as she stood watching, a little horrified, as the students ordered a row of dark amber shots, that were now being lined up along the bar.

'Come!' Jaz shouted in Kitty's ear. Holding Kitty's hand, Jaz weaved her way through the crowd in the opposite direction of the amber shots. Once the girls had made it out of the initial scrum, Kitty spotted that they were headed towards a set of stairs that she had not noticed before. The stairs curled up to a second level above, part suspended over the floor they were now on. At the bottom of the stairs stood a burly guard checking names. Clearly this section of the bar was more exclusive.

The bouncer gave the girls a questioning look as they approached. He was dressed entirely in black, had a disproportionately broad, bald head and a pair of narrow eyes that gave him an unfortunate porcine appearance. The small bits of skin that were showing at his wrists were heavily tattooed. Unfazed by his hostile expression Jaz waltzed straight up to the man and, smiling broadly, leant in close before whispering something in his ear. Once she had finished, the bouncer pressed his left hand against his ear, revealing yet more ink inscriptions, and spoke to a previously hidden microphone attached to the inside of his shirt collar. Obviously satisfied with the response he had received, the man stepped aside and ushered the girls upstairs.

'Second room on the right,' he called as they passed him.

'Thanks!' Kitty shouted back over the music. The bouncer's eyes crinkled and Kitty thought he was perhaps attempting to smile.

Once upstairs Kitty could see that there were three rooms, their entrances highlighted by delicately lit glass arched doors, spaced evenly along the suspended corridor. Jaz pulled Kitty in to the first.

'He said the second?' Kitty questioned.

'They're all connected. Look at this.' Jaz dragged Kitty in to the centre of the first room and turned her clockwise until she was facing another archway. Through this she could see another circular bar and behind that another archway leading on to a third space where a live band was entertaining the revellers. Each room was accented with a different jewel shade and the sound-proofing up here meant that they were now listening to some rather sophisticated jazz style music. It was worlds away from the rave going on downstairs.

There were sofas and arm chairs in the first room, tables around the bar in the second and people dancing in front of the band on a checkered floor in the third. The spaces were fully occupied, but there was no sense of claustrophobia. It was very cosmopolitan. Kitty noticed a birthday party attended by a collection of striking Amazonian beings, who were perhaps supermodels by day. Countless other groups comprised of suited individuals which Kitty deemed to be business men and women entertaining clients, and the remainder of the revellers were some artily dressed folk, whom Kitty had the vague feeling she should recognise from a movie, or television show, as they were definitely not fellow Truro escapees.

As they approached the bar in the middle room, Kitty felt Jaz's arm tense beside her.

Spinning around to face Kitty she checked, 'Do I look ok? No pasta sauce on my chin or anything?' she winked knowing that this was the third time she had asked. Once leaving the restaurant, once when they had arrived and now again.

'You look great. Now which one is he?'

Before Jaz needed to answer, one of the bartenders waved happily at them. A broad grin marked his face.

'I'm going to go with that one,' Kitty said with a wry smile. The girls giggled.

'Buonasera, Jasmin. Kiti, benvenuto, welcome. It is a pleasure to finally meet you,' Beto greeted the girls warmly as they stepped up to the bar, kissing them each on both cheeks.

'Please, per favore, sit down and make yourselves comfortable.'

His speech was heavily accented, making each line lilting and friendly, perfectly matching his features. As the girls positioned themselves on two stools, Jaz stowing her bag underneath hers, Beto set to work fixing them two gin and tonics as requested, 'Traditional with lime? Or limone?'

'Lime's great, Beto. Thank you.'

'Toast!' Jaz called once the drinks had been served. She eyed Kitty as she spoke first, 'May the best of your past be the worst of your future.'

'Thanks, Jaz,' Kitty whispered in her ear, chinking her glass and blinking back tears. Jaz never forgot. Kitty started speaking, trying to curb the sudden rush of emotion, 'So Jaz tells me you're planning on opening your own bar someday?' she smiled at the barman.

Beto talked passionately about his aspirations in between serving other customers. He clearly favoured the quieter, more personal, intimate Tuscan style bars than the big, London sensory overload style rave spaces, like the one below where they now sat.

'For talking, great food too. Not just how you say... ah... raving,' he explained.

Alas for now Beto was stuck working in a bar and not owning one. Kitty wondered why he didn't find a bar to work in more like one he would want to own, but she didn't need to sit there all night to understand that the large tips being passed over the marble worktop were most likely a strong incentive to stay.

'But you are the genius eh, Kiti?'

Kitty raised her eyebrows doubtfully.

'You gonna be a big top lawyer one day no?' Beto looked quickly to Jaz.

'Not at this rate,' Kitty replied quietly.

'But she will.' Jaz squeezed Kitty's shoulders tightly.

The girls had been sat at the bar for nearly two hours when they decided to brave the checkered dance floor in the third room. Beto had been occupied for the last twenty minutes with a group of businessmen who were paying for the full show. The performance had included flaming cocktails, sparklers for their female companions' drinks, juggling and Beto had made it all look effortless.

'He's great, Jaz,' Kitty said, her voice slightly slurring, 'Jesus, Beto makes the G and Ts much stronger than they taste.'

Standing up Kitty felt a slight giddy lightheadedness. *How many did I have?* A sinking feeling took hold in her stomach as Kitty remembered the supper fiasco and considered how little she had actually eaten in her daze throughout the meal. *Oh God.*

'You good?' Jaz questioned holding Kitty's arm, steadying her.

'Yeah, yeah, I'm fine. Honestly, just may give it a miss on the next round. Stay here, I'm going to the ladies… or actually maybe for some fresh air.' Out of the corner of Kitty's eye she could see Beto had finished his show for the businessmen and would be making his way back to them soon enough. She didn't want to take Jaz away now that he was free again.

'Sure?' Jaz pushed.

'Yes ma'am!' With a dramatic salute, Kitty turned to leave. Spinning out of the manoeuvre a little too fast, the room blurred around her. Catching her heel in Jaz's bag strap, Kitty stumbled into the the man who had been sitting with his back to the girls for most of the evening.

All night the man had been rude to the staff, lecherous to most of the passing women and of all the people to bump in to, Kitty thought that she couldn't have picked a worse candidate.

'Sorry,' Kitty squeaked uprooting herself. *Shit. Well at least we didn't end up on the floor,* she thought, grateful for the small mercy.

The man turned around, red faced and furious. His latest Negroni, that he had been pouring down his throat by the bucketload all evening, dripped off the end of his aquiline nose and ran down from his chin. Standing up he started yelling furiously at Kitty, drawing some sympathetic looks from his party. She couldn't understand a word he said. Jaz leapt up to defend her, but before she could give the man both barrels, a spectator to the commotion drew the attention of the furious man, turning him away from Kitty to look at him instead.

There's no way, Kitty thought shocked, her hot cheeks no doubt betraying her. Standing before her was the soldier from the restaurant. He briskly glanced at her before speaking quickly to the angered customer.

With the adrenaline spiking in her system from the unexpected turn of events, Kitty's head cleared and she realised they were speaking Italian. Beto, having seen the commotion, had hastily made his way over to the girls.

'You ok, Kiti?' he asked looking uncomfortably in the direction of the soldier before returning his gaze back to her.

'Yeah, sorry. Just...' she floundered, 'Nothing. I'm good. It's nothing.'

'Don't worry about the fat bastard,' he whispered, making sure he could not be overheard.

Jaz laughed.

Kitty forced a smile. Turning back around from Beto - slower this time - she realised that the angry man and the soldier had vanished. Disappointment washed over her. Beto on the other hand seemed much more relaxed without either of the mens' presence.

Forcing the unwelcome butterflies that had begun to flap inside her to calm, Kitty turned to Jaz, 'I think I'm going to head back. Honestly don't leave though. I'll just grab an Uber and be fine.'

'You sure, Kit? I can come. I don't care.'

'No please. I mean it. Beto is off in an hour and you were going to hang out. I'll be sad if you leave with me. I promise I'm fine. Just tired. Long day.' Before Jaz could protest any longer Kitty continued, 'Thanks for a great night, Beto. So nice to meet you. Take care of Jaz - hopefully I'll see you again soon.'

He kissed her on both cheeks, 'Piacere mio, Kiti. The pleasure is mine.'

Finding comfort in the fact that she had managed to convince Jaz to stay, Kitty made her way back down the stairs, past the porcine bouncer and out into the street. The air, which had turned colder, made Kitty's breath condense. She wrapped up tighter in her coat, breathing out little clouds as she walked. Heading towards the road, Kitty pulled out her phone to order a taxi. It was dead. *Great.*

Head down against the wind, Kitty strode back to the bar's entrance. She had not gone six paces before she walked hard into a passing stranger. The two stumbled, thrown off-balance by the surprise collision of bodies. The stranger instinctively placed his hands firmly on Kitty's upper arms and she felt them steady her.

Looking up, praying silently that she was not about to see the puffy, red face of the crotchety man that she had disturbed earlier, Kitty began her apology, 'Oh my God! I'm so sorry, I don't know what's wrong with me today…' Kitty stared. Her voice trailed off. Her lips stuck parted, she felt the cold air rush unpleasantly down her throat as she took a sudden, sharp breath. Standing before her in composed silence was the soldier.

The memories of their two brief encounters thick with personal embarrassment, Kitty had not before appreciated his sculpted leonine features. He possessed distinct, high-set cheekbones, a tapered jaw and full, almost pouting lips that now, set in a hard line, gave him an indecipherable, imperious expression. The humour she had glimpsed at the restaurant had vanished.

Having restored her balance, the man swiftly removed his hands and Kitty met his gaze square on. She felt an unexpected, but not altogether unwelcome, apprehension sweep over her as she looked at his eyes. They reminded her of frosty winter mornings.

Smiling at her own ridiculous girlishness, Kitty spoke first, 'Hello stalker.' The greeting, an odd and overly familiar choice, had popped out before she had thought it through. She cringed at his answering frown.

He paused for a beat before speaking. 'I was going to say the same to you. Alright then, I'll settle for, "Good evening clumsy."' His voice was smooth and alluring as he coolly mocked her. His expression however was unreadable.

Kitty blushed and his arched dark brows furrowed a little.

Pull yourself together Cleopatra and for God's sake be nice! she scolded herself. 'Really I should have gone for, thank you for saving the situation back in the bar. I thought I almost had him but...' she quipped, clicking her fingers on her left hand as she swung it across her chest in mock frustration. The corner of his mouth twitched a fraction but he did not laugh.

'Well, thank you,' Kitty started again, this time opting for simple sincerity, 'I appreciate it.'

'You're most welcome.' The soldier turned as if to go, before adding, 'Forgive me, but are you alright? You seem...' the man stopped, his face remaining passive as if he had asked out of politeness rather than genuine concern.

Kitty's eyebrows shot up. No matter what the reason, she was rarely asked if she was ok. 'Um, yeah, I'm good. Just been a long day and now my phone's dead and I can't get home,' she began to ramble.

'I can take you if you need? My car is parked just around the corner.'

'Umm—'

'I'm quite harmless. Really. But up to you.'

Something about the man made Kitty doubt this, 'I better just let, Jaz, um, my friend upstairs, know about my phone.'

'Sure. Well I'll be around for another five minutes or so,' he paused, 'i'm waiting for my brother who's got something that belongs to me. He's just around the corner... apparently.' The man shifted his weight from one foot to the other and back.

'I see. Well, I'll come and find you if I need you. Thanks again.' Kitty hurried back inside and quickly made her way to the stairs at the far end of the club. The place was still packed. She fought the overwhelming draw to go with the man and his ruinous, frozen blue eyes. The butterflies in her stomach started to flip.

As she made her way up the stairs, her head was full of Burt's warning voice, *Remember now, Cleopatra, stranger danger,* he would always say whenever Kitty had left the fisherman's cottage. At university, one learnt to quiet these sorts of childhood warnings, as it was impossible to act upon them whilst coming into frequent contact with new people all the time on nights out. Despite this though, there was always the perceived, however potentially false, comforting assumption that they were attached to the University, which made it somehow "ok."

This isn't so weird, is it? she questioned herself, but the indefinable nagging in the corner of Kitty's mind persisted. Scratching at her palm as she walked up the stairs, she began to search for Jaz and Beto. *What would Jaz do?* Kitty laughed to herself - she knew exactly what Jaz would do.

FIVE

Raphael stood outside the bar on Upper James Street waiting for his brother. The weather had been getting colder throughout the past week and tonight it was the lowest recorded temperature of the winter so far. His weather app was predicting a seventy percent chance of snow fall across London. He couldn't remember the last time snow had settled in the capital. If he wasn't skiing, something which he excelled at and perhaps the only activity all of his siblings managed to do together without fighting, he had no time for the white mush and even less time for the complete chaos its presence always seemed to cause in the UK.

Raphael breathed into his hands, trying to warm them up, before shoving them impatiently in his pockets. He kicked at a piece of rough tarmac, nudging a little chunk loose from the pavement. Looking back in the direction that the young woman had disappeared, he felt a strange desire to go after her. *Maybe I am a stalker?* He chided himself remembering her greeting. Shaking his head, his dark hair fell across his forehead. It had gotten long quickly. He had shaved it all off after his last deployment. As if somehow it was possible to physically cut out pain. He should have known better.

Raphael's hair had always grown fast, one of the many things which annoyed his twin sister, particularly in the aftermath of some of her more ill-suited cuts. As a young girl she had never seemed to grasp that, although born at the same time, they were no more related than any of their other siblings, hence their differences were no more shocking. Despite Raphael's constant reminders, Martina had grown up stubbornly determined that anything her beautiful, blue-eyed brother could do, she could do as well… just as well… if not better.

This rivalry had spread to everything. If Raphael was picking figs in the orchard, Martina would pick more. If he was practising piano, she would practise more diligently. She would brush her teeth longer, eat her food faster. One Christmas, when they were twelve, Martina was hospitalised after hiding a fever that had escalated to pneumonia. When challenged by their mother as to her reasons for not coming to her sooner, Martina had merely sulked that she hadn't been as healthy this year as Raphael had been. This level of competition had denied them a particularly close bond. Despite beating Raphael at almost anything quantifiable, she had never gained the respect he could from Luca, nor, she knew deep down, was there the same depth of attachment their mother felt for him. After all, she had confided once, Raphael was named after an angel and no matter how hard she tried, she could never beat that.

It was shortly after this acknowledgement, aged seventeen, that a new, greater chasm had divided them irreparably. Even now, aged twenty-seven and considering everything that was happening to them, they still managed to end up quarrelling.

Joining the army, let alone the SAS, had caused bitter dissension in the family which had only deepened in the nine years since his commissioning. They had always harboured the feeling that he had renounced who he was and in doing so forsaken them. It had not been easy. His was not a family one could simply walk away from.

Kicking the piece of loose pavement into the road Raphael pushed his hair back out of his eyes and looked up at the night's sky. Not a single star was visible. It was thick with menacing cloud. Raphael decided the weather app was going to be correct on this occasion. Before his mind could wonder further, his phone began vibrating in his pocket.

'Ciao, Luca,' he listened to his brother, 'Really? Come on, Luc... I can't. I can't give her what she wants. I just make it worse... Are Martina and Pulce there too?' he listened a little while longer, scraping again at the pavement with his boot, 'Fine. Just say, you don't know... please?... Luca?' The line went dead. *Fuck.* Another chip came loose and he kicked it hard, this one flew far into the road.

'Is this a bad time to take you up on that offer of a lift?'

Raphael spun around. The young woman from before was standing back in the street. His right hand was twitching and he clenched his fist, forcibly stilling the muscles. 'How long were you standing there?' His voice came out harsh and the girl before him visibly recoiled a little. *Well done.* He straightened. Curt seemed to have become his default setting.

'I'm sorry,' Kitty blurted instinctually, 'literally a second.' That was not entirely true, but she didn't fancy confessing to the amount of his heated phone conversation that she had reluctantly overheard. Feeling her heart beating in her chest, Kitty was regretting coming back to find the soldier, but she bit her tongue for she was short on options.

Unfortunately, by the time she had made it back up to the bar, the other barmen had informed Kitty that Beto had managed to wangle leaving early and had already left with Jaz out the workers' entrance at the rear of the club. With no phone and a poor knowledge of London public transport routes, Kitty was now completely stuck.

She changed tack, 'If you just know a bus route I could use, or… if I could just borrow your phone if you have a travel app? I could check that or—'

'No of course not, that was… maleducato. Um… rude.' He paused, 'Where can I take you?'

Kitty watched the man warily as he stumbled awkwardly over the word rude. It was as if he had never verbally apologised for anything in his life. *Not that he had actually said sorry for his terseness*, the little voice in Kitty's head tutted. *He was the one who had offered the bloody lift after all.* Kitty stared for a second at his brow, still irritatedly furrowed, trying to read her contribution, if any, considering what she had overheard, to his now vexed disposition.

Distracted by a group of noisy revellers spilling out on to the street, Raphael looked away from her and she thought she saw a sadness cross his face. When his gaze returned he was composed again, all cheekbones and pouty lips. Despite his recovered poise, his violent, shining eyes betrayed him. Fleetingly Kitty wondered if she would ever decipher their meaning. Feeling a cold breeze bite at her ear, she pushed the thought aside.

'Thank you. Camden please. Literally by the Tube station would be great. Camden Town Tube Station that is,' she said, remembering that there were two. She pulled her coat tighter around her. She knew she could walk back to Jaz's place from that one.

'Fine.'

They walked down the road, past the leafless frames of the large oak trees that marked the end of Golden Square and made a left on to Brewer Street. An awkward silence filled the space between them. He was walking at a brisk pace and Kitty was struggling to keep up, cursing the heels she had been convinced to wear. She followed the man as he ducked into a narrow, cobbled side alley about a hundred metres down the road. Before following him, Kitty took note of the sign above - Farrier's Passage. She had only paused for the briefest of seconds, but he had noticed her hesitance immediately. She blushed deeply. *Well, if he's going to kill me, I'm not sure what noting street names will do about it. Trust and risk Kitty.*

A ghost of a smile brushed his lips, the same mischievous expression she had seen in the restaurant a few hours before. Kitty relaxed.

'Sorry,' she muttered again.

'You apologise a lot for things which aren't your fault.'

'You don't.'

Raphael look down at the impudent girl. His eyebrows had shot up his forehead and despite his attempt at lowering them, his lips remained slightly parted. She was right though. The thought amused him almost as much as her retort annoyed him.

Annoyed at herself, for she was trying to be a gracious recipient of the offer of a lift and did not want to be left stranded, Kitty re-answered the question. She knew full well it had been rhetorical in the first place, but she wanted to talk to the leonine soldier. 'Yeah, suppose I do,' she said before laughing quietly, 'sorry.'

Kitty knew she had done this ever since learning that it was the only thing that could rescue her from the full consequences of her sharp tongue and clumsy social interactions. She had become kinder with age and effort (hers and that of Freddie and Jaz), less peevish, less defensive, even more tolerant. But the habit of apologising had remained.

Miss M reckoned it stemmed from a deep-rooted desire, which she knew was there, despite Kitty's protestations, to be liked. Perhaps even a need to be loved, as often the case with the perpetually abandoned - but she had never confided this in Kitty, for that was not in Miss M's nature.

Raphael looked down at the young woman. Her laughter was soft and enchanting, but there was a sorrow behind it, like the song of a caged bird. He felt strangely melancholy hearing it.

'I really won't hurt you though,' he said before looking down the empty street toward the single parked car.

His words drew Kitty back from her wandering thoughts, finding it odd that the man obviously felt the need to reassure her. His body language exuded confidence, arrogance even. He was muscular as one would expect from a member of the Army and walked with an almost autocratic gait. Yet his reassurances suggested a softer interior than the curt facade which had been on display for most of their time together.

'The trusty line of every good serial killer.' She smiled before continuing, wanting to lighten the mood, 'But… I know.'

Raphael look down at her once again. She was looking at him, grinning. Though, the teasing aside, he was shocked by the confidence in the way she had said "*I know.*" This worried him for some reason. He didn't like it. 'How?' he questioned, his interest piqued.

His mood was vexed again and Kitty felt the easiness that had been growing between them vanish. *Curt, pouting man is back,* she thought.

'Well, you're in the SAS and so on probability, you probably won't be a serial killer as well. Really you should be quite a safe pair of hands, like a policeman.'

'Alright Sherlock. Tell me. How do you know I'm in the SAS?'

'The way you roll your left ankle slightly as you walk. I'm thinking it's pinned. The result of a bullet wound perhaps? Then there's the hair. It's too messy for a regular army soldier so you must work undercover and the eyes… well sir… it's all in the eyes. Open book. Dead giveaway.'

Raphael frowned at her.

Kitty laughed at his bemused face, before taking pity on him, 'I'm joking...obviously. It's the beret. Sand-coloured, downward pointing excalibur wreathed in flames. *"Who Dares Wins."* I don't know where it is now but you had it on the table at the restaurant.' She looked up at him innocently.

Now he smiled, pulling the folded beret from his pocket, 'Nicely done. You are surprisingly perceptive for someone so clumsy.' He gestured curtly to the passenger door of a large black Range Rover that was parked up beside them. 'Get in.'

'And *you* are surprisingly high-handed considering your chivalrous role in rescuing me at the bar.' Kitty raised her eyebrow.

Raphael stopped. This woman was quite frustrating. She confused him. She laughed with caution yet teased with a free bold confidence. It had been a long time since he had been alone in the company of a woman and he was quickly realising that tonight he was not going to get away with any bad manners. He walked forward to open the door for her, but she beat him to it.

Kitty climbed in. The car was enormous with slippery leather seats. Once she was in, the soldier shut the door softly - she thought she had better let him do that, slamming it in his face seemed rude. She watched out the windscreen as he slowly made his way around the bonnet to the driver's side. She saw him take a deep breath, his shoulders rising slightly in response, before he leapt in beside her.

He turned to her unexpectedly, 'I'm Raphael by the way. You can call me Rafa if you'd like.' He extended his hand, 'Everyone else does,' he trailed off.

'Kitty.'

'Kiti.' He repeated before turning on the engine. The car roared to life.

He spoke her name with the same stresses as Beto had at the bar. *What is it with the Italian boys all of a sudden?* Kitty smiled. She liked the way he said her name. His accent was faint, almost inaudible unlike Beto's, but crept out on occasion.

'Where are you from?' she asked.

'Roma. Well half of me is, but I'm assuming you were meaning the accent. My mother is Italian born and bred, but my father, English.'

They drove most of the way in silence. Kitty asked a bit about his family at first but felt as though she was prying somehow. It was the way he answered, simply, politely. It was as though he didn't want to talk at all. Perhaps it was the tense phone call she had overheard earlier making her feel excessively intrusive, but whether it was or not, she respected his privacy all the same. He drove with a calm proficiency despite the heavy traffic, his eyes remaining front the whole time. *How very un-Italian of him,* Kitty smiled to herself.

Out the corner of his eye Raphael could see Kitty smiling down into her lap. He wondered what she had seen. What conclusions she would draw from their brief time together. She had not asked anything for a while. He had told her about the fact that he had lived in England until he was six, and then Italy until he was sixteen. He had revealed that he was the first in his family to join the Army and that his family didn't really approve of the decision. That was an understatement, but he didn't feel like opening up that particular can of worms. His answers had been simple, to the point and she had clearly given up trying to learn anything new about him.

They had been driving for a while, picking their way through the heavy traffic and Raphael knew they weren't far from Camden Town tube station. He was regretting having not chosen a longer route. By now it was snowing as the weather app had predicted and he could have easily diverted, giving some vague excuse about gritted roads. Although having only afforded Kitty practically one sentence answers all evening, he now wished he could have another chance. Raphael couldn't remember the last time someone had asked him about his life, without the knowledge of who his family was. It was a novel feeling to be with someone who didn't want anything from him, and he was frustrated that he had let the opportunity pass.

Pulling alongside the curb, on a side road a short walk from the station entrance, he looked at Kitty and for the first time since he was a child, was unsure of what to say.

'Would you like to come in for a drink… So I can thank you? Jaz's house is literally two minutes from here,' Kitty said. She wasn't quite ready to let the perplexing man disappear just yet. Raphael, clearly hadn't been expecting that. He remained silent for an awkward length of time.

'I shouldn't,' he said.

He watched as Kitty's cheeks dropped ever so slightly. She was disappointed. 'One drink then.' The words shot out of him. He kicked himself.

Kitty sat in her chair. Her curiosity deepening. *I should really let the poor man go but, I don't want to, s*he mused, *Trust and risk.* 'Cool. I really am grateful.'

Kitty directed him to Jaz's student house. None of the lights were on. Turning off the engine Raphael silently followed Kitty inside. It was surprisingly tidy despite its residents occupations and completely empty.

'Where is everyone?' he asked.

Kitty eyed Raphael. She couldn't tell if he was he disappointed or relieved to be alone, 'Well, Emma. She lives on the top floor and has gone back home for the holidays already. Then Liv is staying with her boyfriend or something tonight and Jaz, well… I'm not exactly sure.'

'You should call her.'

'Um… Yeah. Good idea.' Kitty pulled out her dead phone and went in to the kitchen to look for a charger. She fiddled with it in the ensuing silence, willing it back to life. Standing behind her, she found Raphael deeply intimidating - not to mention bossy.

The phone finally came back to life and two messages flashed up.

'She's fine. Oh and she's staying with her new boyfriend tonight.' Jaz had asked Kitty earlier if the option occurred to stay with Beto would she mind. Kitty didn't mind at all, but she was a little surprised that Beto had been called "*new boyfriend*" so soon.

'The barman?' Raphael asked, distinctly unimpressed.

'Yeah, the very same. Do you know him?'

'Not really. Just saw them together. She looked quite… affascinata. What's the word? Yeah… smitten.'

His tone had turned condescending. If Kitty had hackles they would have been standing on end. *He's so bloody superior, he doesn't even know her!*

'Is that a bad thing?' Kitty heard the judgement thick in her own voice as she asked. She was not sure why she cared what this man's view of smitten was. But she did.

Raphael eyed her warily, 'No, not always I suppose.'

He was sitting on the fence.

'You suppose?' she continued, 'Do you have a girlfriend?'

'No.'

'Clearly.'

'If I did I wouldn't have accepted your offer.'

'Have you ever been in love?' Kitty was facing Raphael now. She had unknowingly crossed her arms. He was standing opposite her leaning casually against the kitchen worktops.

He looked at her, as she scowled fiercely. His face spread in to a broad, disarming smile, 'You tell me, Sherlock?'

His smile was desperately alluring and it broke her train of thought. 'Sorry.' Kitty bit her lip, holding back her amusement.

Realising she had been interrogating the poor man, Kitty uncrossed her arms and turned her attention to the drink that she had offered him. Looking around, she realised that the girls had obviously run down their stocks for the coming holiday. *Very sensible, very annoying,* she thought rifling through the poorly stocked cupboards.

'Well, there's tea and… yeah tea. D'you drink tea?'

'My English half does.' This was not exactly true. In fact, Raphael had always found the watery brown drink to be a poor relative of coffee.

Kitty sensed he was being polite. 'I mean there is red wine. Sort of,' she said apologetically holding up a near-finished bottle to the kitchen light.

'Tea's fine.'

Kitty busied herself making the two mugs of tea, unsure of what she was now going to say to the beautiful, difficult man, who had randomly stumbled into her evening. She returned the milk to the fridge, grateful that there had actually been some left. Turning back to the mugs, she saw Raphael was stood, holding them expectantly.

'Where can we sit?' he asked.

The house was tiny and barely had enough room for a full kitchen, let alone the tiny bar that had been fastened to the wall in place of a dining table. The two plastic stools below it looked pitifully uninviting. The girls often chatted with guests in their rooms. People would sit on the beds and, to be honest, they rarely had unknown visitors for whom a sofa to sit upon would have been more appropriate.

'Well…' Kitty began not entirely sure how Raphael would react, 'people usually just hang out in the rooms upstairs.'

He visibly stilled a fraction.

'I won't jump you,' Kitty teased, trying to hide her nagging self-consciousness.

'Kiti, you jumping me wouldn't be something I would worry about. Besides, you should be more worried about your good name, not mine.'

Raphael dutifully followed Kitty up the narrow stairs to Emma's bedroom that she was staying in on the top floor, all the while trying to keep his eyes on the carpeted steps. Kitty was about five steps above him and, a point he was trying to ignore, had an arousing sway to her walk.

'It's this one,' Kitty stated outside the final door. It was stiff and she had to put her back into it to get it to budge. Looking at Raphael as she reversed into the door, she reddened thinking about what he had said downstairs. She thanked Emma silently again for the little black dress she had loaned her.

Once inside, Raphael placed the two mugs down on the small desk squashed in to the left hand side of the room. The ceiling sloped away steeply to the right under which a double bed had been squeezed in, dominating the small space. Kitty sat on the end of the bed, at a loss as to what she should do. The space, often used to host guests due to the absence of a lounge, now felt more intimate than she had expected and she began to scratch at her palms.

'Tell me something about you then,' Raphael started. He made no move to sit next to her and instead stood, leaning his back against the far wall. He crossed his arms behind himself as though in restraints.

Despite the distance he had kept between them, Kitty was pleased that Raphael was seemingly going to be a little easier than he had been in the car. Even if that meant he was the one asking all the questions instead of answering them.

'Well...' she wasn't sure where to begin, 'i'm Kitty.' *Obviously, s*he chastised herself, before she continued, 'I literally have spent nearly my whole life in Cornwall until I moved to Cambridge.'

'Where did you live before?'

Kitty stayed silent. She couldn't go there. Not today.

'Ok. But you like Cornwall?' he continued.

'Umm, sure. It's alright.' This was a lie but Kitty, although not wanting Raphael to leave, was not about to tell the sorry tale of her Cornish life. She could imagine his sympathetic expression and stood in no need of his pity.

'So that's a no.'

'It's not Rome - put it that way.'

'That doesn't sound so bad,' he muttered quietly.

'You didn't like living in Rome?' Kitty asked confused. What she wouldn't have given to have been brought up in a city like Rome. Around every street corner a masterpiece waiting to be admired. The Vatican, the Pantheon. A city literally adorned with angels.

He ignored her question, instead asking one of his own, 'You didn't like living in Cornwall?'

He wasn't going to give up.

'It's small you see, the town I grew up in. Claustrophobic. Everyone knows everything. I lived amongst the same people I went to school with and their families for years. It just… gets boring.'

'So you want an adventure?'

'You could put it like that.'

'So why move to Cambridge?' He looked genuinely confused.

'Well I'm a student there. So—'

'Ah… so you're a smart one.' He was impressed, 'But surely Cambridge is small and claustrophobic too?' he finished, folding his arms more casually in front of his chest.

Kitty eyed Raphael unsure as to why the sudden interest in her fairly mundane life, 'Yeah it is. But they did a good degree and I hoped it would take me places.'

'I see. And did it?'

Kitty's shoulders dropped a fraction, 'No. It was meant to, but my third year trip to Russia was cancelled last minute.'

They spoke about the international relations crisis that had thwarted her plans and eventually Raphael sat down beside her. Kitty was thankful that the conversation began to flow more easily from this point. They discussed Russia and then the Middle East. It was something he seemed, perhaps unsurprisingly considering his job, to know a great deal about. They talked for a couple of hours about current affairs and spy rings throughout history, both impressed by the other's knowledge. Kitty realised that as long as the topics didn't get too personal, he was as passionate and engaging as they came.

Lying now side by side on the bed Kitty looked up at a small crack in the ceiling as she asked her next question, 'What's it like being in the SAS?' She regretted asking as soon as she felt him tense.

Kitty waited for what felt like a long time.

'It's not quite what I expected.' That was the most honest Raphael had ever been about his army career. Of course he had spoken to Alec and some of the other guys in his unit about it in the beginning. However over time they had all learned that it was easier to just not reflect on the jobs they were tasked to do, good, bad or otherwise and trying to explain it to a civilian was not worth the hassle. The things he had seen. *Fuck it's hard.* He wanted to say to Kitty who had now rolled over and was looking at him with sad, apologetically wide eyes. 'Someone's got to do it,' he added wryly. 'What are you planning on doing after uni?' he kicked the conversation back to her.

'I'm not sure.'

'Really? What do you want to do?'

'It's not as easy as that.'

'If it was?'

'If it was I would be a lawyer.'

'Really? Yeah, I can see that, Sherlock.' He smiled widely, 'So if you want to do law so much, why not do it now?'

'The law doesn't want me…'

'You're at Cambridge. Don't tell me you're not smart enough?'

'It's not the exams. It's the interviews.' Kitty could feel her palms beginning to get moist. She didn't like all the questions and was blaming her earlier intake of gin for her candour.

'I don't—' Raphael began.

But Kitty cut him off, instead opening a new line of questioning. 'Tell me,' she began. Looking at Raphael's now concerned face, she stopped. She was running out of dispassionate conversational topics and didn't want him to leave, but this question was bothering her and she needed a distraction from his own line of inquiry.

'Go on.' He was still tense.

'Why did you come in?'

He looked confused by this question.

'As in why did you agree to come in to the house with me, here?'

Raphael thought for a second. He thought about her clumsiness. How Giovanni had shouted at her at the bar and he thought about the paradoxical sorrow in her laugh. He looked back at Kitty, her face so close to his. *You have no idea who I am,* he reflected.

Kitty searched his face for an answer, but he remained silent. The exhaustion of the last few weeks of exams and yet more law school rejections suddenly felt overwhelming. She was bone-tired and felt unusually unsettled by Raphael's silence. *Why do I care!?* she wanted to scream at herself. He seemed to either deeply dislike who he was, or not like her enough to share anything personal and she suddenly found herself feeling crushingly mediocre in comparison to the mercurial soldier lying in the bed beside her. Feeling an unwelcome rush of tears she blinked them back hard. *God this couldn't get any worse.* Deciding it was best to make a break for the bathroom to compose herself, Kitty sat bolt upright. Having completely forgotten about the sloping ceiling above, she smashed her forehead hard into the ageing plaster.

'Shit!' she yelled grasping her brow. Her head was ringing as she squeezed her eyes shut.

Shocked, Raphael sat up next to her. Ducking a little to allow for the low ceiling, he shifted to sit in front of her and put his hands carefully either side of her head. She was now covering her entire face.

'Kiti?' he asked.

'Mmm,' she mustered. The tears were flowing now and although she had the excuse of the mortifying head ceiling collision she couldn't bear to look at him.

'Kiti, look at me.' It wasn't a question. Raphael was serious now. He prised her hand from her face and felt a sharp pain in his chest when he realised she was crying.

Kitty stared at the duvet. She was too tired and embarrassed to work out what to say.

Unthinking he shifted his weight forward on to his knees and cradling the back of Kitty's head kissed her softly. Her lips, wet from her tears, were warm against his. He was pleased when she kissed him back. Her soft hair tangled in his hands. He smelt her perfume and felt a deep, longing stir within him. He needed Kitty. That's why he had accepted her offer. But he needed her in a way and for a reason she could never understand.

Using all the strength he could muster Raphael pulled away. She stared up at him through her tear soaked lashes. He stared back at her for a moment. He hadn't realised until her tears how much he wanted her. In Kitty he saw a chance of something unexplainable. Redemption? But at what cost to her? He needed her innocence and in being with her would no doubt destroy it.

'I shouldn't have done that.'

Kitty smiled guiltily, 'I'm glad you did.'

'Mmm.' He shifted his weight on the bed, 'I should go, Kiti.' He smiled back but this time it didn't touch his eyes.

'Stay.'

Raphael sighed, putting his face in his hands.

'Please?' Kitty pressed further. She didn't want him to leave.

Raphael looked at her. Looking at her wet cheeks and the bruise now starting to appear on her forehead his resolve disintegrated. 'Let me get you some ice for that head,' he breathed as he climbed off the bed and headed for the kitchen.

Kitty was not sure if that meant he was staying, but was relieved that it hadn't been an outright no.

A couple of minutes later, Raphael returned with a half finished bag of frozen peas that he had found in the freezer. Having scooped up a tea towel as he had left the kitchen, he now sat back down next to Kitty and, having wrapped the icy bag, held them gently against her head.

Kitty took the frozen packet from him and lay back on the pillow. This time she tucked herself nearer Raphael's warm body, the temperature in the room having dropped with the passing hours. She felt the welcome calm that accompanied the cold on her bruise. A small 'ah' escaped her.

Raphael sat reticent. Wordlessly watching Kitty. After a while, he gave in.

Losing his unspoken battle, Raphael lay back down beside her, consciously not reopening the distance between them, and then closed his eyes. They lay in the gloom. Just touching. The faint glow of the pendulum light hanging from the ceiling above, with its cheap energy-saver bulb, was doing a poor job of beating out the darkness. Still dressed in his uniform, it felt strange to be lying next to a woman on a comfortable mattress. He only ever slept in his uniform on exercise. In its own way, he thought the evening had been just as eventful.

'Kiti?' he started. He wanted to tell her who he was. He fought to convince himself that he should allow Kitty the chance, with all the facts, to decide if he was worth her time, 'Kiti?' he said again.

Peering up at him from under the bag of frozen peas, Kitty waited for Raphael to continue.

Now desperately trying to read behind her blank expression, Raphael wasn't sure he could survive her disdain. Not tonight. Silencing his conscience, he swiftly removed the peas and, burying his shame, kissed her once more. First delicately on her forehead, the tip of her nose and then more ardently as his mouth found hers. He knew what he wanted from her. She may be an adulterer, a coveter and a thief, he could not know. But he knew she wasn't like him. One learnt to recognise the traits of themselves in others and in that respect she was guiltless.

He wanted to bathe in that innocence and if she would give it to him, he would take it.

Kitty matched Raphael's advances equally. *Trust and risk*, she told herself. She couldn't have explained to anyone why she had reciprocated his kisses, or in truth, why she had spent every moment, from the first moment he had sat down on the bed, hoping he would kiss her. But she did and for the first time in a long while, Kitty was not going to overthink the situation, or let her insecurities hamper her fun. She would trust and take a little risk. *Better to have loved and lost, than never to have loved at all,* she heard Jaz's mantra ringing in her head as she opened her mouth to his warm tongue's explorations.

Gently turning Kitty over onto her front Raphael slowly unzipped her dress, planting a trail of kisses down her back as he revealed each new section of her soft skin.

When he was done, Kitty slipped out of her dress and turned back to face Raphael once more, this time wearing nothing but her delicate lace pants. Leaning beside her, balanced on one elbow, his eyes slowly raked over her entire naked body. With his free hand he traced abstract patterns around her breasts and down around her navel. He had slept with countless women, but none had ever aroused him like Kitty was doing now, without he was certain, her even realising what she was doing. He kissed the delicate space between her breasts.

Her light hands made quick work of undoing his shirt and he lay back obediently, as Kitty pressed him flat against the duvet. Exploring his body, she traced her hands over the defined lines of his muscular arms, then his torso, replacing each touch with a teasing kiss, slowly working her way lower, towards the waistband of his trousers.

She wasn't doing anything in particular, but Raphael was afire. She was so natural, naive even. She wasn't trying too hard. She wasn't trying to impress some mythical, idealised version of him bolstered by the prior knowledge of his family. He realised she was the first woman who was entirely present with Raphael just as she saw him before her, Raphael the soldier. The notion made him giddy. He moaned. She had unfastened his trousers and had grazed the newly revealed patch of skin with her teeth. Feeling emboldened by his response, Kitty was about to move lower again but he stopped her and gently returned her back to the duvet.

Kneeling over Kitty, Raphael began to kiss her feet, then her calves, massaging and nipping his way up the sensitive skin of her inner thighs, his repetitions ever-increasing the tingling ache in her belly. Knowing the truth, his conscience, despite being frequently ignored these days and already once tonight, would not allow him to receive all the pleasure, without duly satisfying the rare creature, who had reminded Raphael that there were indeed some things still worth living for.

Kitty bucked her hips, as Raphael's hair tickled the sensitive skin at the heart of her arousal. She gripped the tops of his sculpted shoulders, her pulse racing. He held her steady and she was lost to the rhythm of his skilful tongue.

Placing one last kiss on her pubic bone before kicking of his boots and deftly removing the remainder of his uniform, he positioned himself over Kitty once more. She had tangled her fingers in his hair, and was gazing up at him, flushed, a picture of dewy charm. Hovering above her ribcage, he eased into her carefully, like a gentlemen. He waited a moment until he was certain that she was comfortable, checking her face, kissing her cheeks, 'Kiti?' he whispered, pecking her right ear.

'Mmm…' she simpered in response.

He settled his lips once more over her smile and brushed an errant piece of hair from her face. That was the last gentlemanly thing he did. This was not love for Raphael, this was necessity. They fell into a savage rhythm. He held her tightly against him and with every soft mew that escaped Kitty's lips she gave him what he needed.

Absolution.

With his back resting against the cold wall Raphael looked down at Kitty. She was fast asleep. Her lips, swollen from his kisses, hung slightly parted and her hair partially obscured her face.

Slowly moving to the edge of the bed, Raphael carefully picked up the discarded bag of now defrosted peas and carried them across the room, silently placing them down on the desk. The two mugs of tea, long cold, were still untouched on the side. Raphael gently lowered himself into the desk chair. He checked his watch. It was four in the morning.

He watched her sleep for a couple more hours. She was restless that night. She tossed and turned as if warring with some invisible demon. *She sleeps like me,* he thought sadly.

By the time the city was stirring under the fresh dawn light, the possibilities of the night before now unimaginable to him, Raphael was gone.

SIX

Thanks to its enviable south-westerly outlook, the villa at Théoule-sur-Mer was drenched in sunlight from dawn till dusk. Situated high up on the hillside just fifteen kilometres down the coast from Cannes, the terrace and pool had spectacular panoramic sea views encompassing the Lérins Islands and the Esterel Mountains. Primarily composed of porphyry rock, the mountains were a deep red in colour, sublimely congruous with their volcanic origin. They sat in striking contrast to the azure waters of the Mediterranean Sea below and the green swaths of the oak forests that covered vast sections of the rugged terrain.

Throughout the last six days, Freddie and Kitty, along with his parents, had comprehensively explored the sandy beaches, colourful creeks and hidden coves nestled into the wild, rocky coast along the Corniche d'Or between their villa and Cannes.

Freddie's family had been coming to this villa long before Kitty had joined them and had nurtured a fondness with the locals. Nowadays they knew the owners, who lived in a villa down the road, rather well. Well enough at least, that they had not been subject to the ever rising prices of the now distinctly gentrified area.

Visiting France each summer was a tradition that Kitty loved more and more each time she came. She now felt nothing short of adoration, for the week she would spend swimming and reading in the warm sunshine each year.

Kitty floated lazily around the villa's infinity pool. Sculling gently with her hands, she felt the relaxing cool of the water as it washed over her hot skin. It was around four o'clock in the afternoon and the sun was beating down unobstructed, a resplendent golden orb suspended in an otherwise empty sky. Anne had just headed off for a nap in one of the air-conditioned bedrooms upstairs, whilst Freddie and his father had ventured off to a secluded rocky outcrop that they had found the day before, to try their luck - which had been lacking this holiday - at fishing. They had been gone since lunch and Kitty reckoned they would be back soon, leaving time to swim, before deciding where the team would go for supper. Most nights they had headed north into the bustling streets of Cannes. But Kitty had the feeling that Freddie wanted to go somewhere different tonight, having already comprehensively studied what felt like every boat in the Port there.

Making her way to the end of the infinity pool, Kitty looked out, past the yachts milling about just off the coast, to the horizon. Since arriving in France, this had been the first time she had really been alone. Closing her eyes, she felt the warmth on her eyelids and smiled.

It was the first quiet moment she had experienced in eighteen months where she hadn't thought of Him. The vanishing man whose name she had banished with the memories of their brief encounter. She had found, with the absence of a name, that she was able to forget him more easily - as he appeared to have completely forgotten her.

Waking up that snowy morning in December, alone in Jaz's student house had really rocked Kitty. More than she had expected and more than she cared to admit. It had been late morning when she had stirred.

Woken by a growing pain in her forehead. Kitty opened her eyes. Due to her tears the night before, her mascara covered lashes had fused tight shut and so she sat for a minute on the bed, picking at the dry clumps with her fingers. Blinking in the darkness she realised that someone must have switched off the light and shut the curtains after she had fallen asleep. She didn't remember doing that. That was when the memories of the previous evening came flooding back to her.

She looked down to her side, sensing then confirming that her mysterious soldier was not there. Getting up, gathering the duvet around her, she made her way over to the small window. She threw back the curtains and felt the sun on her face. It was bright, reflecting off the snow covered roofs beyond, but there was no warmth in it. She blinked, her pupils struggling to focus with the sudden increase in light. Standing at the window Kitty put her hand up to her face. She stroked her lips slowly, remembering the feeling of his mouth, tentative at first, but then passionate on hers. The butterflies, previously satiated, flinched. She admired the delicate frost crystals that had formed along the base of the window panes. Listening to the house, the answering silence told her that she was alone, and some unpleasant instinct told her that this wasn't about to change.

She had been right, but it had been a few weeks before it had really sunk in that he wasn't coming back. No messages, no surprise meetings, nothing. The depressing realisation had crept up on her, when she was alone just after the turn of the New Year.

Kitty had declined Freddie's invitation for Christmas, instead spending the rest of the festive period in a semi-deserted Cambridge. She liked Cambridge better like that. She could investigate, unobstructed, like the alley-cat she was. No false pretences at romance for the tourists, no work, and this year, it had included the added bonus of no one to see her tears, which had returned frequently and unannounced at various locations all over the city. It had taken her a couple of weeks of effort to restrict them to her pillow, by which time, after a barrage of further messages, Kitty had agreed to spend a few days with Freddie and his family for New Year.

Once Freddie's additional family, who had been staying for the multitude of Christmas festivities, had driven away, Kitty managed a hasty retreat to the guest bedroom to avoid Anne. Anne was busying herself furiously tidying, complaining about a never ending list of relatives, whilst Freddie and his father went to the local supermarket to restock.

'The gannets have eaten all the Christmas chocs! Even the ones for Kitty. Drat! That would have been Harry's family. No doubt… his fat mother Marge. Greedy cow. After forgetting the ham too…mmm…no doubt,' Anne fumed.

Kitty had heard her repeat variations of this rant numerous times since her arrival, as Anne stripped beds and plumped cushions, all ending in an insult about her mother-in-law. Even a comment about washer fluid had concluded with a new insult about fat-mother-Marge. Kitty had watched as Anne beat one mauve throw cushion so hard, she had been left in a shower of tiny white feathers. This, unsurprisingly, had done little to lighten her mood, hampered further by the sticky discarded Quality Street that she had then discovered attached to the inside arm of the new sofa. With no immediate family, let alone the zoo of extended relatives people seemed to have spring up at Christmas, Kitty had no practice in consoling a person in the throes of feeling that their festive efforts had fallen flat, or in this case, been too gluttonously taken advantage of.

From the intended safety of the guest bed, Kitty found herself once again staring out alone onto a snowy winter scene and finally was forced to acknowledge the full extent of the loss she felt. The realisation had been creeping up behind her, not altogether unnoticed, like she had been caught in a never ending game of "*What's the time Mr Fox?*" But Kitty had still tried to stave off the unwanted knowledge. She felt used. Worse. She felt abandoned - again - and the fact stung, deepening a chip on her shoulder she had been trying hard to close up. *Trust and risk… fuck that.*

She hadn't known him. In truth all she could confidently express about him was just how little she had known. Yet Kitty mourned for a sort of, lost future, that for some irrational reason, now it had escaped her, she desperately wanted. She couldn't explain it to herself, it was just an indefinable, deep fervour within her. It was as though she had won the lottery and, at the last minute, someone had cruelly snatched away her winning ticket. She wanted him back and yet she also never wanted to see him again. Kitty had never spoken of the events that evening to Jaz nor anyone else. She knew it would sound crazy to anyone who couldn't literally feel what she felt. She thought it bordering on deranged herself. The depth of loss disturbed her. On top of this, Kitty knew she could not bear to hear herself explain what had actually happened and make it irreversibly real.

Nevertheless, by the time the daffodils had made cheery yellow carpets throughout Cambridge, the sadness had turned to a potent indignation. She was angry at him for cruelly vanishing, she was perhaps angrier at herself for allowing for all these months to have felt so forlorn. And by the time summer came around, all that remained was her wounded pride and the irksome knowledge, she had allowed herself to believe, that the evening they had shared, at the time so passionate and trusting, was anything more than the actions of a difficult man, consoling a crying, disappointed woman.

Kitty had ploughed long hours into her dissertation throughout her final year at Cambridge. Creating an unnecessarily perfect masterpiece and securing a high first, had both proved easier than risking social interaction with anyone new, or having to think about the whole embarrassing ordeal with Him. A fact, for the life of her, Kitty could not rationally unpick. Subconsciously and slowly, as the months went by, she healed. Only now with the French sun warm on her eyelids did she realise that she had. She smiled.

A muffled ringing sound, coming from underneath the towel on her sun lounger, broke her train of thought. Opening her eyes, Kitty swam quickly to the steps wondering who would be calling. Making her way to the lounger, she carefully unfolded the rumpled towel and picked out her phone. Unknown Number. Briefly pausing she assessed the number on the screen. It began plus-four-four-two-zero so Kitty surmised the call was coming from London. Clicking the green, accept-call symbol, Kitty held the phone up to her ear, 'Hello?'

'Hello. Is this Miss Cleopatra May?' a clipped female voice answered.

Kitty felt a small twist of disappointment. *Almost healed then,* she thought, annoyed.

'Hi, yes it is. Please may I ask whose calling?' Kitty's voice turned formal, matching that of the unknown caller. She sat, perching half-on-half-off the sun lounger.

'Good afternoon Cleopatra. My name is Lucille. I'm calling from the Daring Corporation HR department in London. We would be delighted to offer you a spot on our inaugural graduate placement scheme here in London.'

'Wow! Thank you so much.' Kitty was shocked. She hadn't heard anything after the final telephone interview she had completed last March for the Daring Corporation and had supposed that it had been as unsuccessful as her other attempts to find employment.

It had turned out, without the final exam grade, a Russian degree, even from Cambridge, had been much less appealing to companies than Business and Economics degrees. Students studying the more vocational courses had breezed through selection at the top companies where Kitty had been repeatedly rejected. Talking to the careers team at Cambridge, they had stated, something which they routinely neglected to mention to prospective students at the university open day, that they often found their language students struggled in initial applications, for they couldn't prove their skill until they had received their final mark. Albeit frustrated, Kitty had been comforted by this and thanks to her final grade, both her and the careers team were confident that the situation would be very different when the September applications opened.

Having been faced with an impromptu, perhaps endless, amount of time with no commitments and with her tenancy in Cambridge ending with her graduation, Kitty had been forced to return to Truro. Anne had once again filled her house with Freddie's father's relatives and so Kitty had found herself living back at Burt's cottage, a situation she had promised not to repeat, for the four weeks in the lead up to the holiday in France. The four weeks in the crumbling cottage had been a painful reminder of her abandonment. It was as though the walls themselves had been built out of grief and plastered with the memories of the missing. Desperate to escape the confines of the pokey rooms, packed with the paraphernalia of Burt's life, Kitty had spent almost everyday fishing - an activity she detested - and eating crisp sandwiches, washing them down, as always, with copious amounts of Ginger beer. While most people may have found a few weeks of reliving their childhood past times comforting, as the days had passed, Kitty had become suffocatingly frightened and progressively more certain that she had needed to leave. And leave soon. She could not allow herself to become trapped.

Burt knew this had been the cause for Kitty's increasingly bad temper. That and Roger unhelpfully tearing the corner off her leather luggage case - a most unfortunate turn of events. But there was not much else he could do for her, so Burt had silently soldiered on beside her. Buttering sandwiches and hoping for something good to come her way.

'The team here at Daring was particularly impressed with your linguistic ability,' Lucille continued, unaware of Kitty's wondering mind, 'It was decided that our selection board would wait until final university marks were published before we made any firm offers. Hence we are getting in contact now. You also scored exceptionally highly on the psychometric tests.'

Kitty had slightly zoned out. *Wow... I'm free.* The application for Daring had been long and confusing. There had been many varied questions about interests and experiences, and at no point had she been able to illicit what specific type of candidate they were looking for. The initial forms had then been followed by long, online psychometric tests and then two phone interviews, the sole purpose of which, seemed to be to question where she had worked before and what she had learned from these previous experiences. Kitty had been stumped as to how she could embellish her past employment history which included just one title. Barmaid.

'Hello?' Lucille asked.

'Hi! Umm... hello. Yes, sorry,' Kitty took a quick breath, 'I would be delighted to accept. Thank you.'

'Excellent. I'll have our team email you the contract. While that's signed, we will undertake our background checks. Criminal records checks, that sort of thing. Then assuming that's fine, you'll be good to go.'

'Great. Thanks. I mean thank you,' Kitty said again. 'Oh - just one thing. When does the scheme officially start?'

'As it's the first scheme Daring has run, subject to checks going smoothly, you will be starting August first. We plan to have you complete a four week introduction plan ending early September, and then we will assemble the graduates to begin streaming and mentoring shortly after. Does that work?'

'Sounds perfect.'

That would give Kitty a few weeks to find somewhere to live, with the rest of her savings, she could probably move to London as soon as she had found somewhere suitable.

'Fantastic. Well thank you, Cleopatra. I'll have the necessary documents sent over at once.' With that Lucille hung up.

Kitty lay back on the lounger reeling a little from the sudden turn of events.

The next thing she knew she heard Freddie's ecstatic tones. Waving the glazed-eyed bodies of two shiny silver fish in her face he beamed, 'Kit look! How awesome's this. Dad got one too... Kit?' he frowned at her, 'Everything alright Kit?'

Freddie had seen this distracted look on Kitty's face many times since the December before last. He was pretty sure something, or someone, had really upset her. He knew it must have been bad, as Kitty was rarely visibly affected by the opinions, or even actions of others. It was one of the things he loved about her. Yet she had been overly sensitive for eighteen months at least by his count. He was not one to pry and Kitty sure as hell not one to open up freely, so Freddie had done a good job at pretending not to notice. He had covered for her when his mother had asked why Kitty had almost exclusively remained in their guest bedroom each time she had stayed recently and even lying that he had been with her on most of the occasions that Anne had referenced. Despite, in truth, having spent much of Kitty's stays in his own room - alone as she had been. Freddie was also pretty sure that Kitty had not noticed that he was aware of anything strange about her, which had been even more unusual.

Staring at his best friend, her hair tied in a messy, wet bun on top of her head, he was relieved, on closer inspection, to see that it was not the same sad distance that he had become accustomed to seeing in her eyes. She was instead in shock.

'Oi!' he teased, clicking his fingers.

Kitty looked at him, 'Sorry. Amazing! Congrats! I… um…'

Freddie waited patiently, not sure exactly where she was going with her train of thought. Then she smiled and all his worries melted away.

'I was just offered a job. At The Daring Corporation would you believe?'

'Shit. That's awesome, Kit. Nice work.' Freddie embraced her.

'Argh. Gross. Thanks, Fred, but those fish absolutely reek. I'm here escaping Burt and his smelly creatures, remember.'

She pushed Freddie and his silver fish away.

He laughed - she was back.

'Afternoon, Kitty,' Harry called, having just made his way out on to the terrace, his sunglasses sitting nestled in the rapidly vanishing golden strands that crowned his head.

The day out by the water had turned Harry's face a rich salmon colour, which although smiling now, would be painful come this evening. Kitty noted that she would need to find him some moisturiser.

'Did Fred tell you?' he continued.

'Yeah he did. Great job with the fish!'

'Speaking of jobs,' Freddie elbowed Kitty.

Harry was lost.

'Oh. Yeah. I got one. How mad's that?'

'That's great! Well done.' Harry made his way over, taking his turn to hug Kitty.

'Fish! Get rid of the fish. They stink!' she cried.

The three of them laughed together, each delighted for their own reasons. Harry was thrilled that he had caught a fish, Freddie was relieved he seemed to have the old Kitty back, and Kitty was relieved, for she had found an escape which would save her from having to return Truro.

Hearing the commotion, Anne appeared at the upstairs balcony, 'What have I missed?' she called down to the trio.

'Kit got a job,' Freddie called up, 'and we finally caught some fish,' he added waving his two madly in the air.

'That's wonderful! Give me a second.' Anne made her way quickly down to the terrace and embraced Kitty, 'Well done sweetheart.' She then moved to embrace her boys, 'Are we going to eat in tonight? Cook the fish on the barbecue or something? Or Fred did you still want to go down to see the boats at Saint-Raphaël?'

Kitty stilled, 'Where?'

'Saint-Raphaël. It's just the next port along. We had that beautiful meal there your first year. Or was it…'

Anne continued trying to remember which year they had explored Saint-Raphaël, but Kitty had stopped listening. Interrupting Anne's ramblings, gaining her a disapproving frown, Kitty said, 'Yeah, let's stay in. I'm up for a barbecue. We can go to the little shop to pick up some salad bits. You know, the one past the villa with the brown shutters.'

Surprised by Kitty's readiness to stay in for dinner, which was most out of character, and delighted that he would not have to fork out for another restaurant supper for their final night, Harry quickly piped his support.

With both his father and Kitty firmly in the remain camp, Fred happily obliged.

From her seat by the pool, Kitty watched the merry trio make their way inside to prepare the fish. Kitty kicked herself. *It's just a stupid name.* Alone again, she reclined on the sun lounger. The padding was warm against her back, having been exposed to the sun all day under the cloudless sky. Closing her eyes Kitty rubbed at her temples. *New job, new start, Kit.*

Later that evening, after the barbecue dinner, Freddie had convinced Kitty to come out to a cosy wine bar a short walk from the villa. The place, only open at night, was expectedly busy and it had taken them a short while to secure one of the small outside tables made from old wooden barrels. Here they had sat, perched on high stools, for the past ten minutes, in the sublime evening warmth, watching the street sellers and passing tourists funnelling into the building towards the bar. Serving only a *trio de croque monsieurs* consisting of layers of ham and white truffle, foie gras and onion confit and yakitori prawns, Kitty regretted having agreed to a barbecue.

'Kit,' Freddie began warily.

'Just say it,' Kitty said, her tone flat. She had been waiting all evening for his questions.

'It's just that... I just... well...'

'Fred. Spit it out.'

'Are you sure taking the job at Daring is the right thing for you?' he mumbled, rushing his words.

'I'm not going round this again.'

'But you've wanted to be a lawyer. A prosecutor like.' Freddie stopped himself on seeing Kitty's bottom lip tremble. Once she had gained control, he started again, rephrasing, 'You have wanted it for as long as I've known you.'

'Well we don't always get what we want.'

'I just meant...' He raised his hands. Beseeching.

'Fred. I know what you're trying to do and it's sweet. But I need to get out of Truro. I've tried and tried to do the law thing and I'm going to let it go.'

'You can live with me and—'

'I'm going to let it go, Fred.'

Kitty took a sip of her wine. She pretended not to notice when she saw Freddie clear his throat once more to say something and then stop himself having thought better of it. She knew a part of her had hoped to have been rejected from all of the large corporations that she had applied too. A reason for her to try once again to follow her passion. But the four weeks in Truro had solidified her resolve. She would never be trapped in the house again. She didn't care if Miss M thought she was just running from the memories instead of tackling them head on, or whatever bollocks she had talked about the first few times they had been forced to "*talk.*"

'Do you mind if I cut in there for a sec, mate?' A handsome black man, tall and lean approached the table. His crisp white shirt was undone to his throat, his expression was one of serene confidence as he spoke directly to Freddie. A glass of red wine hung his hands.

'No…umm…' Freddie looked from the man to Kitty. 'I'll just get us some more wine ok?' Freddie made his way toward the bar, not waiting for Kitty's response.

'I might,' Kitty said curtly, looking cooly up at the intruder. She didn't like that the man had not asked her directly.

'I apologise.' The man, having taken up residence on Freddie's stool stood up again and walked away.

Kitty, alone, and not wanting to invite anyone else's attentions picked out her phone from her pocket. Vaguely she scanned the screen for for texts or missed calls - of which she knew there were none.

'D'you mind if I have a seat there, mate?' a voice called.

The man, now wearing a cheeky sideways grin, was back looking even more pleased with himself.

A touch amused, Kitty allowed the man to once more take up residence on Freddie's stool, 'You can have a seat. But I warn you now, I don't leave bars with strangers anymore.'

'Good thing i'm 'appy to stay at the bar then,' he winked, 'Elliot.' He extended his hand.

Kitty rolled her eyes, 'Kitty.'

'Kitty. What brings you to France then?'

The conversation flowed surprisingly easily for the next five minutes. Elliot was, in a cocky sort of way charming, a fact even Kitty had to acknowledge. He was carefree and his London accent didn't make everything sound stupidly silken and smooth. Her name sounded normal when he spoke it. He seemed normal and, with a disarming candour, he had even managed to get the news of her new job offer out of her. Before her assessment could continue Freddie returned, she heard his bad tempered breathing as he sidled up to the table, re-armed with two new glasses of chilled white wine.

'You all done?' Freddie asked Elliot.

'Yeah, we're done,' Kitty replied.

Elliot chewed on his lip. He shook his head laughing, 'You warned me.'

'Yes I did.'

'Well 'ave a lovely evenin' then.' With that he grinned and climbed off the stool. 'See you around.'

'Not likely,' Kitty added.

'You're movin' to London though.'

'It's a big place.'

'Not that big,' Elliot winked. Raising his glass in toast to Kitty he looked sincerely into her eyes. All previous humour gone he lowered his voice, as though out of respect, 'May the best of your past be the worst of your future.'

Kitty felt her mouth fall open. She scrambled around, trying to work through the confusion. Had she read him wrong? Had she heard him wrong? But by the time the shock had subsided enough for her to focus her attention,

Elliot had vanished. She turned to Freddie who had taken his stool back, 'Fred did you—'

'Anyone could have chosen that toast, Kit,' he answered.

'He knew, Fred.'

'Kit…' Freddie warned.

'He knew.'

Kitty had spent the rest of the evening trying to find Elliot again. They had checked all the bars along the promenade, and those that dotted the older twisting side passages, but he had vanished as quickly as he had arrived and eventually Kitty had been forced to accept this.

The *"new job, new start"* mantra - despite having been replaced by the curious meeting with Elliot, eventually returned to her and it was this little phrase that kept Kitty going through the last of the long summer days.

She spent her time, once back from France, in Holloway with Jaz. Jaz was now working as a sales assistant, in a different branch of the same accountancy firm as Mr Taylor. Despite having been there for a year now, Jazz had remained forceful in her reminders to her parents that this job was a temporary stopgap and she would be travelling the world soon. 'Most likely with a backpack, a tattoo and a lover,' she would add on the nights she felt her parents were failing to take her seriously. These rants had made Kitty laugh. She was relieved to see, despite her ever increasingly serious relationship with Beto, that Jaz had not lost her independent adventurous streak.

Freddie, having completed his degree that same year, had secured himself a job in Southampton. Working for a respectable firm building boats down at the docks, he had found himself with much to learn and little time to spare. Nevertheless, he had managed to see both the girls on the last weekend in July.

Kitty had never possessed many things, but she still appreciated the company Freddie and Jaz had provided on the day she had moved into her rented room, barely bigger than a closet, just down from Market Row on Coldharbour Lane, Brixton.

Now standing suited in The Daring Corporation's headquarters. Kitty knew she was completely ready for this next chapter of her life. The shortcomings and difficulties that had haunted the past eighteen months all but melted away, carefully locked up alongside the troubles that had followed her since the interrupted trial of Monsieur Renard the stuffed fox, as she strode without a backward glance into the impressively imposing atrium. Life was going to get better. She would make it better.

SEVEN

'Cocaine.' Vasili spoke calmly. He saw no point in lying to the man sat opposite him. *Well*, he qualified, *no point in lying about this*. Vasili needed him to know his cargo would be illegal. He wouldn't have requested this conversation be held in the privacy of his own home if it was not.

The man opposite knew this well too. It was the only reason he had made the time for Vasili, and why he had agreed to meet here, out of his way, in the typical, ostentatiously furnished living room of a young Russian too rich to have taste and perhaps, he speculated considering their meeting so far, common sense. Additionally, he was all too aware that even his own office most likely harboured unsympathetic ears and with this kind of work, the only ears he wanted hearing anything at this stage, were his own. For Nero Ossani had learned a long time ago, that trust in others, was a luxury in life he had not been given.

Sitting back in a studded, metallic damask armchair, Vasili waited impassively as Nero's gaze moved toward the window. He did not speak as Nero took a lengthy drag on his now half burnt cigarette, nor did he react as the man nodded, almost imperceptibly, as though communing with some invisible third party, whose views Vasili was not privy too. He continued to watch as Nero silently took the cigarette twice more to his lips. After an inordinate amount of time, the man returned his hooded gaze to Vasili.

Knowing he had Nero's attention once again, Vasili continued, 'We require three containers. One, each month travelling by boat from Novorossiysk Port into port of your choosing in UK.'

'Sounds like a lot of cocaine. Surely you can not have that quantity in one place eh? Anyway, we don't have that kind of sway with the Port authority in the UK,' Nero rasped, nothing in his tone to suggest that what he had said was anything other than the truth.

Vasili tilted his head. Looking up he stared for a moment directly into the dark, unwavering eyes of the man opposite him who had thus far treated him with ferocious disdain. Vasili hadn't thought much of the "*great Nero Ossani*" on first meeting. His physique markedly unimpressive, his oiled hair greying, his hands soft and now he was lying. But Vasili knew the man sat before him was resourceful, he had an unparalleled reputation and a skill set that Vasili needed. He was proven. Proven many times over.

Vasili thumbed the arm of his chair. He breathed leisurely, fighting his impatience. Ignoring Nero's pretence he spoke again, 'The drugs will be coming from Cauca. My team will move them across border to Venezuela. By boat they will be brought to small fishing town on Barents Sea. Here cocaine will be placed in crates of premium brand Vodka bottles. We bring them to the port, load them side by side with genuine vodka. You ship them.'

'That is much effort for a drug that's only getting cheaper.'

Vasili knew that Nero was wanting to know what he was set to gain for his compliance. 'Not too cheap. We already have buyers line up in London. High net worth individuals, private clubs, that sort of thing. Effort simple. Reward big. You will do well.'

Vasili had been promised that Nero Ossani's aggressive greed was the only thing greater than his felonious reputation. He continued hoping those same promises had been correct, 'Yes cocaine is becoming cheap at street level. Hence big volume. But pure, uncut, from reliable source…' he smiled displaying a full set of yellowing veneers, 'it still has high value if you know the right people who want it… If they trust you.'

'And they trust you?' Nero quizzed. He twisted his spent cigarette into the ash tray that had been set next to him by the pinch-faced, excessively short-skirted maid and brushed off a smattering of ash, that had landed on the arm of the chair, onto the parquet below.

'Yes,' Vasili continued, ignoring the slight, 'in three months we ship one hundred sixty five individual packages of cocaine, weighing twenty-three kilos before splitting into vodka bottles. Total—'

'Three point seven tonnes.' Nero sounded mildly impressed. The amount proved the Russian must be in business with a big cartel, making him either foolish or well connected.

'Correct. Total value, around two hundred sixty million dollars. US. In your registered containers with your influence. It won't be checked going in to UK. Big Ports with lots of containers much better than the shit fishing boats most use trying to cross undetected. It won't be picked up.'

'Half and I control the transportation routes for the whole process.'

Nikolay, who had been patiently observing his brother's negotiations from his position by the door, moved to object. His large frame coming into full view, Vasili raised a silencing hand. 'Of course,' he responded, once more revealing the veneers.

With that the two men shook hands.

'My representatives will be in touch within the week.'

Vasili nodded and watched his new business parter slither to the door.

Not a second before Nero's ebony Mercedes saloon had crawled away into the night, did Vasili turn his attention to the two men who had played witness to his meeting.

Speaking now in their native tongue Nikolay pulled at his hair, 'Half. Fuck. Half... really you've gone mad this time. By the time we've paid the Colombians and the border officials and the bottlers we'll have made nothing. Fuck's sake!'

'I don't understand, Vasili. How does this help?' Pavel spoke for the first time, moving from his spot by the bay window. He was more measured in his approach. Having seen what Vasili could do, he would not risk letting his passions get the better of him.

Before Vasili could answer, Nikolay spoke again, 'He's mad, Pavel. You've thrown away at least a hundred million if not more. The bastard would have settled for less. You didn't even bargain.'

Vasili settled back into his armchair and eyed his brother cooly. Nikolay's face had turned an ugly puce and, wrinkled from his laboured frown, he now resembled a foaming bulldog. Vasili decided he would encourage his brother to lay off the truffles tonight. As a child and now a man, Nikolay had always been impulsive, short-sighted and easily stressed. Losing a little weight would, if nothing else, help prevent the untimely stroke that was no doubt looming determinedly, like the iceberg that sunk the Titanic, in Nikolay's future. Vasili found his brother's attempt at living pathetic and he refused to be left caring for a cripple - for he was certain fate would not be kind enough to stop his brother's life-force outright. No, it would be much worse, he would survive, someway maimed, but alive. If they had not shared a mother, Vasili would have distanced himself from Nikolay, or perhaps disposed of him a long time ago. He had silenced people, their dreams and aspirations ended, for much less. Nikolay, egotistical to the point of blindness, had no grasp of this.

'Fuck!' Nikolay punched at the wall. Fragments of plaster cascaded from beneath his fist.

Vasili spoke now, pushing all thoughts of icebergs and strokes from his mind, 'Nikolay. My God brother, such little faith. Open your eyes. Think. The money - pah!' He waved his hand dismissively. 'Irrelevant. Nothing. Pavel's father. Our uncle, Christ even Yakov with his clever

103

bankers and smart accountants could get that for us through their offshore Caribbean accounts in a week. Three days maybe. Nothing. It's not what we need.'

'Maybe you, brother. With your grand aspirations. I just want to be rich.'

'Nikolay. Tut-tut. So short-sighted. What is the use of money without power? Influence? Real power mind, not the kind bought by a house full of staff kissing your bollocks. Besides, Nikolay,' Vasili sneered, 'where will you go with your money? Russia? I don't think so. You're as tarnished by Irina's father's crime as much as I. What you need, what I need…we…' he waved in Pavel's direction, 'need, is a secure shipping route. One that won't get checked. Nikolay, look at me.' Having walked over to his brother he now took his plump face in his hands, 'We need a back door in to London. A back door into London, will become a front door to Moscow.'

Pavel's ears pricked, 'This is about Молча?'

Vasili turned, slapping his brothers cheeks as he did. It sounded like a fillet hitting a chopping board, 'There we go.' He pointed a pale bony finger toward Pavel.

This disclosure silenced Nikolay. He took out a cigarette from the near-spent packet in his pocket and began puffing madly.

Pavel took his opportunity to find out what Vasili knew, 'I thought it wasn't possible. Us? Молча? My God, Vasili, you are mixing with some serious men. When?'

Vasili walked back to his chair, 'The third container. If both the first two go through fine. In the third we make our move. It is going to work. Don't underestimate that man Nikolay. He has built much in his life. He has done things and gone to places where a bullet in the knee caps would seem like a thank you card. Once we do this, our uncle will be able to get us round the table with the people who can get us home. If we prove what we can do brother. We prove what Молча can accomplish. Where others have failed these past few years. We will have their ear, and Moscow's ear. We can go home not simply rich, but with a place at the table. A place to keep hold of our money.'

'Pha,' Nikolay dismissed, 'It's a dream, Vasili. You're a fool.'

Pavel stilled.

'Get out,' Vasili spat, a vein swelling on his right temple, 'Come back when you find your head or not at all.'

Nikolay stormed out of the living room, huffing like a spoilt child, he slammed the door petulantly as he left.

Pavel stood in uncomfortable silence. He waited, assessing Vasili warily, like a historically beaten dog assesses its new owner. Vasili's mobile buzzed on the table, breaking the silence.

'Yes. Ok. Let her come in,' Vasili answered. Hanging up he turned to Pavel, 'Call your cousins. We may need their influence.'

With that Pavel scurried out of the room, grateful that Vasili had not unleashed his frustration on him.

He was not long gone when the door opened again.

Pressing the vein in his head, Vasili rose from the chair.

'Papa!' the small girl shrieked, running straight for her father.

He scooped her up in his arms, 'My little Sofia. You look so well. How was Paris? Did you get everything you wanted?'

She folded her arms and pouted at him, 'I'm a *big* girl now papa.'

Vasili smiled, 'Ah I see.' He bowed his head, pressing himself nearer to her petal-soft flesh, 'My apologies Sofi. Forgive me.' He kissed her on the cheek. She wriggled and he set her down.

'Mama. I'm big aren't I?' The little girl raced over and grabbed the manicured hand of the elegant woman now standing in the doorway.

Her nails freshly painted and make-up perfectly applied, for these were the only remaining areas of her life over which she could still exercise control, Irina bent down to kiss her young daughter, before ushering her from the room and back to the ever-present nanny. She could see in her husband's expression that now was not the time for distractions.

Walking over slowly, like a young foal, she gingerly pecked Vasili's cheek as though they were nothing more than acquaintances.

'Who was here?' she asked, having noticed the Mercedes, one she had not seen before, parked outside the house on her arrival.

'Irina,' Vasili warned.

'Tell me. I never see you, Vasili. When are we going home?'

'Irina. Not now. I have to work. Leave. This is important.'

'For who? You? Me? Sofia?'

Vasili's vein was back. He looked at his wife's hand which had just started to gesticulate wildly. Her engagement ring, a large, blood-red ruby surrounded by a myriad of white diamonds, once a perfect fit now hung loose and upside down on her finger.

'If you want to talk about strange men, Irina. Let's talk about yours.'

Irina stilled. Her eyes widened.

'Sofi. Come.' Vasili called.

Irina took a step to leave but he held her firm. His nails pinching at the bare skin of her forearms, 'Sofi, tell me about the nice ice-cream man? Does mama know him?'

Having run back in as fast as she could at her father's call, gleefully escaping her nanny, a comical glower marked Sofia's delicate face, 'I told you Papa! He buys mama ice-cream too. And when she spills it, he licks it off her. That's what you do when you're big.'

Vasili smiled at his daughter, 'Ah yes of course. How silly of me. Off you go now.'

With that Sofia left the room once more.

'You bastard,' Irina muttered still frozen.

Vasili slapped her hard across the face, 'You bitch. You should be more careful, Irina. Sofia told me all about the nice English man. He's lucky it was only his business he lost.'

'Vasili,' Irina entreated. Her wounded cheek, still stinging, had flushed a vivid pink.

'No. No, Irina. It is your fault we are here in this fucking country. He was your fucking father. So don't "Vasili" me. Get out.'

EIGHT

Overlooking one of Mayfair's finest garden squares. The Daring Corporation's London headquarters were housed in a striking Georgian building. An architecturally imposing site, block work, embellished with ornate stone pillars covered the entire front of the structure. Over the central porticoed entrance, a large, claret flag hung, emblazoned with the corporations now iconic, golden logo - the double-headed god Janus. Below the omniscient, floating icon, a set of sleek copper letters spelled out *Daring Corporation* and could be seen illuminated twenty-four hours a day, seven days a week.

Kitty had found the exterior to be much more reminiscent of a five star hotel, or akin to one of the embassies that frequented the area, than that of the headquarters of a modern, international super-company. But this was only the facade. On entering the building, one was welcomed into a vast marble lobby in keeping with the age of the exterior. In time, Kitty learned that off this were multiple grand meeting rooms, bedecked with the same period features, large fireplaces and gilt-framed oil paintings. However, beyond that the whole building had been completely remodelled. The first time Kitty had first seen the secondary space she had been quite awe-struck. It was a beautiful layered structure of interwoven glass and steel. By her count the central atrium must have been at least seven stories high. Huge wraith-like structures, suspended at various heights decorated the space, their slow rotations causing the hair on the back of Kitty's neck to stand erect each time she paid them more than the briefest snip of attention. On her first day, seeing Kitty staring at the artwork, the receptionists, with their tailored dresses, tight buns and model cuticles, had dutifully explained to her that the atrium was often used to exhibit world famous art.

'Daring sells and manages various pieces under custody,' the first had stated.

With a second chiming in, 'This space is like a shop window for when we receive important clients. It sends a message that Daring can acquire such pieces, and have so many, that we may also decorate the offices with quite literally millions of pounds worth of art.'

'It's a status symbol. One that shows Daring is doing well,' a sleek brunette had added with an easy, perfect smile.

The first few weeks of work had gone fine. It had been fairly manic. There were twenty graduates, ten male and ten female who had all studied wildly varying courses and were from an equally varied set of countries. Unlike most companies, instead of sending the American graduates to the New York Office and Chinese graduates to the offices in Beijing, or perhaps Hong Kong, Daring had decided to bring them all together in London for their inaugural program. The purpose of this was to create a more boutique, insightful and hopefully interesting experience for the graduates involved - Daring's future leaders, as they were continually called.

It had been four weeks of three day rotations, allowing for introductions throughout the main departments. Founded in 1838, The Daring Corporation had begun life importing copper ore from Chile and Cuba into the lower Swansea area and the Neath Valleys for smelting. The Daring family, having made a fortune from the burgeoning success of the Welsh Copper Industry in the nineteenth century, had then begun exporting the smelted copper to overseas markets across Asia. With each successive generation investing wisely, adding to their transportation network and diversifying the materials that they imported and exported, the corporation had been well placed to survive the decline of the UK industry. As smelting works were established nearer to the mines which formerly supplied the ores, they had re-employed their fleet of vessels so that, by the nineteen-thirties, The Daring Corporation was a leading player in the ever-expanding ocean liner shipping market.

The Corporation today, as they had now been told on several occasions throughout the past four weeks, had highly diversified interests. These included a presence in a range of sectors covering: property, retail, luxury hotels, motor vehicles, construction and transportation. Nevertheless, shipping, with nearly forty thousand employees, across one hundred and eleven countries, remained the largest operating unit of the conglomerate, providing end-to-end transportation to every corner of the globe, these days by sea and by land.

It was a variant of this same spiel that the graduates now sat listening too from one of the primary sector heads. The sinewy, owl-eyed man had been linked to the successful hotel chain that Daring had recently acquired, and was explaining which opportunities would come from this growing sector. 'Our sector manages a combination of long-term property assets and cash generating activities,' he said, gazing down his nose into the audience from behind the podium, which had been erected in one of the Georgian conference rooms on the third floor.

Kitty listened to the gentleman and the three speakers that came after him. All of the graduates had been assembled since nine o'clock that morning and Kitty was becoming increasingly aware of the pins and needles that had begun an assault on her bottom as Lucille from HR, the lady who had offered Kitty the position whilst she had been in France, returned to the podium.

As it turned out, Lucille had been running the whole four-week program. She was the graduates' point of contact and was responsible for their timetabling and streaming. Kitty and Lucille had gotten along very well. Kitty reckoned Lucille was about forty and extremely good at her job. She was efficient and professional and had put hours of work into preparing the graduates before they had met each department head.

'It's amazing you get to meet all of these senior executives. An experience that few new joiners to a company get,' Jaz's father had stressed one evening to Kitty. He had taken her and his daughter out for supper, during which Kitty had expressed doubt over her future at Daring. Anne had voiced the same opinion in her good luck card which had arrived a week or so later, proving that Mr Taylor had been in contact. For Anne had no knowledge of graduate schemes and placements. Suffice it to say, Kitty had stopped telling people that something didn't feel right.

It wasn't that she didn't like the company employees, who on the whole had been welcoming, or that she wasn't impressed by Daring's exponential growth throughout the last forty years, which was a frequent topic in the press. It was just a feeling that the corporate life wasn't going to be for her.

As with any business, as Kitty had become well aware, the root concern was about making money. Because of this, throughout each rotation it had become increasingly clear that the directors emphasis was on maximising profits and creating a team that "*fit*" their vision for achieving this. There appeared to be no freedom to do anything differently. Conformity, not just in the smart attire and near identical suits worn by all the employees but even, Kitty had started to feel, in personality, was what the directors were after. Each one in their own way had begun gently massaging out the variations between everyone, to create one unified body. The workforce was like Daring's army, and it needed workers who could follow orders from above. Kitty wasn't convinced that she would want to, or even could conform in this way. On more than one occasion she had found herself wondering if she had made the right choice. Not that she had been blessed with a myriad of options.

About three weeks in, Kitty had expressed her concerns to Lucille. It had been after two dreary days with the finance department looking at account structures and budget setting. Kitty had been pretty sure that in the streaming, due to her lack of experience in this field, that Avery, with her accountancy major from Harvard, or Max with his degree from the Mannheim Business School, would be streamed that way. Nevertheless to make sure her forced manners were not confused for genuine enthusiasm, she had booked a time to meet with Lucille.

'I'm just not sure that I fit in here.' Kitty had begun their meeting by explaining how grateful she had been for everything Lucille had done and how insightful the program had been so far. Kitty had moved on to explain how she just felt, that the whole corporate structure was something she couldn't get her head around.

'We need leaders not just followers, Cleopatra. People who grow through the ranks and become expert in their field.'

'I get that, Lucille. Honestly. I just feel that at the junior level there's less client interaction than I'd hoped for. Less opportunity to be creative.' Kitty had thought that perhaps if she could be streamed into a client facing role, then at least that could be more interesting.

'Cleopatra, you are very talented. Nearly all of the department heads that your group have rotated through have expressed an interest in you. Are you saying you're interested by none of them?'

Kitty had been rotating in a sub group alongside four other graduates. This included Max and Avery, whom had been a part of her "buddy structure." Her and Max had struck up quite an easy friendship. He was straightforward in his approach to everything which was refreshing and had a knack for unknowingly putting his foot in his mouth - something Kitty found deeply amusing. Unfortunately, Avery had proven to be about the most unsupportive "buddy" Kitty could have hoped for. She was smart, at times a little too brash, but above all desperately ambitious. Kitty knew she would have to watch her own back.

'I just don't see a role that would allow me to use my Russian for example. A client facing role,' Kitty had continued, feeling that she wasn't explaining herself particularly well. She also knew Lucille would be a useful ally at Daring and Kitty really did appreciate everything that she had already done for everyone and so was not trying to cause offence. Besides, Lucille had helped Kitty once more escape the clutches of Truro, and she would not be sent back for bad manners.

'The mentoring process will be really excellent. I'll make sure I find you a mentor in some sort of client-facing role. We were going to try and keep all the graduates shadowing managerial positions within HQ, but I'll have a look at perhaps what some of our other holdings have got which may interest you. Then you can spend the six months with them before any decision needs reassessing. How does that sound?'

'Thank you, Lucille. I really do appreciate it.'

'Thats quite alright, Cleopatra. It is my job after all. We aim to please in HR and I really believe you could go far with Daring. Just keep doing what you're doing and I'll sort the mentoring. Your contract ends at the end of the six months anyway, so you will be free to decide after that.'

Kitty had thanked her once more. Lucille was clearly very proud of the graduate scheme and Kitty was well aware that she wanted to make it a success, beat the common natural attrition accepted in these schemes and retain all twenty graduates by the end.

The room broke into a muffled applause signalling the end of the morning's speeches and Kitty dashed out of the conference room. She knew they now had an allotted hour for lunch and wanted to walk off the pins and needles and avoid the networking which was to ensue over nibbles. She felt today her polite conversation would be found severely lacking.

Outside in the sunshine, Kitty crossed the road and headed for the wrought iron gate that led into the garden square - one of the work perks that she had taken advantage of on a regular basis. Walking head down, wondering who Lucille had paired her off with, Kitty didn't notice the man leaning casually against the gate posts until it was almost too late.

'Fancy seeing you 'ere, Kit,' Elliot said, stowing his phone in his pocket, 'what a coincidence. Seems London ain't so big after all.'

'Coincidence is it?' Kitty asked dryly, the scepticism clear in her voice.

'Maybe not,' he shrugged, 'Got five?'

'You can have three if you answer one question?'

'Shoot,' Elliot smiled and Kitty guessed he knew what was coming.

'Why did you make that toast in France?'

'To impress a girl I quite like.'

'Seriously. Why that specific one?' Kitty crossed her arms, delivering Elliot a determined scowl.

Elliot shook his head before answering her. His voice turned sincere like the night they had met, 'I think you know.'

'So you did know.' Kitty bit her lip. She didn't understand, but was glad she hadn't been going insane this whole time, 'You may be a bit older than me, but you definitely aren't old enough to have known him.'

'Didn't need to, to know that. He's a legend.'

'Was,' Kitty corrected.

'Is,' Elliot countered firmly.

'What do you want, Elliot? Your three minutes have started.'

'To offer you a job.'

'What?'

'I'm 'ere to offer you a job.'

'I have one thanks.' Kitty began to walk away. She didn't know what game Elliot was playing but wasn't in the mood. He didn't follow her.

'But you don't like it,' he called.

Kitty stopped in her tracks and turned back, 'You have no idea what I like or don't like.'

'I do actually. You want to be a lawyer.'

'Do I?' Kitty scoffed.

'Well you applied enough times.'

'Well if you know that, then you know that the law didn't want me.'

'I do. But Kitty, if you do this for me, the CPS'll sponsor the whole training, qualifications, everything.'

Kitty couldn't believe what she was hearing. She had applied, on top of her other applications, six times to the Crown Prosecution Service Trainee Scheme and had been denied entry on all six occasions. Elliot must be bluffing.

'Bollocks,' she countered.

'It's true.' Elliot walked forward now and handed her a piece of paper.

Kitty eyed the document. He wasn't lying. In her hands she held a signed contract. She couldn't believe what she was seeing, 'Why were you in France?'

'Because you were more likely to talk to me if you already knew me a bit.'

'So it wasn't a coincidence?'

'About as coincidental as this.'

'How did you know I was there?'

Elliot smiled but stayed quiet.

'How did you know I was going to be here?' Kitty asked.

Elliot raised his eyebrows.

'What do I have to do?'

'It's easy. Listen. Lemme know anything you think might be…of interest? Simple as that.'

'You think Daring is doing something illegal?'

'No evidence to suggest that.'

'But you… or someone more senior than you thinks it.'

'Kitty. Deal's on the table. Take it or leave it. You've a six month contract with Daring that will take you to the end of the mentoring scheme. It's the perfect opportunity to—'

'Spy.'

'Network.'

Behind him, a dark tinted car pulled up twenty or so metres down the road, its tyres making a satisfying hiss on the damp asphalt. Elliot took this as his queue to leave, 'Don't worry, you're not our only hope.'

'I haven't agreed yet,' Kitty called after his retreating figure, still holding the contract tightly in her hands.

'I'm betting that you will,' he called back to her over his shoulder.

'So I'm not just a girl you quite liked then?' she quoted him.

'I said our meeting wasn't a coincidence. I didn't say I lied about anything.' He winked as he disappeared into the waiting car.

Back at the lunch buffet, Kitty stood to one side avoiding eye contact with anyone looking to "network." Suddenly she was looking at all of her colleagues through a different lens. *Could Elliot be right?* She shook her head. Lost in thought Kitty jumped when Lucille appeared behind her.

'Cleopatra, I have the best news!' Lucille peeped.

Before Kitty could ask any questions, Lucille continued, 'I can't discuss the particulars but the Chairman and CEO found out about our mentoring scheme and agreed to be a part of it. I heard what you said about wanting to try something a bit different and I thought this could be perfect. Just Perfect!'

Kitty didn't know what to say, but Lucille hurried off before she could say anything and Kitty soon found herself returning to her seat as the assembled group was ushered back for the final part of the programme. *Well if anyone knows about anything illegal it'll be at the top,* she thought as she moved slowly amongst the line of people, all swapping final comments of conversations, the subjects of which she hadn't been party-to. For the first time since seeing Elliot, a tiny buzz of excitement fizzed within her. Perhaps she might be a lawyer after all? Perhaps Elliot would provide the bridge to doing something actually meaningful with her life. *Something meaningful like Dad did.* Kitty swallowed, feeling an unwelcome lump rise in her throat.

On the podium in front of her twenty fresh-faced graduates, and many of the global heads and managing directors of various departments, beaming with pride at how well the event had gone so far, Lucille prepared to welcome Mr Daring to the stage to make his address - a surprise addition that had catapulted her project to the highest echelons of the Daring mega-structure.

Seated near the back of the room next to Max, Kitty had pretty much zoned out, focussing instead on how she was going to contact Elliot, when Avery slid in next to her. Whispering to them both, while Lucille filled time waiting for a now late Mr Daring.

'This. Is. Huge! I just went to the bathroom and one of the HR secretaries in there told me that Mr Daring is on his way and I've heard that he's apparently going to mentor one of us. How freakin' mad is that?' Avery squeaked.

Having only been told by Lucille moments before Kitty had been required to sit down for the next round of speeches, and having been in a daze throughout the last few minutes of the luncheon, Kitty had not been able to tell anyone that she had been assigned to the Chairman and CEO. Deciding it was better to come clean, than risk the certain worse wrath of Avery if she didn't, Kitty whispered back, 'Yeah. umm. I was literally just told at lunch. I'm going to do it.'

Avery looked as though she had been slapped.

Max smiled, as usual missing the mood change, 'Good for you Kitty. I'm hoping for a place in Murray's team. Seems as he reports to the Chief Operations and Service Delivery Officer, would be a good fit for me. I spoke to Lucille, so we'll see. Avery you'll get accounts or treasury for sure, you're so good at it.'

Kitty cringed. Avery didn't want accounts and everyone knew with her background, she was going to get it. Deciding to play it down to Avery, who now looked like a coiled snake ready to strike her at any moment, Kitty continued, 'Nice one Max. Hope Lucille pulled that off for you. To be honest I'm not sure that shadowing some old dude who'll probably be too busy to even notice I exist will be that great.'

Max shrugged in agreement.

'He's not old,' Avery hissed, 'How did you get the job? Who do you know? I thought you had no connections—'

'Avery seriously. I've no idea. I know no one here. I didn't even know he wasn't old,' Kitty said. It was true. Kitty had no idea who the board were. Why would she? It hadn't come up in her interviews and wasn't necessary. She had never expected to meet one of them.

'God you know nothing. How did you even get this job?' Avery eyed Kitty suspiciously. She was about to open her mouth to say something else when a man from the row in front gestured to silence them. Tutting disapprovingly over his crooked nose.

Coming to the end of her thank yous Lucille finished, 'Now it gives me great pleasure to welcome Mr Daring to the podium. He has graciously offered to be a part of this inaugural mentor scheme with all of you and I know that with his contribution, we will all have a constructive and illuminating adventure together.'

The room erupted into applause and Kitty, having hidden her face from the displeased man in front, now looked up to the podium.

There's no way, she thought.

NINE

Kitty stared opened mouthed at the stage, her hands frozen in her lap. She was the only one in the room not clapping. In her peripheral vision Kitty could see Avery glaring at her. She forced her mouth closed and looked down at her still frozen hands, keeping her eyes away from the podium.

'Yeah, I don't know who he is. I don't know anyone on the board,' Avery muttered mockingly impersonating Kitty. 'Bullshit,' she spat.

Kitty ignored her and Max, who was also now looking at Kitty's ashen face, his expression perplexed as the applause died down. Trying desperately to compose herself, Kitty looked back to the front of the room. She felt sick. Standing at the podium, in a sharp, perfectly tailored, grey suit was Raphael.

'He look's like a freakin' god,' one of the graduates seated the other side of Max whispered, a little too loudly down the line, responding in some more shushing and tutting from the row in front.

'Good Afternoon ladies and gentlemen. Thank you for letting me be a part of this important scheme. The company my father inherited forty years ago, when he was a little younger than I am now, has always been at the forefront of innovation. We have always striven here at Daring, to be the best in everything we set our minds to and we take this same approach now to the graduates and their development here with us.'

Kitty scratched at her palms. She didn't understand what was going on. Raphael continued to speak eloquently for a few minutes, but Kitty didn't hear a word of it. She felt seriously unwell, confused. She thought she must be visibly green, or red with steam coming out her ears like the animations she used to watch in cartoons as a child. The anger she had felt for so long, and finally successfully suppressed, was once more bubbling furiously within her. This time, Raphael's appearance had not awoken the butterflies in her stomach, instead he had stirred a swarm of killer bees.

The room once more filled with a torrent of applause and Kitty was called back from her thoughts of cartoon animations and insects. Raphael had finished speaking and with this concluding the day's speeches, the audience was being ushered into the adjacent meeting space where the lunch buffet had been served a few hours before. Slinking into the room, Kitty saw that the buffet had been cleared and instead, the space was now dotted with small circular waist-high tables. Around each one people were gathering and conversing. Kitty again thought of bees. Waiters and waitresses danced around the tables offering canapés and serving wine. Whilst Lucille, beaming like a proud mother, merrily introduced each graduate, one at a time, to their assigned mentor. Kitty knew that she needed to grab Lucille before she had the chance to introduce Kitty to hers.

Sheltering behind a tall potted palm, Kitty scanned the room for Lucille. She was grateful to note that Raphael had appeared to have disappeared once more. Spotting Lucille with Max on the far side of the room, Kitty started to weave her way through the mass of people towards them. About half way towards her target, Kitty felt a hand tug on her arm. She spun round praying it was not Raphael. Having kept her head down throughout his address, she was certain he had not seen her.

'What's going on?' a voice screeched in Kitty's ear. It was Avery. Kitty relaxed a little, relieved. Although now she had to work out how she could placate the harpy at her side.

'Honestly, I don't know him Avery,' Kitty pleaded with her. She didn't want a scene and had hoped that, in time, her and Avery would manage to find some common ground upon which they could have built a friendship, or at least an understanding. Considering they, along with Max, were to be "buddies" for the next six months and would no doubt be seeing a lot of each other.

'You're a liar, Kitty May,' Avery practically spat.

'Avery. I was just shocked he was so… young.'

'Yeah he's young and hot, if you didn't know that too.' Avery's glower broke a little. She was smitten.

Kitty pitied her, she had no idea what an arse he really was.

Deciding that further denial wasn't going to bring Avery onside anytime soon, Kitty instead settled for blatant flattery, 'How do you always know so much? You always seem to know more than the rest of us. I wish I was like that.'

Avery, still suspicious, scowled at Kitty's change in demeanour. Nevertheless, her stroked ego couldn't resist answering, 'Knowledge is power Kitty. That age old phrase. I make it my business to know things.'

Well she's not lying, Kitty thought unkindly. Avery was a busybody. She had witnessed it on numerous occasions with the other graduates.

'Well maybe I should take a leaf out of your book Avery. Then I wouldn't be so shocked by these things. Sorry... if you'll excuse me, I just need to catch Lucille.' Kitty tried to turn away but Avery's talons dug into her arm. The harpy was still vexed. Kitty turned back, her expression beseeching now.

'I know you're—' Avery's voice broke off.

Behind her Kitty could now hear the high-pitched croon of Lucille, 'And here we have Cleopatra who will be your mentee for the next six months. Cleopatra?'

Kitty turned slowly. Stepping back as she did, so that she was in line with Avery's now entranced body. *Fuck*, Kitty cursed, knowing that she had well and truly missed her opportunity to catch Lucille in private, for standing beside her, in all his leonine glory, was Raphael.

Kitty stared at Raphael for what felt like an awkwardly long amount of time, but could only have been a few seconds in reality. His eyes, just as violent and confused as the night she had met him, stared back at her.

'Kiti?' He seemed as shocked as she and now Lucille was.

Kitty felt the resentment flowing hot off Avery, her body had gone rigid and she couldn't bring herself to look at her.

Lucille wasn't sure what to say. She had never called Cleopatra by her nickname, to her face nor on email. She had repeatedly expressed to Kitty herself that she felt it wasn't conducive to gaining respect at Daring to use her childhood nickname at work. She didn't introduce herself as Lil. Kitty and the other graduates had ignored her on that front, but Lucille had held firm in calling Kitty Cleopatra for all her work-related interactions and introductions, and she knew that she would certainly not have called her Kitty in any of her exchanges with the Chairman and CEO's office.

'You know each other?' Lucille asked poorly covering for her surprise.

'No,' Kitty answered, feeling that it wasn't exactly a complete lie, as she really knew very little about the man before her.

Mortifyingly Raphael picked a different answer.

'Yes,' he replied a fraction of a second after Kitty's chosen response.

Avery's mouth audibly popped open.

'No. We don't,' Kitty insisted, now glaring at Raphael. She wasn't sure why she was hanging on to this, but the anger she had felt for so long against this man was now freely raging within her.

'Well we...' Raphael began. Assessing Kitty's face he wisely concluded on letting the subject drop and instead smiled at Avery. She blushed deeply, shutting her mouth.

Oh please, he's not that great, Kitty thought, pushing away the unwelcome memories of how she had first found him.

'Your name's Cleopatra?' Raphael smirked looking back at Kitty. He thought she didn't suit the name. Too long, pompous. He was under no illusions, despite Kitty's protestations, that it was now apparent to Lucille and the other blushing girl beside Kitty that they had met, and the question had just popped out of him. As his thoughts always seemed to around her. His question had evidently made Kitty even more vexed, which he gathered by her answering wordless stony glare.

Breaking the increasingly awkward silence Avery piped up. She had collected herself and had seen an opportunity worth exploiting, 'Mr Daring. It's a pleasure to meet you. My name's Avery Williams,' she began.

Raphael wasn't looking at her and instead was still staring intently at Kitty who had taken to avoiding eye contact with all three of them.

Avery pressed on undeterred, swishing her copper ponytail, 'Lucille, I would be very happy to exchange my place with Cleopatra if that would make things easier for everyone.'

Finally Raphael looked at Avery. She answered his attention with her well-practiced, doe-eyed, I-rescue-orphans type smile.

Cleopatra? Since when has she ever called me Cleopatra? Kitty thought temporarily distracted by Avery's vamping. She was pouting as she spoke and fluttering her lashes at Raphael. Kitty thought her behaviour shameful. *Perhaps that's his thing though*, she mused. *Who knows, clearly the crying and head smashing into the ceiling didn't do it for him.* Kitty smiled. Looking back it was all rather embarrassing. *Better laugh than cry... again*, she decided. *God this is so ridiculous.* A small snigger burst out of her at the thought. Avery, her face now matching the colour of her red hair, glowered at her once more.

Raphael, who had turned politely to Avery to hear the rest of her pitch, snapped back to Kitty. Kitty thought she saw a moment of confusion cross his features before he turned once again to Avery. This time utterly composed, all traces of surprise gone.

'Thank you, Miss Williams, but I fear we wouldn't want to ruin Lucille's master plan. It was a pleasure to meet you.' With that he shook her hand formerly, ignoring her pitifully indignant expression.

Avery opened her mouth to persist but Lucille, taking that as Mr Daring's agreement to keep Kitty as his mentee, irrespective as to whether they did or did not know each other, interjected, 'Thank you, Avery, but our European Accounts Head is very keen to meet you.' When Avery didn't move she insisted, 'This way.'

Leading Avery off to find her mentor, Lucille disappeared into the crowd without so much of a backward glance. The same could not be said for Avery who looked back so frequently, it was a marvel she didn't stumble into anybody.

'Kiti?' Raphael began warily.

'No. We need to sort this shit out. Now.' The fire inside of Kitty was now fully ablaze, bees in full attack mode and she clung on to this sudden burst of inner strength. A cluster of staff, whom Kitty had not met before, turned on hearing her bad language. They each took a moment to look stunned when they realised who she was speaking too. Raphael laughed it off and the group thankfully returned to their prior conversation. Turning back to Kitty, he did not look impressed. She swallowed, *remember the bees*.

'Can we talk somewhere private.' His voice was smooth but threatening and Kitty realised he wasn't actually asking.

'No. I need to speak to Lucille.'

'Later,' Raphael replied curtly, gesturing to the door.

Kitty decided that she wasn't going to argue here. The whole situation had been embarrassing enough as it was and she didn't want to attract anymore unwanted attention. Following Raphael to the door, Kitty waited patiently behind him as he had to make the many customary handshakes and stately greetings with various members of his staff as they left. Mortifyingly the last man by the door had been in-charge of Kitty's most recent rotation and began gushing about how enthusiastic she had been. Kitty wanted the world to swallow her up.

Once in the hallway, still in uncomfortable silence, Raphael, who decided correctly that he wasn't going to be able to convince Kitty to come all the way to his own office, instead walked to a nearby vacant meeting room and held open the door for Kitty to enter.

Kitty spoke first. Turning to face him the moment she heard the latch click shut behind her. He could no doubt see that she was mad. Less than twenty minutes before she had been ready to accept Elliot's offer, but that was the last thing on her mind now.

'So what are you then? Millionaire? Or Marine?'

'Special Air Service and… billionaire actually. Although I thought you would've deduced that Sherlock,' Raphael replied, his voice completely deadpan.

Kitty stiffened. He was laughing at her.

Eyeing her persistent frown Raphael changed tone, 'Kiti—'

'No stop. Don't "Kiti" me like we're friends, or like you know anything about me,' she said, mimicking the way he said her name. Soft, as if caring. 'You left me remember. Vanished. No note. You know, embarrassingly, on more than one occasion in the months after, in trying to work out why you never called, I thought you may have been killed in some hell hole in Syria or wherever you SAS people go. If you even are… or… were SAS.'

Raphael stayed silent.

'God… was I that bad?' Her voice broke a little and she kicked herself. She didn't want to be upset. She didn't want to care what he thought and she certainly didn't want to let him know how used she felt. But she couldn't lie to herself and standing before him, despite everything that had happened, Kitty felt the same irrational draw to him, just like she had after the first time they had kissed. Before he had left. Fortunately her resolve was bolstered by the same extreme resentment coursing through her. He had left. The bees would beat the butterflies.

'No,' Raphael answered sincerely. He took a step towards her but she stepped back and he stopped himself.

'I can't have you as my mentor Raphael. I don't care whether you're the CEO of this company or not.'

'Ok,' he said calmly, 'but, Kiti, if you give me a chance, I can make a real difference in your career.'

'I don't want your help, Raphael! I don't want to do well at work because I fucked the CEO on some weird night out.'

'It's not like that. I didn't mean,' Raphael clenched his jaw.

Kitty looked into his face. She was furious that much she knew was obvious. But standing before her, she thought Raphael looked almost wounded by her casual dismissal of their previous encounter. It was like he was only now realising that she may have been hurt by his disappearance. He had caught the spite in her tone and now looked at her differently somehow. Wide-eyed. Vulnerable. An unsolicited sympathy welled in Kitty. She had been pretty impolite, but she couldn't accept his mentorship. It would be weird, besides, whether an overreaction or not, he still provoked a fervent anger within her and whilst that was the case how could she do what Elliot was asking? Or even, how could she stand to be in the same room as him?

'I'm not after an explanation as to why you left,' Kitty began again. This was wholly untrue, but her immediate priority was to extricate herself from this surprise and unwanted reunion. 'I just need you to understand that I would like a new mentor.'

'Lucille is never going to understand why you would turn down being my mentee. I'm just saying. Let me mentor you. Or at least join my team and I don't know,' he paused, 'i'll keep it professional.'

'I'm not sure I can,' Kitty replied quietly. Honestly. Then annoyed that she had expressed her thought out loud.

Raphael cocked his head. He was frowning again.

'Please,' she said, her exasperation filling the silence. She waited for him to respond, hoping that she had appealed to his better nature. If he had one. *Why does he even want this?*

'No,' Raphael concluded, 'if you turn me down there will be rumours. No one would understand, they will draw conclusions. It'll ruin your reputation here and possibly somewhere else. I'm not being responsible for that.'

'My reputation again? Funny.'

'Yes, your reputation.'

'Or yours, Mr Daring?' Kitty snarled.

'Yours,' he practically growled in response.

'Great. Well that's that then,' Kitty said turning her back to him, her voice thick with sarcasm. She knew he wasn't going to change his mind. She could hear the finality in his words, see it written all over his face and she was pretty certain, with the little she did know of him, that he was accustomed to doing exactly what he wanted.

'I have to go. Monday morning. Nine. I'll see you then,' Raphael paused.

Kitty remained quiet. She wasn't sure what to say. She was infuriated and couldn't bring herself to turn back to Raphael for fear the sympathy, or worse, the unexplainable draw to him would return. After a minute she heard him leave and the thought that Elliot may be her fastest ticket out of Daring took up position at the forefront of her mind for a minute, before being pushed aside by a momentarily more pressing matter - how she was going to get out of the building without seeing Lucille, or worse, Avery.

Monday morning came around all too fast.

Throughout the weekend Kitty had busied herself running errands, trying in vain to forget about Raphael and the no doubt awkward exchanges they were set to endure for the next six months.

On Sunday, Jaz had met her for lunch, but Kitty hadn't been able to find the words to express quite what had been troubling her. She had kept her and Raphael's meeting a secret, a secret she wasn't ready to share, and the whole Elliot issue was another secret - this one she couldn't share - and so Kitty now found herself unable to explain why she was so distracted. In the end, Kitty had settled on saying that she had stupidly just kissed someone at work and now they had been streamed together for the next six months. Jaz had laughed, but understandably brushed it off as merely unfortunate. Kitty knew that Jaz had experienced many similar situations and was not surprised that she thought it rather amusing that for once, the same had happened to Kitty, who in recent years had been particularly, even by her usual standards, mistrusting and prickly. Fortunately, Jaz had also been blinkered by Beto's surprise appearance and so Kitty had not been hounded too hard for information throughout the rest of the day. Despite envying their easy closeness, it didn't stop Kitty enjoying spending time with them both. She was genuinely happy for Jaz. She put up with her for one thing. She deserved someone special.

Now in the elevator making her way to Raphael's office on the top floor, Kitty focused on her breathing, a meditation technique she had observed Miss M trying to master, to varying degrees of success, on many occasions. She had come to the logical conclusion that, knowing herself, she was probably always going to harbour some resentment towards Raphael for vanishing and always going to be annoyed at herself for caring as much as she did. But focusing on those annoyances forever was not going to help. She planned instead, that she would simply do the best job she could for six months and then get as far away from Daring as possible. With a glowing reference from the CEO of course - after all, it was the least he could do. And if something Elliot might want came up before then, well so be it, for Kitty felt it was exactly what Raphael deserved.

'Welcome, Cleopatra,' a slight, long-necked secretary said as soon as Kitty had made her way out of the lift. 'Mr Daring is in his office finishing a call and will be ready for you in a few minutes.'

She was swanlike, even more immaculately presented than the girls based in the front lobby, a feat Kitty had not thought possible, and spoke in a warm, kind manner.

'If you would like I could show you where you'll be working?' she asked smiling.

'That's alright Natalie. Ciao. Hello, Kiti,' Raphael spoke as he breezed from his office.

Kitty was a little taken aback by his seemingly relaxed manner. He had practically purred her name and appeared genuinely pleased to see her. Natalie seemed a little surprised as well.

Turning to Kitty she asked, 'You've met?' She seemed irritated, as if Kitty had somehow intentionally concealed this from her.

Kitty wasn't sure what to say.

Raphael calmly interjected, 'On Friday. We were introduced at the mentoring event.'

'Of course.' Natalie seemed satisfied with this and took her leave.

Kitty was relieved with Raphael's answer. He was clearly trying to be less difficult.

'This way,' he ushered Kitty towards his office door. 'Take a seat. I'll be with you in one second.' With that he disappeared.

Situated at the rear of the building, within the remodelled part of the headquarters, the office had floor to ceiling glass windows along its far wall. Modern in its design the room was palatial. One side was dominated by a huge, dark wooden desk around which, three pale leather armchairs were placed. The other half had been laid out to create a chic sitting room stationed around a Kilim rug. The walls were painted a soft shade of grey and the floor was covered with sleek white marble tiles.

Kitty assumed that some renowned interior designer had been called in to assemble the space, to create the correct impression, as they had done throughout the rest of the building. For she struggled to find anything personal about the room. It was impressive for sure, but the space could have belonged to any Fortune 500 CEO.

Deciding to sit at one of the desk chairs, Kitty made her way to the far end of the room. She admired the assortment of buildings and rooftops that she could see through the wall of glass. London was undeniably an inspiring city. A melee of architectural styles, meant even in the carefully regulated Mayfair, there was a couple of centuries worth of variation to enjoy.

Pulling out one of the two chairs on the guest side of the desk, Kitty sat down. The chairs swivelled unexpectedly and she couldn't help herself from whizzing a full rotation at top speed. She was alone after all. Grinning, Kitty steadied the chair, not wishing to get caught. It had all gone so well so far. She had stayed calm. Relaxed. After her weekend preparations working on controlling the irritation she felt whenever she saw him, she was pleased with her efforts. No bees or butterflies.

Still waiting for Raphael to reappear, she gazed around the room. At the opposite end to her, the space was decorated by three huge canvases. Each one an oil painting of classical, she assumed Roman, architecture. In speckled antiqued frames they sat in appealing contrast to the modern furnishings of the room. *A mildly personal nod to his Italian heritage perhaps?* she thought. Contrastingly, at her end of the room, behind the desk, the wall was decorated with eight black and white prints.

The prints reminded Kitty of Rorschach test inkblots. However on closer inspection she could see that they were semi-abstract portraits. She recognised two of the subjects, Ernest Shackleton and Thor Heyerdahl, but none of the others. She wondered about their purpose, getting the feeling that because the two she had recognised were explorers, these additions may have actually been chosen by the current, previously SAS, incumbent of the office.

Raphael, having silently entered behind her, smiled at her formal choice of seating. *Very professional,* he thought amused.

'Do you like them?' Raphael asked.

She hadn't heard him come in but was getting used to his sudden reappearances. 'I don't recognise some of the subjects.' She did like them, but didn't want to say so in case he did. She scolded her childishness.

'They're all individuals who have survived great feats of human endurance, Kiti.'

Every time he said her name, the muscles in her stomach tightened. It was the slight accent he had. It made her name sound like a compliment, caring, gentle. Kitty focused hard on the prints, 'I recognise Shackleton of course.'

Raphael, having crossed the room now leant against the desk. Standing gazing at the prints over his shoulder. His suit, dark blue this time, was like the last, perfectly tailored and hung handsomely from his still visibly muscular frame. Kitty, momentarily distracted by his hand gently thrumming the desk-top in front of her, suddenly realised she had been right in assuming the prints were Raphael's addition and was quietly glad she hadn't complimented his choice.

'You know,' he began eyeing Kitty, 'in his nineteen fourteen to nineteen seventeen expedition. Shackleton survived crossing the freezing ocean despite his boat, Endurance, being sunk by ice. He camped on an iceberg and journeyed across a mountain range. In all that he didn't lose a single member of his team.' He now moved to the wall and pointed at another print.

'Thor Heyerdahl,' Kitty interjected.

'You know that one then,' Raphael smiled, impressed, and moved to a third print. 'This is Juliane Koepcke. Then Chris Ryan, only surviving member of the ill-fated eight-man Bravo Two Zero mission in the Gulf War. Then we have…' He looked back at Kitty giving her a chance to answer first.

She shook her head.

'Cornelius Rost,' Raphael stated. His voice had turned reverent, 'German soldier. Captured by Russians in nineteen forty-five. Rost escaped a Siberian gulag. He navigated his way through Russia, Mongolia and Central Asia before he reached Iran in nineteen fifty-two.'

Kitty nodded swallowing a smile. Raphael was deeply appealing when he was passionate about something. 'That's incredible,' she breathed. *I'm pretty sure I can manage six months with you then, compared to that.*

'It's amazing what people can do to escape their personal prisons,' he began pointing back through the prints. 'Stranded. Disbelievers. Sole survivor of a plane crash. Mission gone wrong. Prisoner of war...' his voice eventually falling away. Kitty had seen this lost look before. She wondered what personal prison he was trying to escape. Daring perhaps? Or was he talking about her? Who knew?

'So why these paintings? I thought you didn't like growing up in Rome.' Kitty gestured to the decadent pieces at the other end of the room.

'I didn't choose those,' Raphael answered cooly. Hiding his surprise, if he had felt any, that she remembered anything about their night together despite so flippantly dismissing it the last time they had met.

Before Kitty could ask anymore Raphael sat down on the opposite side of the desk, 'So. Miss May—'

She stopped him, 'Kitty please.'

'Not Cleopatra?' His mouth twisted into a mischievous grin.

'No. Definitely not that. Just Kitty.'

'Kiti then. Lucille will be most disappointed.'

Kitty wasn't sure if he was teasing her or not, so decided to stay quiet. She didn't want to end up in another argument.

'I have read through the reports I received from your various rotations. Very impressive. What do you hope to achieve from your six months with me?'

'Umm... thank you. To be honest I have no idea.'

'That can't be what you said in your previous rotations?'

Kitty thought he seemed amused. He was beginning to really annoy her again. What did he expect her to say? He knew she didn't want him as a mentor and he clearly didn't seem to understand that he had turned what had been for her a trusting passionate evening, into a regrettable one-night stand.

'No, it wasn't,' she replied.

'So...' he pushed.

'To be honest, Raphael, I don't understand if you're playing a game, or what you want from me. But I can't discuss my employment aspirations with you. It feels awkward and I don't actually want your help. Besides, I know nothing about you.'

'I bet none of the other graduates know anything personal about their mentors.'

'Yes, but I bet none of them have slept with one of them either.'

'Kiti, I—'

'I know. I mean... I don't know why you're so private and I'm not asking you to open up or even apologise. But please, just give me a job to do and let me get on with it.' *I really want nothing to do with you,* she added silently.

'Fine.' Raphael picked up the phone on his desk.

Kitty watched him hesitate for the briefest of moments before he held the receiver to his ear.

Waiting for it to connect, Raphael's pale eyes were cold as he tapped the desk and Kitty guessed that he was annoyed. She had no idea why he now seemed to care so much about her career development. He was infuriatingly confusing. She assumed he could just be trying to be civil, professional as he had promised, but his chance for being nice had disappeared when he had all those months ago, and she had made no such promise of professionalism.

'Ciao, Hugo. Is the desk still empty by you?' he waited, 'Perfecto. I'm going to send you my graduate mentee… Kiti yes. She can help with the New York preparations.' With that he hung up. He turned back to look at Kitty, 'Happy?'

'Thank you… Mr Daring.'

Raphael nodded and walked her silently to the door.

TEN

Raphael sat behind his desk looking out over the empty office, staring at nothing in particular. His computer screen was blank and phone lay idle in his hands, its screen flashing on and off, heralding the ceaseless inflow of messages. Messages he should be checking.

It had been two weeks since Kitty had joined Raphael's private team at Daring and her attitude towards him hadn't changed. Still stubbornly refusing any kind of assistance from him, she had remained resolutely frosty. Any conversation that had occurred, a few brief and stilted remarks in a corridor or lift, had only arisen due to the misplaced encouragement of another employee, the presence of which forcing some sort of collusion between the pair. Both silently agreed, despite their differences, inviting gossip about their personal lives was something to be avoided at all costs. Even then, these moments had been tense, each party competitively polite. Raphael often receiving little more than a tight smile from his newest employee.

Despite his promise of professionalism, one he remembered her not making in return, Kitty's desire for distance was having the opposite effect on him. Making little progress at work had become the norm. His days were besieged by memories. The faint echo of her laugh, the arousing lilt in her walk, her smile, her…

At the click of the door latch disengaging he glanced up. It was Natalie, delivering a fresh pile of post. More messages that required his attention. His spirits dipped. *Pathetic,* he scolded.

Natalie's heels clicked loudly on the stone tiles. Then softly as she passed over the rug. Then loudly once more as she left. Turning his attention to his phone, ignoring the stack of unopened missives, he scanned his contacts. Finding the one he wanted he pressed dial. He wouldn't waste any more of his day at Daring.

Raphael hadn't seen Alec since his mother's funeral. With everything that had happened in the twenty or so months since, he just hadn't had the time. A subtle apprehension drifted over him as he waited for the line to connect.

'Turtle!' Alec answered, 'What's up man? How can I help?'

Raphael shook his head. He hadn't heard that nickname in a while. Alec always tried to amuse him, 'Just meet me?'

'Now?'

Since the explosion, Alec had been working freelance security. Without one of his legs he could no longer serve in the SAS. It had been a big knock to him, but he had dealt with it as admirably as one could expect of a man whose only ambition in life had been to serve in the Army. After months of physiotherapy, followed by many more months of counselling. Alec had gotten himself to a mental place where he was able to focus on the fact that he was still alive, rather than looking at what he had lost. This did not mean he didn't think about those things, but for reasons he had kept private, he wanted to live more as he was with his missing parts, than not at all. Now between jobs, and refusing to accept one from Raphael. Alec was training for the London marathon. He had run it numerous times before the explosion and wanted to prove to himself that he could still do it.

'If that works with your training?' Raphael pushed as Alec had still not accepted.

'Hungry?' Alec sounded hopeful.

'Falcon then.' Raphael hung up.

A relic of a pub, hidden down a narrow side street, a short walk north from Mile End Park, the Falcon existed quietly. A dusty haunt for regulars only. The faded faces of obsolete celebrities and bygone sportsmen, their inked signatures faded from view, covered the walls alongside the dark wooden panels that lined the interior. To some it was a sacred space, a once grand temple to anti-temperance, still free from the modern trappings of the hipster evolution that most London hostelries had been dragged through in order to afford rising ground rents. To others, it was an antique, a cigarette-smoke stained, gold chintz-accented wart on a neighbourhood trying to claw itself out of a rough past.

Alec, after a few years of army quarters and hard saving, had bought a shoebox flat, third floor, one bedroom, with a lounge that doubled up as a kitchen, dining room and entrance hall where a tatty leather sofa overlooked an unloved park. Here Raphael had slept whenever their leave periods had crossed over. He had never considered going to his own home on these occasions. It was during one of these stays that the two men had been charmed by the Falcon and after each deployment it had become an honoured tradition to return and have a drink with Alf the landlord.

Alfred White, or simply Alf as his friends were permitted to call him, was the fourth generation of his family to call the Falcon home. Now in his seventies, his marriage having borne no children, he would be the last White to man the tap handles. Childless but not loveless, Alf's marriage had been the happiest time of his life. Never having been accused of gushing, it was only at Nenet's funeral that he had wondered if she had known how much he had loved her. Still loved her.

Born in Arish, the largest city on the Sinai Penninsula, Nenet's family had moved to London during the large scale emigration after Egypt's defeat in the Six-Day War. Their romance had alienated her from her family, and in a way had done the same to Alf from his own community. The barrels of beer in the basement had certainly needed changing less often after she had moved in. But he hadn't cared much. "*It is what it is and so we carry on*" was Alf's mulish mantra.

144

It had been eleven years since her freckled hands had tickled the ivory keys of the piano in the far corner of the pub where, hidden from the bar, she had sung on quiet nights, and longer still since her ebony tresses, the first thing she had lost to the illness, had tangled the old vacuum cleaner. But her presence could still be felt, among the dried lavender Hydrangeas she had nestled into the fireplace, which remained despite now being cancerous with cobwebs, to the inclusion of a selection of pies (the only part of British cuisine she had come to cherish) into the Falcon's offerings, which had before excluded all food products - something Nenet had never been able to understand. Even the sign hanging above the entrance on the street paid homage to her heritage. Unchanged for more than a century, the community had bustled and gossiped long after the day the board had been repainted with Nenet's design. In place of the dowdy brown bird, a golden illustration of Horus, the falcon-headed Egyptian god hung proudly and below it, his large all seeing eye, painted in black, watched all who entered. Alf had taken a while to get used to the shining image, but now passed below with a reverential demeanour.

Now strolling under the sign, the little that remained of the original gold paint glinted in the low autumn sun, Raphael rolled his eyes. Alf had hammered its meaning into Alec and himself many times. '*Perseverance and Life when the world around you doesn't seem conducive to either,*' the landlord would insist, harping on about how Horus would bring him good fortune one day - something Nenet had convinced him of perhaps. Raphael, unfailingly sceptical, had never given Alf much time on the matter. Alec, perhaps feeling a strange responsibility for Raphael's bad manners, had always indulged the old man. So the importance of perseverance and stories of Nenet had been a regular topic during their visits.

Knowing the trouble Alf had gotten in over the years with local gangs and loan sharks, something Alec knew nothing about, Raphael felt quietly reassured as he passed under the sign's unblinking gaze, that the eye and disfigured god above had no divine powers.

Entering the Falcon, the air permeated with the fermented smell of beer, like overripe fruit and the curtains holding on to the memory of once permitted indoor cigarettes, Raphael coughed quietly, his nose wrinkling at the stale miasma, before assessing the booths.

Empty.

The barmaid, having noticed his entrance, began to shift uncomfortably. She glanced repeatedly between Raphael and the man, the only visible customer, sitting on a stool in front of her. Her hair, tipped a seaweed green, was pulled into a messy ponytail revealing a clear row of gems, getting progressively larger, which sparkled down her right ear. On her left lobe hung a feather, below which the tattoo of a hummingbird spiralled around her collarbone, its tail disappearing beneath her top. The man on the stool swivelled to see who had entered.

Raphael waited calmly, watching as the man, thick-set, baseball cap, calculate his chances. The man's eyes flickered. His right hand balled.

'Wes!' was all the barmaid said. But the fight had left him and instead he strode out. Puffing out his chest, soft with the fat that hadn't been there in his twenties, his cheeks reddened.

Raphael stayed put, his face impassive, his position forcing the man to walk around him to reach the street. Raphael tried not to smile. That wouldn't help.

He stayed frozen until the last of the street noise, a distant siren blaring above the low rumble of car engines and a dog barking somewhere, had once more disappeared behind the heavy wooden door.

The barmaid, now fiddling with the dried green ends of her ponytail moved to clear the pint, half finished, which had been left on the bar, 'Can I umm... get you something... umm sir?' she mumbled, tripping over her words and then her feet as Raphael closed the space between them.

Before he could answer Alf appeared. Wheezing into the archway behind where the barmaid perched, 'That's alright Ruby. Take ya lunch break,' he coughed. Still catching his breath from having climbed the stairs from the basement. A pipe had leaked and one pint sold wasn't going to pay to fix it. He wondered if the football would draw a bigger crowd this evening. He couldn't remember who was playing. Then he remembered the television had been taken in the robbery.

Ruby, not having waited to be asked twice, had darted out the front door, giving Raphael a wide berth. The dog's barks once more invaded the space, distracting Alf from his thoughts.

'The man who was in here before. He's one of Darren's guys no? Are you having trouble with them again?' Raphael asked, seeing no need for drawn out small talk.

Alf shook his head. Wheezing some more, 'No no... That one's just taken a shine to our Ruby.'

Silently nodding Raphael turned around and headed in the direction of the private section of the pub, where the piano lay unplayed and the booths were hidden from the door.

'Don't get any trouble these days,' Alf called after Raphael, coughing again, a lifetime of cigarettes having caught up with him, 'Not since it got out the Falcons under new ownership.'

Raphael turned on his heel. 'It's not,' he said coolly.

'It may be my name on the deeds, but it ain't me who pays the bills.'

The old man was taunting him now. Today Raphael wasn't in the mood. 'I don't pay the bills,' he replied calmly. Slipping behind the bar, Raphael took down a tumbler and bottle of Irish whiskey. Pouring himself three fingers, he swallowed the smokey amber fluid in one, welcoming the soft burn in his throat. Placing the glass back on the bar, Raphael bent to the small hidden fridge compartment and helped himself to a bottled Peroni. Standing up again he turned to Alf and placed a twenty pound note on the bar, 'This does.'

Raphael didn't want to have this argument again. Alf was a friend. He had loans that needed paying and he couldn't pay them, nor protect himself from the men wanting payment, whereas Raphael could do both. Easily. Alf's pride was the reason he had sorted the problem without his permission. The old man would never have asked for help or agreed to it.

Watching Raphael make his way back to the booths at the back of the pub, Alf remembered the boy he had first met. Gobby little shit. A swell of pride washed over him seeing him now. Smartly suited. Calm. His skin free of the old, seemingly endless cuts and bruises it used to endure. Alf cleared his throat, 'Not eating?'

'Old Golden Bollocks is coming back, Alf. He'll have pie don't you worry,' Raphael called back without turning, oblivious to the broad grin now planted across Alf's crinkled face.

Having loaded the pie into the oven, wishing he hadn't sent Ruby out for a lunch break, Alf returned to see Alec entering, his shoulders flecked with rain, he rubbed his shoes on the mat by the door. Always so polite. 'Got a pie on for you, stranger.'

'Cheers, Alf,' Alec smiled apologetically waving from the door. 'Sorry it's been a while,' he added, wiping the rain from his forehead.

Having already pulled a fresh pint for Alec's arrival, Alf held the glass up for Alec to see. He knew, unlike Raphael, Alec would not be so heinous as to take one of the foreign, bottled jobs, he had hidden away below the bar - another of Nenet's additions. Making his way up to the bar to collect the pint, Alf now noticed the stiff, unbending limp in his friend's walk, 'You hurt yourself this time?'

'You could say that.'

'Bad one?' Alf frowned, concerned.

Pulling up his trouser leg to reveal his prosthetic Alec tapped on the plastic, 'Missing.'

Momentarily, Alf was lost for words. Caught between sadness and the archetypal British trait of jesting in the face of adversity. 'Sticking power remember,' Alf settled somewhere in between, pointing to his eye.

Alec nodded, 'Perseverance.'

'Bloody right son.'

Alec raised the beer to Alf, fully aware that was the old man's way of saying he was glad Alec was alive, he had always been particularly fond of the two of them. 'You're doing alright here, Alf? Persevering?'

'I had a bit of help,' he nodded in the direction of the back of the bar.

'Rafa?'

'Don't tell him I told you. But I wouldn't be here without him.'

'That makes two of us.'

Raphael had not been waiting long when Alec found him at their old spot by the piano. Despite this he was still regretting agreeing to meet. He wanted to see Alec. But despite being far away from the office, his mind was still besieged with his earlier distractions.

'How have you been?' Raphael began. He had been pacing in the empty space beside the booths, unable to settle and only on speaking did he force himself to stop, gripping the top of the piano to hold him firm. The dust transferred to his fingers.

'I'm good. Still unemployed and before you ask, happily so.' Alec slouched into the the leather booth, gratefully taking the weight off his prosthetic, temporarily easing the aching throb where it joined what remained of his right leg. The marathon training was taking its toll.

Raphael moved to object, 'Why won't you let me help you?' he paused, leaving his perch by the piano and taking up residence opposite his friend, 'I owe you everything Alec.'

'No you don't owe me anything. Anyway, if you really feel that, then you more than made up for it when you saved my life back in Syria.'

Raphael frowned and Alec took his opportunity to move the conversation away from him and find out what was troubling his friend.

He could tell something was the moment he had entered and found himself once more staring, at an albeit slightly aged version, of the confused nineteen year old Raphael he had first encountered. A boy who, until today, he had thought he wouldn't see again. For behind Raphael's big, ridiculously blue eyes, a pair which, despite his repeated disinterest in women, had made him such a hit with the ladies, Alec knew him to be a troubled, perhaps even broken man. As far as Alec was aware he always had been. He can't have been born broken, Alec had eventually decided, but by the time he had met him he was shattered, with so many pieces of himself lost, that Alec suspected sadly he could never be truly fixed.

On joining the army, Raphael had been wild, all mouth and angst. He had been a live wire at training, acting more like a cornered wolverine than anything human, solely driven by an unspoken desperation to prove himself. A trait which had eventually, after many scuffles and dressing downs from superior officers, finally tamed or more, channeled his unbounded aggression. Alec had been fascinated by him from the outset. He had never encountered a person born with such a massive silver spoon in their mouth, such advantage, and yet so hopelessly determined to distance themselves from it.

Raphael had never spoken in too much detail about his family, and if it were not for the Daring surname and customary high-end Range Rover that Raphael never went without, Alec might not have known he was from such privilege. But privileged or not, Alec knew that whatever Raphael's family had done, or failed to do, by nineteen Raphael had been royally screwed up.

It had not been the usual kind of confusion found stereotypically in rich children, who had spent their lives palmed off with nannies and tutors in place of their disinterested, absent parents. In fact, Raphael had never once appeared to doubt nor question his parents love for him. From what Alec gathered, his mother in particular had been an ever present and loving force throughout his childhood. It was something else that had driven him away from his family and into the Army after practically vanishing for a year post school.

Alec had given up trying to understand it a long time ago and instead had focussed on helping, as much as he could, in shaping the man he had always known Raphael could be. In truth, it wasn't until he had seen Raphael kill his first man on a mission, that he had started to appreciate the depths of his friend's inner torment. Raphael had dealt with his first military sanctioned assassination like one deals with taking out the rubbish. Dispassionately. Systematic. Even familiar. He dealt with it, Alec remembered, like he had seen it all before.

Alec had never questioned his friend on this topic and instead was simply forever grateful that Raphael had been on his team, rather than the enemies. Over the years, Raphael had become good, perhaps the best soldier he knew at compartmentalising tough situations and concealing his own emotions. He had perfected this until he was almost completely unrecognisable from the feral, electric boy Alec had first met.

The extent of Raphael's refined self-control was evident the last time they had seen each other. It had been Raphael's mother's funeral, where throughout the whole proceedings, Raphael had been unwaveringly the composed, resolute CEO that people had come to see him as. He had been polite to all the guests, gracious with their well wishes, but never once joined them in their grief. In reality, behind his carefully constructed facade, Alec, having lived the best part of the last decade side by side with him, throughout some horrifying ordeals, had seen that he simply wasn't mentally present. He was somewhere else. Physically in the room, but mentally checked out. No doubt missing some more of himself, a new piece, broken off and irretrievably lost to the world.

Now seated beside him. Alec looked at his friend for a clue as to what had broken through the barrier, which Alec had thought had become impenetrable, 'Rafa, what's up?'

Raphael's face broke into a frustrated half smile. Alec had always been able to read him. More than his own brother could for sure. Rubbing his hands over his face he groaned, 'Argh, Alec. I think I fucked up.' He pulled at his hair, 'No… I did fuck up.'

Alec was taken aback. He had never heard Raphael say something like that. Not in this tone. He waited for him to continue.

'There's a woman.'

'Really?' Alec interrupted.

Raphael raised a questioning eyebrow at Alec's now shocked face, 'Is it really that shocking?'

'Well yeah. To be honest, Raf, I'd sort of come to the conclusion that you genuinely weren't ever going to go there. It's been a while mate.'

Alec knew that it wasn't a genuine disinterest in women that stopped Raphael entering relationships. He had proof enough of his friend's debauchery. But he didn't want to misjudge the tone by voicing now, how he still thought Raphael was of the view, one that he had expressed on a very drunken night when they were about twenty, that he for some misguided reason felt he wasn't deserving of someone's love. *Not undeserving of their virginity mind,* Alec counted in his head. But of a genuine love, the kind one would hope to foster in a faithful relationship. The kind that could spin you out.

'Yeah…' Raphael muttered looking down.

'Come on then'

'There's not much to say. I did go… *there*. As you put it so… cavallerescamente. Um… chivalrously.'

'When?' Alec pushed

Raphael sighed. What had he expected? Alec clearly wasn't going to let him drop it now he'd started, 'Soon after my mother was diagnosed. You were busy in rehab. Christmas before last.'

'Mistake?'

'No. Well sì. Yes… but no,' Raphael stopped, trying to focus his thoughts. He was not used to asking for advice or opening up, but he was beginning to realise that he needed another perspective and there was no one he trusted more than Alec. He rested his head on the back of the booth.

'So what? You slept with her?'

Raphael looked across at Alec. His eyes burning. He nodded. He looked deeply ashamed. Alec had never seen him like this. Especially not with regards to a woman he had slept with and this one nearly two years ago.

'And now?'

'Now she works for me,' Raphael continued ignoring Alec's burst of chuckles, 'it's messed up I know. Genuinely pure coincidence. I didn't know and...' he paused briefly, '...and now she won't speak to me. She barely looks at me.'

'Wow... maybe you're not as good as you look, Turtle,' Alec teased. Raphael knew he was waiting for more of the story.

'Funny,' he took a deep breath, 'I left the next morning, before she woke up.'

'And you did a runner didn't you?'

'Pretty much.'

'I'm not surprised she won't speak to you. That was fucking rude. Be honest. You're not that surprised? This isn't the first one-night stand of your life though, mate. What's the problem?'

Raphael had considered that fact too. But this one he couldn't shake off. Or he had well enough, until he had seen her at Daring, looking as radiant as the first time he had seen her giving the waiters the run-around in one of his restaurants, 'I did it *for* her, Alec. But this one... Ah I don't know. She's different. I was still in the SAS. My family...well...' He didn't want to go there. 'She's...' he finished the sentence in his mind. He shook his head. 'Special,' he offered.

'You never said anything even remotely close to that to her though did you?'

'No.' Saying this all to Alec, Raphael suddenly felt like the prize idiot, Kitty no doubt thought him to be. He had been so caught up in his own issues, that he hadn't really considered the conclusions she would draw from his disappearance. Or the consequences he may have to live with.

'So—' Alec began.

'I used her, Alec. I used her and she won't let me make it right.'

Both men had agreed not long after their first deployment, that being in the SAS wasn't conducive to starting relationships. But Raphael had always thought it more than simply a hindrance. He thought it reckless, even selfish of the guys in his unit who had partners back home. He had been forced to deliver bad news to so many of them. The worse part being, that due to the sensitive nature of the job, he was never at liberty to explain what had really happened to their loved one. He had watched as the women, one by one became broken. Unable to fully move on and heal for they lacked the knowledge of what had even happened. He refused to do that to anyone. And his family, he didn't want to bring that up with Alec, but he knew he equally hadn't wanted to expose Kitty and her trusting innocence to the darkness he had been exposed to by being a Daring. Now knowing she had passed the Daring Corporation's stringent criminal records checks, he knew she was no thief. Even if he couldn't yet answer if she was an adulterer or coveter, the familial issue was still a concern for him. Being a Daring, or involved with one, was not all holidays, parties and expensive cars as the magazines like to suggest.

'When I was in the hospital in Birmingham…' Alec glanced at Raphael. He was staring back at him. Waiting

156

silently to see where the story was headed. They had never spoken about this time before.

* * *

The venetian blinds tapped periodically against the window panes. Pushed and pulled by the breeze flowing through the opening at the bottom. I felt it tickle my eyelids. It felt nice. Soothing after weeks in the scorching desert. *Is this it? Am I dead?* I opened my eyes. Squinting at the strip light above my head, it was too bright. I blinked three or four times before the room began to come into focus.

It was white. Everything was white, the walls, the blinds, the ceiling. The linoleum floor began to turn smoke coloured as my focus returned, contrast slowing leaking back into the world. The yellow waste bin, the silver of the taps at the sink on the far side of the room all coming into view, began to stand out to me. I looked down. A pale blue blanket covered my legs.

A doctor stood at the foot of the bed. The stethoscope curled around her neck a clear indication of her profession. Not looking at me, I watched her as she scratched her neck, bent over a stack of papers bound by a dull brown file. Adjusting her tortoiseshell glasses so that she was able to better read the notes balanced in her hands. A strand of hair, similar in colour to the linoleum, fell from its prior placement behind her ear. Now partially obscuring her vision, she wiped it away, all the while continuing her study. The brown file was large. Huge. I looked once more around the room wondering whom the notes belonged too. Realising that there was no one else in the room, an uneasy feeling snarled from the pit of my stomach. *Panic?* I wondered. *The file must be mine.* Before I could speak, I realised the doctor was assessing me, her glasses now resting on her head, revealing creased, dark purply bags under her bloodshot eyes.

She spoke first, her voice calm and assertive, 'Good morning, Mr Page. My name is Dr Hazel. I was not here when you arrived. You're at the Royal Centre for Defence Medicine or as we call it RCDM. How are you feeling?'

She waited patiently looking at me. Not moving her steady gaze from mine.

I blinked a few more times, 'I'm alive?' I managed. Hearing my voice weak and slurring compared to hers, I lifted my hand to rub my face. Trying to help wake it up.

'Ah!' I cried out as a sharp pain shot up my arm. It stung and I bit down on my lip to numb the sensation. Looking down, I saw a cannula protruding out from the vein in the crook of my right arm. My eyes followed the clear tube until I found what I was looking for. A bag of morphine hung from a frame. *That explains the deliriousness.*

'You have been unconscious for a few days. You lost a lot of blood. It will take you some time to get your strength back.' Dr Hazel said, dragging my attention back from the morphine. She moved to stand beside the bed, 'Do you remember what happened, Mr Page?'

'Alec. Please, just Alec.'

'Ok,' she smiled. Her camomile scent washed over me, the subtle perfume caught by a gust from the window, 'Do you remember what happened, Alec?'

I nodded and began to slowly work through what I remembered about the explosion. I laughed a little at the end. It was not a lot apparently.

Once I had finished telling my story she took her leave. A strange moment of déjà vu passed over me. I tried to remember where I had seen the doctor before, but the morphine decided otherwise.

I was not sure how many days passed this way. Sleeping and healing. They told me about my leg. About how it had needed to be amputated. About how Captain Daring's bravery had saved my life. I thought of Raphael often, hoping that he now considered the strange debt he had always felt he owed me had now been paid.

He visited me a few times in the first week. He sat at the end of my bed telling me about his mother's illness amongst other things. He was so lost on those visits, his face a near constant picture of sadness. It took me a long time to realise that he was mirroring my own.

At the end of the first week they removed the cannula. Then the physiotherapists came to visit and we began working with the prosthetic leg that they had built for me. I stood up almost straight away. It wasn't anywhere near as hard as I had imagined it would be. The physios didn't seem surprised by my quick mastering of the prosthetic, so I quietly readjusted my glee, assuming that most patients were able to adapt in the same way.

There was a small garden at the back of the building I was staying in. Walled on all sides and planted around the edges of the lawn with neat borders of rose and hydrangea plants, it was a quiet sanctuary. A pocket of Eden, at odds with the clinical, soulless surroundings of the hospital and the daily bustle of Birmingham beyond.

Sitting on the garden's only bench, embellished with a small brass plaque marking the life of a now deceased Army Major, I closed my eyes. The sun was warm on my lids and the wooden slats beneath my thighs provided a welcome relief to the throb of my stump.

'Hello,' a quiet voice called out to me.

My eyes flashed open. Panic stirred within me. Registering my alarm the woman who had spoken instantly apologised, 'Sorry. I didn't mean to startle you.'

'I didn't mean to be startled,' I replied, forcing a brief smile and adjusting my hospital pyjamas.

'Do you mind if I sit down?' she asked.

I moved aside creating a bit more space. The woman was clearly not well. Her frail body was heaped over a zimmer frame, her face pale and eyes glassy. For a moment I wondered if she could see at all, but the absence of a guide or stick answered my unspoken question. She lowered herself onto the bench. I watched as she placed her arms, mummified in bandages into her lap. Only once she was settled did she speak again. A little out of breath.

She told me about her injuries. Her name was Jane but she had spent her lifetime being called Annie thanks to her ginger curls which flowed, unruly down past her shoulders. She insisted I call her Annie too. On the day that she turned fifteen years and seven months she had applied to join the Army. Her fellow soldiers had become a sort of family for her and six years ago had encouraged her to follow her passion. Retraining as an Army Medic, Annie served two tours in Afghanistan. On the last day of her final deployment, a roadside bomb had taken out three members of her section and badly injured two more, including herself. She had third degree burns up her arms and along her torso and shrapnel lodged everywhere. She took my hands in hers and carefully lifted them to her face.

'See,' she squealed, 'I'm all lumpy.'

I carefully moved my hands over her cheeks and it was true. There were hard lumps hidden beneath the surface.

'Will they not take them out?' I asked, my hands still tracing the pieces of metal and plastic.

'They have taken out as much as they can for now. Some will continue to surface and escape all on their own.'

'You seem so happy. Underneath it all.'

'I'm alive aren't I?' she breathed.

Annie's candour was unnerving. I removed my hands from her face and placed them down in my lap, mirroring hers.

'Why are you here, Alec?'

'How do you know my name?' I felt my eyebrows pinch together. Confusion.

'Sorry, that was weird. I'm in the room opposite you.'

I told her about the explosion and showed her my amputated leg. I couldn't tell her much about what I had been doing in Syria as it was classified. Thinking about it, I hadn't yet been debriefed. The thought lodged in my mind. *I should chase that up.* Out of the corner of my eye I saw Annie's shoulder's slump. She seemed disappointed. Perhaps she had been hoping for a more thrilling tale. She began to turn away, positioning the zimmer frame to help her stand when she turned back.

'There is a story about a thirsty crow,' she began, 'he is scouring the countryside when he comes across a pail of water.'

'Why are you telling me a children's story?' I could feel that I was beginning to lose my composure. My gut

161

warned me that I didn't want to hear what Annie was about to say. Not that I had much choice. It would take me a while to refasten my prosthetic comfortably, having taking it off to show her the scarring. It had healed amazingly well I reminded myself, as I tried to calm myself down.

Ignoring my question Annie continued to talk. Staring at me with her glassy eyes, 'The crow goes up to the pail but finds the water level too low. He can't reach the water. Just when he is about to give up, after straining and straining to reach, the crow finds another way to drink. He carries little stones, for he can't carry any big ones as he is now too weak, and drops them one by one in the pail. Slowly the water level rises—'

'And he drinks,' I said frustrated.

'He survives. He nearly died but he keeps going. He survives. Who knows what the crow went on to do with its second chance?' she pushed.

I got up to leave, but I had only made it a couple of paces before I heard Annie's voice calling after me. I froze, waging a silent inner war with my manners. I wanted desperately to ignore her. It seemed imperative that I ignored her. Panic.

'Why are you here, Alec? All day I sit across the corridor from you and hear Dr Hazel asking you that same question,' she called again.

I turned on her, 'My leg. I told you. I lost it.' *Like you've lost your fucking mind.* Anger coursed through me. I felt it in my veins. The twitching. *When did I take my pills?* I couldn't remember. I couldn't remember what they were even for anymore.

Annie tried to catch up to me but fell. Her weak arms unable to match the strength of her intentions. I didn't turn back to help her, just left her there on the grass. I thought she was crying but I pushed that thought from my mind. *She's mad.* I repeated over and over in my head. But the question had stuck. *Why am I here?*

During Dr Hazel's next visit, I finally plucked up the courage to ask her. She sat on the end of the bed and lifted my hands up in front of me. I looked down. Wondering if perhaps she had lost her mind too. There was nothing wrong with my hands. Carefully she began to undo the bandages that encased my arms.

'The burns… will they have healed?' I asked.

Dr Hazel stopped. She had finished unravelling my bandages. I knew because I could feel the breeze on my forearms. I looked down. There were no burns. Just a pair of thin matching red ridges running across my wrists. Scarlet scores across the otherwise smooth skin.

'Alec,' she began, 'why are you here? This time, why are you here?'

I shook my head. I couldn't form any words. I felt lost. Cast off in a vacuum with nothing to hold on to. I began to panic again.

'Let me help you,' Dr Hazel offered. My head was still shaking but she continued anyway, 'The explosion. Your leg amputation. Your physio. That was all completed about six months ago.'

It took the doctors a while longer to finally get the answer they were looking for, a full answer. The truth. The memories came back to me in bits, like one sometimes remembers a nightmare after they have woken up. Pieces of some horrific puzzle. Dr Hazel turned out to be a psychiatrist and bit by bit, like the crow and the stones, I began to heal and I survived.

* * *

'You can't blame yourself,' Raphael's voice called Alec back to the present.

'I did it. I was saved and I tried to throw it all away,' Alec muttered.

'The same could happen to anyone, especially with what you went through. Less even. It's nothing to be—'

Alec cut Raphael off, one hand in the air. 'On the day I was discharged I went to see Annie. To thank her and apologise. She wasn't in her room but the book of fables was on the side. So I waited for her. Flicking through the pages until I found the one about the crow.' Alec coughed, 'I fell asleep in that chair, reading about the crow. But it wasn't Annie who woke me. No it was her daughter. The same red hair. Everything. I didn't know she even had one. It was her book you see,' Alec laughed, 'She wanted it back. They only told me later that one of the pieces in Annie's neck. One of the shrapnel pieces had moved unexpectedly in the night… It had sliced her jugular.'

'Alec,' Raphael hesitated.

Alec ignored him. He needed to get this all out, 'It took me a long time to acknowledge the fact of my readmission to the RCDM, let alone the reasons for it.' He shook his head, 'I was so ashamed.'

Raphael had become a statue. Frozen in position.

'But nearly two years on, here I am. And here she's not.' Alec looked up to Raphael now, 'So if I'm struggling. Ha! *When* I'm struggling, I think of the crow. No matter your problem. Big or small. Just tackle it one stone at a time.' Alec wiped his eyes. Forcing a smile he coughed

164

again trying to clear the tightness that had formed in his throat.

Raphael wanted to comment on the story Alec had just shared. Not that he had any idea as to what he should say. Alec was the bravest man he knew. But before he could bring up the topic, Alec's pie and mash arrived. The smell emanating from it occupying his thoughts and he could see his friend was wanting to move on. He had just wanted to share.

Forking a spoonful of steak and kidney into his mouth, Alec leant across the table. He slapped Raphael on the shoulder. Swallowing the pie, he spoke again, 'So. Stop being so fucking stubborn. Stop overthinking this. Apologise for being a dick and go from there. She can't hold a grudge forever.'

Raphael raised his eyebrow, he wasn't so sure. She was the most strong willed woman he'd ever met outside of the ones in his own family. His only other experiences of women, he had found that they had been quite amenable to his persuasions and if those had failed him, his money never had. Whereas Kitty seemed to be having no problems in avoiding him, despite now knowing both of those things.

'Then what? What about everything else?' He knew that Alec would know what he was alluding too, whether he remembered the drunken confession or not.

'It's not up to you to decide whether who you are is good enough for her or not. That's her prerogative. Besides she's alive, and while that's the case, each and every time you see her is a new opportunity to change your relationship. To change her view of you.' Alec now stared at Raphael, 'You're not as bad as you think—'

'Alright. Alright.' Raphael raised his hands in surrender. He didn't want to hear anymore. Alec was always too forgiving, complementary. *If I was even half as honest as you are with me Alec you wouldn't be so kind,* he thought, once more clogged with the weight of his past crimes. Filling his lungs to the brim, he raised his beer to Alec, 'One stone at a time then.'

Alec smiled broadly, 'And make it a bloody big one.' He winked.

ELEVEN

Standing hunched, beaten down by the previous five and a half hours of incessant rain, Marku shook as he tried to breath life back into his sore, nicotine-stained fingers. The relentless weather had breached a formerly unnoticed section of loose stitching in the seam of his anorak, and his once insulating woollen jumper, was now soaked through. His body temperature was dropping and an annoying sniffle had begun in his nose.

Newly divorced, Marku had found himself forced to take on a third job this month and the mind-numbing hours spent labouring away were proving to be not without cost.

His now ex-wife, had somehow convinced the court judge that she would be requiring a not-inconsequential sum of spousal support and Marku had found himself stretched to fund two households, where before he had struggled to keep just one. Marku had no doubts that his wife hadn't worked a single job during their marriage, not for the sake of him or their two daughters, but because she was a lazy, selfish, bitch. The law had decided otherwise. But not before parading his adolescent misdemeanours with alcohol, gambling and disorderly behaviour - none of which having ever resulted in a criminal conviction and so none of which known in his new neighbourhood - around the courtroom for all to hear.

Despite his possessing a clean legal record, the self-satisfied woman had also been awarded sole-custody of their children. Long before Amalia, his eldest daughter, first opened her almond eyes on an unusually warm January day, Marku had regretted marrying her mother. A woman who had fallen pregnant from the briefest of interludes and whom, thanks to his traditional upbringing, he had married out of some - now long gone - sense of moral duty. Saving her from certain social exile and bringing her with him to the UK, to live as an honest woman - or that had been his intention. But no marriage certificate could create honesty where, as it turned out, there had been none beforehand.

With alternate evenings spent delivering greasy boxes of Chinese takeout around the Southampton area for Cheng's Palace, weekends used up painting the newly refurbished science block at St. Davids Secondary School, and the rest of his time spent down at the Docks logging containers, Marku had not seen his two little girls, or what was being bought with the money he was earning, since August.

With Halloween twenty-nine days away, a festival not overly celebrated in his home country, but one Marku had come to realise as another spending-spree beloved by the seemingly insatiable British consumers, he had planned a day off and had squirrelled away what he could to treat his girls. His goal, one he was determined to see through since the divorce, had been to become a figure that in time, no matter what their mother whispered in their trusting ears, his daughters could look up to and even, he hoped, admire.

Six days ago, with the resurfacing of his past gambling habits, Marku had been visited by some old acquaintances. Acquaintances he had long evaded. Acquaintances who possessed more information about Marku's past than he would want shared and acquaintances who had made some very dangerous new friends. It had not been long before the stark realisation had dawned on him, that he wasn't going to become this figure anytime soon.

Now sodden and desperately in need of a cigarette, Marku lodged the biro between yesterday's fresh callouses as he signed off on the twenty foot, unchecked container that had just arrived from Albania. Praying it was the one and only time he would have to do it. Inside, he knew he would not be so lucky. That was not how these things worked.

TWELVE

The graphite sky over London grumbled restlessly as the rain, which had not let up for the last four hours, continued to beat hard against the oversized office windows, like an angry uninvited guest clamouring to be let in. Kitty sat at her desk, cross-legged, spinning slowly in her chair as she watched the downpour. Below her, tiny strangers moved this way and that along the pavements, chasing their errant umbrellas, battling with the wind and hurrying about in an amusingly disorientated chaos. She wondered what they were thinking? Who they were? Where they were going? These were all questions she had been asking herself lately.

One month done. Five more to go. Kitty thought as she flipped over her desk calendar. She was pleased with herself at the small milestone. *At least I achieved something today,* she mused. Having found herself, for the first time in a month, woefully unoccupied, she was not welcoming the thinking time.

James hurried in without a greeting. He looked flustered, his sandy greying hair stuck to his overly round face and a mass of wet dark spots covered his jacket. He was muttering to himself, 'Bloody rain. Bloody Hugo, you'd think he was already on holiday with his current attendance record. Bloody nightmare.' He threw his jacket over the back of his chair and slumped hard into it. It groaned beneath his weight.

Reaching behind her Kitty picked up the unwanted fresh coffee she had made a few minutes earlier, another attempt to distract her from her wandering mind, and offered it to him. His eyes sparkled as he took it from her. An almost visible calm washed over his face as his pudgy fingers enclosed the mug.

'Sorry there… thanks,' he muttered, as his rabbity teeth pinched over the side of the mug, savouring the hot brown liquid.

One thing Kitty had learnt about James, a caffeine addicted colleague who shared Hugo's office from time to time, was that as long as his hand was clasped around a fresh cup of coffee he was pleasant and often rather jovial. Unfortunately Hugo García, the thickset South American with features as disorganised as his temper who Raphael had sent Kitty to work for down the hall, was the complete opposite.

Less satiated with a simple hot beverage, Hugo was a man of few words. Unfortunately those he did utter were, to the untrained ear, practically indecipherable. Since birth, whenever he spoke his tongue protruded unattractively between his front teeth, leaving him with a pronounced lisp. Combined with his native accent the effect was unnerving. His words combined into a throaty almost primeval growl. James had assured Kitty that she would understand him in time, but not to worry too much if she never could, 'Moody bastard, he's got some time off soon anyway. We'll do some practicing then,' James had commented, sticking out his tongue three afternoons ago, mocking Hugo's condition whilst suffering from his second caffeine low of that particular day. Kitty had felt a measure of sympathy for Hugo on her first few days, but this had failed to last the month. He was aloof at the best of times and a figure to avoid at the worst and it was a miracle if she could guess by mid-morning what mood he was in. She had been told he was a savage negotiator when he wanted to be, a fact that had not surprised her. 'A real cut-throat, grade-A bastard when he's making a deal too,' Richard from accounts had told her after he'd had his head chewed off over filing an incorrect expenses claim concerning an international flight. She had supposed it made sense, the Daring Corporation bought and sold assets all the time and they were intent on making a profit on every transaction, so perhaps Hugo's savagery was sometimes needed to get the job done - it certainly wasn't his charm that would do it.

Kitty had decided against telling either of the men that she would be resigning after her six month contract ended, if she hadn't already managed a way out before then, for fear that her excuses would be pitifully transparent. Instead, they had bumped along without major incident for four weeks and begun to sow the seeds of a manageable rhythm. This had been helped immeasurably by Hugo's ever-increasing absences. Kitty had not been asked to assist on whatever project he was currently working on. In fact, she realised, she didn't even know a single piece of information about whatever he was he was spending his time doing. *Real inspiration,* she sighed.

Once half the coffee was finished. James spoke again. This time without muttering, 'He loved it by the way. They had a great time.'

It took Kitty a second to work out who he was talking about.

'New York?' she asked.

'Yeah. What else?' James scoffed, 'The whole event went off without a hitch. The charities loved it. They raised millions. They all got back today.'

Kitty felt a small elevator drop in her stomach. She had been enjoying Raphael's absence for the last fortnight. The two weeks prior to his trip, despite a rather good effort on her part, had still been punctuated with a few too many awkward run-ins for her liking. Something bound to restart now he was back.

James had continued speaking, oblivious to Kitty's mood change, '…they said that! Can you believe it? Praise from *both* Luca and Martina Daring.' He lowered his voice and checked over his shoulder despite no one else being in the room, 'I never thought I'd see the day. Usually it's Hugo who gets the credit and even that's muted. That man knows more about the Darings than anyone I'd reckon. It's weird sometimes…' he trailed off, sitting back in his chair, licking his lips he sipped the coffee at a more leisurely pace.

Kitty smiled weakly as she turned back to her computer and began scrolling numbly through her unread emails. James didn't notice.

The preparations for the Charity Art Fair, something Daring had sponsored two years in a row, had been surprisingly difficult not least because of the complexity of trying to get three of the four Daring siblings in one place at the same time. Aligning their diaries had been a feat overseen by Hugo with great interest but little action on his part.

The fact that Raphael was in possession of so many siblings, something he had neglected to mention the night they had met, had surprised Kitty. She had before imagined him to be a lonely only child, for she had deemed him too troubled, too self-contained, too stubborn and certainly too self-righteous to have been raised in such a large brood. In her eyes, Raphael did not fit what she would expect from a man who must have grown up with the hourly compromises and rivalries of life amongst multiple siblings, nor the support she had assumed that must bring. The security and feeling of belonging that surely accompanied being a member of such a team, bound by blood, seemed to have evaded him entirely.

In her planning she had learned that the group comprised of Raphael's elder brother Luciano, more commonly referred to as Luca, an exceptionally glamorous twin sister called Martina, Raphael of course and another sister Sienna. Sienna was seven years younger than the twins, and was the only Daring not directly involved in the business and the only one without a seat on the board. Kitty had heard that she was studying at an Art School somewhere.

Luca's diary had been the easiest to work with. Despite his senior position within the corporation, he appeared to have very little to do with the day to day running of the company. Kitty had wondered why, as the eldest, he hadn't taken the role of Chairman and CEO for himself. Although she didn't ask, as time had passed it hadn't been hard to see that Luca was less of a businessman and more of a party animal. He often spent time abroad on fancy yachts and could be seen arriving, on the rare occasions he did come to the Mayfair office, in a loud scarlet Ferrari befitting of his much remarked upon public image. On one occasion, with Hugo absent once again, she had asked James why Mr Luciano was able to spend so much time on holiday and, despite finally receiving an answer, she had been warned about that sort of talk.

'Don't let other people hear you asking those sorts of questions in this office in particular. The Daring family keep their affairs and decision making very private. They don't like being discussed,' James had said. Although later, after Kitty had discovered his weakness for caffeine, he had added quietly, 'But between you and me. Most of the people he's meeting on his holidays, at least the ones I've had a hand in organising, are seriously wealthy individuals. It's Hugo whose worked his way up to manage this kind of thing, but from what I saw, we're talking Russians, Chinese, Arabs… people with influence from all over. So I suppose if you want to grow as a company…' he gestured with his hands, 'you need a client base and partners and Mr Luciano seems to have happily accepted the mantle of client entertainer.' He winked before being serious again, 'But seriously, be careful who you ask about the Daring family. It can get you in to trouble.'

Despite the surprising fact of Raphael's siblings existence, it hadn't surprised Kitty to discover how private the whole Daring family was and until today James hadn't spoken of them again.

Kitty, who had begun rechecking her emails for the third time, now noticed a small red bubble of a reminder bouncing at the bottom of her screen. Clicking on the bubble, her heart sank once more. She was meant to be meeting Lucille with her placement buddies today to discuss the first month of the mentor scheme.

As if reading her thoughts James piped up, 'You got that HR crap today?'

'Yeah,' Kitty replied.

'You better say nice things about me,' he winked as he stood up to leave the office.

'Only the best,' Kitty delivered a mock salute.

James laughed before looking serious, 'I'm sorry I can't get you out of this one like the last one. And I bet Hugo's been no help. This meeting I'm off to…' he waved his hand in a blasé fashion. 'Just clearance shenanigans. Confidentiality bollocks. Unfortunately until you're full time after these six months I can't get you in.'

'It's alright, James. Thanks anyway.' Kitty fought to keep the disappointment out of her voice. She had been hoping he could have helped her get out of the grilling from Avery she was no doubt in store for, having avoided her entirely successfully since the mentoring event.

Alone again, Kitty pressed the button on her phone. The screen lit up. Nothing. Elliot hadn't been in touch for three weeks. He hadn't messaged since she had accepted his offer and despite requesting some help as to what exactly he needed she had been left out in the cold with regards to any assistance.

Despite this, she had kept her ear to the ground as he had requested and, an idea she had been quite proud of, even used one of the contacts she had made throughout grad-scheme rotations, one of the gossiper accounts technicians to get a run down of how the money streams were structured across the various revenue streams. It had all been, as far as Kitty could tell, well and truly above board.

'Oh this stuff is so restricted, regulated, checked, double checked, triple, you name it,' the technician had explained to Kitty, 'you couldn't sneak fifty pence in or out of this company without someone like me knowing.' With her home-knitted jumper and pictures of her "*fur-babies*" as she had called them, two drooling pugs, framed on her desk, unless it was a good cover, Kitty was pretty certain that this lady wasn't pulling one over on her.

The red reminder began bouncing again in Kitty's periphery and seeing the time, she realised that she now had twenty minutes until she needed to be in Lucille's office in HR and decided that she would get herself a tea in the meantime. She knew the walk would do her good and it would also negate the possibility of her being given an extra task by Hugo, if he returned from wherever he was. She was not busy, but her distractions had left her with no appetite to work excessively hard today and the slow workload wouldn't last. Rising from her desk she headed for the lifts.

The space that Hugo's team occupied was located further down a wide corridor from Raphael's palatial office. In between, a set of swanky panelled boardrooms lay hidden behind frosted doors, a collection of very senior managerial offices whose spaces Kitty had never entered, the bathrooms and a coffee come refreshment centre were all housed. Walking along the corridor Kitty noted the stream of closed doors. *Lots of meetings today*, she thought idly.

At the end of the corridor, the space opened up into the Chairman and CEO's entrance lobby, at the back was Raphael's office, and to the right there were the lifts. Here Natalie sat organising Raphael's diary and Georgia, or sometimes David, two junior receptionists, also perched. The latter two spent their time welcoming and sorting refreshments for the senior business men and women fortunate, or at least important enough, to be involved in meetings either with Raphael or the board in this part of the building.

As Kitty rounded the corner in to the lobby, pleased to note Raphael's door was shut like all the others, Natalie caught her eye. She was just about smiling from behind her desk, some of her hair had fallen out of her usually neat twist, and was waving Kitty over, her free hand flapping up and down. Kitty thought of circus seals waving for fish - not the image Natalie usually exuded.

Looking for the cause of her distress Kitty noticed two middle-aged business women sat in one of the sofas that filled the designated waiting section of the lobby. They did not look up as Kitty entered, engaged in their own private conversation. Still fielding the phone call, Natalie made a drinking gesture to Kitty before she had quite reached her. Clearly Georgia or David had been held up somewhere else. Without needing to be asked twice, for that was not something often required or expected at Daring, Kitty gave up on her idea of the impromptu twenty minute walk and tea. Politely introducing herself to the waiting women, she offered them both a drink.

Returning a short while later from the coffee centre with one white frothy cappuccino and one soya latte as requested, Kitty carefully set them down on the table with the requisite Daring smile. She now had fifteen minutes remaining to cross to the other side of the building to HR and so turned to make her way to the lifts.

Kitty stopped short when behind her, the door to Raphael's office burst open. She was not the only one who turned to look in the direction of the office. The heavy door having made an intrusive clang as it had hit the wall, beating out the previously hushed tones of the lobby.

A strikingly good looking woman wearing a structured, form-fitting cinnabar dress, hissed in Italian as she made her way out of the office and strode towards the exit. Natalie, having just ended her call, leapt up from behind her desk and darted to press for a lift.

As she strode past Kitty, the woman looked her up and down, no doubt unimpressed by Kitty's stare and in their brief exchange, Kitty realised that she was looking at Raphael's twin Martina. The woman had the same defined bone structure and unusual pale, stormy eyes which were now, like the rest of her body, raging. Despite having not said a single word to her, the immaculate woman was quite probably the most formidable person Kitty had ever encountered. She was even more intimidating than Raphael - a thought which suggested that Kitty had perhaps over-romanticised the idea of a childhood with many siblings - especially if they were all like this.

Having not been personally present at whatever meeting had just concluded in Raphael's office, Kitty could not be certain of its outcome, but the look still marking Martina's face suggested it had not gone her way and Kitty did not want to find herself standing like a gooseberry in the lobby if Raphael should follow his sister out.

She waited until Martina had disappeared before she risked pressing the call lift button again. She had decided against sharing, but before her escape could be executed, Natalie beckoned her once again, this time audibly. Kitty silently cursed under her breath.

'Kitty,' Natalie called a second time. The lift hadn't arrived and Kitty couldn't ignore her twice. Giving up on her hopes of freedom, she turned on her heel and headed for the desk. Only once she had closed the distance between them did Natalie continue.

'Thank you for fetching those drinks. David was called to serve refreshments in the meeting room. A member of the waiting staff failed to appear. One of those days.' Natalie refastened her twist, catching all of the stray hairs that had fallen loose.

Kitty smiled as she heard the soft ping of the lift, signalling its arrival behind her, thinking that Natalie had in fact just wanted to thank her. The tea was back on.

'I'm just going to…' she began before the phone started ringing again. Kitty risked a glance at Raphael's still open office door and knowing that Natalie would have to answer the call, she hoped she could catch the lift, whose doors were still open waiting for a traveller. Seeing Natalie reach for the handset, Kitty turned to go. She was surprised when Natalie leant over the counter and caught her shoulder.

'Oh, Kitty. Please can you take this in to Mr Daring? It's just arrived for him.'

Great, Kitty thought annoyed. The worst thing about being the most junior member of the office was that she couldn't say no to anyone. Unable to come up with a justifiable excuse on the spot and with Natalie, having begun the phone conversation, now staring pointedly at her. Kitty sighed and took hold of the parcel being thrust toward her. Making her way slowly towards Raphael's office, she nodded at the ladies on the sofa who had been rather amused by Martina's departure. Kitty surmised they probably knew who she had been, and for all she knew, perhaps had seen it all before. 'Siblings,' she thought she heard one say to the other rather tickled as she passed.

Standing outside the door, Kitty settled on knocking despite it being open.

'Yes.' She heard Raphael answer. She couldn't see him, but could hear the frustration thick in his voice. *This will be fun,* she thought sardonically.

Raphael was seated at his desk and with his head cradled in his hands, Kitty could not see his expression. She had made it about half way across the room when he looked up.

'Kiti.'

She thought she saw the ghost of a smile cross his face. He looked tired.

'Natalie asked me to give you this,' Kitty said nonchalantly, placing the parcel down on the desk, avoiding eye-contact with Raphael. He didn't seem particularly interested in the package and Kitty wordlessly cursed Natalie as she saw him push it into a draw, never once taking his gaze off her. Whatever it was, there had clearly been no urgency.

Having ignored Raphael's curious blue stare, Kitty was passing the seating area on her way to the exit, when suddenly Raphael started speaking behind her.

'Sit down.'

Turning back to look at him, she hadn't heard him move, but now saw that he had left his desk and was walking towards her gesturing to the sofas.

'I'm not sure,' she countered.

'Kiti. Please. Just sit down,' he said exasperated.

A little shocked, Kitty took a seat on the edge of the nearest sofa.

Raphael walked passed her and, paying no attention to the two waiting middle-aged women smiling in his direction, he slowly shut the door. Returning to Kitty, he gracefully sat on the sofa opposite and removed his tie.

His previous meeting had not gone well with Martina and the silk had become a tight and uncomfortable corporate noose around his neck. He lay it on the spot beside him and looked back to Kitty. Undoing the top button of his stiff, white shirt he breathed. He didn't want to fight, but after a long fortnight in America, he had decided he needed to talk to her. He needed to try and explain.

'Raphael, I have a meeting in about ten minutes.'

'I'm not sure anyone really explained to you what the title of CEO is,' he said cooly scowling. 'I'm the boss Kiti. If I say I need to speak to you, then other meetings don't matter.'

'Right. Of course, your royal highness, how silly of me. Whatever Raphael wants he gets right?' Kitty replied acidly.

Raphael took a slow breath and stared out into the rain, still falling heavily across the city. This hadn't been exactly how he had planned on starting this conversation but, suppressing his frustration, which he knew was due to Martina's endless demands and not Kitty's sharp tongue - a feature he actually quite liked - he decided to ignore her reply and start again, 'I'm sorry.' He looked back at Kitty.

She was almost gawking at him now, her mouth slightly parted.

'Is it that shocking hearing those words?' Raphael thought of his last meeting with Alec.

'Yes.'

Looking at Kitty, Raphael couldn't work out if she had accepted his apology or not. She hadn't smiled that was for sure, 'Is that all you're going to say?' he asked. 'I am sorry Kiti.'

Kitty looked down at her lap. Raphael's voice had become deeply sincere. However he had reached this apology, Kitty could tell he had obviously thought about everything. She looked back at him bracing herself. He was clearly going to wait this time for her to say something. Unsure of what she should say, Kitty settled on how she felt. He obviously wasn't going to let her leave and so be-it. *He wanted to bring it up. He can take it,* she decided.

'It's not good enough.' Her voice had come out a touch more broken than she had expected. She looked away from Raphael, whose face now matched how she had sounded. Although having wanted to sound calm and assertive, her broken admission felt like someone had just opened the floodgates on her carefully locked away emotions. Kitty could feel an unwelcome hotness in her eyes. *Don't fucking cry*, she ordered herself.

'Kiti, I—' Raphael began.

But Kitty cut him off. Meeting his embattled stare her eyes filled with tears, 'I've never felt so used in all my life.'

Raphael stood up and came to sit next to Kitty. He didn't touch her despite feeling a burning desire to put his arms around her. 'Let me explain.'

'Please don't. I really just want to move on.' Kitty wiped her cheek as a tear escaped over the edge. She wasn't looking at him and hoped he hadn't noticed the errant fluid.

'Just let me make it up to you.'

'You can't.'

'Yes I can. If you'll let me. Please. I can see how you feel that what I did was wrong.'

'How I could *feel* it was wrong?' Kitty asked incredulously at Raphael's backhanded remark. 'We slept together then you vanished. On what planet do you think that's ok?'

Raphael stood up, running his hands through his hair he made his way over to the window. 'I left *for* you.'

Kitty stayed quiet, something in his voice told her that he really believed what he was saying. Like somehow him disappearing was the least selfish decision he had ever made. She recognised the tone, for she had often imagined what her mother would say should they one day be reunited and had, in her younger days, hoped that it would have sounded something like that.

She watched as Raphael continued to stare out of the window into the storm. She didn't want to have this conversation here... now... ever. In her mind they couldn't get back to before he had vanished, and she couldn't work out what he desired from her now, let alone what she wanted from him. *He's a young, disgustingly rich man with the face of a bloody angel. If he wants a girlfriend, he surely can find a very beautiful one somewhere and if he now wanted a friend, well...* Kitty was hopelessly confused. She had spent nearly the whole of the last two years avoiding social interactions and had become unaccustomed to dealing with the fluctuating emotions she was now feeling. Shock and anger had guided her through the first surprise reunion with Raphael. Careful preparation the second. But this time, she wasn't ready.

Still standing at the glass wall, Raphael stopped himself from turning around to face Kitty. He couldn't bare the reflection of his shame which he saw in her eyes. He began again. His voice pained but still forceful, 'I left because I thought it was the right thing to do. You don't know me. My family. It's not...' Raphael was struggling to find the right words, unsure of how much he could risk. He checked himself, he wanted Kitty. He wanted any piece of her that she would give him. This time... he would risk it all.

In that moment of realisation the door to his office burst open. Raphael turned to it seething.

Kitty wiped her face. She did not look at first to see who had entered, but her ears were assaulted by a torrent of deep Italian snarls.

Slamming the door shut behind him, the interrupter turned back and fell silent upon noticing Kitty seated on the sofa. Kitty looked up, having done the best she could at composing herself, she now saw the scowling face of Luca Daring. He was still wearing his coat which was speckled with rain and whatever was the cause of his animation he had clearly just come in from outside.

Kitty felt Luca's stare boring in to her and knew he was waiting for her to leave. She got up to excuse herself when Raphael spoke.

'No. Sit down,' he ordered.

Caught by surprise, she found herself obeying. She looked between the brothers. Luca looked genuinely dumbfounded.

'Luca, what the fuck...' Was all Kitty understood before Raphael slipped into Italian.

Practically snarling at each other, the two men reminded Kitty of stags readying for a fight, as she had seen once on the television at Burt's. The men, tall, muscular and both wildly annoyed, faced one another. Luca was not the angelic leonine figure his brother was. He was the same height, but thicker set and had hazel eyes that reminded Kitty of burnt caramels. His hair was pitch black rather than mahogany and cropped shorter than Raphael's around his even face. Despite not looking exactly like his brother, he was still - by normal standards - exceptionally handsome.

Separating her thoughts from the ranting that was continuing over her head, Kitty took the decision that she really ought to leave, and began her third attempt of the afternoon to reach HR - a destination that had become increasingly more inviting. Now pretty certain in the knowledge that Raphael's childhood was about as far from the *Swallows and Amazons* style setup that she had imagined having many siblings would entail, she stood up.

'Siediti!' Raphael commanded turning his attention back to her. 'Kiti, sit down…please.'

Kitty, having been prepared for such a command, ignored him this time and started walking to the door.

Raphael looked furiously after her until she disappeared out of the office, shutting the door behind her.

With his hands on his hips, Raphael turned back to his brother who had now moved to slouch down on the sofa which Kitty had vacated.

'She's a fucking intern, Rafa. What's wrong with you?' Luca looked at his little brother. He was not sure what sort of a meeting he had just disturbed, having noticed the discarded tie on the sofa, but was deeply vexed that his brother had tried to send him away. Family first, that's what they had been taught. That is what they had always been taught. *Not that Raphael had always been very good at that concept,* Luca thought. His little brother had basically disowned them all for the last decade and then returned as head of the family.

In truth Luca did not envy his brother's role as head of the company, thus the family. Despite being three years younger, Raphael was a natural born leader, and although he would never admit it, Luca had always looked to him to make the final call, even as children. In childhood games and now in life, Raphael was and always had been the boss. It was why, despite Raphael's determination to sever all ties with his family, Luca had kept seeing his brother. He needed him. He loved him no matter what choices he made. On occasion they would meet for dinner and Luca had always kept Raphael in the loop with family and for that matter, company news. Always praying he would one day return.

Although not the CEO title, there were many things Luca did envy about his brother. His bravery for one thing. Another being the bond he had shared with their mother. This second had been much harder to live with, for Luca had been forced to watch her mourn Raphael's absence for ten long years, and live with the crippling knowledge that he was entirely unable to fill the void Raphael had left behind. A third aspect was the fact that, as the younger brother, Raphael had even been allowed to choose a different path from the one to which they were born. This had grated on occasion - not that it had subsequently worked out. And fourth, the fact that he had lied for him. Then again, Luca acknowledged, sitting up straighter and trying to control his often disorderly temper, Raphael had killed for him.

'Brother, talk to him. Per favore?'

'I don't see what this has to do with me? The decision's been made,' Raphael growled, still annoyed at Luca's unannounced arrival and Kitty's disobedience. It had not been how he had envisioned his apology going.

Luca had been informed about an hour previously that their uncle, who since Raphael's return to the family had returned to his role as Vice President of the Daring Corporation, had taken the decision that Luca would represent the family at an upcoming investment event being hosted in Abu Dhabi. To anyone else it would seem like a dream assignment. Horse racing and yacht parties all providing the backdrop to agreeing some of the most lucrative investment opportunities in the United Arab Emirates. But a couple of years back, Luca had been involved in a hotel room brawl in Paris, that had resulted in the hospitalisation of a young Emirati named Khalifa Al Zayed, which was why he did not relish this particular assignment.

Khalifa had discovered that Luca had taken his sister's virginity after a fashion show she had been attending. During a drunken night out clubbing, Luca had boasted unknowingly to her fiancé about the tryst and the discovery had brought shame upon Khalifa's entire family. Not to mention his little sister, whose wedding was then called off. Khalifa had managed to track Luca down before he had left France and despite warnings of reprisals, had challenged him to a bare knuckle fight. Luca had all too happily accepted, relishing a physical challenge. Although Luca had sustained a broken nose, Khalifa had ended up with a broken collar bone, four broken ribs and a fractured leg before Luca had been prised off him.

'You are going to make amends. We need the Al Zayed family's allegiance in the region. For two years they have been using their connections to hamper our new investments.'

'You are Mr CEO. Why don't you go?' Luca stared at his brother.

'It's not my problem, Luca.' Raphael walked over and put his hands on his brother's shoulders, 'You should think yourself lucky. If we were Muslim you would be marrying the sister... and her monobrow.' Raphael playfully shoved his brother, 'Our uncle has spent the last two years rebuilding the relationship. I heard he even found the girl a suitable high-ranking husband. God knows how.'

'Fine.'

Raphael flopped onto the sofa beside his pouting brother, 'Stop being a fucking baby. You owe him, Luca. I've already had Martina whinging today. I can't deal with you as well. Per favore.'

'Well I'm not thanking him. Khalifa Al Zayed deserved his broken bones. Slimy fucking Arab,' he muttered petulantly. Luca knew that Raphael was right. *When was he not?* he sulked.

THIRTEEN

Kitty checked her watch. Seeing that it was already five o'clock she decided that she could get away with leaving half an hour before her usual time. She had seen Hugo leaving early on her way back up to the office, so he wouldn't have a view on her departure time and having survived Raphael, followed by a thorough interrogation from Avery, the tenacity of which even Lucille had managed to do little to hinder, Kitty felt that she had given enough to Daring today as she readied her bag.

The rain had stopped by the time Kitty had made it out of the office building, the large puddles that punctuated the pavement the only reminder of the ferocious storm that had only recently let up. Fixing a wisp of hair that had blown across her face, Kitty took a long deep breath. She loved the damp fresh smell that always hung in the air after it rained, and the calm it brought as she let the soft moist air saturate every corner of her lungs.

'Miss May?'

Kitty, wondering who had called her, scanned the pavement for the source of the inquiry.

'Hello?' she said quizzically, having zeroed in on a dark suited gentlemen who had approached during her searching and was now standing smartly six feet in front of her.

Satisfied he had identified Kitty correctly, a polite smile spread across his face, 'My name is Clint Wilson. I'm Mr Daring's driver. Please follow me.'

So close, Kitty sighed. After the emotions of the day she was too tired to argue and followed Wilson without a word to the familiar parked Range Rover. *He's only following orders,* she repeated to herself in a small loop. She felt a touch of pity for the smartly presented man, despite his seeming perfectly comfortable with her silence. She supposed his boss wasn't much of a talker either.

Once they reached the car, Wilson gently opened the rear door and ushered Kitty in. She thanked him with a generous smile, hoping this would make up for her lack of conversation. He replied with a polite nod. Satisfied that Wilson was a man of few words and had not been offended, she slid into the back of the car and turned bewildered to look at Raphael. His face had never looked so angelic, his eyes wide with a childlike caution.

'I'm sorry,' he said quickly before she had a chance to say anything, 'Have dinner with me?'

'What are you doing?'

'I didn't get a chance to finish my apology.'

'I give up.' Kitty slumped in her chair. *If this maniac wants to do this then who am I to stand in his way.*

'Is that a yes?' he pushed.

Kitty remained silent.

'You are free to leave if you don't want to,' Raphael continued. There was something melancholy colouring the sincerity of his voice.

Kitty sensed that he was desperately hoping not to be rejected, 'I'll have dinner with you.'

Raphael relaxed his previously tense shoulders and sat back, letting himself be supported by the soft leather behind him, a breathtaking smile spread across his face.

Caught off-guard by his reaction, Kitty looked out into the street. She counted the Daring employees, now filling the pavement and making their way home for the evening, trying to fill her head with the mundane images of suit variations and umbrella styles. But it was no use, for in Kitty's mind even Michelangelo's David, should he have been given life and come to join them, would have looked prosaic and middling in comparison to the now smiling Raphael. She scratched at her palms and forced herself to continue to count. She was not ready to acknowledge the attraction.

Raphael tapped on his window, his knuckles lightly rapping on the glass, and Wilson, who Kitty now pleasantly distracted by the tapping noticed, had been waiting outside the car.

He took up his position in the driver's seat, 'Where would you like to go, sir?'

Raphael eyed Kitty gingerly as he answered, 'Home.'

Kitty was surprised, but settled on the conclusion that whatever it was he wanted to say to her, Raphael obviously didn't want to say in a public place or risk being interrupted by anyone this time. She was not sure how she felt about being alone with him again, free from the possibility of interruption.

Lost in thought, they drove the whole way in total silence. Kitty acutely aware of the re-emerging draw she felt to be near him - to understand him. With both of them sitting in the back, despite not touching, the atmosphere was charged around them and she wondered if Raphael could feel it too. If he did, he was not showing it as he stared impassively out into the darkening evening, mirroring her silence.

'What would you like to eat?' Raphael asked softly as Kitty took a seat on a large, plush L-shaped sofa.

'Now?'

'No, later. For dinner.'

'Whatever you have in.'

Raphael laughed a little, 'We have anything you want.'

'Are you a good cook?'

'Don't worry, Sherlock. I won't be cooking.' He flashed his white teeth.

'Ahh, I see.' Kitty couldn't help but grin, remembering the second time he had called her Sherlock, when she had grilled him on his love life and his views on the word smitten - a topic she was surprised to notice she still wanted his opinion on.

Having discovered that Raphael's meaning of "home" had meant an enormous, cream painted, Italianate villa in Kensington Palace Gardens, Kitty was not overly surprised to learn of the existence of in-house chefs. It was the most beautiful building she had ever been in.

A long avenue of plane trees, illuminated by the dim golden glow of victorian gaslight style street-lamps, stood still like sentries on the approach to the embellished cream frontage of the house. Set back from the road down a drive of granite sets, it had taken a moment before Kitty had been able to see the whole building. The central rectangular block - whose porticoed entrance sheltered the heavy black door that they had entered through - was evenly covered by seven large sash windows on the upper floor and three either side of the entrance on the ground floor. Two wings, matching in style, with their own further sets of sash windows, extended out from this central block creating a symmetrical facade reminiscent of a dolls house. The grounds in front of the house had been heavily planted, appealingly softening the huge edifice and down the inside of the traditional iron railings that ran along the pavement, a thick hornbeam hedge had been planted, providing further privacy. Due to the abundance of vegetation, Kitty had temporarily forgotten that they were in the heart of London altogether.

The interiors were equally remarkable, with detailed cornicing and plasterwork covering the high ceilinged rooms, and in the most part wooden floors, of which some were partially covered by thick patterned rugs, providing a canvas for the furniture. As Kitty had followed Raphael across the entrance hall, a light stone-tiled space dominated by two mirroring serpentine staircases that curled up the walls, she had peeked through the open doors of the ground floor rooms that had evenly fanned off around her. The style chosen in each, was an intelligent mix of traditional shapes with modern twists. Overall the colour palette throughout was an array of charcoal, paler shades of grey and fresh off white with accented colours including navy, shamrock and gold picked out in the artwork, soft furnishings and chandeliers. Someone had managed to take a museum and create a refreshing, inviting home. A real home, despite the grand scale.

Later Kitty would come to discover the hidden basement with its wine cellar, the twenty-five metre pool, gym, underground carpark and various manicured gardens that circled the property, whose emerald parterres sheltered by Norwegian maples, sycamores and lime trees she had glimpsed through the windows, as she had been shown to the sofa where she now sat nestled amongst a sea of embroidered, tasselled cushions.

Admiring a collection of cubist paintings that adorned the walls of the charcoal room in which she now found herself, the interior reminded Kitty of Raphael's office and, just like his office, despite his perfectly tailored suits, he seemed out of place in it.

'You live here?' she asked forgetting that he was trying to decipher what she wanted for dinner. In truth, considering her track record of recent conversations with Raphael, Kitty did not particularly want the chefs to go to the trouble of making dinner for her.

'Yes.'

'You bought it?'

Raphael cocked his head.

Kitty explained, 'What I mean is. This house. It's beautiful don't get me wrong. It just doesn't really seem very… you?'

Raphael laughed, 'It was my parents' house. My mother chose it and had it renovated and furnished. She loved interior design, she actually went to art school herself. It had been in a pretty bad state of disrepair when they took it on. The building is very old, eighteen fifty or thereabouts,' he said running his hand along an ornate carved fireplace mantle positioned in front of where Kitty sat.

'That makes sense,' Kitty said. A sadness passed over her as it suddenly dawned on her that from his use of words, Raphael's parents must both have passed away.

'Why?' he asked.

'I said. You just look… I don't know. Out of place.'

'Story of my life I'm afraid, Kiti,' Raphael joked, but Kitty heard a sourness tinge his reply.

'Now dinner, what will it be?' He flashed a smile again, rescuing his mood.

'Pizza,' Kitty grinned.

'Pizza?' he said, raising his eyebrow.

'Yeah you're Italian. Must be an option. Besides I love pizza and after the day your bloody company has put me through. It's a pizza kind of day.'

'Pizza it is… and I can only apologise for my company,' he paused. 'I blame the leadership.' With that Raphael disappeared off to the kitchens.

What a day, Kitty thought, exhausted. Looking around the room, she continued to be impressed by it. Raphael's mother must have had great taste. After having let her emotions free earlier, Kitty now felt more relaxed in Raphael's company and was beginning again to find herself once more intrigued by the curious man he was. How he could have all this and be so confusingly troubled escaped her. Before her thoughts could take her anywhere, Raphael returned holding two glasses and two bottles of wine.

'White or red?' he asked politely. 'Or tea?' he joked.

'Just tea.'

'Really?' He raised his eyebrows again.

'Yep.'

Setting the bottles down, Raphael disappeared laughing. He had definitely never met anyone like Kitty before.

A couple of minutes later, Raphael returned carrying a pretty silver tray supporting a china cup and saucer, little tea pot and silver strainer, beside which sat a small jug of cold milk. As he set it down Kitty smiled. They obviously didn't just do mugs in this fancy house.

Raphael poured himself a glass of red wine and sat beside Kitty on the sofa.

'I don't want to fight,' he began. 'I know I hurt you and I would like to make it up to you. I'm not always such an arse… or I didn't used to be…believe it or not.'

Deciding to just roll with whatever was going on in Raphael's head, a place that she seemed to be continually reminded she barely understood, Kitty smiled a little, 'Can I ask you something then?'

'Anything,' Raphael replied quickly. A little too quickly.

'Really?'

He frowned, concerned by her excitement, 'Well, almost…'

'I want to know why you left?' No tears followed this question. Their last meeting had lanced the final boil - he knew how she had felt used and sad and so now, for the first real time, Kitty realised she was ready to move on. Providing he was honest of course and preferably didn't vanish this time.

'That seems fair.' Raphael looked down into his glass as he spoke, 'After you fell asleep I watched you for a while. I wanted to stay. Trust me.'

He looked up at Kitty now and she noticed, despite their cool blue colour, there was a new warmth in his eyes.

'You see, Kiti... I've never been with anyone before who hasn't known anything about me. My family. The money.' He waved around the room.

'I'm not interested—'

'I know,' Raphael laughed. 'You found out I was a billionaire instead of a severely underpaid soldier and then you wouldn't speak to me. Kiti, you are very... insolita... unusual.'

'You've been hanging out with the wrong women.'

'I see that. But you see, those women require... less risk. Time with them is more like a business transaction than anything more serious. Ceasing when it no longer remains pleasing to both parties.'

'Who would want that though?' Kitty pushed, ignoring the fact that she herself was risk averse when it came to relationships.

Raphael returned her comment with a knowing grin, he knew Kitty better than she thought and knew she was no open book. That much of himself he could recognise in her.

She blushed. Changing tack Kitty continued, 'Surely because I don't care about this crap, or didn't know, that should have been a good thing?'

'It was. It is. But you see, it's complicated.' He was serious again.

'Please try.'

'I am… the thing is…' Raphael wrestled with his internal dilemma. Earlier he had decided to risk telling her everything if that is what it took to get her to smile, but now, with Kitty sitting fairly happily in front of him, he wanted to lie again. He didn't want to risk her dismissal. His better half won out, 'Kiti… the truth is that I'm not a good person.'

A small snicker burst from Kitty. He was staring at her now. His face previously determined, she saw a slight shift in his features. Relief, but beyond it, something more intense.

Raphael knew he could not trust in her laugh.

Composing herself, she returned his expression. It was not what he had said that had been amusing, but rather the ridiculousness of the situation had momentarily overwhelmed her. She didn't believe anymore that one thing could be either good or bad. Life was a kaleidoscope, each person continually moving upon a sliding scale. Each choice affording a new opportunity to move one way or the other. Sadly, Raphael clearly held no such view. Something in her decided that she was going to have to change his mind. The sadness of this realisation helped her recover her poise, 'I don't—'

'No Kiti. I'm not. I've done some terrible things.'

This time Kitty did not laugh at him, but Raphael had begun and he knew, whatever it meant he must continue, 'I have spent the last ten years running from who I am. Then I met you and suddenly I wanted to stay right where I was and I didn't… I still don't know how to do that.'

Raphael was still staring at Kitty, trying to gauge her reaction. She didn't open her mouth, so he continued. Filling with a strange mix of pleasure and despair that he may finally be getting through to her, he continued, 'I'd just finished my leave period and some rehabilitation after a particularly bad deployment that had gone to shit. We'd all had rehab, we'd lost guys. Good ones. Some of them friends. I come home and discover my mother, whose heart I broke in joining the army, and who for the previous decade I'd seen only on rare occasions had been diagnosed with an aggressive cancer and had but a few months to live and—'

Kitty couldn't stop herself interrupting, 'I'm so sorry, Raphael.' Without thinking she extended her hand comfortingly, but almost as soon as it touched Raphael's knee she withdrew it.

He either hadn't noticed or pretended not to, but instead continued to speak, 'The night I spent with you was the last night my mother was alive.'

Kitty's lips parted, 'Oh my God. Raphael, I don't know —'

'I didn't go and see her, Kiti. I couldn't. She was dying and I couldn't go.' Raphael hung his head.

Kitty stared at him. She had never seen someone look so ashamed, 'Why?' she asked warily, assuming that she may be pushing her luck with that question.

The side of Raphael's mouth twitched up into a tiny smile. *Well she's not run out yet,* he thought, pleased but confused. Looking back to Kitty, who by now looked very sad, he smiled more, reassuringly. He didn't want to upset her. That is not why he had chosen to share this information. He could lock away the shame on his own.

'Let's just say my heart was broken too,' Raphael concluded.

Kitty knew that there were some serious holes to his story and that he was not telling her half of whatever was going on. But inside she knew that it had taken a lot for him to share even that and she felt touched. There was something about how he had shared a very private piece of himself with her that made Kitty feel very special. She knew herself well enough to know that if they were to be friends one day, that she was going to need a bit more, but for now, She was happy to lighten the tone and allowed the conversation to move on when the chefs invited them through to the dining room for dinner.

The pizza was truly exceptional. Kitty hadn't realised how hungry she had been until she had tasted her first bite. They didn't talk a huge amount while they ate, both deep in their own thoughts about the evening's revelations. Nevertheless, Kitty could feel Raphael's eyes cautiously on her throughout the meal.

The times they did speak, it was Raphael asking about Kitty's life. She had chosen to answer his questions about Cambridge, Jaz and Beto, what she thought about Daring and bits about Cornwall, all the while avoiding her own orphaned status - he didn't need to know that just yet.

When she had run out of interesting things to share, within the parameters of honesty that she had quietly set, they had moved on to discussing music, films and the other easy, trivial topics people usually talked about with friends. Travel had been the most fascinating, for Raphael had been everywhere. He spoke of childhood holidays sailing with Luca in the Caribbean, playing in the orchards of their family villa in Tuscany throwing overripe pears at his sisters, elephant encounters in India and the time he had snorkelled with manta-rays in Bora Bora. Kitty had privately once more re-adjusted her views on his *Swallows and Amazons* childhood. Although comforted in once sense that she had not completely romanticised the idea of having siblings, his wondrous stories did not explain his troubling nature now, nor how his mother had broken his heart. He had eluded to a darker truth hidden within the Daring family, perhaps the real reason he felt he was not a good person, but she knew she would have to wait a bit longer to work out what it was.

The rain was clattering hard against the windows again as Kitty got up from the table. She hated the weather at this time of year, the repeated soakings so dreary, and the damp bone-chilling.

'Thank you for supper,' she began as Raphael walked her back across the huge stone tiles to the front door.

'Kiti?'

'Yeah?'

'Why didn't you become a lawyer?'

She stood still for a second before she turned back to Raphael, 'You remembered?'

'Of course.'

'Well…It never worked out.'

'Why did you want to be one?'

Kitty stilled. She felt he had earned the answer to this. An answer she had never openly expressed to anyone but Freddie and Jaz.

'My father was one,' she breathed deeply, 'we used to play at it all the time. Putting my toys or my dog on trial. Running trials and appeals and sentencing hearings.'

'Was one?'

'He died,' Kitty said, looking down at her feet.

'I'm so sorry.'

'Now you're the one whose apologising unnecessarily.'

'Kiti—'

'Why did you come back to run Daring? Why not just stay in the Army.' *One for one*, Kitty thought, hoping he would answer.

Raphael's eyes widened, 'It's a long story.'

Kitty waited.

Raphael rolled his eyes, 'Well. Short version, this company means everything to my family. And even if they don't think it, they mean everything to me.'

Kitty nodded, 'Thank you.'

Raphael cocked his head.

'Honesty,' she replied to his unanswered question.

'Are you sure I can't drive you home? Or at least get Wilson to?' he pressed, 'Or you can stay?'

'No. Thanks though. But I'm good,' she smiled.

'Kiti—'

'I'm good,' Kitty replied strictly. 'Anyway it's gone midnight, Wilson may have gone to bed.'

Raphael's lips curved in quiet amusement. Kitty really had no idea how the whole staff thing worked. For Raphael harboured no doubt, that if he was asked to, Wilson was available for chauffeuring services at all hours of the day and night. Nevertheless he fought the desire to insist. Kitty clearly didn't like being told what to do and he did not want to spoil the evening. It had gone so well so far, in part, he thought shamefully, at his neglecting to reveal the entirety of his dark history, having stopped far short of the truth. He pushed the unwelcome thought aside.

Opening the door for her, Raphael watched begrudgingly as Kitty stepped out under the covered entrance.

Kitty turned to say goodbye but before she had spoken, Raphael leant forward and kissed her on the cheek.

'Buona notte then, Kiti. Let me know you're home safe,' he breathed.

Kitty froze. She hadn't been expecting that and the contact had sent a rush through her body. She looked up at Raphael and flushed.

He held up his hands in mock surrender, 'Italian. Scusa. Sorry.'

'Mmm… half,' Kitty chastised, knowing full well that he was chancing his luck. Formally putting out her hand she thanked him once again as he shook it.

Very professional, he thought bemused.

Having thought of Raphael's honesty the whole way home. On making it to her bed Kitty fished her phone out from her bag. It mattered who she was. Not what. Hammering away at the keys she sent one very short message to Elliot.

I can't do this.

FOURTEEN

The Duplex apartment on Coldharbour Lane was positioned above a twenty-four hour mini-cab firm in need of more than a lick of paint, whose flashing neon "open" sign did little to entice many, if any by Kitty's count, customers and a permanently shuttered convenience store. Kitty could not be certain how long the convenience store had been closed. The sign indicating the store as a place to send money worldwide still spun, like someone had forgotten to turn off the power, indicating a recent departure, but the shutters suggested a longer abandonment. Once plain, they had become a thickly layered canvas for local graffiti artists, the majority of which had not quite reached the artistic talents of Banksy or Blek le Rat, instead opting, in the most part, for abstract aerosol scribblings with a fair smattering of misspelt profanities and "was ere" motifs. The rest of the adjacent buildings and those opposite, which Kitty could see from the small window above the sink in the kitchen come living space, housed a Jamaican Jerk Barbecue joint, a new Thai takeaway, one nail bar, one nail spa, two estate agents and an off-licence. The three residents of the apartment were equally diverse.

Behind the peeling stiff door, routinely papered with advertisements for local music or comedy events, the worn treads of a staircase covered by a mousy floral carpet connected the hall with the secondary entrance to the duplex above.

The first floor housed the landlady, Edinburgh born octogenarian Mrs Smeaton's bedroom on the front of the building, the bedroom of a raven haired Asian girl named Ying at the back and sandwiched between the two was Mrs Smeaton's day room. This included the small screen that connected to the buzzer on the front door so that the landlady could be alerted to any and all comings and goings. The second floor comprised of the shared bathroom, equipped with a full pampas green suite. A basic ageing kitchen and small four-person dining area finished with the same mousey carpet. Off this Kitty's room had been, not entirely successfully, squeezed in at the very back of the building.

On arrival Kitty had been welcomed by Mrs Smeaton. The hunched lady, her hair exclusively white and often pulled back into a wispy bun like a summer cloud, that floated at odds above her still dark brows, was approaching ninety and had thrust a key into Kitty's hand, with surprising strength, before Kitty had even managed a hello.

'There ye go now lass. No changing yur mind now!' she had cackled. A crooked smile had revealed a dark stained set of false teeth.

Despite her fluffy hair and woollen attire, Mrs Smeaton had proven herself to be as sharp as the sewing needles that filled the box in her day room, a place where nowadays she spent her afternoons making potpourri. Having found a deep pleasure in the tangy smell of dried citrus fruits, oranges in particular, Mrs Smeaton spent many hours perfecting her arrangements. In between drying sessions, she busied herself dusting her collection of china dolls (a previous fascination) and religious artefacts. The produce of her hobby, her dolls and as it turned out new-found - as often the case when one was swiftly approaching death - religious fervour decorated every inch of the small flat, her bedroom and day-room having failed to provide sufficient space.

Mrs Smeaton herself did not see the harm in spreading her beloved treasures around the duplex, for since her children had left home and her wayward husband had passed, the dolls and dried petals and spices had provided a comfort of sorts, a temporary balm for her loneliness. It had only been recently, after she had learned of the existence of Airbnb that she had decided to fill her two spare rooms with living artefacts instead.

Her youngest child, soon to be grandmother herself, had helped list the property and Mrs Smeaton had enjoyed a steady string of foreign language students since then. Kitty was a refreshing change. With both rooms let, not that she would mention this to the girls for fear of being overbearing, she was once more reinvigorated by the prospect of young life back in the flat. The challenge and hubbub that accompanied it and this time, someone who may even speak to her.

Freddie and Jaz had been - Kitty remembered, amused as she wolfed down a bowl of porridge - disturbed by the eery china painted faces that peeked out from behind the ever-growing collection of carved crucifixes that decorated the corners of various shelves throughout the flat. It had taken them all of about five minutes, once certain that they had escaped the old lady who had delivered what had turned out to be the first of many lectures on the degradation of morals in modern society, whilst squished onto the quilted single bed in Kitty's botanical papered room, to stress that Kitty could live with Jaz's parents in Holloway for free until they found her a better place.

Kitty had ignored their mutterings. Overcome with a quiet joy - which she still felt now - that she had finally found a place of her own. One she could easily afford and the first in a very long time. The small space would be her home and, ignoring the fact that the interiors, and as she had recently discovered fixtures and fittings, had not been updated since the 1950s (some even before that) Kitty was determined to make it work.

In truth, she could think of nothing worse than moving in with Jaz's family. No one could deny that Mr and Mrs Taylor were kind and generous and would be more than gracious hosts, but Kitty had waited her entire adolescent life to be free from the views and rules of adults trying to care for her, untroubled by the direct line of enquiry and concern that had clearly been set up between Mr Taylor and Anne. It was her chance to be the adult, answering to no one, pitied by no one. Free. And no amount of memorabilia, even the kind more commonly found in horror films, would take away this freedom.

The hearty welcome from Mrs Smeaton could not have been more opposite to the sullen stare Kitty had received in place of a greeting from Ying. The girl who now sat cross legged on the kitchen counters in front of Kitty. To say the slight Asian was a woman of few words would have been a gross understatement. Ying was a women of no words. It was for this reason that, despite Mrs Smeaton's insistence, Kitty was not entirely certain the girl was Chinese.

As Kitty sat finishing up her breakfast in silence. Mrs Smeaton bustled into the small room and parked herself at the end of the table. She began her day as she always did with "her charges" as Kitty had overhead her calling them to her daughter on the phone.

That morning Mrs Smeaton commented on the raising of skirt hems, the multi-cultural state of the nation and how she had come to be here, falling in love with an English tradesman as a young girl in Scotland and following him down to the big city.

Kitty found her musings quite endearing. Taken out of context her individual comments could be interpreted as evangelistic, old fashioned, querulous and at times even racist. But really, Kitty knew the old woman was simply trying to pass on the wisdoms - however unwise - that she felt she had learned throughout her life. When explaining the pitfalls of sex before marriage Mrs Smeaton was not in truth shaming the loose morals of modern women, but was rather trying to express the point that one can become trapped with the wrong man should they fall pregnant.

Kitty guessed this may have happened to Mrs Smeaton, for she was not too complimentary of the late Mr Smeaton. When talking about how, '*One must watch out, for there are foreigners everywhere in London,*' a statement Mrs Smeaton would accompany with a not-so-subtle point at Ying behind her back, or would follow with a reference to '*The African Man*' and his family who lived next door, Mrs Smeaton was not intending to be racist, nor make them feel unwelcome, in fact - although this point had taken Kitty a while to unpick, and so had made her frequently thankful for Ying's near constant use of in ear headphones (one of the few things that had certainly escaped the landlady's attentions) - Mrs Smeaton was trying to say how the Bible had taught her to be accepting of others. 'You shall not wrong a sojourner or oppress him, for you were sojourners in the land of Egypt,' she would say to her audience of two.

Last Wednesday, Kitty had finally met "*The African Man*" whose wife worked at the nail spa down the road, and had been wickedly amused when he had introduced himself as Patrick who turned out to be a Phlebotomist at King's College Hospital on nearby Denmark Hill and who, although Kitty didn't have the heart to pass this on, hailed from the Caribbean and not Africa at all. Furthermore, Patrick had informed her that he was the third generation in his family to have called Brixton home and so, Kitty thought if questioned, would have no doubt declared himself less of a *sojourner* than the Scot who lived next door. Nevertheless, the message of tolerance was what Mrs Smeaton had been trying to get across, of this Kitty was certain.

Having finished her breakfast, apparently unaware of any of Mrs Smeaton's lessons, Ying jumped off the countertop and quietly returned to her room below, reattaching her iPod to her speakers. The faint thrum of music vibrating up through the floor was the only indication she was there at all.

Kitty had no complaints about Ying's unsociable nature. In fact, once the three had settled into a comfortable rhythm, the silence no longer feeling bloated nor awkward, Kitty had enjoyed the lack of questioning - a welcome change from Truro. There was however one of Ying's traits that was a little harder to live with. One that had cast a shadow over the entire weekend.

Having shown herself to be a women of restraint, Ying's only indulgence had turned out to be in the taking of long and excessively hot showers, the steam from which would billow out from under the bathroom door and had added immeasurably to the growing patches of slimy mould on the bathroom ceiling.

The Chinese, Japanese and Korean for "turn on the fan," translations Mrs Smeaton had worked on, having spent a not inconsiderable amount of time at the local library undertaking the necessary research on three successive Saturdays, each after her weekly trip collecting food and potpourri supplies from Brixton Market, had fallen on deaf ears.

Unfortunately it was not only the growing mould that was the issue with Ying's bathing habits. The old Victorian iron pipes, not updated when the pampus suite had been fitted in the bathroom, would creak and groan under the quantity of scolding water that Ying would flush through them, and after would cease to provide any warmth for Kitty's own showers.

Kitty had never been one for long showers at Burt's. The old fisherman's cottage never had had sufficient pressure nor heat. But after one severe infestation of nits, her bathing routine had become somewhat ritualistic, despite no scientific evidence that frequent showers would stop a similar event. It was this one particularly unfortunate infestation, causing no end of scratching, that had earned Kitty an earlier edition of the moniker she now bore proudly. In its inception, her name had been changed from Cleo to Cat, for the children at her school had deemed that she was flea-ridden like the stray cats of Truro that they were always warned against playing with at the beach. Kitty, still young, had tried to argue that fleas were not the same as nits, but as she would become acutely aware, children could be mean, and possessed a bad habit of choosing which facts of life were acknowledged, and which ignored to better serve childish nastiness. Kitty had actually known that the invisible creatures had come from Bethan, whose elder sister had suffered a positive infestation the week before, but no one had cared about the truth. Jaz, whose friendship had blossomed around this time - she was the only girl who would not hiss at Kitty in the playground - had renamed her Kitty-cat. Eventually Kitty had stuck with everyone, including Kitty herself, who now quite liked the name, for she felt a great affinity with the wild strays of Truro. Flea-infested or not.

However, even Kitty's ironclad resilience had frayed that Friday night coming home after dinner with Raphael. She had been drenched, thanks to her stubborn refusal of a lift, and so had been more vexed than usual to find her suspicions about the aged pipes correct.

Ying had indulged in one long shower too many and the corroded pipes had burst, flooding Mrs Smeaton's day room below. The landlady had arranged to have the bathroom fixed the following week, but a cold, shivering Kitty could not wait that long. Plaiting her rain soaked hair and squeezing as much of the dampness out with her towel. Kitty had packed herself off to Jaz's flat for the weekend. Here she had stayed up until Sunday night when Beto had required the other half of Jaz's double bed.

Unfortunately Jaz had been in an annoying mood throughout the weekend. Jaz and Beto had endured their first series of real disagreements. Kitty had thought that none of them had seemed particularly important. But nevertheless Jaz had wanted to examine and reexamine them in minute detail. Kitty had never been very good at this, but listened dutifully as payment for Jaz's hospitality and warm water, for which she was deeply grateful. When Jaz had fully exhausted her ranting, the crux of which seemed to be about her desire to travel and Beto's lack of finance, Jaz had asked about Kitty's job.

'Yeah it's ok. Busy,' she had begun, deciding that now was not the moment to enlighten her friend on the existence of her wildly frustrating but fascinating CEO. She was also not entirely sure how she would begin to explain, considering the secrecy of their first encounter, which now finally seemed buried in the past.

Kitty's luck had remained resolutely scarce however, for Jaz had replied to Kitty's vague mumbling with a hundred more questions and comments, only this time focused around the handsome Raphael Daring.

214

'I was so bored at work. Honestly Kit, my job sucks. So I googled your job - well, the company. I did Freddie's but ships aren't really my thing. And then…W-T-F girl!' Her face lit up, her previous annoyance at Beto all but forgotten.

Kitty remained wide eyed. Feigning innocence.

Jaz didn't buy it, 'That man is hot, Kitten.'

'He's a really talented businessman. He's actually really smart, Jaz.' Kitty was not sure why she had suddenly defended him and flushed deeply.

Jaz was beaming now, 'You know he owns the bar Beto works in. I asked him if he knew him at all. He said the Darings all keep to themselves.'

What a surprise, Kitty thought sarcastically.

Jaz, having given up waiting for Kitty to contribute, spoke again, 'So I pushed him on it. Beto that is. I'm telling you Kit, he doesn't much like them. He said you should stay away from them when I said you worked there.'

Kitty waited.

Fortunately either Beto hadn't remembered or had simply refrained from telling Jaz that Raphael had been at the bar the night they had all gone out. She didn't want to have this conversation at all and so, feeling a touch bad, denied the existence of any closeness. She explained that she was just the most junior member of his wider team. Too inconsequential to be noticed. Jaz seemed satisfied for once, ranting off about how she was still the most junior member of her office too and her patience for making coffee was running thin. Kitty had nodded along in agreement before making some excuse about needing an early night.

Kitty sat at the dining table beside Mrs Smeaton, an empty bowl in front of her. She had caught herself staring into nothing again. Elliot had never replied to her message and after Jaz's warning from Beto, however annoying she had been, Kitty couldn't help but consider whether she had made the right call. If there was something wrong, didn't she want to be the person to help uncover it? Wasn't that the exact kind of person she wanted to be? These thoughts persisted, in a constant loop as she made her way to the office.

Thankfully, for Kitty was not sure she could politely endure another soaking, the storm had passed over the weekend. Frustratingly however, the sky was still a dull, pewter grey, something Kitty noted behind worried eyes as she made her way out of Green Park Tube station and began the short walk through the refined, well kept streets of Mayfair on her way to the Daring Headquarters.

Even under sunless skies, Mayfair was indisputably delightful. Not only the buildings, but the people too seemed somehow more polished with their expensive clothes and hair cut with seemingly spirit level accuracy. It still amazed her that the location where she lived and the other where she worked were in the same city. She felt the added spring in her step that this realisation always gave her. Variation had become insatiably thrilling to Kitty. The kind of variation she had been devoid of in Truro and, for that matter, Cambridge. She felt no preference for the refinement of Mayfair over the diverse, quick tempo of Brixton, knowing she most definitely looked and felt more at home in the latter. Instead, she was simply thrilled that the two existed so close together and that she could reside in both.

Her recent positivity was not entirely down to the enticing contrasts of London life and Kitty, once more smugly noting how well the unplanned dinner with Raphael had gone, practically beamed in recognition of this. The memories were a welcome break from the loop of worry that seemed to have been stuck on repeat.

A couple of streets from the office, Kitty heard a voice that put the loop firmly back in motion.

'You're done?'

Kitty turned to see Elliot, bedecked in a dark trench coat striding up behind her. He stopped a few steps in front of her. A little too close. She didn't need to ask to know he was angry.

'So you do exist then huh?' Kitty asked, allowing the annoyance she felt at all her unanswered messages to be heard.

'You know, Kitty, I really thought with everything I'd heard about Claudius that you'd be different.'

'You're crossing a line, Elliot,' Kitty warned raising a finger.

Turning to leave he caught her arm.

'Kitty! I'm sorry.'

Kitty turned to meet his dark gaze, 'Really? Cause you don't sound it.'

He chewed on his lip, 'I am sorry. But I am disappointed.'

'Disappointed now! Wow,' Kitty fumed incredulously, 'who are you?'

'I'm disappointed because I need you, but you're letting your feelings get in the way of doing what's right.'

'Yeah, and what's that, Elliot?' Kitty stepped towards him. 'Because I looked and asked and kept my ear to the ground and as far as I can tell, everything is above board. Way above. And that's what everyone thinks too. And truth be told, if it wasn't, I don't have the access or security clearance or seniority to even see the things where anything dodgy could even happen.'

Elliot shook his head disbelieving.

'What?' Kitty asked, annoyed.

'You don't have the clearance?' Elliot began to laugh.

'What's so funny?' Kitty snarled.

'You.' Elliot ceased his laughing and glared at Kitty.

'Me? Right. Goodbye, Elliot.'

Spinning on her heel Kitty made it about six paces before Elliot called after her again.

'You're the CEO's mentee and from what I hear...'

Kitty stared back at Elliot. She quickly scanned the street. It was empty. Her voiced was raised as she began walking back towards him, 'You have no idea what you're talking about.'

Elliot shook his head, 'You didn't think you were the only person I've got in there?'

'Is that a threat, Elliot?'

'No.' This time his anger broke. His voice was softer as he continued, 'Kitty. I know he can be charming and —'

'You think I'm distracted by his charm?'

'Are you not?'

Kitty didn't answer. Instead asking her own question, 'I thought we were investigating the company?'

'It's one and the same.'

'I can't do this, Elliot.'

'Just keep an open mind,' he implored, 'That's all I'm asking. Your father—'

'You didn't know him,' Kitty cut him off.

'I know enough to know that Raphael Daring and his whole scum family are exactly the type of people Claudius spent his life putting away.'

Kitty didn't want to hear anymore, 'Fine.' She stared for a moment longer into Elliot's dark eyes. All anger had left them and she could see he needed her. 'But if I find something. I want to be fast-tracked. I'm not waiting till the start of the next program after my Daring contract expires.'

Elliot's face broke into a lopsided grin, 'Whatever you want.'

With that Kitty left and hurried off to the office. Elliot was right. If there was something wrong, her father would never let anything get in the way of stopping it.

Once installed behind her desk, trying to calm her reeling mind, Kitty began to sift through her emails. One caught her attention. It was just one simple line.

So you are alive.

Kitty looked around for the sender. She had not seen Raphael yet this morning and wondered when he had obviously seen her. Deciding he couldn't surely be serious Kitty quickly tapped out a response.

Last time I checked.
Kx

An hour later Raphael had still not replied and her intuition was beginning to sense he maybe had been serious. She didn't want him to be cross, wondering if he

219

had the same fierce temper as his siblings, so qualified her response. Albeit a little irritated.

> If you're referring to me getting home safely on Friday, I did thank you.

> If you're referring to me not alerting you to my safe arrival, I don't have your number.

> Thank you for dinner.
> K

Kitty removed the kiss this time. She had sent the first in error, her thumb typing the addition automatically, having recently texted Jaz wishing her a good week and confirming their plans for the one ahead.

It was not until Kitty had been heading out to grab some lunch that she had realised the extent of just how mistaken she had been.

A hand shot through the lift doors just as they were about to close. Kitty having previously been the only occupant, inwardly groaned, knowing she would now potentially be waylaid on her way for food. It was later than usual, as Hugo had been unusually demanding today, preparing for his time off, and her stomach was not feeling particularly pleased at having to potentially stop at another floor before it was fed. Deciding also that she was not in the mood for polite conversation, still irritated from Raphael's silence, Kitty kept her eyes down, focussed on her phone, something she had noted many business people seemed to do when wanting privacy, as the figure walked in beside her. She didn't need to look up to sense who it was.

'Hand me your phone?' the cool voice of Raphael growled.

'I'm sorry?' Kitty looked up, 'You can't actually be seriously cross?'

Raphael glared down at her bitterly. Extending his hand, he continued to stare without a word.

Kitty gave up. *So he does have a temper then.* Handing him the phone and dramatically folding her arms, hoping he would register her displeasure at being treated like a truant teenager, as he hammered his number into her contacts.

'Raphael you're acting like a child.' She knew her comment would elicit a similar reaction to poking an angry bear, but couldn't help herself. Nevertheless, without realising it she had taken a step back, noticing his jaw clench at the reprimand.

The lift pinged announcing their arrival on the ground floor.

'You could have emailed,' was all he said, handing her phone back and stalking out of sight without a backward glance.

Kitty stood a little aghast, all thoughts of food temporarily erased, she did not register the curious gazes of the employees waiting for her to leave so that they could board the lift themselves.

He was named after the wrong angel, she thought bitterly.

221

FIFTEEN

'Are you going to tell me? Or should I guess?' Sienna breathed, gently pecking her brother on the cheek, before returning to her position leaning against the teal painted railings outside the entrance to Hertford House.

'Sienna,' Raphael warned.

Sienna pursed her lips and folded her arms. He rarely called her by her birth name, instead of the silly childhood nickname he had given her when she was four, thereby confirming her suspicions that he was indeed in a bad mood. She could always tell when Raphael was frustrated because he would become distant, his posture overly formal, tense and would - something she wasn't sure if he was aware of - flex his right hand or tap it against something, as if somehow trying to massage out whatever was getting to him.

Their plan, as had become something of a happy routine for the pair, was to investigate the Wallace Collection for the afternoon. Housed in a beautiful historic townhouse in Manchester Square, just around the corner from the Daring Headquarters. The collection comprised of twenty-five galleries' worth of eighteenth-century French painting, furniture, porcelain and a world class armoury.

Sienna knew perfectly well that her brother held no affection for the arts, at least not in this form, but she also knew how much he enjoyed indulging her and she couldn't resist his attentions. Hence why he had accompanied her to almost seventy galleries, collections and exhibitions all over Europe since leaving the SAS.

However, now, with his palm twitching and subtle glower she was not sure she would get him inside this time if she didn't halt her inquisition.

Raphael eyed Sienna carefully. Her stance reminding him of his recent encounter with Kitty, he shook his head. Not wishing to discuss the cause of his current vexation with his little sister, he gestured stiffly up the path to the entrance of the museum.

'Pulce. Per favore? Would you like to show me around?'

Sienna accepted his spoken offer and the unspoken plea to, as the English liked to say, *Let sleeping dogs lie* - at least for now.

They wondered around the beautifully preserved townhouse, each room still decorated with classic silk wallpaper and curtains, gilded door frames, ornate mantlepieces and gilt cornicing. Slowly admiring each piece, Raphael remained a few steps behind Sienna the whole way, allowing her to set the pace and choose wherever she wanted to go. He did not come to the galleries with an agenda in mind. He simply loved spending time with her, being in her aura. It was comforting, she was to him the only uncorrupted Daring and something in that felt immensely precious.

He knew it was the same view that had made him an often overbearing and certainly overly protective elder brother. She would no doubt accuse him of scaring off many potential suitors, but Luca had had some bizarre notions as to the acceptable behaviour of a young lady, and with no father and their elder brother unwilling, Raphael had taken on a sort of paternal role, even if a little too vigilant a one. Above all, making Sienna smile was, until recently, his favourite pastime. Not, he noted, that he was doing a fantastic job of it today. A small laugh escaped him thinking of the poor young men he had chased away.

Sienna heard the small outburst, but restrained herself from turning around. Usually Raphael recovered his own moods in his own time, and she knew if she showed too much interest too early that he would stew for longer. Instead she sauntered into the next room.

'Che bello! Oh great!' she peeped.

Raphael, having become distracted, followed his sister's line of sight as she tugged him across the room, her small hands clasped tightly around his wrists.

'Look at this. This is one of the reasons we're here.' Sienna looked up at her brother and wagged a slender ringed finger in his face smirking, 'So pay attention. Educating you is becoming a full time profession.'

'Mmm. Is that what we're doing here?' Raphael frowned, dutifully inspecting the miniature crystal sculpture mounted in gold and colourful jewels.

The piece depicted a young child sitting cross-legged on a cushion. The child's right hand supported his head and on his lap Raphael saw the figure of a lamb. Feeling his sister's eyes now on him, he read the sign below, '"The Good Shepherd, Ceylon or Goa, circa 1600." Lovely,' he muttered sarcastically, knowing Sienna was bursting to tell him about it.

Sienna let out a long dramatic sigh - for his benefit and her indulgence - before she launched into her appraisal, 'So it's carved out of rock crystal and mounted in gold—'

'Yep I got that,' he smiled devilishly, 'I have been paying some attention.'

'Bene. Good. Well you're better than Luca.'

'Luca has been taking you to art galleries?' Raphael queried, instantly distracted. The image of his brother strolling around a museum amused him.

'Why? Would that give you a let out?' Sienna asked, a touch frustrated that he had interrupted her appraisal.

'Well sì Pulce. Yeah. I'm a busy man these days.'

Sienna's mouth dropped open.

Now Raphael really laughed, 'Calmati, bambina. Calm. Please,' he snickered, again dodging a swipe from her left hand, 'I would never... subject you to Luca's company in an art gallery.'

Sienna turned back to the sculpture.

Raphael closed his arms around her. 'Pulce. There is nothing I would rather be doing.'

She smiled in his embrace, 'It was when you were away. He came with me to a small exhibition, all marble sculptures. He managed ten minutes and by the end still had no idea what he had seen or what the pieces had been made of.'

'Still ten minutes of marble is…'

Sienna pushed out of Raphael's arms and silenced him with a warning glare.

He smiled, 'Tell me more. What are we looking at?'

'It's an exceptionally rare figure of the Christ Child as the Good Shepherd. The presence of the lamb characterises him as such.' She continued for a few more minutes, lost in awe of the specialist gem carvers, goldsmiths, and ivory and ebony carvers who must have toiled to create the piece.

'What it symbolises,' she added, 'is the christian belief that Christ, on behalf of God, will forever shelter and protect his flock of believers.' She turned to her brother who had gone quiet, 'Rather nice don't you think?'

Raphael was grateful that Sienna had not waited for an answer before returning to her musings about the subjects revival in the Indo-Portuguese art of the Renaissance and the Jesuit involvement in the conversion of the native population in Ceylon and Goa, for he could not have joined her in her comforting assessment. Instead debating in his head whether God was a good shepherd or not. P*erhaps I am simply a very bad sheep,* he concluded.

'Rafa?' Sienna called. She had crossed the room and had realised that he had not followed her. On this occasion she decided she had finally found a piece of art he actually liked. She was wrong.

They made their way through more of the gold and silk rooms, each one more opulent than the one before, creating a perfectly majestic time capsule, past countless

Old Master paintings and through a room dedicated to Marie Antoinette housing many of her treasured belongings. Their tour ended in a powder blue room, surrounded by a collection of French Rococo paintings.

'At the beginning of the seventeen-hundreds, the end of the reign of Louis the Fourteenth, the aristocracy in France returned to Paris, abandoning Versailles and so began a culture of luxury and excess perhaps best epitomised by indulging in romantic intrigues like those depicted in the art of this period. It's all very erotic,' Sienna stated, pleased with herself for remembering what she had learnt about the time period last summer.

Raphael glanced around the room. One of the smaller paintings caught his attention and he made his way over to it. Before he could read the name plate below Sienna was at his ear. He remembered why he had named her Pulce.

'*The Swing*. Originally known as, *Les Hasards heureux de l'escarpolette*. Lucky Happenings on the Swing. It was painted by Fragonard. He's perhaps one of the greatest of all the Rococo artists.'

Raphael waited for Sienna to go on, knowing she would, as he admired the painting of a beautiful young women in a billowing peach dress, swinging in an overgrown garden.

'The message of this painting is one of desire, infidelity, hence the swing as a symbol, and erotic love. Notice the presence of Cupid. And look here,' Sienna pointed to the bottom left hand corner of the painting, 'concealed in the foliage, illuminated under the women's skirts we have a young man, most likely her lover, admiring the view as she deliberately flashes her legs apart above him. How naughty!' Sienna laughed, 'And how sad.'

'They both look pretty pleased with themselves,' Raphael stated impassively, distracted again.

'They do indeed, Rafa, but look here.' She now pointed to the far right of the painting where an older gentleman had been painted in amongst the shadows, 'It's decided that this second man has no idea of the presence of the one hiding in the bushes.'

'Well he's a fool.'

'Are we not all fools in love?' Sienna pushed.

Raphael sensed she had come to some unspoken conclusion about his bad mood and was revving up to sharing her thoughts. He braced himself. Considering now whether in his current entanglement with Kitty if he was the hidden lover or foolish observer, he suddenly realised how little he knew about her - about her current relationship status for one. For all he knew she had a boyfriend. He scowled.

Sienna interrupted his thoughts, 'So she is either the object of desire, or an instigator of romantic intrigue. Or perhaps both?'

'Who?' Raphael questioned, having missed the start of Sienna's sentence.

'Well,' Sienna smiled. She had him. 'The girl in *The Swing* of course…' She moved in front of her now brooding brother forcing him to look her in the eye, 'Or your intern?'

Raphael sighed. Rolling his eyes he gazed down at Sienna, 'Don't let me stop you.'

His tone was dark but she did not let that halt her, 'So Luca told me about your new intern.'

'Did he now? And what did our dear brother have to say?'

228

'Well, that doesn't really matter. Although I can say he wasn't impressed that you tried to kick him out of the room when he interrupted whatever was going on between you... come to think of it...' She delivered her most perfect smile, 'What was going on?' She waited but when Raphael didn't answer she tried again, 'I heard there were tears.' She let this last comment sit for a while. She was not trying to incense Raphael, but was curious and it wasn't hard.

Of course her brother had had many flings but never something which would have elicited the kind of reaction Luca reported that he had witnessed, 'You can't ignore me forever.'

'I'm deliberating it,' Raphael snarled.

'Ok. Let's do this a different way. I'll tell you what I know first. Her name is Kiti. She's very attractive—'

'Intelligent,' Raphael interjected, 'Wait what? Luca said that?'

'Mi dispiace. Apologies, she is very *intelligent*. The usual foundation for passion.' Sienna rolled her eyes.

'Stop, Pulce. It will never work.' He started to make his way out of the room.

He had decided to pursue Kitty. In truth he felt more that he wouldn't be able to stop himself pursuing her. But he hadn't wanted his probable failure, and her certain future rejection if he ever truly opened up, to be common knowledge.

'What will *never* work? My probing or your relationship?'

Raphael did not answer.

Sienna ignored his now dejected expression and, skipping alongside him began again. 'How defeatist. I

229

think a relationship is just what you need,' she stated, wondering how much she should push her luck. She really did believe he needed someone. Raphael had a bad habit of excluding himself. 'We aren't designed to be on our own.'

'Sadly I'm not on my own.' He waved toward her, crossing into a crimson panelled room.

'Mama would want this for you. She would want you to be happy.'

Raphael stopped still.

Sienna's call had filled the room which was fortunately, considering it was well before the close of the working day, empty.

He turned to her. 'If Mama wanted me to be happy, she would have let me run a thousand miles from the family business and not insist I return as CEO,' he said acidly, taking a step toward Sienna. 'If Mama wanted me to be happy.' He stopped.

Tears had welled in his sister's face and he knew that sharing the truth with her would be too much. He refused to corrupt the image of their family which, somehow mercifully, she had retained.

'Perdonami. Forgive me.' He changed the subject away from their mother. Fearing Sienna's tears, he chose to indulge his sister a little, 'Kiti is the most intriguing, difficult woman...' he laughed and Sienna laughed with him. 'I have never felt about anyone how I feel about her. But Pulce— '

'But nothing! You're so obtuse. What do you think relationships are?'

Raphael was confused. He had not been expecting a lecture on love from his sister and, having been caught up in his own self-loathing recently, had forgotten her view of him.

'Trust built on honesty. Honesty built by sharing. Being there for someone when they need you. Accepting someone with all their flaws, idiosyncrasies and failings.' Raphael moved to interject but Sienna continued, she wanted her brother to hear this, 'You are not meant to be alone Raphael. You are a better person—'

'Stop.'

'No you stop. You're a better person than the one you think you are. I'm not completely naive, I know you and Luca and Martina don't tell me things. I can work more of them out than you think. But I don't need to be told this. Mama loved you and despite whatever happened between you, she always hoped you'd find someone. Trust someone. Did you ever read her letter?'

Raphael looked away. He had not read the letter, written on thick cream parchment that Isabella Daring had left for him on her deathbed, its contents still a secret.

Sienna saw her brother glazing over. She was losing him. 'I don't know what it says. But I don't need to read it to know that she would want you to follow your heart.' She smacked him playfully around the head.

Raphael was surprised.

'You overthink way too much anyway.' She was desperately trying to lighten the mood, 'So I look forward to meeting her. The flea and the cat...we shall get on famously.'

'Ok Pulce, back to the art.'

'Well... the outstretched left arm of the young man in the bushes has an obvious, phallic significance—'

'Great. Thank you for that. Enough of phallic significance for one day I think.' And with that he led her from the room and into the covered courtyard which housed the restaurant. His mind a jumble of peach dresses, bare legs, Kitty, the potential of a rival and the letter from his mother.

SIXTEEN

'It's going ok. I'm not doing much really. I barely see Mr Daring at all,' Kitty said, trying to placate Avery for the countless time that morning. Having slept poorly the night before she had diverted via the nearest Starbucks on her way in to work, hoping a caffeine hit would see her through the start of the day. She was now regretting this move as it had unfortunately resulted in her bumping into Avery, who she should have known was a Starbucks regular.

Avery had questioned her all the way to the offices and now, standing in the huge glass atrium below the spectral installations, she was cross-examining her again. Only this time two of the other grads, who Kitty had not seen since the mentoring assignment event, had gleefully joined in.

Equally prying. Equally annoying. Avery must have spread something.

'So how was it you know Raphael Daring again?' one of the haughty girls, whose name had escaped Kitty, asked, sipping at her latte.

Kitty gripped her cup, her nails were digging in to the cardboard, leaving a neat row of crescent shaped indentations, 'I really don't know him. We bumped into each other once but I didn't realise who he was. That is literally it. We are certainly not friends or anything remotely close to that.'

With Raphael's terse elevator performance the day before, and with what Kitty was considering doing, Kitty was not sure she was entirely incorrect with this last remark.

'But you like him?' Avery pressed, searching for a weakness in Kitty's defences.

'Sorry?' Kitty half laughed - these girls would not give up. She struggled to see what the three-pronged inquisition was hoping to gain and was readying an excuse to leave when an oddly familiar voice interrupted her.

'Kiti. Buongiorno.'

The voice did not belong to Raphael, but spoke with a similar intonation, if only a little harsher, a little lower.

Following the voice, Kitty stood speechless, watching as a smiling Luca Daring waltzed toward her. His burnt caramel eyes were positively glowing. Reaching her, he pecked her warmly on both cheeks. Kitty remained stock still throughout, wilting a little under the intense scrutiny of the three observers, whom she had just spent the last half an hour or more desperately trying to convince of her lack of relations with the Daring family, and whose expressions now resembled those more akin to being found amongst the baying crowds of a Salem witch trial.

Luca, even less interested in commonplace office civility than his brother, did not turn to acknowledge the three gawking onlookers. Instead he kept his fiery gaze fixed on Kitty.

Despite his smile, something about Luca Daring was unnerving. Frightening even, Kitty thought as she realised this was the first time she had really looked at him. She couldn't put her finger on it, but there was something undomesticated and feral about the man. His aura unsettled her. She was not sure if this was down to his temper, which she had witnessed once before, his muscled physicality and burning eyes or whether she was letting the warnings of Elliot, Jaz and Beto colour her judgment. *Then again,* she thought unhelpfully, *even Raphael tried to warn me off his family.* The list was getting worryingly long.

'How are you this morning?' Luca inquired, drawing Kitty's attention. His voice was disquietingly cool.

'Umm... Fine, yeah. I'm good,' Kitty nodded, completely lost as to what was happening.

She had never before shared a single word with Luca Daring, and this couldn't have been a worse time to amend that fact.

'I have someone who is dying to meet you,' he continued, oblivious to Kitty's discomfort.

'Really?' Kitty began, surprised, but before she could ask the name of the mystery person, a lightly freckled, blonde-eyed figure bounded up from behind Luca. She had the widest, whitest smile that Kitty had ever seen, framed by bold scarlet lips.

At the woman's sudden arrival, Avery and her cronies had been forced to retreat a few paces. Nevertheless their expressions remained shamefully curious, doing little to hide their fascination at the scene playing out before them.

Kitty turned her back on Avery to face the visitor.

'Kiti!' the figure purred.

The girl was charmingly winsome, clad in a pastel pink coat under which a soft cream cashmere hoodie protruded, making her stand out against the dark smart suits that filled the rest of the building. After embracing Kitty, she returned to stand beside Luca. That was when it clicked. Kitty realised this must be the fourth Daring, Sienna. She had the same plump pouting lips as Martina and Raphael, and shining mahogany hair which flowed over her shoulders. Her eyes however, were not their icy blue but instead were a kinder version of Luca's. Less burnt caramel more molten honey. She was also not Amazonian in height like the other three. In fact, Kitty thought, if she had removed her heeled boots she would be not much taller than herself.

Sienna too seemed immune to the burning eyes of an increasing cast of onlookers, three of whose faces Kitty couldn't bare to look at.

Kitty knew this bizarre encounter would circulate throughout the interns' gossip circles for weeks, if not longer. Nausea swelled inside her when she reflected that the Darings didn't usually talk to anyone in public, rarely showing anything other than serene refinement or disinterest, and Kitty feared this encounter, with Avery as lead witness, could spread beyond the circle of graduates. She cringed inwardly.

'You are even more beautiful in person,' Sienna smiled broadly, 'Will you have lunch with me?'

Kitty thought she heard Avery gasp. Even Luca looked a little taken aback by Sienna's request.

That was when Kitty felt a presence behind her and realised it was not what Sienna had said which had caused the group to freeze.

A firm hand gently gripped her elbow and Kitty turned toward the pressure.

'Sienna. Luca.' Raphael nodded towards his brother and sister, 'I need my assistant back.' His was tone menacing, threatening. Providing the only answer Sienna was going to get to her offer of lunch.

Before she knew it, Kitty found herself being escorted across the lobby at a brisk pace.

Raphael breathed deeply as he marched Kitty to the farthest elevators, his free hand twitching. He wasn't looking at her and she knew it wouldn't take a genius to realise he was furious. Kitty felt a small pang of pity for the jolly Sienna.

Raphael did not feel such an emotion. He would be having words with his little sister. And for that matter the Ferrari owning maniac who had agreed to bring her in the first place.

'See you later Kiti!' Sienna called after her across the atrium.

Kitty felt Raphael go tense all over and heard his teeth meet as he set his jaw. *Oh dear,* Kitty thought.

A few heads turned in the direction of Sienna's call, the noise dancing around the usually quiet atrium. The lift pinged announcing its arrival.

237

Raphael turned to Kitty, his expression brooding. 'I'm so sorry. Scusami. Will you go to my office?'

He did not wait for the reply. Instead he doubled back towards his siblings who had not yet vacated the spot where they had accosted his mentee.

Watching his brother stalk towards him, Luca was under no illusions that Sienna's plan to encourage the budding relationship between Raphael and his intern, despite whatever the two had spoken about during one of their arty trips, had gone badly and he no doubt would be chewed up about bringing her in the first place. *I knew Raphael wouldn't have wanted her bloody help,* he cursed feeling foolish.

Luca, like all the other Darings, was far from immune to Sienna's wiles. Their mother had decided that it was something about being the youngest, and by such a margin, that had given Sienna such astute powers of persuasion. She was able to make one not only do what she wanted, but feel like they had actually wanted to do it on their own in the first place.

Avery and her companions, having retreated to a more appropriate distance from which they could continue to stare, now waited in anticipation. Avery was green with envy at Kitty's apparent personal relationship with the Daring family. *What a pretty little liar,* she thought, begrudgingly rather impressed.

Aware they could be overheard, and not ignorant of the sea of curious eyes filling the corners of the atrium, Raphael forced himself to temper his frustration. He was not surprised by Sienna's actions, she was a law unto herself, but nevertheless he was still furious. He thought he had made it quite clear that Kitty was a no go on their way home from the Gallery. The last thing he wanted was Kitty getting a false image of his family by meeting the only innocent soul of the whole damn lot of them. Apparently Sienna had decided otherwise. He would spell it out for her later.

Reaching his sister, Raphael forced a smile and spoke in as hushed a voice as he could manage, 'Sienna, what are you doing?'

'Encouraging you to grow a pair,' she smiled back brazenly. 'Besides I warned you yesterday. I wanted to meet her before you scare her off with your nonsense about not being good enough. And I realised this morning was my last day in London for a while. So I thought lunch.'

Her tone was innocent, but Raphael knew her better than that, 'Thank you. Pair grown. Now please leave. You're causing a scene.' With that he surveyed the crowd that had gathered in clumps throughout the room.

Luca looked too, following his brother's gaze. The clumps, including Avery's trio, swiftly dispersed.

Raphael pecked Sienna on the cheek, clearly signifying the end of the office entertainment. But all three of the siblings knew this discussion was far from over. He gestured to his brother, 'Luca, please.' He waved toward the doors.

Understanding, Luca turned to escort Sienna out of the building, grateful that he had been spared a public scolding. Raphael caught his arm at the last minute. He braced himself. Sienna had begun crossing the marble and was already about six feet away, heading for the street.

'Next time she has a bright idea and asks for your help, or the next time you decide to lower yourself to family Pot Stirrer,' Raphael leaned in and growled acidly, 'don't.'

Kitty was standing by the wall of glass windows looking out over the city when she heard Raphael come in behind her.

So she can do as she's told. Raphael's mood lifted at this realisation.

Kitty did not turn at first when she spoke, 'So are you being nice today?'

'Mmm.' He slumped onto the sofa.

'Is that a yes?' She turned.

'Yes. You did as you were asked.'

'So that's the criteria? I should warn you, Mr Daring, I'm not very good at doing what I'm told.'

'I don't doubt it.' His mouth twisted into an alluring smile.

Kitty folded her arms behind her back, as if this would somehow help stretch out the knot developing distractingly in her stomach. She remained standing, waiting for Raphael to explain whatever had just happened in the foyer, but slowly crossed the office until she was positioned behind the sofa opposite the one he occupied.

Raphael began his explanation. His tone frayed, 'My family… well my little sister, as I'm sure you noticed, is very... excited. At our…umm…friendship.'

'Is that was this is?'

'I hope so,' Raphael answered, his voice entirely sincere.

Caught by his change in tone, Kitty found herself locked into his frozen stare, searching for the unspoken. 'What did you tell Sienna?' she pushed, hoping his answer may unveil what Raphael wanted from her. His honesty caught her again.

'That I've never felt about anyone how I feel about you.'

'And how's that?'

'I want to spend every minute of the day with you. I want to make you laugh. I find myself worrying when I don't know where you are. I worried all weekend because I didn't know if you'd got home safely. I was furious you never said.'

'Oh I didn't notice,' Kitty replied sarcastically.

Raphael narrowed his eyes, 'Mi dispiace. Apologies. I'm not usually so emotivo. Emotional.'

Raphael watched as Kitty walked around the end of the sofa and came to sit opposite him.

'So what about the, *I'm not a good person Kiti!*' she exaggerated his accent.

Raphael frowned. For him, one fact did not change the other and right now he did not want a reminder as to all the reasons he should leave Kitty well alone, 'I'm not. But I'm selfish too. And... I can't seem to ignore you.'

'Mmm.'

'You don't believe me?'

'Nope,' Kitty shook her head.

'I'm doing the best I can to be *better*—' he began before being interrupted.

'I have so many questions.'

Raphael waited.

'Ones I know you won't answer,' Kitty stressed.

'Like?'

'Why is being a Daring such a bad thing? Why did your mother break your heart? What did you do that is so bad?

Because I don't believe that it was only not seeing your Mother the night she passed?'

'I see. Perhaps, for now, can we just forget all that?'

'That's a big ask.'

'I know.' Raphael hung his head.

Kitty was not sure she had ever seen Raphael look so vulnerable. The knot in her stomach tightened, waking the butterflies. She swallowed as Raphael continued.

'I'm asking for a chance to prove to you and myself that I can separate the past from my future.'

'And how do I know you won't change your mind tomorrow? Or in a weeks time and just disappear.'

'Well…' Raphael grinned, 'you know where I work… and where I live.'

'Not to mention your number,' she added reminding him of her scolding the day before.

'Yes that too.' Raphael visibly filled with chagrin.

Rising from his seat, he moved in front of Kitty. Bending down, so he was almost kneeling he waited till she looked him in the eyes, peering up at her through his thick lashes. 'Give me a chance.'

'One.' Kitty paused before smiling, 'And only because I like your sister.'

Raphael hung his head again, fighting an amused grin. Shaking his head, his hair falling in to his eyes, he laughed deeply. Without realising it, Kitty was joining in with the laughter. His happy peels were catching.

A cough in the doorway startled both of them, and the two looked to see Natalie standing awkwardly in the doorway.

Raphael looked angry again, all traces of humour gone. 'Yes?' he asked curtly for Natalie had not spoken.

'Sorry... yes. Umm your ten o'clock is here, Mr Daring. Sir.'

'Fine. Send them in two minutes.'

With that Natalie hurried from the room.

Raphael looked back to Kitty who had hidden her face in her hands. He peeled back her palms and her crimson blush was so irresistible, he leant in to kiss her. She broke her hands free from his grasp and caught his jaw.

'No no, Mr Daring.'

'Why? I thought I had a chance?'

Kitty sprang a few steps away from him and smiled coyly, 'Your ten o'clock is here. Besides, you only have *one* chance. So let's not risk anything too soon.' With that she disappeared from the room.

Ignoring Natalie's quizzical frown from behind her desk, Kitty hurried along the corridor to the bathrooms. It had taken every ounce of self control to not leap into his arms, bury her face in his and give herself entirely to him. But she was once bitten, twice shy and he would have to do more to earn her affections this time. Besides, there was still a lot more she wanted to learn, despite having decided on giving Raphael the same open-mind that she would give Elliot.

Much to Kitty's delight, the rest of the week had passed without incident. She had not had to endure any more awkward encounters with any of the Daring siblings, and, due to Hugo's holiday leave commencing soon, her enhanced workload had kept her from being able to attend a graduate internship event that was designed for the graduates to swap stories from their respective departments. Kitty had been dreading the event since Tuesday's atrium performance with Luca and Sienna Daring, as she was certain no one would be listening to her discuss her involvement with charity art fairs in New York, or her new task of organising the Daring Corporation members and friends St Moritz winter extravaganza to celebrate another year of business, instead she was sure all the questions would be aimed at her *involvement* with the CEO.

Less pleasing to Kitty, Raphael had also been under an increased workload, and so she had not had much opportunity to discover what he was planning to do with his one chance. *If he even really wants it,* she muted again the thought that had settled cynically in her consciousness.

Since Tuesday's ill-timed ten o'clock appointment and after persevering through another seemingly endless board meeting, which had filled the rest of his morning, Raphael had tracked Kitty down. Finding her in the office alone, he had asked her to join him that night for dinner. Unfortunately, having agreed to attend a girls-only night at Jaz's place, Kitty had been forced to refuse. Raphael had accepted her refusal in a surprisingly pleasant manner, for a man who had proved he liked getting what he wanted, however, a fact Kitty had not overlooked, he had refrained to ask her again since.

By the time Friday lunchtime came around, Kitty, finally on top of her work assignments for the week, forced herself to stop thinking about Raphael as she made her way to the lifts in search of food.

Raphael, having just returned from a meeting in the Vice President's office on the other side of the building, was standing in the lift heading back to his own office. He was still annoyed that Kitty had refused his offer of dinner. For Raphael, disappointment was an emotion he was poor at acknowledging and instead he had let the feeling fuel his irritation. Waking on Friday morning, alone, he had vowed to swallow his pride and try again. He still had to find out if she had a boyfriend, a nagging concern that had bothered him since his viewing of the painting of the woman in the peach dress on her swing.

The doors slid open and Raphael was surprised to find a courier standing lost in the hall. Natalie was not at her post and apparently no one had passed since the deliverymen had arrived.

Having no idea who he was talking to, the courier sprang upon Raphael as soon as he was free of the lift.

'You work 'ere?' he asked, his tone besieged with annoyance. The man was sweating profusely along his brow, and two stains were now darkening the armpits of his polo shirt.

'Yes,' Raphael answered cooly.

'Kitty May work 'ere?'

Raphael's curiosity piqued, 'She does.'

With that the short sweating man thrust a large gaudy bouquet of sunflowers into Raphael's arms.

'Give her these mate. Some of us only get paid per delivery.' With that he tutted away, disappearing into the lift Raphael had just departed.

Raphael set the bunch down on Natalie's desk, cursing in Italian as he noticed the streaks of shimmering dust that now marked his jacket. 'Che palle!' *As if the flowers aren't*

offensive enough, some moron has covered them in glitter.
He shook his head. Brushing at his jacket to no avail,
Raphael noticed the small note that had been staked
amongst the flowers.

Kit,

*I'm sorry you're hating your job. Hope these will brighten
your desk and your day.
And remember you can always quit at the end of your
contract and come and live with me!
Love Freddie x*

Grabbing the bouquet, Raphael turned to see Kitty
staring at him.

'You should try a smile if you're after Natalie's role.
It's more welcoming,' she laughed.

'Who the hell is Freddie?' Raphael growled back.

'What?' Kitty replied, shocked by the question.

Raphael did not wait for Kitty to answer and instead
silently passed her the sunflowers and stalked into his
office.

Kitty looked down at the flowers, confused. Then she
saw the note. *Oh shit.* She turned and followed Raphael
into his office.

Raphael was standing by the windows and did not turn
to face her as she walked in.

'Let every fox take care of his own tail,' she began.
'Isn't that what they say in Italy?'

Now he turned and Kitty felt very small under his
intimidating gaze.

'I'm sorry about the note. I'm sure it was meant to have been put in an envelope,' Kitty whispered awkwardly. 'It's also very misleading. It's not the people here—'

Raphael had closed the distance between them and now put his finger to her lips, 'Who. Is. Freddie?' He repeated harshly.

Kitty sighed, pulling Raphael's hand away. She smiled, 'Just a friend.'

'Just a friend?' He raised his eyebrows.

'Yes.'

'Not a boyfriend?'

'Absolutely not. More like an annoying brother.'

Raphael was smiling now, the corners of his eyes creased with understanding.

Annoyed, Kitty continued, 'Do you honestly think I would entertain *this* if I had a boyfriend.'

'And what is *this*?' Raphael asked, waving between them as she had just done.

Kitty pursed her lips. She would not be tricked into acknowledging her feelings, especially while Raphael wore such a smug look.

'Are you unhappy here?' his eyes still twinkled wickedly.

'The note is really misleading.' Kitty took a few steps away from Raphael, unsure of his expression or where this conversation would turn. She wanted to be able to make a quick retreat if required. She was keen not to argue, fearing it would rock the foundations of their budding relationship. With Raphael she was never sure if she was on stone or sand. It was one of the reasons she found his company exhilarating but it also challenged her self-confidence. He matched her retreat with his own advances.

247

'Are you unhappy Kiti?' he turned serious.

'It's also out-of-date.'

Raphael took hold of Kitty's arm, halting her retreat. She had been about to knock into the back of one of the cream sofas and was grateful to have been spared the embarrassment.

'Per favore siediti. Sit. Please,' he gestured, leading Kitty around the end of the sofa. She sat, placing the sunflowers on the low table. Raphael sat beside her.

'Just tell me. Are you unhappy?'

She looked up trying to read his expression.

'Kiti?' he sounded a little exasperated.

'I just… I'm just not overly sold on the whole massive conglomerate, corporate structure type environment.'

'I see.' He looked troubled.

'It's really my fault for not doing a whole lot of research before applying…' she paused.

'Are you interested in any of your projects?' he questioned.

Kitty smiled, 'Recently, one is proving to be rather interesting. It's requiring a lot of patience though.'

With her reply Raphael's face twisted into a crooked smile, 'Really? Well that project is late for a lunch meeting.'

'Sure thing.' Kitty, pleased they had not argued, made a swift move for the door.

'You're not leaving those in here,' Raphael called.

Kitty turned to see him, his nose wrinkled, as he glared at the flowers which she had left on the table.

'Freddie has poor taste in flowers,' he added.

'Everyone likes sunflowers!'

'Kiti, guy *friends* don't send female *friends* flowers unless they are after a one way ticket out of the friend zone.'

'Thats a lot of use of the word *friend* there.'

'To secure such a ticket, one doesn't send sunflowers. They're gaudy, cheap—'

'Ok ok. Jesus. Since when were you such a florist? Christ! Well he should have enlisted your help then if you're such an expert.' Kitty hadn't denied that Freddie was indeed after such a change in status.

Raphael noticed, 'I shall be helping no man, however woefully unequipped, in that department or any other concerning you.'

'Are you jealous, Mr Daring?'

Raphael once more handed Kitty the flowers, gentler this time, and walked from the room. 'Lunch,' he called over his shoulder.

After her own lunch break, having been distracted by thoughts of Raphael's potential jealousy, Kitty returned to her desk to find Raphael leaning against it, talking to Hugo. On seeing her in the entrance way, the two men looked toward her. Raphael looked pleased with himself, whilst Hugo looked a little annoyed.

'Kitty. Forget the skiing itinerary. You're going to shadow Mr Daring.'

Hugo seemed a little lost. For a brief second Kitty almost pitied him. Perhaps she was not the only one who experienced the ever shifting sand that was life with Raphael.

Raphael closed the topic, 'I have a bunch of meetings and I need someone to take the minutes,' he said as he escorted Kitty from the room.

Only once he was sure that Hugo could not hear. Raphael leant into Kitty's ear as they walked along towards his office. 'Besides, I'll get more work done where I can keep an eye on you. So I won't be worrying which next gentlemen is going to make a play for your affections.'

The afternoon passed surprisingly quickly. Filled with three back-to-back meetings, Kitty scribbled down everything she heard, all the while trying to not be distracted by Raphael. He was an astonishingly good businessmen, born to negotiate, passionate, engaging. He commanded every meeting and got exactly what he wanted out of them. His prowess was insanely appealing especially coupled with the fact that she witnessed nothing remotely shady or backhanded in his dealings. Nothing that would interest Elliot.

Raphael slouched back into the leather desk chair after the last meeting concluded, having already escorted the attendees to the door. Checking his watch, he groaned.

Kitty smiled. It was comforting to see the private Raphael again, behind the facade of perfect charm. 'Would you like a cup of coffee?' she offered, correctly judging his tired expression.

Raphael blinked, 'That's very *graduate intern* of you.'

'I'm feeling nice,' Kitty purred.

He smiled, 'That is very nice.' His voice dropped, 'But unfortunately for me I have to go and meet Martina now.'

'Have fun.'

'Mmm.'

With his refusal Kitty left. The price for a front row ticket to Raphael's performance was now the mountain of notes she had to type up. She was not certain as to when they were expected and so thought she better finish them before leaving for the weekend.

Kitty was not sure what the time was, or how long she had been asleep, when she felt a warm hand gently shake her shoulder.

'Kiti?' Raphael breathed.

Stirring, the office came into view. It was dark outside, the sun having fully set, and the desks were empty. She remembered having seen Hugo leave, unusually he had been the last, after spending hours hunched behind his computer, mumbling unintelligibly. She remembered his departure as he had received a late phone call and for the first time she had seen him smile. The memory of his smile even now made the hairs stand on the back of her neck, it had been strange, the upturn of his features had felt more like an animal baring its teeth than anything friendly. She was not sure how long she had stayed awake after that, the rest was a blur. The long nights of thinking about Raphael and his family had caught up with her.

'Let me take you home.'

'What?' Kitty asked, only beginning to get her brain functioning again. 'Oh,' she realised, 'I'm sorry. I must have—'

'Fallen asleep, yeah.' Raphael put out his hand and hauled Kitty onto her feet. 'Let me take you home?' This time he was asking.

'It's honestly—'

'Humour me.' A full smile adorned his face. Kitty knew she couldn't refuse this and, in truth, she didn't want to.

Throwing his jacket on, the remnants of the sparkles from Freddie's flowers glinted as he wondered through the deserted atrium.

'You look good in glitter,' Kitty laughed softly, clutching her sunflowers protectively, despite Raphael's suggestion that she bin them on the way out.

Kitty knew she must have drifted off again, because before she knew it they were pulling up outside the flat on Coldharbour Lane.

'Hey. We're here.' Raphael frowned.

Kitty yawned, 'You really are a stalker. Did I tell you where to go before I fell asleep?' She couldn't remember.

'It's in your file. Payroll… Insurance… I didn't want to wake you again.' He was still frowning as he surveyed the area.

Unsure of where she found the sudden surge of confidence, Kitty unfastened her seatbelt and slid over the back seat until she was touching Raphael. She pressed her fingers onto his forehead, and smoothed out the creases. 'It's not that bad,' she soothed, reading his judgement of the place she was now calling home. 'And besides, no one likes a snob.'

A group of teenagers spilled out of the taxi firm. Their slurred shouts were unintelligible, but the gist of their frustration was clear, as one of the workers followed them out, shooing them away with equally strong language, pointing to a large pile of vomit which one had obviously just deposited. They kicked the metal shutters of the neighbouring convenience store as they took off into the night, the racket filling the street.

Raphael's brow creased again, 'I would be happier if—'

'Stop. It's fine. Thank you Wilson.' She slid back to her side of the Range Rover and before he could stop her hopped out. Darting around the back of the car, she met Raphael as he opened his door.

'Kiti…' he started.

Stepping up onto the edge of the Range Rover, Kitty gently pushed him back into his seat. Raphael obliged her. Then she placed her hands once more either side of his head, 'And thank you for a wonderful day.' With that she kissed him.

SEVENTEEN

The Mercedes E-Class saloon sped southward toward the M1, the beam of its high-resolution LED headlamps providing the only source of light on the wet asphalt road. Beyond the curb, the conical-shaped silhouettes of partially leafed alder trees, full conifers and passing hedgerows sat dark against the fading light of the encroaching evening.

After a short time the road widened and came to a roundabout. Here, the black vehicle was joined by other cars, each taking the same right turn before accelerating down the now visible slip road toward the motorway.

Only once entirely consumed amongst the fast moving traffic, feeling sufficiently invisible, did Vasili permit himself to exhale. Reliably busy, the mass of red tail lights in front of him all added to the feeling he was hidden, a tiny, inconspicuous cell travelling along a great vein flowing into the beating heart of the city beyond.

With the driver's eyes fixed on the way ahead, and nothing but the sound of the air conditioning gently fluttering through the vents, Vasili silently touched his face. He pressed carefully around the swollen flesh, still stinging and no doubt visibly red, along his right cheekbone. He didn't think it was broken. Responding to a tickling sensation in his nostrils he wiped his nose with the back of his hand. He winced. It was bleeding. Again. With the blood running down his fingers, Vasili realised that the dark red fluid had already escaped his clutches, leaving already partially-dried stains along his shirt collar.

The sight brought back a rush of childhood memories. Christmases. Birthdays. Days when it rained. Days when it didn't rain. The difference now being that, having always been faster than his brother, it had usually been Nikolay's shirts stained whenever someone had needed a beating, or as they had been told as boys, "A *reminder of their morals.*" These days he was not used to being scolded. He was not used to bleeding.

Recognising in himself the early stages of his often disorderly temper and general dislike of humankind, Vasili, having temporarily stemmed the flow from his nose, made himself remember the mission, the purpose of all this kowtowing and rushing about. Returning his arm to its resting position against the door, he subconsciously began to chew impatiently at his nails. They tasted metallic. For all his bluster, for all his allusions of control, Vasili was not in control. He hadn't been for a long time and he was scared.

Thankfully, the first container had been imported successfully, with all its cargo unchecked and intact. Nero's contacts, including the perpetually cigarette-puffing port worker, had proven true and now Vasili's newly bolstered forces were busy with preparations for the second and, most importantly, the third shipment. However, Nero's unavoidable interference in choosing specific ports and containers, allowing for no deviations, had resulted in unfortunate repercussions. Vasili had been forced to request further help from a contact with whom he had conversed with only a few times before and whom he had hoped he would not have to trouble again. He had vowed to check all of his logistical decisions with the contact before altering any arrangements - a vow he had broken in approaching Nero.

A figure with no name, no physical appearance and no past, whose sole future belonged in service to one specific organisation. An organisation whose ventures into the dark web and beyond had incurred global repercussions. Vasili had been informed before that, having started out as a faceless hacking group, молча had found success, not to mention incalculable financial incentive, and had since diversified. Now internationally - and to any Russian speaker aware of their existence, incorrectly - called MONYA, the results from their exploits, if you knew what you were looking for, could be found frequently spouting from the mouths of news anchors all over the world, pasted on the front pages of newspapers, the subject of political satires, and a mainstay amongst the most avid conspiracy theorists. The most recent of these had involved the supposed rigging of a Presidential election.

Having approached Vasili in a low moment about a year before, after hacking his laptop, MOYNA had promised him a prize so valuable that he hadn't wanted to refuse. Just sober enough to remember to protect himself, he had requested proof of their capabilities. They were asking for no small amount of money or assistance. In proving themselves worthy of Vasili's investment, they had shown him proof of their existence amongst the official jottings of confidential documents belonging to a raft of national security agencies.

The FBI, NSA, CIA, French Direction Générale de la Sécurité Extérieure, MI5, MI6, the NCA, the Brazilian SNI, Indonesia's Badan Intelijen Negara and even Shin Bet and Mossad in Israel, were just a few of the agencies who had all found themselves both the victims and purveyors of MONYA's ventures. Vasili had been impressed with each new document that had popped up, as if by magic, on his screen over the following weeks. A written narrative, appearing in an emerald dialogue box which had opened as soon as his server had been accessed, explained the documents and the harrowing facts each contained in minute detail. They had been so absorbing, that Vasili had curbed his drinking in order to digest each properly.

Knowing few organisations had found themselves the subject of security service agents' entire careers, and fewer still were so embedded into the global political structures that even public acknowledgement presented an impermissible threat to the veneers of control governments held up in times of crisis, Vasili had been engrossed in conversation with the faceless emerald dialogue box.

257

'Would it not be frivolous, Vasili, to place MONYA on a watch list? Go public. Stir panic. Give something else for people to worry about. To fear perhaps? Or fix their fears to? When at the end of the day, there is no one to watch.'

There is no one to watch. This parting sentence, appearing across the screen of Vasili's laptop which was no longer under his control, had stuck with him long after it had vanished. The words had disappeared only moments after they had first shown themselves. Seconds later the totality of the evidence, the classified documents that had consumed Vasili for weeks, had been wiped forever from his reach. It didn't matter though. He had already agreed.

Since that day, Vasili had encountered various representatives of MONYA, "Bodies" who provided the necessary muscle to make certain operations possible.

Employed with a single purpose, anonymously appointed through the untraceable tangle of the dark web for a set price, they knew nothing about the organisation. Nothing about any greater plans. They couldn't hack anything, they couldn't trace their employers and they were never assigned more than one tiny job, which, on its own, was untraceable to the wider mission. For this reason, Vasili had never met the same "Body" twice.

Despite not meeting a Body again after he or she had served their purpose, it had not taken Vasili long to realise what made MONYA so dangerous. Why, even within the corrupt, vast and varied world of organised crime that he had been born to, it was an organisation only contacted as a last resort. Bound by something far more profound and uniting than ideology or faith or even money, these Bodies, these servants of secrets, combined to form a silent global influencer and were, for their silence, offered something far more valuable. Immortality. The chance to be pulled from obscurity into the only form of indefinite permanence mankind had so far been able to harness - fame. For their service they were offered a chance to matter, to contribute to the increasingly infamous notoriety of their fraternity, eternally living on in the memories and annals of the clandestine shadow world in which they inhabited.

Vasili had worked this out. For, in a way, it was what he too sought from his time on Earth. A purpose, a place, power. But in using MONYA to achieve his goals, he had crossed some invisible line and become a soldier operating in a wider task, fighting for someone else's cause he knew little about. He had become a Body and tonight a Body had been sent to remind him of this fact.

EIGHTEEN

It wasn't until Kitty had disappeared behind the faded door that led to her apartment that Wilson gently pulled away, smoothly steering the Range Rover back into the passing line of slow moving traffic. Wilson never required specific instructions regarding the finer expectations of working for Raphael. He was intuitive. Raphael liked this about him. This, and his previous military experience.

Gazing out the car window, his eyes fixing on nothing in particular, Raphael breathed. It felt like he hadn't come up for air since Kitty had kissed him. He hadn't been expecting that. Her soft lips warm against his. His hands tangled in her hair. Her perfume filling the air around them. His arousal. And then she had vanished.

'Wilson. Turn around.'

Though Wilson's face rarely betrayed much expression or private emotion, instead resolutely fixed in a steely focus with the occasional polite, yet subdued smile, Raphael knew Wilson would be laughing at him on the inside.

'Very good sir,' Wilson responded, characteristically neutral, but, thanks only to their long standing relationship, Raphael had caught the tiniest note of surprise in his voice.

Raphael rolled his eyes, knowing the ever watchful Wilson would catch him in the rear-view mirror. The situation was laughable.

Silently the driver had been wondering what his boss would do about Kitty's kiss. He had been rooting for the brazen young women since he had first witnessed the effect her presence had imbued on his previously hard-hearted charge. She filled him with life, in-keeping with his youth, a certain spirit that suited him, and one Wilson had never seen before. Something like carefree. *Or perhaps caring?* he mused, keeping his eyes fixed on the road. Kitty took control of Raphael, spoke to him in a way no one else did or ever dared - besides his mother of course. A quiet melancholy suffused Wilson and he tightened his grip on the steering wheel, seeing an opportunity to make a U-turn.

Isabella Daring had been the most wonderful woman Wilson had ever had the pleasure of knowing, and he had witnessed the deep wound, incapable of being healed, that her passing had left on her son. This brilliant young man who hated himself so utterly. She would be forever missed.

The weekend after Wilson had driven Kitty to dinner at the main house, Raphael had been erratic, distracted and grumpy in the extreme. She had moved him. *And annoyed him,* Wilson remembered, this time having to physically restrain a chuckle.

He had worked for the Daring family for a long time and had, for the last couple of years, enjoyed working for Raphael, whose previous SAS career he greatly admired. Their shared military experience had made his unspoken role of bodyguard much easier, despite, as he had come to realise, Raphael did not need much protecting. Although, with his family excelling in a very particular line of work, they had no shortage of enemies and so the two of them shared a tacit agreement, the simple fact that two guns were better than one. As Raphael had quietly accepted Wilson's presence, so too had Wilson formed a quiet attachment to the young man, as one might a son, if one's own life was devoid of such a relationship. Although the later paternal fondness was one Wilson could not accept. It made the job too difficult.

'Would you like me to wait?' Wilson queried, still neutral, having found a space to park alongside the curb. Kitty's faded door was once again just a few short metres away.

Raphael smiled, he could tell Wilson thought the whole situation hilarious. 'That's probably for the best.'

Climbing out of the car, Raphael made his way toward the shabby door that he had seen Kitty disappear through. He could not explain to himself exactly what he was doing, but he knew he didn't want to spend another weekend alone.

Raphael pressed the buzzer beside the door. After a few endless minutes, having forced himself three times not to walk away, he pressed the small round button again.

Still no one answered.

A simmering frustration bubbled within him. Judging by the state of the outside of the building, he knew that perhaps the damn thing didn't even work. Raphael held himself still for a few minutes longer, trying in vain to remain calm, before turning to make his way back to the car.

As Raphael took a second step toward the Range Rover, back to Wilson, who had politely turned away from his failure, the door opened behind him and Raphael was engulfed in a torrent of abuse. It took him a moment to process the words as he turned back to see a small, craggy-faced old lady, with furrowed dark brows and a tight mouth. Her thick Scottish accent had caused him to miss the majority of her tirade which, he had discerned correctly, was aimed at him.

Aside from a lot of finger wagging and tutting, he had managed to catch something about the lateness of his call. A secondary point about knocking and running and the woman had ended, he thought, with a tirade about her home not being a brothel, or something along those lines. He clenched his fist. *This night just gets better and better,* he thought sarcastically.

Kitty, who had been fixing herself a cup of tea whilst trying to control the swarm of ecstatic butterflies now blossoming in her stomach, had heard Mrs Smeaton head down the stairs. The buzzer had sounded a few times and the women had decided it must be the local youths - for knocking and running off, or in this case buzzing and running off, had become a Friday favourite on the evenings when their fake IDs had failed to secure them entry to one of Brixton's clubs.

263

Kitty clasped her hands around her mug, the warm ceramic helping to ease the fluttering in her stomach, as she made her way to the top of the stairs to see who Mrs Smeaton had caught. The stream of abuse she had been yelling indicated that, for once, the woman had actually caught someone.

Standing at the top of the stairs, Kitty looked down through the open door. She gasped, before erupting into peels of laughter. Deliberating how long she could continue to watch Mrs Smeaton berate Raphael before his mood was spoilt for the evening, Kitty decided she better rescue him sooner rather than later.

'And do ye have nothing to say for yurself lad?' Mrs Smeaton waggled her bony finger in Raphael's face.

Kitty heard this last harangue before she hurried down the stairs.

Raphael had no idea what to say to the old lady. He could hardly berate her back, his manners being better than that, but he had smiled, knowing that whatever he said she wasn't going to be listening. She reminded him of some of the matronly nuns who used to pace the halls at his school. His smile had gained him a kick in the shins. Now he frowned.

'You think this is funny? You smug little—' Mrs Smeaton continued.

Kitty caught the woman's arm and she turned.

'Kitty ma dear. I caught one of the blethering scoundrels.'

Kitty bit her lip. Raphael looked stunned. On seeing his now wide blue eyes up-close, she laughed. Mrs Smeaton looked very confused.

'Mrs Smeaton.' She clutched the lady's shoulders, ensuring she was following, 'Please let me introduce you to Raphael.'

'You ken this laddy, Kitty?'

'For her sins.' Raphael risked a second smile.

Mrs Smeaton turned her beady eyes back on him, 'Well what time do ye call this young man?'

Raphael's smile faded.

'He called earlier. I should have told you. It completely slipped my mind. He needs a place to stay.' Kitty leant into Mrs Smeaton, 'So disorganised I know. Can't get his shit in one sock this one. But what can you do?'

Mrs Smeaton chortled.

Raphael looked a little unimpressed at his given description, but when Mrs Smeaton looked back to him he raised his hands in surrender.

'Useless.' He hung his head dramatically.

'Is it alright if he stays the night?' Kitty asked. She was not sure why Raphael had come back, but it obviously was to see her and she was too tired to go out.

Mrs Smeaton raised her bushy eyebrows, 'Kitty I—'

'He's my cousin.' The words had shot out of Kitty before she had even thought them through. *It might work.* In her peripheral vision she could see Raphael raise his eyebrows. He was not so convinced.

'Well why did ye no say lassie?' Mrs Smeaton threw her hands up. 'No fuss. But mind the mess now, our eastern friend had an accident.'

Kitty knew that Mrs Smeaton was referring to Ying's shower disaster and knew that Raphael, who was smiling charmingly at Mrs Smeaton again, nodding politely, had no idea what she was on about. Although the bathroom was up and running again, the day room had not yet been repaired. This had meant that the dining table, just off the kitchen, had become Mrs Smeaton's potpourri making and artefact cleaning station.

Following Kitty and Mrs Smeaton inside, Raphael gallantly offered the old lady his arm on the stairs. Although having been refused, the gesture had made the scot soften in her demeanour toward him and with each step nearer the duplex, it had not taken Raphael long to realise what Mrs Smeaton had been talking about. A strange antiseptic smell hung in the air, which Kitty explained was emanating from the bowls of sodden potpourri that had been damaged. Mrs Smeaton was apparently still hoping to resurrect the sorry displays. The oranges had begun to rot and so the strange odour, reminiscent of cleaning fluid, had reached most corners of the house.

Mrs Smeaton waved Kitty and Raphael off at the top of the stairs with a hearty smile. It was late and so she declared that she was off to her room. Smiling smugly as she kicked off her pomegranate slippers, now in the privacy of her bedroom, Mrs Smeaton settled on the side of the bed and patted out a crease in the lilac throw. *Cousins!* she laughed, *Young people these days*. Feeling satisfied that she had given Kitty every opportunity to refuse to entertain her visitor - who was clearly not her cousin - she was pleased that the young lady, whom she had grown quite fond of, had an admirer. She was also glad that she hadn't scared him off. She had known as soon as she had seen him that he wasn't a Brixton youth, but with her stiff hips taking most of the joy out of city living these days, she hadn't been able to resist. It felt

266

better having scolded someone, for she knew sadly she would never again be quick enough to catch one of the real pranksters.

'Well... this is home,' Kitty waved around the kitchen, finishing off her explanations about Ying's bathroom antics and Mrs Smeaton's hobbies as she lead Raphael to her small room. 'And this is my room,' she pointed in through the open door. 'Can I get you a drink or...?' she faltered, unsure what to do next. Her earlier boldness had gone, and she wanted Raphael, who had gone very quiet, to talk about why he was here.

'I'm fine. You look tired.'

'Thanks for that,' Kitty muttered. 'What can I do for you, Raphael?'

'I want to spend some time with you. Not at work. I had intended to invite you out but...' Raphael drifted off, knowing Kitty, who had just experienced the same moment, did not need to have explained how his plan had been derailed.

Feeling emboldened by his honesty, Kitty smiled, 'Well, seeing as you're staying,' she smirked, turning her voice sickly sweet, 'Dearest cousin. Please come through.'

Making her way into her room, she swallowed. A nagging self-consciousness trickled into her spirits. 'You can leave if you want... it might be quite a squeeze,' she said, apologetically looking toward the single, three-foot bed which was pushed up snugly against one of the walls.

'I'm game if you are,' Raphael grinned.

Kitty relaxed. He looked so young when he did that, so untroubled. The complete opposite of how she often found him to be.

'Cool. I'm just going to get out of my work stuff.' Feeling a second wave of shyness, Kitty gathered up her pyjamas and left the small room having decided to change in the bathroom.

Moving aside to let her out of the bedroom, Raphael sat cautiously on the bed. The lumpy mattress sagged below him. Just before Kitty had completely disappeared he called after her, a sudden idea having occurred to him. 'Do you not want supper?'

Kitty remembered polishing off the remains of a large box of Krispy Kreme donuts before she had fallen asleep at her desk earlier in the evening. The treats had been bought into the office in early celebration of David's birthday that coming Sunday, and now the thought of eating anything else resulted in a mild swell of nauseousness. 'I sort of already ate… in the office. I can make you something if you need—'

'I ate with Martina. Well…' he laughed, '…on my own after she walked out.'

'Why?' Kitty began, a flood of questions returning to her as she stood, leaning against the door frame.

Raphael looked a little startled by her sudden interest.

Well, if this is going to work, he's going to have to tell me something, she thought.

He cut her off though. 'Change. Then we can talk.'

She swallowed a well of disappointment and hurried off to the bathroom.

Raphael watched her until she had completely disappeared. After taking off his jacket, he removed his tie and undid the top few buttons of his shirt. Rolling up the white sleeves, placing his now redundant cufflinks in his jacket pocket, he looked around the room. Besides a holdall with a badly repaired, duck-taped corner, the sunflowers, which Raphael noted with disgust, and small candle which was burning on the windowsill, desperately fighting the aroma of rotting citrus, nothing else in the room looked like it belonged to Kitty. The knowledge of her apparent lack of belongings made him feel sad. But before he could formulate a question to try and account for it, she was back, pulling him from his thoughts.

'You're still here,' Kitty breathed, standing awkwardly again in the doorway.

She had changed into her pyjamas. Fortunately, Jaz had persuaded Kitty to buy some new ones when she had moved to London, declaring that, should she have any visitors, or simply for the sake of her fellow flatmates, her holed t-shirt and tracksuit bottoms were no longer suitable attire. It was only now, in front of Raphael, that she wished she had taken on all of Jaz's recommendations and purchased something a little more alluring. Instead, she wore a cream soft-touch long sleeved top with the matching shorts. The only saving grace was that the set was trimmed with French lace, so she did not entirely look like a little girl. 'This is weird isn't it?' she asked.

'It's really not that weird, Kiti,' Raphael comforted, frowning almost imperceptibly.

Crossing the room Kitty climbed on top of him so that she was sitting in his lap facing him. She felt his body tense beneath her.

'You know you often say one thing and then act the complete opposite way,' Raphael said, 'I thought you were about to ask me to leave.'

'Sorry.'

'It's fine,' he laughed, resting his hands on Kitty's waist. 'I'm just trying to figure out what you want…' He waited, before finishing, 'I don't want to blow my one chance now.'

'Well besides from the obvious—'

'Wanting the answers to your questions?' he checked raising his eyebrows.

'Yeh that. I just want you to stay,' Kitty whispered, unsure of how much she was going to risk tonight. 'The thing is, I don't really trust people much and I still don't trust you. But… and I know I should probably have said this when you did earlier in the week… I've never felt about anyone how I feel about you either.' She buried her face in his shoulder.

Raphael could smell the fresh mint on her breath and felt her smile against his collar bone.

'That said…' Kitty added, feeling her cheeks burn, '…I don't want to have sex with you.'

Raphael hugged Kitty tightly, 'That's fine.'

'I mean I do. But I don't.' She looked up at him now, 'Does that make sense?'

'Not until you trust me right?'

'Right,' Kitty nodded, pushing aside thoughts of Elliot.

Raphael laughed darkly, 'Besides, now we're cousins, I'm not sure what Mrs Smeaton would think of that?'

'But will you still stay?' Kitty wasn't ready for him to lighten the tone, this was important to her.

'Of course.' Raphael flashed one of his big white smiles, 'Kiti, I didn't knock on your door with the aim of sleeping with you. Anyway…' a melancholy filled his voice, colouring his previous happy sincerity. 'It's probably for the best if you don't get too attached.'

'I'm not sure I can promise that,' she whispered, burying her face once more into his shoulder.

Laughing about Raphael's first encounter with Mrs Smeaton, and then about the creepy decorations that littered the duplex apartment, it wasn't long before they had both relaxed into each others company. Raphael, having never experienced anything like this, was almost giddy with the experience. In truth, Kitty herself had never really done this before.

Raphael, with his back against the pillows, closed his eyes blissfully. Kitty had positioned herself between his legs and lay against his chest. With his arms wrapped around her, she fiddled with his hands, tracing the edge of a small gold ring that sat on his little finger. Eventually, she began to drift off to the quiet din of the city outside and his strong, steady heartbeat, which she could hear comfortingly against her ear.

'Can I just ask one question?' Kitty whispered, her voice a little groggy, sleep having begun to take hold.

Still with his eyes closed Raphael smiled, 'One.'

'Did Sienna get in trouble for talking to me at the office?'

'Why do you say that?' He opened his eyes.

'Well you didn't seem too impressed.'

Raphael laughed and Kitty felt the happy vibrations of his chest.

'You don't need to worry about Pulce. She was very pleased with herself.'

'Why Pulce?'

'It means flea in Italian. So far it's just the best description I've been able to come up with to describe her.'

'The flea and the cat. We should get on great.'

'She said the same.'

Kitty smiled.

'Why are you smiling?' Raphael asked.

'Your voice…' she paused, 'it's very sweet when you talk about your little sister.'

'Is it not always?'

'Not really. Actually you can be really intimidating.'

'Really?'

Kitty ignored his surprise, 'Yep. And you definitely aren't as sweet when you talk about Martina.'

Raphael had stilled and so Kitty rolled over to look up at him, 'You guys aren't so close?'

'It's gotten worse. We were never particularly close to start with.' Raphael began to explain the competition between the pair growing up.

'So why has it gotten worse?'

'She did something I can't forgive, because it led to something that I did that is much more unforgivable.'

'I doubt that.' Kitty pushed up on his chest so that she was now sitting once more in front of him.

Raphael met her gaze, 'You need to sleep.'

'I have one more question,' Kitty stated, trying to sound determined. Although in truth, she was getting too tired to care much about anything.

'Why doesn't that surprise me?' he rolled his eyes.

'Make me a promise?' She waited for him to blindly agree. He didn't. So she continued undeterred, 'Promise me that one day, you will give us a fair chance and tell me why you have such a terrible view of yourself.'

Raphael sighed. 'Fine,' he answered finally.

'Fine?'

'Ok Sherlock. I promise.'

'Ok,' Kitty mirrored, 'And in the meantime...' she settled back on his chest, 'I will forget all the silly things you've said and get to know you like I would anyone else... Benefit of the doubt and all that.'

'Benefit of the doubt,' Raphael mused, softly stroking Kitty's hair.

NINETEEN

Andre Hayes was a man not used to being seen. For forty years, since graduating from the London School of Economics with a joint honours in Accounting and Finance, he had quietly navigated his way through a career of blurred lines. Hayes never asked unnecessary questions and avoided ostentation in all its forms. Instead, he occupied his days unobtrusively, meticulously moving a varied range of assets around the world and dependably providing his employers with full accounts, legitimate revenue streams and most crucially, discretion. After four decades, he was one of the most skilled accountants working within the shadow economy. He kept a very small group of friends and an even smaller group of acquaintances. After a personal tragedy, and then in part due to his relocation to the sun-drenched tax haven of Tortola, these groups had gotten smaller still. For this reason, Hayes knew without doubt that the man walking about fifty metres behind him did not belong to either of these groups.

Earlier in the day, whilst the mountainous scenery of the island had still appeared an inviting luscious green, Hayes had first laid eyes on the man. Clad in a pair of torn jeans and nondescript navy t-shirt, the man's face had been partially obscured by a fedora. Resting by the side of the road, on a wooden bench situated between a sprawling cerise bougainvillea and pair of Tyre Palms, Hayes had presumed the man to be another tourist - a little lost perhaps, but a tourist nonetheless. One sheltering from the midday sun in the dappled shade provided by the fan like fronds of the palms, waiting for a passing safari - one of the converted open-air pick-up trucks with bench seating and a canvas roof that passed for public transport.

Despite it being the rainy season throughout the Caribbean, the weather had been kinder to the volcanic archipelago this year. And with the absence of any hurricanes, the cruise ships had continued to dock in Road Town almost daily, bringing with them a steady stream of eager tourists hunting for a week of paradise in the charter-boat capital of the Caribbean.

Now, as Hayes hurried uphill along the narrow street lined with parked cars and single storey colourful buildings that wound away from Wickams Cay in Road Harbour toward Main Street, he saw the man again. A rush of adrenaline followed the eerie sense that he was being followed.

Stop being so paranoid, Hayes scolded himself. It had been a long and stressful three days owing to a troubling discovery he had made whilst checking his affairs over breakfast seventy-two hours earlier. For the first time in his career, an asset had gone missing. In fact, multiple assets.

Eighty-one tons of unrefined Coltan, a dull, tarmac-coloured metallic ore, the extracted elements of which could be found in almost every kind of electronic device from mobile phones to high-temperature alloys for jet engines, and the mining of which having unethical associations with multiple human rights violations around the world, had disappeared somewhere in the North Atlantic Ocean. Whilst one disappearance could perhaps be explained due to inclement weather conditions, this asset had disappeared in twenty-seven tonne portions, on three separate occasions. More worryingly for Hayes, the contingencies he had specifically designed should such an event occur hadn't kicked in. The assets had merely vanished. Hayes himself had only realised by chance, his experienced eyes having noticed some missing figures in a few rarely opened accounts, anomalies too inconsequential to be noticed when one was managing the larger web of operations.

Despite having experienced no consequences for the loss as of yet, Hayes knew his luck would fail eventually and he would need a good answer for his employer when it inevitably did. His employer was a man who had little time for errors, this could cost Hayes his life. *Perhaps it already had*, Hayes considered, feeling the unfamiliar nausea of panic rising within him.

He stole another glance behind him. The man was still there, still tailing him at about fifty metres. Hayes had begun to sweat. His shirt, clinging to his dampening torso, now felt two sizes too small. He stretched out his arms momentarily as he strode on. He could feel his heart beating hard and fast in his chest, his breathing was strained despite having not walked a great distance. He needed to calm down. His employer wouldn't send an assassin. Not for him. No, if he needed discarding of, his employer would have come himself.

Unable to shake the paranoia, Hayes made a quick decision to turn off the street he was on. Disappearing down another narrow passageway which had appeared on his right Hayes sped up. Walking now at a brisk pace, he kept his eyes fixed on the rocky road surface as he raced for the intersection ahead. He couldn't afford to trip on one of the notoriously uneven side streets. Alone with no protection, the man would be on him in an instant. A shiver ran down Hayes' back.

A menacing bank of near-black clouds had rolled in throughout the afternoon, gradually swallowing each sharp verdant peak as they had settled over the island. A storm was coming. The wind was picking up and he could feel it nip against his sweating skin as it channelled along the passageway, rushing between the colourful buildings either side. With each passing vibrant shuttered door his hopes grew for someone to come out, join him in the passageway, but no one did. He would feel safer in a crowd. He would *be* safer in a crowd. Unable to look back for fear of falling, Hayes pressed on, fighting the urge to see if he was indeed being followed.

Spinning around the corner, making a left at the intersection of streets, Hayes smiled. He had made it. However, his elation was short lived. Looking down the road he had chosen, the colour drained from his face. *No. Please not today,* he thought.

The street, home to a large selection of the many bars and restaurants that serviced the tourist market in Tortola, was completely deserted. Devoid of the usual crowds that filled the streets around this time in the evening. The crowds Hayes had been banking on disappearing into. The storm had apparently dissuaded sufficient numbers of patrons to leave the comforts of their hotels in order to make it worthwhile opening at all tonight.

Hayes glanced behind him. Nothing yet. He focussed on his breathing. *It may be nothing,* he began to repeat to himself. Walking down the empty road, Hayes tried to work out the quickest way back to Main Street, or Waterfront Drive. At least there should be some people there, cars with passengers driving home from work. Witnesses. Anyone.

Turning around, knowing it was the only way to reach the harbour, and so the busier roads, bile rose in Hayes' throat. The man in the ripped jeans was just exiting the small passageway he had just left. They locked eyes for a brief moment. A single loud thought became clear in Hayes' head. *Run.*

Just then the spluttering rumble of a cherry red safari rolled around the corner of a building about a hundred yards ahead. As it trundled toward him, Hayes felt tears of relief spring in his eyes. Despite the burn in his lungs and legs, Hayes ran toward the safari, waving manically until it pulled to a stop.

Clambering into the vehicle, he pushed himself into a bench already filled with locals making use of the availability of island-wide transport due to the lack of tourists that evening. Hayes counted seven throughout the bus. As the safari engine roared to life and continued to rumble down the road, Hayes' eyes were fixed on the man, still standing at the entrance to the alleyway. Hayes had stopped breathing.

At the last moment the man hailed for the driver to stop and he too climbed on board. Choosing a seat on the bench furthest back. Hayes stole another quick glance. The man casually pulled out a pair of headphones and seemed to select some music before staring off into the distance. Hayes wasn't convinced of his innocence. Not yet.

The safari continued on, following the winding coastal road, collecting some more passengers along the route, others disembarking as they entered each town or village along the coast. Hayes kept a strict count of those getting on and off, ensuring he would not be left. He was grateful that he had not been living in the house which the company had provided for him. Perhaps, if he could just make it back to where he had been living instead, then he could lie low for a few days and make a plan. He could make almost anything disappear. Why not himself? This thought helped calm his nerves. His heart had slowed to a more measured pace. The man was still in the back of the safari, but he had not looked up once.

Finally arriving at the large bay which he had been calling home for the past few months, Hayes disembarked along with another man. This man smiled and Hayes smiled back. He recognised him, but couldn't quite place the face. Attributing him to the group who lived in the cream block with the green bars and shutters about five houses down from where he was staying, he waved a greeting as the man headed out across the sand.

Hayes skirted the large crescent bay surrounded by pinnate leaved palms. The water turquoise and crystalline by-day was now dark, the cloud blotting out the moonlight, the wind carrying large crashing waves to the beach.

Staying on hard ground for speed, Hayes headed for home. The man in the fedora hadn't disembarked with him, but Hayes knew the safaris could stop whenever someone asked to get off, so he couldn't be sure he wasn't about to disembark any minute.

Looking up to his right, the mountainside rose steeply up. The lights of the expensive guest houses dotting the hills, with the far-reaching sea views, still sparkled through the cloud.

Disappearing into his house, a small wood-clad, single-story dwelling with lilac painted shuttered windows, he stole one more glance down the bay. The safari had stopped. Hayes swallowed.

Listening to the ache of the wooden house, its planks cooling after the heat of the day, Hayes thought he was, unexpectedly, alone. *Good*, he thought, setting to work locking the door. He didn't risk turning a light on. He wanted it to look empty. For a minute Hayes just breathed. That was when he heard a noise coming from the back of the house.

His heartbeat now audibly thumping in his ears, Hayes shuffled as quietly as he could towards the rear of the building, too frightened to call out incase the noise belonged to anyone other than the owner, who usually could be heard at this time snoring in the double bedroom at the back of the property.

Hayes had crept halfway along the small corridor that led into the rear bedroom when he heard the unmistakable clatter of the front door's insect screen. His knees buckled beneath him.

TWENTY

Kitty felt the morning sun, having broken through a crack in her curtains, on her face and stretched. Her eyes snapped open. The bed was empty. He was gone. She looked around for any sign that she had not dreamed their entire evening together. Noticing his glitter streaked jacket hanging on the back of the door she smiled and returned to rest against her pillows.

Listening now, a strange voice filled her ears, its tone spiked with wild excitement. Getting out of bed Kitty opened her curtains. It was going to be a beautiful day, the sky was already a bold cloudless blue with the sunlight highlighting the lampposts and tree branches a vivid orange.

She made her way to the bedroom door. Opening it, Kitty took a moment to take in the scene before her. Mrs Smeaton, as always, was busying herself at the dining table. However, the ornaments had been returned to their shelves and the stinking pile of semi-dried potpourri had been replaced by a huge bunch of soft pink peonies, held in a large cream vase that Kitty had not seen before and she realised that Mrs Smeaton was cleaning and stacking the bowls that had once housed the dried flowers.

In the kitchen, Raphael, clad in a frilly crimson apron, was cooking, and most shockingly, beside him, Ying was seated on the counter, speaking animatedly in perfect, albeit slightly accented, English. Kitty stood speechless.

'One for you,' Raphael smiled placing a plate of food in front of Mrs Smeaton. 'And one for you,' he smiled again, handing one to Ying, who thanked him profusely, almost gushing. Then he noticed Kitty in the doorway. Gathering a tray off the side counter he walked towards her. 'And one for you Miss May,' he breathed, kissing Kitty all too briefly on the lips, ensuring Mrs Smeaton could not see.

Kitty moved aside, allowing Raphael back into her room. She shut the door behind him and took a seat next to the tray which he had placed on her bed. There were two glasses of what smelt like orange juice, a small bunch of blush peonies and a tea pot with one cup. She grinned, she had always thought he was not much of a tea man. Then there was a plate of French toast covered in blueberries, banana slices and raspberries, a smattering of chopped almonds dusted with icing sugar and a small jug of maple syrup.

'I wasn't sure how much you liked,' Raphael said casually. 'Kiti?'

'You cooked this?' she asked, having been stunned into silence whilst Raphael had been explaining what he had made.

'Yes,' he beamed.

'Wow. And Ying talks?'

'Mrs Smeaton seemed a little surprised by that too. Is she usually quiet or something?'

'Yeh, something like that,' Kitty muttered. 'What were you talking about?'

'She's a fan. She actually wants to apply for a job at Daring once her business degree's all done. So tips and stuff for that.'

'She's doing a business degree?'

Raphael cocked his head, confused.

Kitty moved the conversation on. 'Nice apron,' she teased.

'Your landlady insisted. So I didn't ruin my white shirt. I didn't say I'd slept in it.' He smiled crookedly.

'And nice flowers.' She took the small posy to her nose, inhaling the fresh sweet scent.

'Real flowers,' Raphael said.

'So you must like me?'

'Oh no, I like Mrs Smeaton. I just had some left over,' Raphael answered deadpan.

'Well that's good then. Because I'm more a dandelion kinda girl,' Kitty replied with a mischievous smirk, placing the posy back on the tray.

'That's a weed.' Raphael rolled his eyes.

Kitty shrugged, covering the French toast with syrup before forking a portion into her mouth. She was overwhelmed, 'God this is amazing.'

Raphael laughed, 'I'm glad you like it.' Pleased with his offering, for it was one of the few mildly impressive things he could cook, thanks to Pulce and her insatiable sweet tooth.

'What would you like to do today?' he asked, watching Kitty eat.

'I don't mind,' she blinked, helping herself to another portion of food. It really was very good.

'Are you still tired?'

'No,' she lied, worrying he would leave. She sensed the bags she thought she felt under her eyes were a give away. The answering curve of Raphael's lips confirmed her suspicions.

Thinking of sleep, a small pang of sadness crossed her mind. Raphael had nightmares. He had actually turned out to be the worst person to share a single bed with. If the wall hadn't lined one side of the bed she was certain they would have fallen out. She decided against asking him about whatever haunted his dreams. She had promised to start afresh and, in time, he had promised he would tell her the truth. She would be patient. She would keep her promise.

'Outside or inside?'

'Sorry?'

'Outside or inside. Where would you like to spend your day?' Raphael repeated.

Kitty looked to the sunshine, 'Outside.'

'Foreign or domestic?'

'We have two…' She looked at her watch which she had left on the bedside table, '…one and a half days.'

'Plenty of time,' Raphael shrugged.

285

Before Kitty could answer, her phone started ringing. Looking at the caller ID she groaned. 'Sorry,' she mouthed.

Kitty was not on the phone for very long, but Raphael saw in her expression that whoever it was, his grand ideas of a weekend in Paris, Copenhagen or Berlin were about to be swiftly cut short.

'Who was it?' he asked when Kitty hung up.

Kitty moaned, flopping onto her pillows.

Raphael placed the tray of now empty crockery on the floor.

'You're not going to like it,' Kitty groaned, her face still hidden her pillows.

'Try me?' Raphael replied, already suspecting she would be correct.

Kitty sat up, 'It was Jaz wondering where I am.'

'Where should you be?'

'In Holloway, getting ready for lunch with her and Freddie's family. They've come up for the day. Sort of a happy Cornwall reunion.' Kitty grimaced, 'They're really just checking on me as I've been a little off the radar.'

'I see.' Raphael had set his jaw, 'Can I see you tonight?'

'I'm afraid not. We're all meant to be staying over.' Kitty knew full well she would be top and tailing with Freddie on Jaz's spare single in her room - she did not share this fact with Raphael, sensing he would take it the wrong way.

'Sunday night?'

'You really want to?'

'Yes. Thanks to the sunflower kid, I realise I have a lot of work to do to improve employee satisfaction.'

'Oh is that what this is all about?'

286

'Of course,' he teased. He moved closer to Kitty, 'How am I doing?'

Kitty watched him warily. She shrugged her shoulders, 'Alright I guess.'

Raphael nodded. He picked up her hand which was resting on the duvet and kissed it very softly, 'Now?'

'Meh,' she shrugged again.

Leaning forward he brushed his lips along her collar bone and laid a trail of hot kisses all the way up to her ear. A small murmur escaped her.

'And now?' he whispered, nipping at her ear.

'Average,' Kitty teased, forcing the word out in contradiction to the happy sensation filling her belly.

With that, Raphael locked his arms around Kitty's waist and pulled her down on top of him, rolling so that she was pinned beneath him. He eyed her laughing face, her eyes beautifully creased and her mouth coy.

'Can I kiss you?' he asked.

Kitty nodded, laughing.

He smiled before silencing her peels with his kisses.

TWENTY-ONE

The man re-fastened the insect screen behind him. The Caribbean excuse for locks always made him smile. It had been so simple to find Hayes. Painfully simple. *Boringly so*, he thought as he made his way across the tiny kitchen. He had hoped for a chase. He had hoped Hayes would have at least recognised him.

The old, white-washed wooden floor boards creaked beneath his steps as he stroked his gloved hands along the countertops. Opening each cupboard one by one he pulled their contents out onto the floor.

The ceramic crockery clattered and tumbled to the ground. Smashed pieces of pot and plate flew in every direction. *It would probably look like a robbery,* the man considered as he found a stack of blue glasses and began to hurl them across the kitchen into the adjoining living room like throwing darts. He watched gleefully as cascades of transparent shards exploded like little fireworks as each cup hit its mark. One smashed into the small television screen, leaving behind a fizzling crack. *Until they found the body,* he added this time removing a whole draw of cutlery and chucking the contents onto the kitchen table.

He stood for a minute, carefully rummaging through the stack of metal implements until he found a sharp cerated steak knife. Pleased with his choice, for he had always favoured blades over bullets, the man began to search the house. It comprised of only the living space he had just destroyed, two small bedrooms and an even smaller, badly dated mosaic tiled bathroom, so it wouldn't take him long.

He was surprised that Hayes hadn't run at him the moment he had entered the house. That's what he would have done. He wouldn't allow himself to be caught like a rat in a trap. Be hunted so shamelessly. But he was glad Hayes obviously did.

Finishing his checks of the bathroom, the man peeled back the soap stained shower curtain, revealing yet more mosaic tiles. A row of yellow rubber ducks with painted faces smiled up at him from the rim of the bathtub. The smaller of the two bedrooms, the one he had just finished methodically checking, had clearly belonged to a child with its single bed and dangling mobile of sea creatures akin to those he now stared down at. Balancing the smallest of the ducks in his leather clad fingers, the man twisted the creature around.

A sudden clattering from the bedroom at the back of the house answered why he hadn't found Hayes so far. The man smiled. Dropping the duck where he stood, he stalked into the bedroom, the steak knife ready at his side.

Reaching the doorway at the end of the corridor, the man stopped stock still and surveyed the scene that now presented before him. Something was wrong. The double bed, with its unmade, coral floral sheets dominated the space. Down one side a row of slatted wooden wardrobes lined the wall and on the other a small speckled mirror hung, below which a shelf was littered with women's products, a hairbrush, some makeup, a used case of contact lenses, and a packet of half-used contraceptive pills. But what had drawn the man's attention the moment he had entered the space still dominated his now racing thoughts. At the far wall, laughing at him, the previously locked window hung wide open. Its shutters clattered against the back wall of the house. The storm had arrived and the wind was now rushing in, causing the curtains to flap distressed, their pink hue reminding him of a great flapping tongue. Yelling in frustration, the man raced back to the front door. How could he have let this happen?

* * *

Hayes lay crunched, barely breathing, hidden under a pile of clothes inside the cupboard. His chest heaved as he clutched at his pounding heart. He was still in a state of shock. He couldn't believe Caneel's plan had actually worked. He had been wrong about being alone. Caneel had been home already, sleeping like a baby nestled under the duvet. He had woken her with his hand clasped over her mouth and, as he had heard his pursuer destroying the kitchen, she had hidden him before escaping out the back window.

It had been about ten minutes since Hayes had heard the insect screen clatter for the second time that evening and he had waited in silence, hearing nothing but the howling wind since. He was definitely alone this time. Caneel would be at a friends. Now all he needed to do was get out.

Trying to steady his ragged breathing, Hayes wriggled out from under the pile of clothes and made his way silently out of the cupboard. He listened with each step. If he wasn't alone this time he would have no choice but to run - something he knew he was poorly equipped for. With each step toward the kitchen Hayes listened and with each step he was gratefully answered with a calming silence. An invisible weight that had been pushing down on his chest began to lift as he made his way into the kitchen.

A sad crunch made Hayes jump. Looking down at his feet he saw the broken remains of the water jug Caneel's mother had given her. He had stepped on its now detached palm embellished handle.

Gazing down at the mess, momentarily stuck, something out of the corner of his eye gleamed in the dark room. His head snapped into action, following the movement.

Hayes' vision blurred. The thumping returned to his ears and he struggled to draw breath. A few paces in front of him the man from the safari. Not the one who he had thought had been following him, but the one with whom Hayes had disembarked. He was seated, twisting a steak knife slowly, gloatingly, between his gloved fingers. Now he recognised the man. Now he remembered exactly who he was and he did not live five houses down.

'Why?' Hayes asked. His voice barely a whisper. His knees wobbled again, threatening to crumble under his own weight.

'Time to pray old man,' his killer responded rising from the sofa. A sickly grin spread wide across his face.

TWENTY-TWO

'I'm gonna get seriously fat if I spend too many meals with you,' Kitty said. A fresh plate of eggs and bacon, avocado toast and a whole selection of intricately decorated French pastries, the creation of the in-house chefs this time, for Raphael had only just come downstairs, lay enticingly before her.

The pair had spent Sunday evening after Kitty had returned from her Holloway weekend curled up on the sofa. And then again curled up in bed together, after Kitty had indulged in a long, hot bubble bath. Raphael had slept in his boxers only this time and seeing his body, Kitty had used all of her willpower to not cave on her no sex before trust rule. A rule she still believed in, but one which was already proving to be difficult to stick to. Intellectually,

Raphael was appealing. Physically he was a whole other level altogether. Combined, he was practically irresistible.

He smelled deliciously fresh as he kissed her on the cheek, his hair damp from his morning shower. He picked up a croissant as he sat beside her.

'You look very pleased with yourself,' she observed.

'I am,' he replied smugly.

'Care to elaborate?'

'No.' He flashed a quick smile, 'It's my turn to ask the questions this week.'

'This whole week?' Kitty moaned.

'You agreed so there's no use sulking,' he teased.

Kitty vaguely remembered something along those lines. But her memories were rather crowded by Raphael's teasing kisses, a tactic he had discovered was particularly useful in getting her to agree to things.

She blushed thinking of the night before. It was truly a miracle they hadn't had sex. She was pleased with her self control - less pleased it had not extended to protecting her from agreeing to stupid things. She still didn't want to elaborate on the sorry state of her non-existent family. It had taken Kitty her whole life so far to fill the cracks left behind by being abandoned. And now, wanting desperately to impress for the first time in her life, instead of filled, the cracks felt barely papered over. He won't want me when he finds out. The most she had shared with Raphael so far resembled a little more like a highlight reel. In short, the first seven years of her life, the time with her father, the only time she hadn't been alone and her stories of all the incredible things he had done in the name of justice.

'Are you still sulking?' Raphael grinned, misjudging Kitty's downhearted expression.

'No,' she pouted dramatically, correcting her features for fear he might actually ask the true cause of her distress.

'Good. Now I'd love to begin my interrogation, but we might want to head in to work soon.'

Kitty looked at her watch and jumped up from the table, 'Shit. Raphael! It's quarter to ten already.'

Raphael laughed. Finishing the last bit of his croissant he rose from the table, 'I was all for ditching but—'

'Yeh *you* can.'

'Rilassati. Relax. I already had Natalie email Hugo to say we had a mentor mentee meeting in HR this morning. So you don't need to worry about us walking in together late.'

'Thank you,' Kitty sighed, grateful she would not have to construct an excuse on her own.

'No one is expecting you to appear till later. So you can sit. And finish eating.'

Pushing lightly on Kitty's shoulders Raphael returned her to her chair. He walked to leave the room.

'Where are you going?'

Raphael laughed, 'I've got to make a call. Some of us actually take our jobs quite seriously.' He winked before disappearing out of the room.

Raphael's call ended up lasting the whole way into the atrium of the Daring Headquarters. Hanging up he turned to Kitty, who was selecting their floor in the lift.

'Should've ditched,' he breathed, tucking a piece of hair that had fallen across Kitty's face behind her ear.

'Good morning Mr Daring,' a jovial voice bellowed, forcing the lift open.

Raphael removed his hand. Kitty did not recognise the man. Belly burgeoning over his trousers. It jiggled as he shook Raphael's hand excitedly.

'Four,' he called to Kitty.

She nodded back. She was pretty sure she saw Raphael sigh as she turned to press the button for the unnamed gentleman.

The man spoke animatedly at Raphael until his stop, where another employee entered. Equally excited to be sharing the lift with the elusive CEO, this one filled the rest of the time. This employee was meeting with Hugo and so stayed with the pair all the way to their stop. This one also ignored Kitty. Something she was actually quite grateful for, her mind preparing to be professional once again with Raphael. She did not want to slip up. Besides, now back at Daring, thoughts of Elliot had weaselled their way in and she knew she was going to have to make some serious decisions.

As the lift doors pinged open, Kitty saw that the seating area was empty, no doubt because the morning meetings were well and truly underway. The woman, who had been travelling with them, bid Raphael farewell as soon as they arrived and hurried off to find Hugo. There was only one figure, conversing animatedly with Georgia at the desk, whom Kitty did not recognise. Natalie, knowing better than to be caught gawking a second time, nodded formally at Raphael, her face remained politely impassive.

Catching the nod out of the corner of his eye, the man turned. Thanking Georgia for her company, he walked with a lopsided limp straight toward Raphael and shook his hand firmly. Kitty tried to skirt past him but he introduced himself. Stopping her in her path and taking her hand.

'Hi, I'm Alec.'

'Kitty,' she replied, looking to see how Raphael would react. He seemed fine. 'A pleasure to meet you,' she added.

'Trust me.' He flashed a quick glance at Raphael, before returning to her, 'The pleasure's all mine.'

He beamed, as though she were some long lost friend, returned at last.

Interrupting his appraisal, Raphael spoke, 'Is this a social visit, Alec?'

'I was just in the area.' He turned to Kitty, 'I'm Turtle's one and only friend. We were in the Army together.'

If Raphael had not known Alec as well as he did, he would have certainly fallen for his affectation of casual friendliness, but Raphael could see his friend was tired and, despite his warm greeting, something didn't feel right.

'Kiti…' Raphael began.

But Kitty didn't need to be asked, she could see the questions in Raphael's eyes and she knew they weren't for her.

'I'll leave you both to it. Nice to meet you. Have fun… Turtle,' she teased.

Raphael rolled his eyes, knowing he was going to have to explain that one.

Shutting the door to his office behind him, Raphael turned to his friend, 'In the area?'

'Not as such.'

There was no pretence at friendliness now. The air had cooled around them.

'What's going on, Alec?'

297

'A man's been killed,' Alec spoke slowly, staring intently at Raphael.

'Why are you bringing this to me?'

Alec didn't answer.

'Where?' Raphael pushed.

Still no response.

'Alec? Where?' Raphael growled, he was getting frustrated.

'British Virgin Islands… Tortola.'

Now it all made sense, 'And you think I did it…Or ordered it?'

'Did you?'

'My God.' Raphael turned away from his friend, aghast.

'Rafa. I need to know.'

'So that's what you think of me?'

'Not me. But my boss… let's just say she's got less faith.'

'So you found a job then?' Raphael made his way over to his desk and took a seat.

'I'm giving you a heads-up, Rafa. The NCA is coming for you.'

'Those bastards have been coming for me my whole life. I had nothing to do with this.'

'Did your family?' Alec began walking towards the desk.

'No.'

Alec raised his eyebrows questioningly.

'No… I would know.' Raphael countered the unspoken doubt. He knew there was no point pretending to his oldest friend, a friend who he knew was in possession of more information than he was letting on. If Alec was working on a case for the NCA, he would now know not just more, but a lot more, about Raphael's past. Raphael thought of their last trip to the Falcon, wondering if he should have been more honest.

'This was no murder or robbery gone wrong Raf. This was an execution,' Alec continued, drawing Raphael's attention back into the room. He carefully laid out a series of graphic photos on his desk. 'The victim,' Alec said putting another photo down. 'Andre Hayes. Sixty-two. PWC accountant for ten years. Daring accountant for the last thirty. One of your father's hirings. Two years ago relocated to Tortola. He retired six days ago after leaving his job, according to a source, at Inveniam Viam.'

Raphael looked back, his expression blank, not reflecting his feelings inside.

Inveniam Viam, or IV, was a shell company that had its official seat in the offshore haven of Tortola in the British Virgin Islands. Existing exclusively as a name on paper, no office and no employees, it covered a consortium of international trusts and other asset managers who all spent their days investing in natural resources throughout the mining industry. Raphael had set up the company as a way to remove the inherited illegal contracts that had infiltrated every layer of the Daring Corporation. He had reorganised the trafficking and smuggling contracts that previously went through the Daring Transportation networks and instead had hidden them, and the associated clients, amongst the obscure structure of the consortium. Over the last two years, the consortium had successfully functioned as an elite money laundering service. Transforming money from Daring's old roster of clients into legitimate financial instruments, through minerals future contracts, or even commodities in the form of stockpiles. Today, Inveniam Viam's assets under management included multiple highly lucrative coltan mines in Eastern Colombia and also the Democratic Republic of Congo. In the two years since its inception, Raphael had worked hard to pay back debts owed to various clients who had helped Daring grow. It was to be Raphael's way out. At least until today that had been the plan.

'Your boss is surely going to be wondering where you are, Alec?' Raphael gathered the photos without so much of a second glance and handed them back.

'I'm just trying to give you a heads-up, mate. I owe you my life. I officially sign on tomorrow. This is the last one I can give you. They *are* going to investigate the consortium, Raf,' Alec pressed.

'Let them,' Raphael stated matter-of-factly, shrugging his shoulders.

'And when they find a solid link, the NCA will investigate Daring.'

'There wont be one,' Raphael said firmly, as he showed Alec to the door.

Alec bowed his head as he left the office. After the three briefings he had already sat through from his new boss at the NCA, Alec was under no illusions as to the kind of family Daring was and he knew, without a shadow of a doubt, he and Raphael were about to find themselves on opposite sides of a war.

Alone now, Raphael slammed his hands down on his desk. The heavy frame shuddered under the force. He was sure the NCA had something. Alec wouldn't have come unless they already had a link or at least something to go on. It was too big a bluff with too great a risk if they didn't. With the gory images of what had remained of Hayes' face burned into his mind he knew the first job was to find out what had happened to his most trusted accountant. As far as Raphael was aware, the man hadn't retired. The confusing fact added to his deepening disquiet.

Having reached Luca on his second attempted call, his brother was now on his way, but Raphael could not get hold of his uncle. Trying to calm his frustrations, he called Natalie from his desk. She answered on the first ring.

'Natalie. Get Mr Ossani in my office now.'

'Yes sir of course. Which Ossani would you like?'

'My uncle,' he clarified, 'Nero.'

Twenty minutes later, with his schedule cleared for the day, Raphael found himself standing in his office. His brother stood in front of him and his uncle slouched on one of his sofas - he hadn't enjoyed being summoned. Raphael had contemplated since phoning them how much he was going to divulge and had settled on the basic truth.

'The NCA is about to start an investigation into the BVI consortium and apparently…' He took a deep breath, 'Apparently they think they can link it to Daring.'

'Who told you that?' Nero asked.

'A source.'

'A source?' Nero queried.

'That's what I said Uncle.'

The two men scowled at one another across the room. Raphael knew better than to bring Alec's existence into Nero's awareness.

'What do they have?' Luca interrupted looking between the two men.

'I don't know.' Raphael turned to his brother.

'So worse case?'

'Seriously Luca?' Raphael shook his head.

'Fine,' Luca snarled. 'Most likely outcome?'

'Hard to say. If they link the subsidiaries, they could search and seize some of the IV containers. It would halt business, cause a few interruptions. They would find some coltan, but by that stage in the line it should be perfectly legal. In truth, I'm not sure it's minerals they're looking for. The consortium structure's impenetrable. The clients, including ourselves, unaccountable and unlinkable.'

Luca, having listened to his brother, turned to his uncle, unsure of why he wasn't saying anything.

Out of the corner of his eye, Raphael caught a subtle shake of Nero's head. He turned his gaze hard on Luca. His brother would break first.

'Umm...' Luca fumbled. 'Actually, we may have a problem if they do that.'

'If they do what, brother?' Raphael snarled.

'Search the containers.'

'Why?'

'A few of the shipping routes have been...' Luca looked to Nero again, '...borrowed.'

'Borrowed for what?'

'A Daring client.'

'And what did this client want to transport?'

Raphael was being unusually polite. His voice had taken on a silken quality. Luca knew his brother's veneer of control was about to fail. 'A small amount of cocaine.' He looked up, seeking absolution.

Raphael launched himself at Luca. Taking his brother by surprise, he forced him up against the glass windows. Pushing against his shoulders, Luca's head collided into the pane with a hard smack.

Nero stood at the sound and made his way over to the windows, 'I was handling it.' He did not raise his voice.

'Not very well.' Raphael let go of Luca who darted out of his reach.

Returning to his desk, Raphael slumped into the chair. *What was I thinking with Kiti? How was I still so naive?* These questions swirled around his head as the stark realisation settled within him. He was never going to escape this. Looking into his lap he spoke very quietly, 'Stop the deal.'

'I can't do that,' Nero answered.

'You mean you won't do that.' Raphael looked up, 'Tell me Uncle. What was the point in us shutting down all of the illegal activity in Daring if you would risk everything by re-mixing the two?'

'You created a whole new criminal enterprise,' Luca added unhelpfully, still smarting from being jumped.

'To pay off a debt,' Raphael growled. His brother had never been able to see the bigger picture.

'That is not how this works, Raphael,' Nero lectured.

'Because you won't let it.'

'You shame your family with your concern,' Nero said.

Raphael took a long deep breath. He couldn't fight every war at the same time. 'I need to find out who killed Hayes.' Raphael stood making his way to the door.

'*We* need to,' Luca said standing up.

'No, Luca, I'll do it. I want answers not bodies.'

Nero smiled, 'Perhaps we'll get both.'

Raphael rounded on his uncle. Seeing the glint in Nero's eyes, Raphael felt the same toxic cocktail of shame and despair that had marred his entire childhood.

'Raphael I just…' Kitty began as she entered the office, looking down at a stack of papers in her hands.

'Get out!' Raphael growled. The command had burst out of him before he had even turned around.

'Excuse me?' Kitty questioned confused. Looking up, she now saw Luca and another gentlemen. The three men looked very tense and she realised, despite the fact that Raphael was meant to be free, he was obviously otherwise engaged. Perhaps a normal response would have been to run as far away from these faces as possible. But Raphael's rude manners had stirred Kitty's anger. She did not appreciate the disrespect. She did not leave and instead went to open her mouth again, 'What did you just say?'

'Get. Out.' Raphael stared her down.

A hotness began to prick in Kitty's eyes, 'What the hell is wrong with you?' Kitty was not sure if she had the energy for a showdown and instead decided to stalk from the room without another word. 'If he wants to play it like that,' she muttered under her breath.

Elliot had called asking to meet. She had been about to decline but now strode forcefully toward the lifts.

Back in the office, Raphael hadn't moved.

'So that's the girlfriend?' Nero asked. 'Or wait is it the graduate intern?'

Raphael glared at his brother.

'I didn't say anything,' Luca insisted.

'She's got nothing to do with anything,' Raphael spat back at Nero, 'Including you.'

Elliot waited until Kitty had shut the car door before he began his tirade, 'This is what happened while you were fucking 'im,' he fumed, his face set in a deep scowl, throwing a set of photos down onto Kitty's lap,

She picked them up. At first, having never seen anything like this before, she wasn't sure what it was she was looking at. Then she noticed something that distinctly resembled a human eye and she realised she was looking at a man's face - or what was left of it. Bile rose in her throat and she began to retch.

'What are you talking about?' she asked, breathing deeply through her nose.

'Ask your boyfriend about Andre Hayes.'

'Is this Andre Hayes?' Kitty asked looking down at the photos in her lap.

'Ask 'im,' Elliot spat pointing out the black tinted glass to where Raphael was making his way out of the Daring building.

Raphael was scanning the road looking for Wilson when he saw Kitty climbing out of a dark tinted BMW X5. Just before she shut the door Raphael caught a glimpse of the man she had been visiting, and he knew straight away that his problems were about to get a whole lot worse.

Ignoring Kitty's questions, Raphael led her by the arm back into the safety of the Daring Offices. Still in silence he led her past reception and into one of the Georgian style meeting rooms on the front of the building. Hugo and another Daring employee, whose face was familiar to Raphael but whose name had escaped him, looked up from the large oval table, around which a meeting had just concluded. The two men had been speaking very close, leaning in until their two bodies had almost merged, Kitty thought Hugo had been holding the other man by his collar, but they had adjusted so fast she was not certain. A deep frown marked Hugo's brow as he looked up, but he corrected his features as soon as he registered the intruder was Raphael.

'Hugo. We need the room,' Raphael said. Kitty had fallen silent beside him.

She refrained from speaking again until they were alone.

'Who's Andre Hayes?' she picked up the unanswered question.

'Kiti…' Raphael raised a hand in warning, before running it through his hair.

'Who. Is. Andre. Hayes?'

Raphael looked down at her. Her eyes were wide and her face confused. 'You're in way over your head.'

'Did you do it?'

Raphael's mouth dropped opened. Then he clenched his jaw before speaking. His fist balled as his expression cooled to stone, 'Elaborate. Please. Do you mean before or after breakfast this morning?' he spat acidly.

'Oh my God.' Kitty shook her head, 'Tell me you don't know who he is.'

'I can't do that.'

'We're done.' Kitty turned to the door, shaking with adrenaline. She would not let him see her tears.

Raphael called after her, 'You know Kiti, maybe if you stopped judging me and my family for a second, you'd see that your own isn't so perfect.'

306

Kiti spun around. Her expression furious, 'How dare you?'

'Me? You just accused me of something much worse.'

'Don't you dare turn this back on me.'

'Kiti. Your father wasn't the white knight you think he was and Elliot—'

'I can't believe you're even suggesting—' Kitty began exasperated.

'Elliot is using you. Everything is personal for him.' Raphael took a step toward Kitty, 'Kiti, please. You're in way over your head. You don't know what—'

'You piece of shit.' Kitty's voice broke on the last note.

Raphael stopped walking. He stared into her face looking for some way to get through to her, 'I'm begging you. Don't get involved.'

'I'm only going to ask you this one more time. Did you know Andre Hayes?'

'Yes.'

'Then we're done.' Kitty stalked from the room. There was no going back.

Raphael said nothing, consumed by the the sight of Kitty's retreating back as she left the room, allowing a surge of regret to sweep his body. But it was not only pride that stopped him going after her. It was the knowledge that she may have been wrong about Hayes, but she was right about him. He should never have let her in.

TWENTY-THREE

Kitty sat, rocking almost imperceptibly, perched on the edge of a tan leather armchair. Her left foot tapped softly against the hard floor as she stirred a mug of freshly brewed coffee. The small spiral repetitions provided a surprisingly soothing balm and so she kept going, stirring now as though her life depended on it, watching the milk lighten the small whirlpool of scalding dark liquid with a determined focus.

Kitty didn't like coffee at the best of times and she certainly didn't like the gesture that this one had been given with. One of apology. A consolation. Sympathy. Kitty locked her jaw, her teeth pushing hard against one another. She stood in no need of sympathy. Certainly not from Lucille, and she didn't need any consoling either for that matter. She just needed to finish what she had started. This she knew clear as the ugly crystal paperweight that sat on Lucille's desk. Hideous thing.

Kitty could feel Lucille's concerned eyes studying her from across the room. Their restless scanning, now becoming quite irritating, had not let up since the moment Kitty had been summoned to the HR department, after having endured an awkward and rather unexpected meeting with Hugo.

During this meeting, a hastily organised, hush-toned conversation in the first available board room, Kitty had been informed that she had been reassigned to a different department "in dire need of help." She remembered his phraseology. Hugo was a poor actor, the words were not his own and she had struggled to understand his mumbles, but she had believed him when he had expressed his displeasure at her transfer. Since returning from his time off, Hugo had been overall markedly less cantankerous. In moments she had thought he had almost been verging on smug, about what she had not been able to ascertain. He had been keen to ensure she was under no illusions that it had somehow been his call. Regardless of whether Hugo had played a part or not, Kitty had left their meeting certain of two things. One, whichever Daring department she was off too wasn't in "*dire need*" of anything, and two, she would not require more than a single guess to ascertain whose desires were behind her sudden relocation. Not that she had asked for confirmation on either point. Lucille had been prickling with discomfort throughout the whole ordeal, and she hadn't wanted to add to it. That, and Kitty hadn't been entirely sure her own resilience could handle the facts she suspected to be true. Her father had told her on more than one occasion during their time together, guidance which Burt too had later adopted: "*Don't ask a question unless you're ready and willing to hear the answer.*" She hadn't been ready for that one. She bit her lip, ceasing her restless foot tapping. She still wasn't ready. After all suspicions could be wrong - hypothetically of course.

Kitty caught the teaspoon against the side of the mug. A high-pitched tinkling pierced the quiet space, briefly adding the attention of two other HR personnel on top of Lucille's continuing study. Ignoring her expanded audience, keeping her gaze fixed on the small brown whirlpool, Kitty tried to focus on her breathing. She wondered how much longer she would be forced to wait and, vaguely, she considered how much longer she could continue to stir the coffee before she would be forced to take a conciliatory sip. Her nose wrinkled in anticipation.

Three days had passed since her and Raphael's argument about the gruesomely faceless Andre Hayes. She had not seen nor heard from him since. A not inconsiderable part of her had expected him to appear at the Duplex on Coldharbour Lane one night with some semblance of an apology. But despite this, and the fragile hope for some form of reconciliation between the pair - a notion which to Kitty had become like a flower that had unexpectedly bloomed before a late winter frost. Kitty was, now time had passed, mostly grateful he had stayed away.

She told herself it was because it would make everything easier, his absence and apparent lack of remorse allowing her to finally do the right thing. To do what he surely deserved. But, at night when she lay alone, huddled under the duvet which had become a fort sheltering her from Ying's incessant questioning - something which had not let up since Raphael's impromptu sleepover - Kitty was painfully aware it was his slandering of her father that hurt the most. During the attack on the one part of her life she was proud of, Kitty had seen a part of Raphael that she wished wasn't there. Something cruel. And no fortress seemed capable of keeping this knowledge out. Mrs Smeaton had thankfully been much more discreet about his absence.

'Grazie, Lucille.'

The words shot Kitty like a bullet and she looked up, startled by the sudden voice. Having retreated into the mess of her tangled memories she had not noticed anyone enter the office space. Looking in the direction of the new arrival, a moment of recognition centred her mind, grounding her in the present. Walking towards her was the man who had been with Raphael and Luciano in the CEO's office three days earlier, when she had unintentionally interrupted their tense meeting. Fleetingly, she wondered what their gathering had been about.

Kitty stood, setting the untasted coffee down on the table before her. She smoothed the creases from her pencil skirt in preparation for the act of contrition she would surely have to feign in recompense for her disrespectful manners towards the CEO that day. Kitty had wondered how long she could continue to avoid all repercussions for her workplace attitude. It was something which Daring openly prided itself on, and something that Lucille had insisted upon since the graduates' very first day. "*Manners people. Manners. Non-negotiable and here, if found*

311

lacking, can be a sackable offence." She must have heard this a dozen times by now.

The man however did not begin to scold Kitty, but instead smiled as he positioned himself in front of her. He had stopped further back than normal, leaving a good few feet of empty, uneasy space. Kitty assessed his expression. It was not as friendly as she had initially thought, her judgement having been clouded by the relief which had accompanied the apparent absence of a reprimand. In fact, on closer inspection the smile was really more of a sneer. Like a crocodile's. It did not touch his eyes nor was it present in his cheeks, which remained flatly impassive. Just teeth.

'Can I help you?' Kitty asked. The question had meant to come out as unconsidered civility, but instead she heard in her tone a stale irritation, as though his mere presence had caused her some deep, personal offence. On hearing her confrontational inflection, Kitty inwardly cringed. She had never managed to fully control her temper. Never a poker player and, true to form, her manners evinced her hidden feelings. Feelings she would rather not wear on display for the sneering man nor her audience, which had once more swelled to three, to judge.

Nero's smile widened. The young woman was feisty. He could acknowledge the appeal of that. He let her comment sit awkwardly, hanging as though caught on some invisible line between the pair. He relished the discomfort of others, when they had revealed too much and were left floundering in their honesty. Exposed. Vulnerable. He savoured the atmosphere. Wondering how easily the young woman would turn her attentions to him as she had clearly done for Raphael. Women were all the same when your were as rich as he was. Easy. The few who weren't, weren't worth the hassle. Surely his nephew had not been caught by the latter type? Out of the corner of his eye, Nero saw the annoyingly eager woman from HR making her way over to them, obviously thinking, as all the HR staff seemed too, that he somehow needed her help. Vexed at having to break the swollen silence, he spoke first. 'Cleopatra,' Nero mouthed slowly.

Lucille, apparently satisfied by his communications abilities, returned to her perch.

'Just Kitty,' Kitty replied coldly.

'You're going to be joining my team for a while.'

'That being?' Kitty still sounded rude, but now her tone was not solely down to her earlier inner struggles. The sneering man made her skin crawl. Everything about him suggested he enjoyed the power of whatever position he held. Arrogance rolled off him like thunder after a lightning strike.

'I'm amazed you got the job not knowing such a basic fact... Cleopatra,' Nero tutted.

Kitty remained silent, pulling her face into a tight-lipped smile. She would wait him out.

After a minute's silence, on seeing Lucille standing once more out of the corner of his eye, Nero begrudgingly spoke first, 'My name is Nero Ossani. I'm the Vice President.' He waited for Lucille to take her seat again, annoyed he had lost the waiting game. *The first of many,* he comforted himself, before adding snidely, 'I'm also the uncle of your boyfriend.'

'He's not my boyfriend,' Kitty snarled.

'I didn't think so,' Nero replied, the timbre of his voice drowned with contempt. The crocodile smile fixed back on his face. 'This way,' he ordered, turning to leave the room.

Kitty followed Nero from Lucille's office as he led the way to a part of the Daring building she had never ventured into. He did not look back at her once, nor did they exchange a single word the entire journey, so she had ample time to assess the man who claimed to be Raphael's uncle as they navigated the endless Daring corridors.

Kitty had been surprised by that admission, for despite the man's overwhelmingly distasteful manner, something Lucille seemed ignorant of, there was nothing particularly remarkable about the man. He was physically a little shorter and not as muscled as Raphael and certainly not his brother. Nor did he possess any of their grace of movement. Quite the opposite, Nero walked as though having survived a lifetime of surprise attacks, skulking, lizard-like. He appeared to be seeking out corners of rooms and shadows, always protecting the still unusually large distance between them. Even allowing for his superior age, highlighted by the grey streaks lining his heavily oiled black hair, little resembled his nephews. Having given Ossani as his surname, Kitty assumed he must be Raphael's mother's brother, which fitted his heavy Italian accent. But from the one picture she had seen, Isabella had been given all the beauty in the lottery of genetics.

Nero's office sat in stark contrast to Raphael's. Dark panelled, the air was permeated by the bitter fetor of cigarette smoke at war with the sickly, vanilla fragrance of a carefully concealed reed diffuser - no doubt an HR dictate. Five taciturn employees, none of whom were introduced to Kitty, sat busying themselves on their computers outside. Their desks bereft of the usual personal clutter that revealed to new joiners a little about the human within the worker. Inside the furniture was principally antiquated. The only similarity she found was a collection of large, gilded oil paintings not dissimilar to the classical, architectural pieces that furnished the walls of CEO's office many floors above. On closer inspection however, Nero's were of a more macabre design.

Kitty turned her attention away from the depictions of spear wielding cavalrymen and severed limbs, noticing a small desk that had been tucked behind the door. The cheap folding frame appeared a recent addition. It sat out of place with the rest of the room.

'You will work there.' Nero gestured to the desk Kitty had spied.

Her heart sank. 'In your office? With you?' she asked, poorly concealing her surprise.

'I have nothing to hide,' Nero shrugged. An ugly smile pulled at the corner of his mouth, 'Why? Do you?'

'I'm afraid I'm not that interesting.'

Nero ignored Kitty's comment. 'Some of our clients… some of our particularly private clients' interests are monitored through the small team you saw on your way in. One in particular needs a little more *attention* than most.'

Nero had been becoming increasingly tired of one of his client's voracious requests and was pleased with himself for arranging the appropriation of Kitty. She was so perfectly disposable. An orphan with as minimal collateral as he could have hoped for. A rare feeling of contentment filled him as he looked at her.

'How can I help this client?' Kitty asked, interrupting the silence which once again had become bloated and uncomfortable. It seemed like an odd request for someone in her junior position. Having been given no direct contact, aside from the odd providing of refreshments, with any of the clients who had moved through Raphael's team, this would be a first.

'Well, you may not be all that interesting as you say, but you do speak Russian.'

'I see.'

'Yes.' He responded as though her question and delayed understanding had been somehow excessively naive. Placing a business card face-up on the folding desk, Nero continued in the same tone, 'Call this number. Introduce yourself. Organise whatever they want. You will work to their hours of need now. When you require a desk, use this one. When you don't you're free to leave.'

Kitty sensed an unspoken test concealed within his words, but Nero left the room before she could ask anymore. She settled down, enjoying the relief that had followed his departure, to phone the number on the business card.

The phone conversation lasted less than two minutes. A gentleman by the name of Pavel had answered and, in fluent Russian, provided her with a vague description about an upcoming event his boss wanted organising. The call ended with another, equally vague, assurance that he would be in contact when there was something for her to do.

With no other assigned tasks, and no sign of Nero, Kitty, fastening her coat, decided to begin her own plan of action. One she had been working on the last three nights she had been holed up in the small bedroom on Coldharbour Lane.

* * *

Structurally, the design of the bar on Upper St James Street was exactly how Kitty remembered it from the evening she had spent there two years before with Jaz. It was still a well balanced, sophisticated blend of a vintage gentlemen's club and an Andy Warhol exhibition. Only now the place was deserted. Populated only by the staff readying for the night ahead, it had an entirely different ambience. Devoid of revellers, their chatter and the thumping music, the place felt eerily sterile as Kitty made her way up to the oval shaped, double-sided bar in the centre of the room. That night she had come trusting. On this occasion, her motives were fuelled by an entirely opposite emotion.

Kitty was relieved when she spotted Beto drying glasses behind the bar. She had not been sure how she was going to reach him if he had been elsewhere, without having been forced to contact Jaz - something she was keen to avoid. Kitty was not entirely certain what she had got herself involved in, but whatever it was, or could become, she didn't want Jaz entangled in the fallout. Beto was an unfortunate necessity.

He had once expressed his dislike of the Daring family to Jaz, and now Kitty knew that she needed to hear his reasons for herself. If Beto loved Jaz as much as he professed, he would not have told her half of his suspicions. She hoped Beto would not try and protect her the same way. If she was going to do what Elliot wanted,

317

she had to find out about the Daring family her own way, using the eyes of those she felt she could trust. So Beto was the only option. These questions, even if she was not ready, she knew she had to hear the answers to.

Beto looked up, glass in hand, as Kitty neared the bar, the front door clanging shut behind her having alerted him to her presence. 'Kiti. Ciao.'

'Heya,' she waved.

'Are you here to see me?' Beto asked, glancing over his shoulder.

'Was just running some errands, client stuff, and I thought I'd say hi.'

'Hi,' Beto smiled, placing the clean glass into a cabinet behind him and taking another from the countertop.

'Hi,' Kitty laughed, trying to work out how to start her line of questioning without seeming excessively interrogative.

Before Kitty could find the words to form her questions, which had become frighteningly confused, a middle-aged barmaid appeared at the bottom of the stairs which led to the VIP area. With ashy hair cropped short around her heart-shaped face, and arms straining under the weight of a glittering tray of Dom Pérignon champagne bottles, she frowned as Beto called to her.

'Lara, I'm gonna take ten now ok?' Placing his tea-towel and the wet glass back on the countertop, Beto slipped out from behind the bar.

'Sure,' Lara called back, her frown dissipating on spying Kitty. She smiled curiously from under her pixie crop, 'But make sure it's only ten, B. The rest of the champagne's still out back.'

'Certo. Sure.' Beto turned back to Kitty, 'Will you walk with me?'

'Ok.'

Kitty followed Beto outside. Stepping into the road, her mind already ten paces ahead of her, and mentally having already begun the conversation about the Daring family, she jerked backwards as Beto caught her by the shoulders. He held onto her, his fingers pressing into her arm, until her balance returned and the screaming black cab had passed. The driver hurled profanities out of the half open window before he disappeared around the corner. Kitty could feel Beto's unspoken questions as she slipped out of his grip and strode across the now empty street toward the square, her mind once again racing into the future.

She took a seat beside Beto on one of the wooden benches that were evenly dispersed throughout Golden Square. The stone statue of a long-forgotten king stared unblinking down at them and Kitty pulled her coat tighter around her, averting her gaze from the statue's haughty glare. Fiddling in his pocket Beto pulled out a packet of Marlboro cigarettes. He held the small red and white box out to her.

'Don't smoke,' she responded to his unspoken offer.

Beto opened his mouth to say something, perhaps object, but then, returning the cigarettes unopened to his pocket, just looked at Kitty instead, his expression clouded with hesitation.

Kitty waited. Forcing herself to be patient.

'I don't want to overstep the mark,' Beto eventually began. His voice wavered, exposing his wariness, 'Jaz says you don't like being…umm… told.'

'Really I… Jaz is just—'

'You need to stay away from Raphael Daring.' Beto's voice was stronger now, having quieted some unspoken doubt.

Kitty's mouth popped open. She closed it swiftly. It was not shock at the warning - she had heard it enough times by now. It was that Beto had staked his position so soon, without encouragement. Feeling motivated that the conversation might not be so difficult after all, Kitty opened her mouth to speak.

Beto cut her off again. He began to pick at a scab on his right hand as he spoke, his earlier moment of strength fading with every word, 'How well do you know Raphael Daring?' he asked, his eyes resolutely fixed on the crusted scar.

'Not well.' Kitty couldn't decide this time if she was lying or not.

Beto visibly relaxed. Ignoring the scab he spoke looking at her face, 'But you work for him yeh?'

'Yes. I'm a graduate intern at Daring. I help organise events for him, sometimes take minutes in meetings. That sort of thing.' She didn't propound her recent dismissal from the CEO's office.

'And I make drinks in his bar.' Beto waved casually over his shoulder back in the direction they had just come. 'So *"not well"* like me?'

Kitty, assuming by his comments Beto meant not at all, or at least not in a personal manner, decided to afford the barman a little more honesty this time. She was well aware that unless one of them started opening up, that her investigation was going to make slow progress. 'Maybe a bit better than you,' she conceded.

'I see.' Beto returned to the picking of his scab.

Her honesty had engendered the opposite effect to the one she had desired, so Kitty pushed now, trying to save the outcome of her trip, 'Beto, what is it you want to say? What's so bad about the Daring family? Or Raphael? Or whatever it is?'

Beto looked up. Kitty wondered for whom he felt the concern that was plastered on his face. Her or himself?

'Robert Daring, Raphael's father, married Isabella Ossani,' he began.

'Ok,' Kitty shrugged. 'So?'

'Ossani is not a name you would know.'

Kitty refrained once more from mentioning her encounter with Nero, not wanting to put Beto off his stride.

'Where I come from—'

'Tuscany?'

'Italy,' Beto stressed raising his eyebrows. 'That name carries great significance. The closer you are to Rome the more your mother puts you to bed at night with a warning to never cross an Ossani.'

'Why? What do they do?'

'They're one of the most feared crime families we have.'

'Mafia?'

'Esattamente. Exactly.'

'But Raphael's a Daring?'

'Prendere lucciole per lanterne. You misunderstand. They are one and the same. Kiti...' he sighed, '... you cross a Daring or an Ossani, it's the same people taking your body away in the night. The company you work for...' Beto looked agitatedly around the park. Seemingly encouraged by their lack of company he continued, 'Why do you think it's grown so much in forty years huh? Ossani contacts, Daring money and a reputable business to hide behind.'

Kitty shook her head.

Beto, mistaken this time in thinking she was about to disagree, pressed on, his tone imploring, 'Trust me. Drugs, guns, money laundering, who knows what else? They do the whole lot. Trust me,' he repeated, taking Kitty's hands in his.

Beto, mistaken for the second time, took Kitty's silence to mean disbelief. 'Kiti. I am telling you this because I love Jaz and she loves you.'

'I get that,' she nodded.

'Killers, Kiti.'

'Who?'

'They *all* are.' Beto let go of Kitty's hands and took out a cigarette. He lit it, taking two deep drags, before he spoke again, 'Back in the day the uncle called the shots and Raphael executed the plans. Luciano, he's just a dog on a lease with a serious attitude problem, but as far as anyone knows his bark is much worse than his bite... although, his left hook isn't so tame. If you want a good beating go to Luca. But Raphael is something else entirely.' Beto took another drag, 'Now he's in charge, he's judge, jury and executioner.'

Kitty was beginning to understand just how unready to hear the answers to her questions she really was, but something more immediate was bugging her, holding her focus, 'So why come all the way to London and work for them if they are what you say they are?'

Beto kicked at the gravel path making a small trench in the loose stones. 'I can't afford not too,' he answered not meeting her gaze, instead taking another long drag on the cigarette. The tip flashed orange.

'What do you mean?' Kitty pushed.

'Oi, B! You said ten!' Lara, wearing her frown again, called from the edge of the park, her arms folded across her chest. Beto's time was up.

'What do you mean?' Kitty asked again.

Beto stomped the unfinished cigarette into the ground as he stood up, burying the stub in the small gravel trench, 'Kiti, just trust me,' he pleaded looking from her to Lara and quickly back again.

'Fine,' Kitty placated after a long pause. 'I trust

you.'

With that Beto raced off for his boss.

Kitty looked down into her lap. Without realising, her hands had begun to shake and she watched them now, dancing as though an electric current was moving through them. They didn't stop under observation. Pushing the unwelcome memory of Raphael's warnings, piled with those of Elliot, Jaz and not to mention Beto from her mind, Kitty stood up. She needed to learn everything there was to know about the Ossani family. She needed to educate herself as to whom she was now working for. Raphael had completely vanished. Never having been one to listen to idle gossip, Kitty would make her own mind up about him, but for the first time she found herself entirely grateful for his disappearance and knew she needed to find some answers before he reappeared. His voice rang in her mind,

323

"*I did something unforgivable.*" She shuddered. *How can they all be wrong?*

TWENTY-FOUR

Having sunned themselves aboard their yachts all day, the people in the marina had all retreated inside their vessels with the setting sun and the breeze that had accompanied it.

Raphael let his gaze stretch across the bay, the swash of the water and gentle jangling of the yachts filled his ears. Hundreds of halyards clanging against their masts sounded satisfyingly melodic. There were no signs here of the unseasonably ferocious storm that had passed through the week before, nor of the brutal murder of a soft-mannered accountant a little further around the coast. Life for the rich always moved on. The relentless march of wealth was never too far away. The unstoppable hunt for happiness.

He wondered if anyone had found it? Money hadn't helped him.

Turning his back to the marina, Raphael began to navigate the winding streets. The brightly coloured wood-clad buildings, a rainbow of pinks, blues, greens and oranges all pressed shoulder to shoulder, made it easy for him to orientate himself despite the fading light. Where he was headed now, he had only been once before - two years ago, on the setting up of the consortium.

Legally the consortium had not begun to operate until a later, predetermined date, but the site of operations and the administrator had all been discussed and decided aboard Luca's yacht in the marina Raphael had just left. Raphael had personally overseen every detail of the complex project. It was his way out and he had been very careful to ensure its successful launch and continued survival. The better Inveniam Viam had performed, the more clients he had been able to remove from the Daring roster, and the less crooked palms he had been forced to cross.

Thinking about it, he hadn't been back to the Caribbean since. And thanks to a private jet and some fake passports, Mr Raphael Daring remained yet to return. Perhaps money did sometimes help.

Raphael stopped. Allowing a couple who had unknowingly stumbled into his path, displaying ample portions of burnt peachy skin, to move out of the way. Kissing and laughing they smiled embarrassed on noticing Raphael. He averted his eyes swiftly, waiting for them to round the next corner, before he slipped unseen down an adjacent, narrow road. Here he found what he was seeking.

Sandwiched unassumingly between a scuba-diving trips shop and a yacht charter office, the building's banana yellow shutters made it easy to remember. The hoardings outside, well kept, but not so pristine as to arouse suspicion, advertised yet more boat trips and popular bars in Road Town. Nothing about the location suggested it housed the only physical office for one of the largest money laundering operations in the world.

A bell chimed, announcing his arrival, as Raphael shut the door behind him. A new addition, he noted with vague interest. A woman, previously engrossed in the entertaining of two squawking toddlers, looked up at the sound. She didn't speak, nor make eye contact for longer than the briefest of seconds as she herded the small brood from the room and returned to the flat on the floor above. A television, left on due to her hasty departure, continued to play an endless stream of cartoons, punctuating the still air with comedy shrieks and whistles. A broken fan, encrusted with dust, sat stationary on the window sill. The lobby, empty when Raphael had bought the place, had clearly been seconded by the residents above as extra living quarters. He didn't blame them, and what they did was of no concern to him.

Raphael could hear the dull thudding of footsteps moving about above him as he crossed the cheap linoleum tiles that covered the lobby floor. Reaching the far side he slipped through an archway covered by a curtain of wooden beads and bamboo tubes and made his way into the office beyond. A delicate, pale gecko, disturbed by his appearance, darted up one of the walls, before disappearing behind a mirror. He refrained from switching on the light but Raphael still caught his reflection. He looked away instantly.

The small office was almost empty, semi-illuminated by light leaking through the beaded curtain and the last rays of the low sun sneaking through an open window on the far wall. The desk, as befitting a paperless company, lay neat, with nothing but a cigar and a small monitor on top of it. A fuzzy, grey image of the street outside was being displayed - another new addition.

Making his way behind the desk, Raphael pulled open the drawers. The first was locked. The drawer rattled in position but did not budge when added force was applied. In the second he found a stack of cheap magazines. Faded images of topless girls, cars, motorbikes. The third was empty.

The room was almost exactly as he had remembered it, besides the monitor and the withered body of a sad-looking fern which now decorated the window sill.

Seeing nothing suspicious, Raphael breathed deeply as a fresh gust moved though the open window, ruffling the curtains. On the salted air, he caught a whiff of tobacco. He touched the cigar resting on the desk. It was warm.

A tiny squeak of rubber on linoleum confirmed his suspicions and he spun around following the sound. Plunging his hands into the darkest corner of the office, Raphael grabbed hold of the figure previously concealed in the shadow of an empty bookcase.

It was so dark, the figure was little more than a silhouette as it writhed and struggled under Raphael's grip. He thought he had control when one wrist slipped from his grasp. The silhouette swung wildly at Raphael's face, he dodged but the tip of a knife caught his arm. A sharp sting followed as the blade sliced through his shirt and into the flesh below. Releasing the figure, using his now free hands, Raphael punched into the darkness. His right fist connected with a jaw bone, forcing the attacker's head backwards. Raphael punched again, and this time, grabbing hold of a neck, hurled the figure out from the corner of the room.

The silhouette smashed into the desk and Raphael, using his weight advantage, pinned his attacker onto their back. Once flat, both their faces illuminated by the light leaking through the beaded curtain, the two men stopped, breathing heavily. The knife clattered to the floor followed by a deluge of regret.

Ignoring the flood of incessant apologies, Raphael took the man by his collar and lifted him off the desk.

The man scurried to the wall and flipped on the light, 'I'm so sorry,' he began effusing manically, noticing the bloody stain on Raphael's right arm.

Raphael looked at the cut as well, cursing inaudibly as he studied the wound.

'My wife can sort that,' the man offered, aware his apologies were getting him nowhere.

Raphael nodded without comment.

With a shout, the lady Raphael had disturbed earlier returned. This time without the two small children. Her features were still resolutely arranged in horror, which only grew on seeing the discarded knife, lying bloody on the floor, and the wound it had inflicted.

'She's a nurse,' the man, who had taken to pacing by the sad fern, reassured.

It took about twenty minutes for the woman to organise herself, her eyes flickering between Raphael and her husband the entire time. Carefully threading Raphael's parted skin back together, she cleansed his wound with alcohol. Raphael silently drank the rest.

Where Raphael had punched the man, a ruby bruise was beginning to shine on his jaw and a cut above his eyebrow was weeping steadily. Having finished her stitches, the woman moved to fix her husband's injuries. He ushered her away. His could wait.

'How can I help sir? I did not know you were coming?' The man crossed the floor to stand before Raphael like a schoolboy cowering before their headmaster.

Raphael gestured for the man to take a seat again. Thankfully, he complied without hesitation.

'I said nothing to the police,' the man fretted.

'What is there to say?' Raphael looked from his arm to the man.

'Nothing sir. Nothing to say.' His head was now wagging violently.

Raphael knew very well that the man before him most likely thought that he had ordered the killing of Andre Hayes - or done it himself, 'Tell me what you know instead, Jamar?'

'I know nothing.' Jamar began shaking again, Raphael's use of his name having surprised him.

Raphael sighed, clenching his fists, 'Tell me everything you know.'

This time he wasn't asking.

Jamar knew this. Looking through the beaded archway to the door and back a couple of times, he wondered how fast he still was. He had been a good runner in his youth. Some said an athlete. He wondered whether he could make it - of course he couldn't. He knew he would never get out of the room alive let alone the building. Concluding that he

330

was a dead man either way, Jamar decided to give what was being asked of him. Hoping his compliance would spare his wife and children, whose footsteps were once again painfully audible above him.

'Mr Andre was killed sir. His body was found near Smuggler's Cove, but he was killed somewhere else. They traced it…I can't remember the exact… he retired a few days before.'

'Who knew Hayes was retiring?' Raphael asked.

'No one.'

'You?'

'No sir! Not me.'

'So how do you know now?'

A moment of silence filled the room.

'I got these… from a courier.' Jamar hesitantly moved to unlocked the top drawer of the desk. Sliding out a thin stack of papers from a brown envelope, he handed them to Raphael with the only explanation he had, 'Signed resignation papers.'

'Where was he living?' Raphael asked rifling through the small offering. He knew that Jamar would have no idea who killed Hayes, so he wouldn't waste his time asking. The two had very little to do with one another. Occasionally meeting if something needed to be legally signed off. That was the deal Hayes had taken gladly. Big pay-off to leave Daring. Live tax free in the British Virgin Islands. Raphael knew he would have never retired, for despite what these signatures suggested, Hayes was as good as done already.

For his part, Jamar knew little to nothing about the consortium. He simply fielded calls and delivered whatever Hayes needed. He was a go-between, who never really understood what he was going between, but his involvement, his BVI passport and therefore accompanying birthrights, allowed the consortium to be legally registered in Tortola and obtain all the benefits that came with it. The man didn't even know who Raphael really was, having only met him alongside Hayes and a Dutch lawyer once, their purpose having been established by an "*introducer*" based in Cyprus, Jamar had been led to believe that Raphael was simply the muscle employed to keep the operation running smoothly.

'Where was he living?' Raphael repeated.

'I don't know.' Jamar's face creased in panic. His eyes, straying to the footsteps above, betrayed his primary concern.

'Where were you told to send the letters?'

Jamar hastily scribbled an address on the back of the discarded envelope, quickly followed by another scribble - he had remembered where the newspapers had reported the man had been killed.

'And why didn't you send them?'

'Sorry sir?'

'Why didn't you send the letters?'

The man looked affronted by Raphael's question. 'Mr Andre would have told me in person.'

Having checked the address against one Raphael had listed on his phone, he walked out of the room without a backward glance.

Jamar chased after him, stopping him just before he reached the door to the street, his chest rising and his breathing a rapid stream of audible puffs. 'Is that all?'

'For now,' Raphael replied impassively.

Jamar nodded respectfully as he opened the door, the new bell chiming once more.

Raphael pulled his shirt sleeve back over his arm. The cut was fortunately not so deep. Under the bandage it would heal soon, and the alcohol had temporarily taken the sting out of it. He should have seen that coming and he cursed his stupidity. Snaking back through the lanes in search of a taxi, Raphael passed a row of bars blasting the street with music as a steady stream of painted safaris rumbled along the road hunting for tourists. He adjusted the handgun in the waistband of his trousers. The go-between had been more useful than he had expected.

Having paid the taxi driver enough for the evening, Raphael climbed out of the back seat of the dusty coloured Hyundai, and began walking down a curving street that hugged the forested hillside. Despite money usually paying for silence in these islands, Raphael, out of habit perhaps, had still asked the driver to take him to a slightly different address than the one he was now walking to.

The rumble of the idle engine turning over disappeared as he followed the road bending around the hillside. He checked his phone once more. *It must be about here,* he thought, reading the names fastened to the ornate high gates that had started appearing to his right.

Coming to his destination on the map, Raphael looked around. The hunched body of a man, leaning against the base of a nearby palm, caught his attention.

'Leave our gurlz alooonnne,' the man slurred, adding a smattering of profanities as Raphael approached.

As Raphael neared the figure, the man began taunting him again, at first with words and then by spitting a large globule of saliva that landed at Raphael's feet. Then he spat another. That was the last thing Raphael remembered coming out the man's mouth before he punched him hard in the chest. The man began coughing erratically, wheezing and retching in the stench that arose from the fat joint he had just dropped.

Leaving the stoned figure outside, Raphael entered the address he had for Hayes. Perched high on the hill overlooking Palm Garden Bay, the house was designed as two separate pavilions separated by a kidney-shaped, turquoise-tiled swimming pool. Connected to the secondary structure by a covered, white-washed loggia, the main house was built in the shape of a stretched octagon. Inside, the property had dramatic high ceilings and an open-plan living room which swept around to an expensively equipped kitchen suite. Beyond that, a large mahogany dining table sat unlaid with views stretching out to the horizon. The bedrooms, near identical, with gossamer draped four-poster beds, walk-in wardrobes and marbled ensuite bathrooms, were found in the second pavilion.

Having searched the entire property Raphael felt a simmer of frustration return, not entirely diffused from having punched the druggie outside. The place was decidedly deserted, entirely lacking the objects usually discarded and abandoned after a person's unplanned disappearance. No rotting food in the fridge. No dirty clothes ready for washing. No unfinished book on the bedside table. No medications. No-one was living here and by Raphael's estimate, no-one had for some time.

Unsure of what to do next, Raphael was staring out to the horizon, a perfect indigo line hovering over the dark, calm ocean, when an idea came to him.

'Who's running the girls?' Raphael called, crossing the road.

The pot-smoking man, less high and now more frightened, began shuffling back across the tarmac on seeing him. Raphael had guessed by "*girls*" the man had meant prostitutes, and by the look on the druggies face he had been correct. Looking more closely at the figure, Raphael realised he was little more than a boy.

'Whose running the girls?' he repeated, this time offering a stack of dollars.

'No beef man,' the boy shook his head, refusing the money.

'Why did you say that?'

'I want no beef.'

'No. About the girls?'

A flicker of surprise crossed the boys face, 'Lots of girls service some of the houses up here.'

'This house?' Raphael pointed to the one he had just left.

The boy nodded cautiously.

'Where do they come from?' Raphael began again.

'I mean no beef man.' The boy now stood before him. He was short with the weedy stature commonly found in those who'd rather smoke than exercise.

Raphael sighed. He waited for a second, giving the boy a chance to rethink his strategy. He could feel the alcohol from before in his system, untempered by his empty stomach. The boy made the wrong choice. As he tried to leave, Raphael delivered another blow to his stomach. This time with his knee. He pulled the kick, but the boy still doubled over, falling to the floor, coughing again.

'Jesus!' he yelled in between drools of bile.

Raphael bent down next to him. His voice low and threatening, 'Who. Runs. The girls?'

'I don't know.'

Getting bored, Raphael pulled the pistol from his waistband, and aimed it steadily at the boy's temple.

'I can find out!' the boy shrieked instantly. Pulling out his mobile, he began jamming in a number.

'Don't do anything stupid,' Raphael warned.

The boy showed the screen as he dialled the number, 'My cousin's wife. She has a sister whose friend was smacked about the other day. It's not something they talk about man, but we all know how she got her bruises.'

After a brief conversation. The boy turned back to Raphael, returning the phone to his pocket, 'There's a lady, goes by Cherise. If you head down to the bay, she can be found at Ochan. It's a bar...' He launched into a full and detailed description of the place, hoping to placate his interrogator, '...you won't miss it. Ask for Cherise.'

'Why are you up here?'

'I work down at the bay. Waiter in one of the hotels. I come up to smoke, look at the view.'

'How often?'

'Most nights.'

Engulfed in thought, Raphael began the walk back to the waiting taxi. Annoyed that, at this rate, his trip could easily turn into a bloody goose chase.

TWENTY-FIVE

Having spent the last couple of hours showing Nero's client, a businessman by the name of Vasili Nechayev, around a carefully selected array of event spaces dotted amongst the finest acreage in London, it wasn't until they had arrived at Swarga, a large capacity opulently decorated entertaining space, with adjacent roof terrace possessing uninterrupted views of St Paul's Cathedral and the City beyond, that Kitty witnessed Vasili and his wife display any emotion vaguely resembling impressed.

'Pavel was right. This one will work.' Vasili smiled, his yellowing veneers on full display, 'My wife Irina, she will continue to do business with you. But do it in English, she needs to improve.'

Kitty turned to look at the tall slender woman, bandaged in cashmere, who had been practically silent for the last two hours. 'It will be a pleasure,' she smiled.

'Irina, is it not a pleasure to be working with Miss Kitty?' Vasili pressed. He had noticed her silence too.

Irina looked at her husband, her eyes wide like a rabbit caught in the deathly glare of approaching headlights, 'Of course.'

Her accent was thick, disguising any obvious emotional inflection in her tone, but it wouldn't take a genius to see that her body language was more than uneasy. Kitty wondered if the woman had a fear of heights.

'I hope you like Swarga as much as we do?' Kitty asked.

Irina took a long look around the room they had spent the last twenty minutes observing, 'We raise lot of money I sure,' she offered with a weak smile.

Kitty agreed that the space would be a magnificent venue to host the gala being held for the benefit of Syrian refugees. It was a cause close to Irina's heart - or so her husband had kept insisting. Kitty was not convinced, but whatever the reason for their wanting to host this event, most likely to impress the trust-fund brigade, the venue would be spectacular.

Kitty led the pair back out onto the roof terrace for a final look at the view. She moved carefully, keeping Irina between herself and Vasili whenever possible. She didn't like him. He had a lecherous smile and she had found his pale hands brushing hers too often for coincidence. She would be pleased to work with his wife. Though timid, ewes were easier than rams.

Vasili stood behind Kitty. He liked her. Pert bum. Perfect Russian accent. Like a perfectly spoken doll. Nero was a cold hearted son-of-a-bitch. He wondered about her life as he watched her arse swaying to the lilt of her walk. *Who would miss her if she disappeared? Who would miss him?* His phone began ringing interrupting his train of thought. He walked back inside, closing the glass doors securely behind him before answering the call, well aware that Kitty would be able to understand his every word.

Alone, Kitty turned to Irina, 'Have you done a lot for this charity?'

Irina looked at her, startled again.

Kitty waited patiently before deciding to ask in Russian, 'We can speak in whatever language you would like Mrs Nechayev?'

Irina smiled kindly at this gesture. Thanking Kitty in Russian before adding, also in her native language, 'In fact —'

With the distinctive clang of glass on metal, Vasili reappeared back on the terrace, 'What did I miss?' He spread his arms open. His phone was still in his hand, its screen now dark.

Irina's gaze returned to the ground.

Kitty, taking pity on her, and deciding that there was more than a fear of heights troubling the woman, spoke first, 'Mrs Nechayev was telling me about the charity.' She smiled at Irina, but she wasn't looking.

A dark chuckle broke from Vasili's lips, 'Irina is a *strong* supporter.' He kissed his wife on the cheek. She visibly froze under his touch, but Vasili appeared to ignore her reticence. 'Kitty, we must leave. But Irina would love to have you at the refugee shelter tomorrow. You can see the work the charity does first hand.'

'I would love to.'

'Pavel will email you the details.'

'Great.'

With that Vasili led Irina from the balcony and the two disappeared.

Alone, Kitty leant on the metal railing. She pressed her legs against the cool glass below and looked out over the dome of St Paul's that rose up majestically before her. Wren's lead-clad, timber masterpiece seemed to shimmer in the sunlight as though it were touched by some divine presence.

Kitty had never thought a lot about the existence of a God, but she wondered about one now, as the wind blew through her hair. Grateful the first meeting was over she embraced its freshness.

Ever since Nero had handed her the business card, Kitty had been communicating over the phone with the man named Pavel, trying to get an idea of the sorts of places Vasili had wanted to see and, ascertain what exactly it was that they were trying to host. She had not spoken to Vasili until today, but the relayed messages between herself and his agent had been vague and confusing.

Since their liaisons and her conversation with Beto, Kitty had also begun her research into the Ossani family. The office had been empty ever since Nero had deposited her there, so Kitty had found herself with ample time to trawl the internet for answers. Beto, and Elliot, she had accepted reluctantly, had not been alone in their suspicions.

A myriad of tabloid stories, as well as public court documents, pieces of investigative journalism and gossip sites had all painted a worryingly similar picture of the family. Now based in Rome, having returned from New York, incidentally six months after the introduction of the 1970 RICO bill, the Ossani portion of the family could be linked through marriages and cousins to all five Mafia families in New York. It hadn't taken long to find the suspicions that the Daring Corporation's forty years of unprecedented success was thanks to Isabella Ossani's "*colourful*" connections. The more reliable reports had not been able to suggest anything stronger than colourful, for no hard evidence had been found. It was all speculation and clearly no one had wanted to chance a libel suit.

Speculation or not, Kitty had found it completely unbelievable that these types of families were believed to still exist. She felt a little embarrassed at the naivety her sheltered Cornish upbringing had allowed to flourish.

Until late the night before, sheltering beneath the duvet fort at the duplex, she had devoured research paper after research paper and various articles about the modern mafia. Conspiracy theories abounded about the clandestine underworld that they inhabited and how these organised groups influenced everything around them through branches of law enforcement, politicians and the finance sector. Only when her research had become decidedly Dan Brown-esque, with references to the Masons and the Illuminati controlling people's day to day lives, had Kitty called it a night.

Rubbing her tired eyes, she turned to leave the balcony. The thought of some divine intervention, a higher justice, suddenly seemed rather appealing.

341

Despite being desperate for a hot tea, Kitty avoided the beckoning of the Starbucks as she passed it on her way back to the office. The thought of seeing Avery today was too much to contemplate.

Taking a final left and crossing over into the garden square, another venue she had become accustomed to avoiding - this time thanks to Elliot's discovery of the haunt and not down to the preppy American - Kitty made her way to one of the benches. A chubby, flint-coloured pigeon leapt off, disturbed and decidedly disgruntled for a few seconds, before returning to scratch hopefully around her feet.

She was not sure how long she had been sat there when she caught herself scratching at her palm, staring at the double headed Janus insignia, billowing on the flag which could be seen above the neatly trimmed, privet hedge-lined railings. The two-faces now seemed sadly appropriate. She wondered which face was Raphael's true one. *Which was hers?* she asked herself, unsure of what she cared more about these days. The fact that Raphael was apparently the monster mothers warned their children about at night, or the fact that whoever he was, he hadn't called. Was he his past, or the future man he had kept promising he was trying to be? Was that what he had meant by the future one? Not a killer? Kitty shivered. It had turned cold, she told herself.

'I thought it was you!' A voice called from behind.

Kitty turned to see Max jubilantly waltzing toward her. She watched forlornly as the pigeon, now outnumbered, flew away, before she forced herself to smile. 'Hey Max.'

Reaching the bench, Max sat beside Kitty, embracing her in an awkward sideways squeeze. He seemed to not have noticed her discomfort, 'How's it going? Working for the big boss man?' he asked.

'Yeh fine. Working for the VP actually at the moment.'

'Nice.'

'How's yours going?'

Max waffled on about how great his placement had been so far, dedicating an excessively large portion of his update to what he had eaten on a business lunch the week before. Listening to his rambling about the virtues of various cuts of beef, Kitty realised how much she valued his uncomplicated manners. She usually hated small talk, but with everything else going on, Max's simplicity was a welcome change and his unencumbered vitality was impossible not to like. Briefly, under the double gaze of Janus, she wondered why she couldn't be attracted to someone like Max. As soon as the thought was fully formed, the image of Freddie followed swiftly behind it and she buried both. Knowing she needed to call the latter before he physically tracked her down to check she was still alive.

Max continued to enthuse about steak and business strategy until they had reached the entrance to Nero's domain. With a cheery wave, jovially unaware of her dampening spirits, he left Kitty and made his way back towards the lobby.

Assuming she would be unaccompanied as always, Kitty did not look up until she was firmly reinstalled at her flimsy desk. The frame wobbled precariously as she positioned herself behind it. Only then did she notice Nero staring at her from behind his own desk, leaning back in his large leather chair, like a great outstretched spider.

'Miss May. What a pleasure.' His tone did not match his greeting.

Kitty's heart leapt into her throat. She looked to the door and the thought, *if I scream would anyone hear me*, crossed her mind. *Grow up*, she chided herself silently, having become tired of the tension. There was no reason Nero would do anything wrong. At least, there was no reason he would do anything wrong within the Daring building.

If Kitty had known anything about the man sat six feet away, she would not have been so reassured by her surroundings.

'Mr Ossani,' she nodded politely, having been unable to come up with anything more flowery.

'Are you a tease?'

Kitty stared at the offensive man, 'Sorry?'

'I want to know. Are you a tease or do you actually put out? Sexually of course.'

'I don't know what you're talking about.'

'I think you do,' Nero sneered, rising from his desk.

Kitty remained silent. Her heart beat out a quickening rhythm as Nero stepped closer.

'Our Russian friend is very pleased.' Nero tapped her desk with a ringed finger, 'Although I would have picked the first venue you searched for. The website wasn't great though I'll give you that, and I suppose he's a bit of an ostentatious twat.'

A sick realisation overwhelmed Kitty. Her Daring issued laptop was tracked. She kicked herself, her heart hammering now at top speed. How could she have been so idiotic? She wondered what else Nero had seen.

As though reading her mind, he answered this question as he left the room, 'It's only four of the New York families. There was an acrimonious divorce... and a couple of deaths. Now do try to stay on task Miss May. We wouldn't want an unfortunate misunderstanding.'

He had seen everything.

TWENTY-SIX

Marku rubbed his calloused hands together, kicking one heavy, steel-capped boot against the other as he sheltered in the shadow of the container. The unit had been fastened onto the back of a lorry, a change from the first two that he had signed off, and he was currently stuck waiting for the driver to get moving.

He waited alone, the driver having disappeared off for a piss behind a nearby building. It had been five minutes at least since his departure and Marku was becoming nervous. This was the last container he had been told about and he wanted his part in the whole affair done. After all, he had his girls to think about, and Halloween had gone so well. They had been thrilled with the pumpkin shaped chocolates and witches hat candies that he had found for them. Even his wife had welcomed his involvement these last few weeks. Everything was really starting to turn around.

Another five minutes passed and a gnawing curiosity had begun to scratch at him. Lighting his third cigarette, Marku crossed to the other side of the container. There was no sign of the driver and in this part of the port he appeared to be entirely alone. It was a good time of day for moving freight out of the docks. With the new loads arriving in their tonnes at this time, this area was all but deserted. Marku felt a bubble of pride at his suggestion as to the timings of the shipments. He had been right.

Stopping his pacing at the rear of the lorry, Marku wondered what all the fuss was about. Drugs? Illegal liquor? The curiosity continued to grow and, encouraged by his isolation, Marku wrenched open the hulking metal doors. He had watched the men check the load earlier and had seen them leave it unlocked. He had thought that odd.

Staring into the gloom, waiting for his eyes to adjust, Marku took a sharp intake of breath, 'What the…' he began, his heart spiking hard.

A pair of shining dark eyes was the last thing he remembered seeing. Then everything went dark and somewhere in the last vestiges of his consciousness he knew he had just witnessed something terrible. At the end, one simple fact burned in his mind. He should never have looked.

TWENTY-SEVEN

Thanks more to the knowledge of the local taxi driver than the description afforded by the half-stoned youth, Raphael found Ochan. Housed inside a traditional, tangerine painted, wooden, hip-roofed building, the bar was positioned firmly off the tourist trail. No frills, no themes and no excessive attention had been paid to any aspect of the decor, service, nor refreshments offered. Yet the place thrived as a haven for those wanting to enjoy local produce, talk shop and forget that the beach, a few streets away, had been forever lost to the rum-fuelled, full moon parties beloved by the instagram obsessed. On the surface, Ochan, named after a creole drinking toast, seemed like a harmless joint. A little tired, but much loved. Underneath, it housed something far more seedy. Something that sold better than any of the overpriced, rum-soaked cocktails for sale down the road - sex.

Reggae music was thumping out of a large pair of cheap speakers as Raphael entered the bar. The crackle of the poor quality electrics audible, even over the din of the clientele. A few suspicious eyes, having lost interest in their female companions, followed Raphael as he approached the bar.

He had made it halfway across the room, and had garnered the attention of almost every eye in the joint when an elderly woman, wide as she was tall, strode out through a door positioned behind the bar and came to meet him. Two younger men, youthfully muscled, followed her. They flanked her as she stood staring up at Raphael. He surveyed them. They were too flinchy. Too keen. Their wild darting eyes and twitching biceps betrayed their inexperience. Cherise had obviously made some very recent additions to her staff. They wouldn't help her, he thought unconcerned.

Raphael looked down at the woman, as she eyed his knuckles. He followed her gaze. They were bleeding and he hadn't even noticed. Checking his arm, he realised that the bandage had become soiled. He had been a little overzealous with the pothead. That didn't come as a surprise.

When Raphael was a young boy, during the summer holidays, he used to sneak out of the villa in Italy and head down into the nearby town. There was a woman there who lived in a small, dilapidated house by the bakery and he would visit her whenever he could. She had a son not far off Raphael's own age who always cared for a litter of puppies each summer. Little, soft creatures, with tiny wagging tails and an insatiable appetite for play. The boys would spend hours rolling them onto their backs and rubbing their chubby, milk-filled bellies.

One summer, when Raphael was ten, Nero had found him down at the tired house. Picking up one of the smaller puppies, Nero had handed it to Raphael. It had snuggled into him and he had held it all the way back to the Villa. For the rest of the summer he and Luca had played with the dog in the orchard and carried it around the house. They named the dog Nano, because of its small stature compared to its litter mates. At the end of the holiday, much to Raphael's horror, the puppy had been returned to the lady by the bakery, as Nero had told him it couldn't come with them to England.

The next year, when summer came, Raphael went back to the tired house in search of Nano. Unable to find the small pup he asked his uncle what had happened to his dog. That evening, Nero took Raphael to a nearby town he had never visited before. In a warehouse on the outskirts, under a half-lit strip light, his uncle showed him what had become of the happy puppy.

Raphael had watched as Nano, unrecognisably large, hugely muscled with a thick neck, and missing half an ear, the dog he had tickled and played with, tore another dog apart before a baying paying crowd. It had been reconditioned. Exposed to so much violence that it no longer understood anything else. It was a long time before Raphael understood what had happened to Nano, and even longer before he realised that the same had happened to him.

The track booming through the speakers changed and Raphael looked back to the woman, 'Cherise I assume?'

'Mmm. I was told you were coming.' She glanced toward her new hires, 'I hope we're not going to have a disagreement young man?' Her tone was matronly. Patronising.

Raphael estimated that Cherise must have been in her seventies. Despite her dyed hair, an artificial jet black, the lights of the bar illuminated her milky cataracts and her face was heavily creased from decades in the sun.

'I'm sure we won't,' Raphael replied evenly.

Cherise continued to stare for a while, assessing him. Finally, apparently satisfied, with a flick of her wrist she gestured for him to follow. 'Sit down,' she ordered the boys behind her. They looked set to disagree but she delivered them a look of matriarchal finality and they obliged her without dissent.

Following the woman, who moved at a surprisingly swift pace in spite of her years and weight, Raphael entered the room Cherise had first appeared from, leaving the sea of curious eyes behind them.

The room was painted dark red, a fan slowly whirling from the ceiling in place of air-conditioning, two worn-out faux leather sofas positioned either side of a small mahogany coffee table, upon which an unfinished card game remained. Two girls. Twenties. Silken ebony hair and unmarked skin. They slinked off the sofas as Raphael entered, mistaking him for one of the owners of the luxury villas that supplied the girls with the majority of their work. Cherise tutted them away, hectoring like an old nun and the girls disappeared back into the bar. Raphael thought he heard a wolf-whistle.

Cherise, muttering about the mess, continued to the back of the room and disappeared through a pair of barred doors that opened onto a small, concrete-paved patio.

Raphael joined her, taking a seat on one of the plastic arm chairs that had been left on the unkept pavers. A small patch of dirt stretched out beyond with two stubby palms and an unlit building sat at the far end.

They remained in silence. It was a clear night and away from the parties taking place on the beach, the stars could be counted in their thousands and the bugs, shrieking and buzzing in the jungle, could be heard loud and clear.

After what felt like a very long time, Cherise spoke, 'Have you come to kill me?' She did not look at Raphael, instead continuing her appraisal of the stars with no audible concern in her question.

'If you thought that, why didn't you bring your two boys back here?'

Cherise sighed, 'I know your type.' She licked her teeth, 'And they are far too young and certainly far too stupid to die tonight.'

Raphael continued to look at Cherise until she met his gaze. 'I need to know if any of your girls were servicing a man named Andre Hayes?' he asked, once satisfied he had her attention.

Cherise pursed her lips. Any semblance of matronly care was gone. She was a businesswoman after all. She ignored Raphael's question and instead began with one of her own, 'Do you know who is on our nation's flag?'

She waited.

Raphael exhaled audibly.

Cherise ignored his frustration, 'Saint Ursula.' She smiled to the sky, 'St Ursula framed by eleven oil lamps

352

representing the eleven thousand virgins after whom these beautiful islands were named.'

Raphael's patience was wearing dangerously thin, 'Well, fortunately for me, I'm not looking for one of those eleven thousand.'

Cherise glared at him. A deep frown creased her already line forehead, 'I pity you.'

'You don't know anything about me.'

'I know your kind. I can see it in your eyes. A curse, under the guise of an angel.'

Raphael leaned forward, 'So tell me what I want to know.'

Cherise sat back, the sun bleached plastic chair groaned underneath her, 'I am ready to die young man.'

'But are your grandsons?' Raphael cocked his head.

Cherise's eyes popped.

Raphael was pleased that his guess about her two newly appointed heavies had been correct.

Failing to regain control, Cherise's voice wobbled tellingly as she spoke, 'You're so confident you could brawl them both, even with a bad arm?'

The blood was really showing now. Jamar's wife's stitches had completely failed.

'Oh I wouldn't bother *brawling*.' Raphael removed the pistol from the back of his trousers and collected the suppressor that had been in his pocket. He sat back, screwing the suppressor into position. Without looking at Cherise, who he could see clearly, squirming in his periphery, he asked again, 'Andre. Hayes. Who was he fucking?'

Cherise stole a quick glance toward the barred doors.

'You know what's on the BVI flag?' Raphael asked. 'Below St Ursula and her lamps?' He waited a long few seconds until Cherise's frown was deep and unattractive, '*Vigilate.* Be careful. You should heed your own motto.'

Cherise moved in her seat. The plastic protested loudly once more under her shifting weight.

'You won't get far enough to even shout.' Raphael cocked the pistol with a satisfying click, 'Trust me. No one's ever ready to die.'

Cherise looked once more to the doors, 'Ok. Ok. Unity.' She held up her hands, 'It was Unity. Come with me.'

With Raphael in tow, she bustled across the dry patch of dirt into the building situated at the back of the lot. Three girls sleeping on a bunk bed did not stir as they entered.

Without comment, Cherise kept walking. Raphael followed until they came to an office. She held the door for him and he entered. He heard the latch click shut behind him, stirring an earlier thought.

Cherise gave Raphael a wide berth as she skirted past him. Moving to a safe on the far wall, hidden behind a painting of a Tortolan fishing scene, she slowly entered the digits and opened the metal door.

Raphael leapt to his right as the shining blade of a large knife flew past his head. It only narrowly missed his face and instead lodged in the door frame. Splintering the old wood. Cherise's aim had been unexpectedly accurate and if his suspicions hadn't been raised by the sound of the door locking, the blade would have hit him between the eyes.

Cherise stared at the knife protruding from the wooden frame.

'Why?' Raphael shook his head, his gun raised to her forehead. He saw the fear.

The woman opened her mouth to scream, but before the cry for help had made it past the first letter, Raphael lunged forward and thrust the frame of the pistol into her temple. Cherise's unconscious body made a loud thump as it hit the floor, jackknifing on a chair.

'You stupid old woman.' Raphael ran his hands through his hair. 'Fuck,' he hissed, checking for a pulse hidden within the rolls of her limp neck. Not everyone, especially someone her age, woke up from that kind of hit. He could only hope.

Making his way quickly to the open safe. Raphael unscrewed the suppressor and stowed the weapon back in his waistband. The scabbard of the thrown knife lay in the alcove. Below it a second lay untouched. Behind these Raphael found what he was looking for. Flicking through a heavy, faded ring-binder, he skipped passed the deeds to the property, various letters regarding bank accounts and utility bills, before he found the details of the girls Cherise kept on her roster. His eyes quickly slipped to the Madam. She was still out cold.

Unity's page was near the back. A photo of the woman smiling had been stapled to a torn sheet of A4 paper. The image had obviously been provided for business purposes and in it Unity was wearing a black and red harlequin leather bikini. Despite her smile, her face seemed sad. Her cheeks drooped and her eyes were dull as though her heart wasn't in tune with the set upward curve of her lips. *Whose would be?* Raphael supposed, feeling sorry for the girls, whose pages he had flicked past. Taking note of Unity's address - a few disconcertingly familiar lines - he returned the file to the safe. He had no time to work out the cause of the déjà vu.

Unlocking the office door Raphael slipped back the way he had come. On the bunk bed, now tangled together on the bottom level, the three women stared. They had heard Cherise's fall. He raised a finger to his lips. They nodded, shaking in fear. The message was universal.

Raphael continued out onto the patio and jumped over the small wall that stood between the property and the road that ran around the back of it. Once there, heading in the direction of his taxi, he reached for his phone. The line connected almost immediately.

'Yeh I need a full clean…' he began to explain.

A voice spoke swiftly on the other end of the line and Raphael listened intently before responding, 'Now,' he growled.

He needed to get the old lady's body checked and, if need be, removed, before anyone came looking. He was banking on the other women's silence. Having seen the majority of the pictures, and the disparity between what they were getting paid compared to what Cherise was taking, he doubted they would feel any undue concern for their Madam. That and the windfall they were about to receive when the "cleaners" arrived should help.

'No I won't be here,' he responded to a question from the other end of the line. 'Take the location from this call…Ok yeh… Two guys out the front at the bar. Brothers. Twitchy. Only ones not drinking. Twenty something,' He saw his taxi waiting in the distance, the driver, having a fag out the Hyundai's rolled down window, having kept the engine running as requested. Raphael picked up his pace, 'No. Leave them. No killing. You got that?' There was a pause on the line. 'Just remind them how good it feels to be alive. Have you got the location? Good.' Raphael hung up.

Holding out the address to the driver he climbed into the backseat. Incase the girls didn't stay quiet, Raphael couldn't risk them warning Unity and so didn't have time to ask the taxi to drop him somewhere else nearby. He prayed that wouldn't prove to be a mistake.

It wasn't long before Raphael got his first glimpse of the village. A collection of lights huddled together by the waters edge alerted him to its presence. Having descended to sea-level, the taxi pulled to a stop beside a large crescent bay. Small wooden dwellings curved out before him.

The driver pointed in the direction of the address, 'I can't get you to the door. Old houses these. No roads. I wait here.' He waved once more toward the ocean, lighting a cigarette.

Raphael nodded, before deciding to relieve the driver of his services for the night. He wasn't sure what he was going to find, but having disclosed the address, he would make a different way back.

Having crossed the sand, Raphael found the home listed as Unity's. The lights were off and the place looked as deserted from the outside as Hayes' had. He hoped she hadn't moved. The front door was locked, but the old latch mechanism was easy to break. Letting himself in he pushed open the insect screen. It fell shut behind him with a clatter.

Scanning the kitchen, Raphael felt a wash of relief. She hadn't left. Food in the fridge. Fresh laundry. Flowers.

Raphael walked through the empty rooms. She hadn't left, but she wasn't here.

Arriving at the final room, a double bedroom with fixed wardrobing lining one wall, he inspected the surfaces. There were condoms, a hairbrush, birth control pills. Having already seen a child's room, Raphael doubted that Unity saw her clients here. The place felt like a home.

Raphael slipped a hand under the mattress. He felt three papery stacks of money. People were always the same. He smiled before his fingers grazed something cold. Metal. Pulling it out Raphael eyed a watch. Rolex. Expensive. On the back, just visible in the darkness, he read the initials. AEH.

Raphael smiled to himself. Hayes had been here.

Then it hit him, the reason for his déjà vu, and the smile vanished as quickly as it had appeared.

TWENTY-EIGHT

Kitty sat, drying her hair in preparation for the weekend. She yawned. She hadn't been sleeping. Lulled by the warmth, her mind wandered back to the day before as the warm air funnelled through her damp strands.

Having to swallow her fear of inciting an inquisition, or perhaps her pride, which had been immeasurably knocked since Raphael's dismissal of her and his subsequent disappearance, Kitty had tracked down Avery. With promises that the task was for Raphael himself and that certain recognition would no doubt follow should she deliver, Kitty had asked for Avery's help to compile a file on the Daring client Vasili Nechayev. She had vaguely explained Mr Nechayev was having some big event planned that Raphael cared very deeply about - she would come to regret that comment.

Kitty herself had spent the week, since the meeting at Swarga, pulling everything she could find on Vasili. If the world was right about the Daring-Ossani family, something of which she couldn't find any solid proof, then perhaps Nero's "*private*" client might be as colourfully connected. Restricted to having to use her phone to search the internet, for fear of Nero's tracking, Kitty had not found an excessive amount of usable intel.

Google had delivered a bit of fairly questionable information on the Nechayev family as a whole. There was one Nechayev listed as a government official, and some links in various Russian articles that she had found talking about their associations with the oil industry. But aside from that, the Nechayevs seemed to have avoided much of the scandal the Ossani family had apparently thrived on.

Kitty's search into Irina had proved a little more fruitful. Irina's father had been caught embezzling party funds in Russia two years ago. A web forum, where students could be found railing against the easy deals of the wealthy, how they were made to leave Russia whereas the normal person disappeared without a trace, had much to say on Irina's father's crimes. But Irina's father's misdoings, although perhaps circumstantially interesting, didn't really mean anything about Vasili - except perhaps explain why he was in London. The forum certainly failed to prove some illicit link too Daring that would interest Elliot. It was this dead end that had forced Kitty to go to Avery.

From under her copper hair, Avery had eyed Kitty suspiciously. She had heard what was being promised and rather fancied another chance to impress the CEO. She had impressed the whole of the Accounts team with her abilities, but she harboured greater aspirations and was planning on achieving them in record time. It was this that had secured her compliance.

Friday evening, whilst leaving the office for the weekend, Avery had caught up with Kitty.

* * *

Slightly out of breath Avery puffed as she spoke, 'You got a sec?' she asked, tapping Kitty on the shoulder.

'Sure.' Kitty followed Avery into the Starbucks. Understanding what was expected of her, Kitty bought them both drinks and followed to a corner table.

Setting Avery's caramel latte down on the table, Kitty spoke first, 'You haven't done it already have you?'

'Well actually I ran into a bit of a problem.'

Kitty's heart sank. Avery was talented but she couldn't work miracles. If her clearance at Accounts hadn't allowed her access, then Kitty's investigation was over before it had even begun. Avery wouldn't understand this fact, for she would simply suggest Kitty ask Raphael for clearance - an obstacle which obviously couldn't be overcome. Kitty sipped at her tea waiting for Avery to explain.

'It's weird,' Avery began. 'Most clients have loads listed about them. We usually have everything. Bank details. Addresses. National Insurance Numbers. God, on some we have marriage certificates. The size of their mortgages. Their assets valued down to the small change in their cars left for parking—'

'So…?' Kitty pushed. She didn't understand.

361

Avery looked at her as though it was obvious, 'Mr Nechayez has by the looks of things avoided the usual checks and due diligence.' Avery stared, 'Completely, Kitty!'

'Is that such a big deal though?'

'Yeh, massively. If we were a bank for example this kind of negligence can get people sent to prison.'

'But we aren't.'

'Not in the traditional sense. But we manage client's assets and are required legally to check that those assets are not being used to funnel illegal money. It's odd.' Avery concluded.

'What did you find?'

'Nothing.'

'Nothing nothing or... nothing of interest.' Kitty couldn't believe Vasili's file was empty but was trying not to heighten Avery's already spiking suspicions. With everything she had been reading over the last week, this revelation wasn't surprising at all. Perhaps she had actually found something.

'Just some shipping arrangements.' Avery rummaged in her bag, 'Here I brought them for you. I thought maybe...?'

Kitty took the documents. Almost forgetting Avery's clear, unspoken question, 'Oh yeah don't worry. Mr Daring will still know how much you've helped.'

'Maybe there's a loophole if they're a sole shipping client...' Avery began muttering to her latte.

Kitty, shuffling through the small stack of papers, didn't hear a word of what Avery was saying. On initial inspection she was holding photocopies pertaining to three different shipments.

'Thank you. I'll let Mr Daring know.' Kitty got up to leave.

'And the meeting?' Avery looked longingly after her.

Kitty had forgotten she had vaguely promised something about getting Avery into a room with Raphael. She kicked herself - that had been overstepping the mark. Deciding she could work something out another time, Kitty reassured Avery and headed for the tube.

* * *

A knot of hair produced a sharp sting, bringing Kitty back to the task at hand. Turning off the hair dryer she reached for her brush and began to smooth the tangled strands. She had spent all night trying to understand the papers on her own, but they still meant frustratingly little to her. Seeing them on her bedside table she reached for her phone. A swell of guilt presented uncomfortably in her stomach.

'Hey Kit!' Freddie answered on the first try. He sounded thrilled that she had called which only worsened her guilt.

'Hey buddy. I can't really talk now but—'

'Are you alright?'

'Yeh, yeh I'm fine—'

'Kit?' his voice was thick with concern.

'Fred, honestly - I'm fine. I just need some help with something for work.'

'It's Saturday?'

'I know.'

There was silence on the other end of the line.

363

'Freddie, please? I know I've been beyond useless since I moved here. I've just been trying to find my feet and—'

'Ok! Ok. What can I do?'

Freddie hated emotionally charged comments like that. He wanted to help - always. Kitty had been banking on this. The guilt notched up again.

'If I wanted to know what was in a container and where it was coming from for example, what would I need?' she asked, trying to sound nonchalant.

Not needing to be asked twice, Freddie launched off into a detailed explanation. Having understood some of what he was saying, Kitty read out the numbers she thought were the containers identification tags, 'So they're forty foot Daring containers right?' she asked, having garnered this information from the documents.

A minute's pause followed.

'No, your numbers must be wrong... ummm... let me check.' Freddie came back on the line a moment later, 'Yeh, these are twenty footers and they're not Daring.'

'What?'

'Your numbers must be wrong, or the filing of them is. These aren't Daring containers.'

'Whose are they?'

'I can't see that. I would have to...' Freddie started fiddling with something, the crackle audible over the phone.

'Don't worry. Where are they now?' Kitty asked, her hopes spiking.

'I would need to be at work to find that out using the correct logins and—'

'But you could find them?'

'If they came to the UK, should be able to. Perhaps it's just a clerical mistake your end?'

'Perhaps.' Kitty fell silent for a few seconds. Freddie refrained from interrupting her thoughts. He was decent like that.

'Fred, thank you. I have to go.'

'Skype soon?'

'Course.' The guilt reached peak level.

'Love you, Kit.'

'Yeh you're the best.' Kitty awkwardly hung-up.

Registering the time, Kitty realised she was running late for the meeting that she had agreed to attend at the shelter with Irina. *Shit*, she cursed, blasting the hair dryer to full.

Waiting under the awning of a small news agents, Kitty, thinking about her freshly washed hair, scowled at the grey clouds looming overhead. She checked her phone. She had made good time, now Irina was the one who was late. The memories of her conversations with Avery and Freddie weighed on her mind as she watched the approaching weather front.

A woman exiting the news-agent's caught her attention. She was carrying a large rainbow umbrella - the kind Burt used to have. A present from his wife given to brighten up his rather drab fisherman's overalls on a rainy day. Burt had hated it, but like everything to do with his late wife, he treasured it as he had treasured her. Kitty felt another pang of guilt. She knew a call to Burt was also well overdue.

Pushing all thoughts of responsibilities from her mind, Kitty turned her attention to the news agents. It wasn't a chain, but one of the independent shops that could still be found amongst the outer fringes of the city. Its windows were a clutter of local advertisements, Jobs mainly and a sorry piece about a lost cat. Newspapers spilled out of the racks outside.

The headlines had not changed much since her Cambridge days. The Syrian crisis continued to dominate the front pages. Disagreements between Russia and the West over how to tackle the growing problems. Lurid photographs. Reports of the government shelling civilians. One newspaper was still carrying the poisoning of an ex-KGB spy in some city in the south of England, squeezed in between photographs of scantily clad women.

The growl of an expensive car engine pulled Kitty's attention. Luca flitted across her mind, but it was not a scarlet Ferrari that had pulled to a stop. Irina had arrived. Climbing out of a heavily chromed Maybach, parked across a stretch of double yellows, the woman looked ill-prepared to be handing out soup to the Syrian refugees who had by some miracle made it to the UK. Wearing a tailored, crease-free, trouser suit, her cream shirt had a pussy-bow collar and her jewellery sparkled even in the dull light.

Swapping simple pleasantries - all in Russian - Kitty followed Irina into the shelter. Up close Irina was not the image of cream sophistication that she had appeared from afar. Her eyes were puffy, their whites criss-crossed by a basket of tiny, red lines. It looked as though she had been crying or at the very least hadn't slept well for days. It was hard to tell, but as Kitty held the door open for her to enter, she thought she saw a bruise in the hollow of the woman's cheek. The smudge had been well covered by make-up, but was still just visible under the glare of the shelter's harsh institutional lighting.

The shelter was sparsely decorated. A repurposed youth engagement centre with an old parquet floor. The stage at the far end, once a platform for amateurs looking to impress at the Christmas pantomime or seasonal talent show, was now covered with piles of clothes and bags of all kinds. Fragments of old lives lived in a foreign land. To the left a stack of camp beds had been piled to create sufficient space for eating, and refugees of all ages sat in small groups, some in chairs, some on the floor, conversing inwardly to one another. Loosely arranged and visibly tired, they mirrored the scene on the stage above.

The shutters on the servery, built into the right hand wall, remained rolled down, but already children were beginning to cue up against the wall. Two volunteers handed out an assortment of donated crockery and when that ran out, paper plates were retrieved from the kitchen still hidden by the servery shutters.

Kitty remembered having once been to a children's party in a hall just like this. She wasn't able to recall whose it had been, but she remembered the cake. A neat row of multi-coloured candles wedged firmly into a smiling hedgehog sponge. She remembered balloons, disco lights and she even remembered crying when she had lost at musical chairs. Kitty wondered if any of these children had ever been to a party like that. She began to scratch at her palm.

The steadily growing wails of a young boy, seemingly disappointed at having been given a paper plate compared to his sibling's china one, were reaching fever pitch by the time Kitty had been robed for the kitchen. Hair scooped into a net, she stayed for three hours, handing out food and later fresh blankets. Some of the refugees who came in to eat were sleeping rough. The shelter couldn't accommodate them all. Most were unable to communicate with Kitty, some through fear like those who were too frightened to come up to the servery and whose food she had hand-delivered to the corners of the hall, others due to the uncrossable language barrier.

Irina, despite looking woefully out of place, had tried with the refugees, handing out bowls of soup and letting the children play with her bracelets. One little girl was so mesmerised by the sparkling diamonds that Kitty had had to convince her for a good long while to give them back. Irina hadn't seemed to mind, and Kitty supposed the little girl had never seen anything so grand. Kitty knew she hadn't.

When it was time to leave, Kitty felt pleased with how she had spent her Saturday. For the first time she felt like she had actually given something back to society. She had done something meaningful and it felt overwhelmingly satisfying. Scrunching up her hair net and placing it in the bin by the kitchen door, Kitty returned to the hall where most of the refugees were having to sleep at night. A few from the new round of volunteers were setting up makeshift beds. Standing by the exit, Kitty stole one last look into the room before she left. The local Imam had arrived and they were about to start the late afternoon prayers - Salat al-'asr.

The door smacked into Kitty and she was forced back into the room. Three powerfully built men shoved passed her without a second glance. They made no attempt to apologise for the way they had knocked her. She watched as they made a beeline for one of the families who had set up a camp in the far corner of the hall. The children had been too shy to collect food, and so Kitty had delivered their allocation to them directly. They hadn't spoken a word of English except the eldest gentlemen in their group. He had possessed a little of the language and Kitty had tried as best she could to make him feel welcome. They had only arrived two nights before.

Their worried faces amongst crashing ocean waves filled her head as she exited onto the street.

Back at the duplex on Coldharbour Lane, Kitty flicked through various apps on her phone, the crusts of a sandwich having long since dried up and begun to curl on the plate rested on the bed beside her. Trying not to trouble Freddie, or really, trying not to use him again, Kitty started a new investigation to see if she could work out where the containers had gone.

Two hours of searching later, she still couldn't work it out. Having searched through reams and reams of shipping entries scanning for matching codes, she was about to give up and get an early night, random clips on Youtube having called her attention in her frustration, when her phone buzzed.

The words "unknown number" flashed on the screen.

Kitty answered after only a moment's hesitation. Her nerves settled when she heard Avery's distinct American drawl.

'Hey Kitty. How's it going?' Avery asked. She did not wait for Kitty to respond, instead continued to speak at top speed, 'So I kept looking. I know it's Saturday but I was by the office and had nothing to do. I hate it when my parents visit and you need a desktop server to get personal files, and, and, and... yeh anyway, so like I was saying,

369

kept looking, you know for something on the containers or anything on Mr Nechayev…'

Kitty for once found herself exceedingly grateful for Avery's insatiable nosiness. She had wondered what Avery was going to do about the strange account Kitty had led her too. It would have been very out of character for her to have ignored it completely.

Avery continued unaware of Kitty's increasing gratitude, '… so yeah, nothing. Then found three invoices. Numbers matched the containers. They had been listed in another file under a different name. Without knowing about the account for Mr Nechayev, and knowing *you* in particular were working for him, then it would have been impossible to have found these.'

'What do you mean *me* in particular?'

'The other account. The one with the invoices in. That's the one the money has actually moved through, and you're listed as the name on it. Not Mr Nechayev. I just put two and two together. You must have messed up filling in the forms.' Avery moved on. Unaware of what she had just said.

Kitty felt her stomach drop. Something was very wrong, 'Avery what did you say the invoices were for again… specifically?'

'Lorries. Different types. To Southampton Port. No onward address. Just from us to Southampton.'

'Thanks so much. I must have screwed up. God, you really saved my ass.' Kitty tried to steady her voice. Keep out the panic that was stirring in her gut. Her name shouldn't have been associated with any accounts nor any lorries travelling anywhere. Nero's sneer entered her mind. She beat that away as well.

'You're welcome honey. It's an easy mistake to make…
I suppose,' Avery made an attempt at consolation.

Kitty could practically hear the woman beaming as she hung up and she made a mental note to figure out how to organise a meeting for Avery and the elusive CEO sooner rather than later.

Lying under her duvet in the dark, feeling more in need of a fortified sanctuary than ever before, Kitty's mind was racing uncontrollably. A longing for Raphael had been replaced by a nagging self-doubt. She considered that perhaps her imagination, Elliot's craziness and Beto's warnings had just led her down the convoluted road to some grand delusion. That she was seeing things where there weren't any. Maybe every wisp of gossip she had heard, every assumption she had made added up to nothing.

Unable to answer the millions of questions that plagued her, she knew there was really only one way to find out if there was anything strange going on. She knew she had to find the containers and answer the only portion of the question she could for now. Were any of the people she was working for involved in some sort of criminal activity? And so was Raphael really the prince of some shady underground world?

Kitty rubbed her temples and buried her head in her pillow. *Would I be happier if I let this all go and walked away? Let every fox take care of its own tail*, she remembered saying to Raphael, but she knew the answer as soon as the thoughts had fully formed in her head. In that respect, she knew who she was.

371

It was late when Kitty, feeling she had no choice, picked up her phone. She would deal with any fallout down the line. She had to know.

TWENTY-NINE

It had been three days since Caneel had been back to the house she had once called home. She had tried to stay, make it normal for her son, but vicious dreams and phantom shouts had haunted her nights and woken her at all hours screaming and drenched in sweat. Today, she would try again.

Making her way across the sand, the small grains tickled her toes where her sandals opened. The young boy raced about in front of her, bringing her washed up shells and discarded sea flotsam like offerings to some grand temple. She kept her head down. It wasn't until she was about six feet from the door that she noticed the latch was broken.

Grabbing the child's arm as he raced passed she began whispering to him. He wailed at the dig of her nails, but she couldn't worry about that now, 'Duane listen to me.'

He continued to wail and she spanked him on the bottom. It was not hard but the shock of it made him listen. His small round eyes popped wide with surprise.

'You know where your Tantin is?' Caneel stressed, trying to keep her voice level. Assertive, 'Yes Duane?'

The little boy nodded.

'Down the beach at the bar. You say to her I will be there soon ok? Ok?'

He nodded again. 'Wiv the turrtlus,' he sniffed.

'Yes. The turtles on the side.' She tried to force a smile, 'Go find Tantin. Go find your Aunt. Go Duane,' she encouraged.

Caneel waited until the child had disappeared past the neighbouring house, before she turned back to the one she used to call home.

The insect screen banged against the wall as she walked in. She stepped carefully, like a young deer on a dew covered lawn.

'Hello?' Caneel called. 'Hello?'

Assuming she was alone she straightened and, depositing her stuff on the kitchen table, breathed for the first time since leaving the beach. There was no indication anyone had been there.

'Hello, Unity,' a man answered from behind her.

Raphael was still standing at his position beside the window where he had witnessed a young child, previously making a direct line for the house, race off down the beach. He was glad it hadn't come in. Children complicated everything.

He had remained in the house where Hayes had been murdered - the fact which had stirred the uncomfortable familiarity on seeing her address - positioned by the front window save necessary trips, for the last three days hoping for Unity to return. He had been coming around to the idea of leaving when he had spotted her walking along the sand.

'You live here?' Raphael asked the frozen woman. He knew the answer. It was definitely Unity. Her face matched the one from the file.

'Take whatever you want.' Unity began to panic, 'I have cash. Take the cash.'

'I don't want your money.' Raphael took a few steps toward her. His hands raised trying to assuage her clear desire to run. A diet of leftovers from the fridge had left him in no mood for a chase.

'You want my stuff? I have a new television. A phone?' Unity closed the distance, trying in vain to thrust her belongings into Raphael's raised hands.

The phone hit the wooden floor with a thud.

'I don't want your stuff.' He bent and picked up the discarded handset. She wouldn't take it from him, so he set it down on the kitchen table next to the unpacked shopping.

'You want sex?' Unity asked, her voice strained to breaking point.

Raphael pulled out one of the chairs and sat down. 'I want to know why you would sell your body before this?' He pulled the engraved Rolex from his pocket.

Unity gasped.

'You know what it's worth?' Raphael continued.

She nodded like a scolded child.

'And the owner's not coming back for it is he?'

She stared without nodding this time.

'But you know that don't you?' Raphael breathed, 'Don't you?'

Unity looked to the door before nodding again. This time singularly.

'Did they offer you this if you gave up his location? And now what. You can't sell it? A bit too rare? Not too many buyers of dead men's Rolexes.' Raphael shifted in his seat, 'I could find a buyer for you.'

Unity started to cry. Big sobbing wails accompanied the large tears beginning to stream down her reddening cheeks, 'No no. I…' Her voice caught.

'You don't want me to sell it? But then how can you cash in?' Raphael pushed, but he had made a mistake.

Unity sunk to the floor, her whole body heaving with her sobs.

'Who killed Hayes?' Raphael asked.

'I don't know.' She looked up at him.

Raphael waited.

'I don't know. I don't know… urgh…' She struggled to breath through her crying, 'A man. A man came.'

'A man? You're going to have to do better than that Unity. Did you give him up? Who did you give him up to?'

'I loved him.' Unity shouted. Her voice clear for a moment before the sobs broke back in, 'He loved me.'

Raphael aware of the distinct lack of soundproofing in the old wooden beach house, and now his school boy error in assuming a prostitute had no feelings, changed tack - he didn't want any undue attention and found himself believing the woman. Standing from the chair he offered Unity a hand off the floor. She slapped it away. Sighing he clamped both his hands around her shoulders and lifted her onto the nearest kitchen chair before retuning to his own.

She looked at him shocked, 'I told him it would end badly.' She began coughing.

'What would?' Raphael asked, allowing a touch of concern to colour his words.

'The job,' She said to her hands.

'What job Unity?' Raphael ran his hands through his hair.

'You knew him?'

'My whole life.'

She looked up with soft, dark eyes, tears still running down her cheeks, 'A man killed him. A man with a strange voice.'

'What do you mean strange?'

'I don't know. Awkward. I never saw him. I was in the bedroom. Andre was living here. He came back in a panic that night. He had been offered a lot of money for something some time before.'

'When?'

'Maybe a few days. I don't know what for. He said he wouldn't do it.'

'What happened the night he died?'

'He came back in a panic. Thought he was being followed. I was asleep. Then he was in our house.'

'Who was?'

'The man with a strange accent. I couldn't understand him. I thought I had hidden Andre when he came looking. I don't know what happened, I left through the window and then...' She started weeping again, but the energy had left her and she sat slouched, her body no longer rocking to the now noiseless sobs.

'Did anything else happen?'

'When I came back the next day the house was full of people I have never seen before. Authorities,' she whimpered.

'The police?'

'Not the local police.'

'I watched them remove stuff from the house.'

'Your stuff?'

'No things that hadn't been there the night before. Sacks. Little bags. It looked like salt.'

'Salt?' Raphael repeated, fearing where this was going.

'But it wasn't salt. Because people started talking. It was—'

'Cocaine,' Raphael answered. Some of the cartels had a habit of leaving drugs behind when someone had crossed them. A warning to others thinking of doing the same, but something felt wrong. 'How long have you been servicing...' Raphael corrected himself on seeing Unity's expression, '... in a relationship with Andre?'

'Eighteen months. Almost the whole time he's been here. I have been with no one else.'

'And in that time did he ever have cocaine in the house?'

'Never. He hates drugs. His son—' Unity began but Raphael nodded.

He didn't need to hear her reply, 'I know.'

Hayes' seventeen year old son had died from taking a bad pill at a festival. Ecstasy cut with god knows what else. The boy's death had nearly broken Hayes, but he wasn't sentimental, nor a talker, so to have told Unity they must have really known each other very well indeed.

Raphael handed Unity the watch, 'This belongs to you.'

She took it with both hands and cradled it as though he had handed her the most precious object in the world. He turned to leave, knowing she couldn't help him anymore. The cocaine. The gruesome nature of the murder. This was cartel business and if Hayes hadn't crossed one of the cartels, then Nero's deal had been with the wrong supplier. Raphael knew, having wanted no part of it, that he needed to know where the cocaine he had just unknowingly shipped to the UK had come from. He was going to have to ask around, but not here.

As Raphael crossed the threshold he turned back. 'Unity?'

'It's Caneel. My real name is Caneel.'

'Caneel,' he nodded. 'Get a different job.'

'I'm trying.'

Raphael sighed as he left the house.

THIRTY

There was the tiniest bit of warmth in the sunlight as it beat through the closed window, the rays magnified by the doubled glazing. Kitty felt them on her cheeks as she stood looking out, her eyes fixed on the horizon.

Before her Southampton Port lay in all its tangled glory, like the rusty remains of a giant child's playroom. Metal containers like oversized lego bricks were piled on top of one another, being moved and stacked by a menagerie of mechanical arms. Tiny figures wearing yellow hard-hats and high-vis jackets appeared and disappeared around the oddly constructed towers. Their individuality disguised by their uniforms, they too seemed bizarrely unreal from this distance. At the water's edge the ships were lined up as though the skyline of some vast marine city. Having deposited their wares, now sitting lighter and higher in the ocean, the red bottoms of their hulls, smothered in crustaceans, were once more visible.

Despite the vision before her, all Kitty could hear was the rhythmic tapping of Freddie furiously typing away behind her, and all she could think about was what he was about to find.

He had been at it some time, searching for the containers. She was grateful he had been so easy, he hadn't asked a multitude of questions she couldn't answer. But unfortunately this had also done little to alleviate her guilt. Freddie had been so excited to see her at the train station and their hug had lasted far too long.

Kitty turned from the jumble of cranes and ships and looked at him working away for her. She looked at the line of his nose, how his hair flopped over his forehead. She had forgotten she was staring when he looked up.

'You alright?' Freddie asked.

There it was again. It was written all over his face. The way he looked at her. Jaz had commented on it once. Burt had too - numerous times. The day she had left Cornwall for Cambridge he had looked exactly as he did now. The day she had returned for the first time since leaving, he had looked exactly as he had at the train station earlier.

'Kit?' Freddie cocked his head.

'Yeh, I'm good.' She frowned, 'How're we doing?'

'I've found them on the system. They definitely came through Southampton.'

'Ok. Let's go.' Kitty headed for the door.

Freddie jumped up from his seat and grabbed hold of her arm, 'Kit.'

'What?'

Freddie remained still. Staring with a raised eyebrow, he stood lightly shifting his weight from foot to foot.

'Fred, what is it? I need to see what's in those containers.'

He remained silent.

'Please?' Kitty smiled.

'You need to tell me why first,' Freddie said having found the tone he was looking for - one of affected severity. Stopping his shuffling he waited for her response.

'Why what?' Kitty feigned innocence.

'Why you've suddenly come down? You're worried about something.'

Freddie knew her better than she had hoped. She didn't know why it always surprised her, 'I just want to know who it is I'm working for.'

'Why *these* containers? They aren't Daring.'

'Maybe not.'

'But?' Freddie crossed his arms.

His determination was almost comical but Kitty felt no desire to laugh. The situation was less amusing. She gave in to his enquiry - only after affording him a dramatically deep sigh, '*But...* they're the only records kept on a Daring client and something just feels, I don't know... off. Call me crazy but—'

'You're not crazy.'

'Thank you.'

'You're insane,' Freddie said as he lead the way out of the room. He didn't want to fight. He never wanted to fight and knew, as they both did, that tackling Kitty head on would only end one way. She was a fighter plain and simple.

Freddie talked about everything he had found out about the containers as they walked through the port, but it wasn't until he mentioned their registered contents that he recaptured Kitty's wandering attention.

'What's Coltan?' she asked, her interest piqued.

Pleased she was talking again, Freddie launched into a lengthy tirade about the morally ambiguous, grey metal. It took them a while to reach the container. Plenty long enough for Kitty to fully understand the listed contents.

'Here it is,' Freddie announced. The bolt seal had already been cut, so using all his strength, he heaved opened the heavy metal door.

Kitty entered the large metal box. Her heart sank immediately. The unit had been cleared of its contents. Just the empty shell remained, answering nothing. Returning to the light, something cracked beneath her boot. Bending down Kitty picked up a small hard fragment.

'Ow!' she cursed. A red blob of fresh blood welled on her finger. 'Glass,' she said looking at the clear shard in her hands.

Freddie took the object. Pulling a tissue from his pocket he held it out to her. 'Looks like a piece off a bottle,' he said inspecting the shard. 'There's a brand name, but you can't see what it said.'

'But Coltan wouldn't be transported in glass. That's weird no?'

'Kit.' Freddie raised his eyebrows, 'Some people drink around here.'

'Fine.' Kitty crossed her arms at Freddie's dismissal of her suspicions, 'Where's the next one?'

The next container was located on the other side of the port. Rounding a grey, prefab structure Kitty fell backward as Fred snatched at her arm. Having pulled her off-balance, he dragged her entire weight back behind the building until she could steady herself against one of its walls. Their bodies pressed against one another, Kitty frowned until Freddie removed his hand which he had placed over her mouth. He held a finger to his lips.

'What the fuck,' Kitty mouthed, nodding her compliance only after Freddie had once more clasped his hand over her face.

Freed, Kitty snuck a quick look around the corner of the building. Vasili's second container was otherwise occupied.

'I'm assuming these aren't port workers?' Kitty whispered turning back to Freddie.

Six dark-clothed individuals were swarming every part of the container and surrounding area. Kitty hadn't been able to see if the contents of that one had been emptied yet.

Freddie shook his head.

'I knew something was weird.' Kitty felt a rush of adrenaline. She was finally getting somewhere, 'Where's the third one?'

'You must be joking, Kit. Look at those guys. They're armed.'

'And I told you something felt off,' Kitty answered Freddie's incredulity with a dollop of her own.

'This a little more than *off,* Kit.'

'They might be the ones clearing the containers. We need to get to the third before they do.' Kitty pulled out her phone. Peering once more around the building, she snapped a picture of the six figures. She was brazenly going for another when Freddie pulled her back.

'What are you doing?' she hissed.

'What are you doing? Kit, enough. You need to step away from this.'

'Why?'

'Why?' Freddie laughed quickly. Throwing his hands in the air, he proceeded to drag Kitty by the arm in the opposite direction of the container. He waited until he was sure they couldn't be overheard before speaking again, 'Because, I don't know, you could be in danger. They have guns.'

'And? I'm not planning on fighting them.' She met Freddie's gaze square on, 'Fred this could be illegal.'

'Why do you care?'

'Why don't you?' Kitty looked away from him. She thought of Raphael. Of Elliot. Of the CPS Training scheme. Of just how much of the story she hadn't told him. She changed tack, 'I just do and you said you'd help me.'

'I'm not going to help you get into something that you can't handle.'

'Can't handle?' Kitty was getting bored of people saying she was in over her head.

'If you had a family you'd understand.'

'What's that supposed to mean?'

'What I mean is, people care about you. I care about you. About your safety and whatever this is.' He waved vaguely in the direction they had just come, 'It's for the police. Or... I don't know. But not for some girl from Truro on some ill-conceived mission to set the world to rights.'

'I'm not from Truro. I have no family. Like you so gallantly reminded me. Being abandoned somewhere isn't quite the same thing.'

385

'Kit, that wasn't my point and you know it.'

'Wasn't it?' Kitty stalked off.

At the sight of her retreating figure, Freddie's resolve crumbled. 'It's not here,' he called after her.

Kitty turned back to look at him, a murderous expression still marking her face.

'The third container,' he qualified. 'It's not here. It was moved to this address.' Freddie offered up a crumpled post-it note that had been hidden in his jacket.

Kitty took it and looked at the information he had scribbled down. 'That's not the same code.'

'No,' Freddie replied. 'So I can't be sure. That's why I was taking ages this morning. It's not the same code but I'm pretty sure it *is* the same container. The weight, size, arrival time. It's the same. And it came from the same place as the other two. So—'

'Thank you.' Kitty embraced Freddie. She felt him tense beneath her.

'Look after yourself.' Freddie muttered kicking at the ground, but she was gone. Like when they were younger. Always disappearing before he had the courage to say what he felt. He thought of the day she had first left Cornwall for Cambridge. She never listened to him then, so he was not sure why he was always so surprised.

Only once installed on the train, in the emptiest carriage she could find, Kitty called Elliot. 'Elliot?'

'Yeh, I'm here. You come to your senses?'

The voice on the other end of the line sounded harsh, but Kitty pressed on undeterred, 'I don't know about that but I need to ask you something.'

'Before you do,' Elliot's tone turned softer, 'I should apologise. I was way out of line the other day. I just…' he paused, '…I just know you can be *so* much more than that arsehole's girl Friday.'

'I'm a graduate intern not a secretary,' Kitty corrected, not entirely sure why.

Elliot laughed, 'Well more than that too. Kitty—'

'Elliot, it's fine. Look—'

'No, it's not. I let my feelings cloud my professional judgement, but I'm not wrong, and I'm hoping you've kept that open mind I asked for?'

'Well that depends on something,' Kitty began.

'What?'

'I need to know if this is personal?'

There was a minute pause before Elliot spoke again, 'Is that what Raphael said?' he asked. His tone was still calm.

'Would it matter? I'm asking now.'

'Kitty. It ain't personal. He may seem great. But it's not right what they do, and I'm going to find the proof to stop it. To stop Daring.'

'So it's not personal?'

'It's professional. I may personally have a hatred of criminals, but this case is straight down the line,' Elliot answered.

'So if Raphael has nothing to do with anything then he walks?'

'Of course. If he's innocent then he's not my problem. But—'

'But something's wrong. I get it.'

Elliot laughed quickly.

There was a silence as both refrained from speaking. Kitty deliberated her options. The list was short. 'I think I have something,' she finally offered. She had made her decision.

* * *

'We have one,' Mac said standing by the container. Five other members of the team, appearing from all sides of the large block, gathered around him waiting for the small machine to fire up. 'It's being checked,' he assured the waiting faces, flushed from the cold.

The image of a young woman flashed up on the screen.

'Our tail,' Mac announced smugly.

'Any associations?' The question came from inside the container.

Mac checked the screen one final time, 'We got her working at Daring.'

A palpable ripple of excitement ran through the group.

THIRTY-ONE

Vasili was pleased with himself at the site he had chosen to implement the final preparations required to complete his task. A disused meat-packing factory in the forgotten outer- belt of poverty that still circled part of the city. Each time he visited the building he struggled to believe that he was technically within the clutches of the capital, the northern perimeter perhaps, but still London. One day, the old brick shell with its industrial, nineteen-twenties windows would perhaps become an apartment block or office complex. The rusted meat hooks, which still hung in rows above his head would be removed, and the mass slaughter that had happened here daily would be all but forgotten. He found the space sublimely poetic.

Making his way to the centre of the room, the light, having been filtered through the layers of dust and grime that caked the windows, gave the space a strange buff-coloured hue like being caught in a perpetual sandstorm, Vasili picked up the jacket. It was lighter than he had expected. Smaller. Minimal. He returned it carefully to the table shaking his head. The Chechen's always provided the crazy ones. Movlid Varayev - d'yavol'skiy portnoy as Vasili knew him - had proved to be no different.

Standing to one side, Varayev picked at his dirt encrusted fingernails. He was sweating heavily, despite the freezing temperature inside the cavernous room, as he waited for the appraisal of his creation to be completed. Having excavated each nail bed, he moved to scratch at his balding scalp where the skin was red and irritated.

'It works?' Vasili asked.

Varayev nodded respectfully, returning his hands to his sides.

'Deliver it today.' Vasili turned to Pavel who had just entered behind him.

Having spent the last twelve hours finalising his master's plans, Pavel looked tired as he took up his position to Vasili's right and began directing orders at the bodies that had been helping clear the factory. *It would all be over soon,* he comforted himself, rubbing his puffy eyes. Once the last of the cocaine was finally distributed and the body of the stupid dock worker disposed of - another thankless task - there would be nothing left of their dealings.

A strangled shout, followed by a series of panicked wails sliced through the silence, interrupting Pavel's progressively fatigued train of thought. The increasingly exhausted pleas, echoed around the room disturbing the sites only remaining inhabitants, a flock of nesting pigeons, who in turn added their own discordant chanting. Disturbed, the three men looked toward the origin of the noise, their expressions devoid of concern, they looked more as one gazes at a passerby from a cafe window - mildly interested, nothing more. Without needing to be asked, two of the bodies made their way to the location of the yelling.

Pressing at the vein that was beginning to swell on his forehead, Vasili waited for the screaming to stop. Their guest must have broken free from their restraints. They would be put out of their misery soon enough.

Only once silence had been restored and the pigeons had returned to their roosts did he speak. 'When will you be finished?' he asked Pavel, returning to the task at hand as though nothing had happened.

'The recordings were completed this morning. We can move out in half an hour.'

'Good.' Vasili began to smile but stopped on seeing his brother entering the room with apparent distress, his heavy steps disturbing the birds.

'We have a problem brother,' Nikolay called, huffing loudly as he thrust his phone up to Vasili's face.

'When was this taken?' Pavel asked having seen the photograph illuminated on the screen.

Vasili remained silent, stroking his forehead.

'This morning,' Nikolay flustered.

'Who are these people?' Pavel began to fidget, subconsciously mirroring Nikolay's stress.

'According to our friend. These three are with the NCA. Haven't got recognition of the other four.' Nikolay looked at Vasili, 'And her?'

'I'll sort her,' Vasili answered turning to leave the room. Taking out his own phone, he forwarded a copy of the image Nikolay had just shown him to Nero. He added one accompanying message.

We have a curious little cat.

Sliding into the Maybach, Vasili slumped against the pre-heated leather, welcoming its embrace. It had been a long day indeed. Before he was able to fully relax, Pavel appeared again, rapping his knuckles against the dark tinted glass of the car window. Vasili reluctantly rolled it down a fraction.

'What do you want us to do with the factory?' Pavel asked, forcing his face into the small gap.

Vasili considered his options before answering, 'Burn it,' he decided. *No one should ruin this place with apartments.*

'And Varayev?'

'Do I need to ask?' Vasili peered up at Pavel through the gap in the window.

Pavel hung his head, removing a cigarette from a packet in his pocket, he tried to hide his shaking hands.

Vasili began to roll the window up, 'Just make sure you remove any link to us. That's the main thing. Once this happens, we've done our bit in the chain and the authorities are not going to have time to concern themselves with a little cocaine.'

Peering through a window so covered in grime and cobwebs it was almost opaque, Kitty struggled to make out anything in the factory. Her searches had revealed the place had once served as a meat-packing facility abandoned in the late sixties. Despite the London postcode, its location had been deemed too undesirable to be considered worth developing, and so Kitty thought it rather remarkable the building was still standing at all. Mother Nature had done her best to reclaim large sections of the complex, tangling roots through windows, breaking panes in the process, and peeling back roof tiles. Yet despite this, the outer-structure was well preserved - eerily so.

The Uber driver she had used from the station apparently agreed. 'Not many folk head up 'ere no more. Real rough area. You sure you're meetin' someone? It's spooky that old factory,' The woman had repeated in between efforts to retune the radio of her Toyota Prius.

Having failed to open a door, which Kitty had found on the far side of what appeared to be the main building, she now tried another. This one, partially obscured by overgrown shrubs which had managed to find their way through the cracks in the concrete covered ground, was also frustratingly locked. It did not budge in its frame as she forced her entire weight against it.

Not disheartened, Kitty returned to what she thought was the front of the factory. Once there, she continued to peer into some of the other ground floor windows. Adrenaline spiked her system as she thought she saw a figure moving through one of the rooms, but on seeing little else, she couldn't be certain that it hadn't been simply a trick of the fading light. There was no sign of a container, despite this being the address Freddie had given her. Nor any pallets or anything else that suggested a recent delivery of metal - or something more sinister for that matter.

Kitty made her way to the the next ground floor window. This one, almost completely concealed by more tangled foliage, had been broken and multiple panes were missing from the lowest level. She lay on hands and knees in the plants blinking into the din, her coat keeping out the prick of the thorns that lined the brambles like barbed wire.

The room beyond was fairly dark. Rows of old meat hooks still hung from the ceiling standing as a disturbing reminder of what once went on inside. Using the torch on her phone, she swung the beam of light around the space until it caught something shining. Reflecting the beam back toward her. Metal? Her hopes lifted.

Flat on her belly, Kitty edged closer to the broken window. She sized up the gap, seeing if she could fit through without cutting herself on the smashed glass. It was too small. Turning her phone light on again, she focussed the beam on the metal object, trying to work out what it was. It was too new to have been abandoned when the rest of the facility had been. The meat hooks were long since rusted and tellingly dull. She stopped. It was a pair of handcuffs.

The roar of an engine filled her ears and Kitty rammed her phone back into her pocket, hiding the light. Her heart began hammering in her chest, another surge of adrenaline coursing through her veins. Someone was here. She hadn't noticed any vehicles. Then again, she qualified, the factory complex was large and she hadn't searched the whole premises. Kitty stayed low, pressing herself as near to the ground as possible, as the glare of headlights illuminated a section of wall up ahead.

By the time the car had passed, her night vision so disturbed that she hadn't even noticed the model, she realised she had been holding her breath.

Kitty sat up. Gasping for air as though she had been held underwater. *Breath*, she told herself over and over. *Breath*.

Her heart jumped again as her phone began to ring and she scrambled to silence it. Wrenching it from her coat pocket, Kitty saw various messages from Jaz filling the screen. Each notification bubble becoming decidedly more anxious - Freddie had clearly not kept quiet about her sudden trip south. Returning the device to her pocket, Kitty put the phone on silent. Their worrying was the last thing she needed.

Spooked by the car and the discovery of the handcuffs, she began to make her way back to the road. None of it made sense and now, seemingly an impossibility, the idea that this was all some grand delusion had become alarmingly appealing.

THIRTY-TWO

'Where's Kiti?' Raphael asked as he entered his office.

Natalie, following close behind with a stack of missives, teetered on her heels as she tried to keep up with his brisk pace, 'She was reassigned.'

'What?' Raphael turned to face his secretary.

Registering the confusion on her boss's face Natalie stopped stock still, 'There was a project… at the VP's office—'

'Get me Nero.'

'Of course sir.' With that Natalie left still carrying the envelopes, her usual appearance of calm efficiency broken.

Having flown back into London that morning, Raphael was tired as he sat at his desk, waiting for his uncle to show his face. He needed to know which cartel Vasili had sourced the cocaine from, and he hoped to God that Nero had bothered to ask. Raphael had made various agreements with an array of cartels when he had stated that he would no longer be transporting their products through the Daring network; assurances that were intended to be pleasing to any disappointed parties - they had all been *disappointed*. The agreement to take these gangs on as clients of the consortium had only just stemmed the flow of grievances. He had also been obliged to agree that he would not ship any rival's products down the line, no matter how lucrative the deal offered. This had been an easy thing for Raphael to agree to do, but if Nero had broken the deal, it could have dire consequences for them all. Rubbing the sleep from his eyes, Raphael worried that these consequences might have already begun, on an isolated beach, with a semi-retired accountant living in the Caribbean.

Ten minutes had passed before Natalie reappeared at the office door, picking at the corner of a small notebook.

'He's not here is he?' Raphael asked becoming tired of her fidgeting.

Natalie lowered the book, 'Mr Ossani's office say that he's taken a few personal days.'

'Fine,' Raphael sighed. 'Is Alec here?'

'Mr Page is in the waiting area,' Natalie beamed, pleased with her first positive answer of the morning.

'Send him in.'

Alec appeared moments later. His limp had become quite pronounced.

'You alright?' Raphael asked.

'Marathon's probably going to be off the cards this year.' Alec extended his hand.

There was a pause before Raphael shook it - they both noticed.

'You alright?' Alec asked eyeing Raphael's hands. The ridges of the knuckles were cut and purpled with bruises, so far the only tangible results of his trip west.

Raphael ignored the question. 'Hayes was killed by a cartel,' he began.

'Which one?' Alec asked as he lowered himself onto the nearest sofa, relieving the pressure on his leg.

'I don't know.'

'And the proof?'

Raphael stared down at Alec. He clenched his jaw. They both knew he didn't have any.

'So why then?'

Raphael mulled over his options. He couldn't admit to having just been in Tortola, not even to Alec. 'I asked around,' he offered.

'You asked around. That's great,' Alec retorted.

'Alec, there was cocaine left in the house *after* Hayes had been killed.'

'Yeh, but what does that mean?'

'It's a warning.'

'To whom?'

Raphael stopped. Alec's initial response playing over in his head. 'You knew?' He suddenly realised Caneel had been right. It hadn't been police scouring the property in the days after Hayes' death.

Alec looked out the window, fixing his gaze on some far off building.

'What else do you know?' Raphael continued.

'I can't tell you that.'

'Alec—'

'Tell me something first.' Alec stood, returning his gaze from the city skyline.

'No. This wasn't me before you ask again,' Raphael pre-empted testily. 'And I can't clear my name if you won't tell me what it is I'm up against.'

'Is that what you've been doing?' Alec asked, once again eyeing Raphael's injured hands.

'Some people weren't as forthcoming as others.'

Alec ploughed his fingers through his hair. 'There's *some* DNA evidence.'

'What kind?'

'Some.'

'Your boss isn't interested in it though, am I right?'

Alec chewed on his lip before answering, 'She wants the top of the pyramid. She's not interested in catching a killer who was clearly paid to do it. Without proof I can't help you, Raf.' With that he turned to leave.

Raphael caught up with him by the door, 'How long were you investigating Hayes?' The question had been bugging him throughout the long flight back to London, the NCA must have been going some time to have got so close and they likely had found help on the inside.

'I'll see you soon, Turtle.' Alec waved as he left the room.

THIRTY-THREE

Climbing the carpeted stairs to the second floor of the duplex on Coldharbour lane, Kitty recognised a voice, deep in conversation with Mrs Smeaton, that she hadn't been expecting.

'Ooo Kitty m'dear, if I was a few years younger,' Mrs Smeaton hailed as soon as she entered the room. The tangy smell of dried oranges following close behind.

Kitty looked apologetically to the blushing face seated on the far side of the dining table, beside the beaming scot and her latest batch of potpourri. An indifference to compliments was something they both shared.

'Hi Burt,' Kitty said once the two were alone. Mrs Smeaton had thankfully taken Kitty's surprise as her queue to leave.

'Cleo,' he smiled, but Kitty could see the worry etched in his expression.

'Fred called you didn't he?'

'Aye Cleo, he did. The lad's a bit worried.'

'He shouldn't be,' Kitty hissed.

'Should I?'

Caught off guard by Burt's concern, Kitty felt overwhelmed by the weight of all the recent sneaking around and lies of the last few months. 'I'm fine,' she started, but her voice cracked, betraying her.

'Cleo.' Burt rose from the table. Balling his fists determinedly, he crossed the room and embraced Kitty in an awkward hug - they didn't do that sort of thing. 'Fred wouldn't tell me what you were doing but he said—'

'To be honest, I don't even know what I'm doing.' Her shoulders slumped forward.

'How so?'

Burt followed as Kitty led him into the small single bedroom. She shut the door once inside, well aware it was really only a pretence at privacy, and took a seat on the bed. Burt copied her, his weight causing the old mattress to sag beneath the two of them, drawing them together. Kitty felt his large shoulder warm and strong against hers and smelt the ocean salt on his clothes. She was surprised by the comfort she found in it. 'I need you to tell me about Dad,' she began after a moment.

In all the years Burt had tried to be the family Kitty had lost, she had never asked him to talk about Claudius. Not once. 'He was a good man,' Burt began, as though qualifying some unspoken accusation.

Kitty noted the word "*good*". She wasn't sure what that meant anymore. 'I think I'm old enough to get a bit more than that.'

Burt settled his back against the wall, opening up the space between them. Kitty mirrored his movements, feeling the welcome cool of the mildly damp wallpaper.

'Claudius was the best prosecutor this country's ever seen. I mean really Cleo. He was ruthless and, one crook at a time, he cleaned up his jurisdiction.'

'But…' Kitty felt it hanging in the air. Tense and obtrusive.

'He didn't want *you* to be any part of fighting crime. So if that's what you're doing then—'

'That's not true,' she countered.

'Yes it is.' Burt's voice had a force to it that Kitty had never heard before.

'No it's not. We used to play at it all the time. It's all we ever did.'

'*Play* Cleo. You used to play.' Burt cocked his head, his brows deeply furrowed, 'The real world doesn't work on the same principles. There's no '*right*' way of doing things.'

'What's that supposed to mean?'

'It means he didn't want you to have to be in the position he was.'

'That being?'

Burt remained silent. He began to pick at a loose stitch on his trousers.

'Burt,' Kitty pushed.

The man, who now seemed to have aged dramatically since her move to London, opened his mouth but then hesitated.

'Burt,' Kitty tried again.

'He crossed a lot of lines,' Burt offered at last, with a look suggesting it had injured him somehow.

Kitty felt a nausea swell in her stomach, 'Lines?'

'Claudius had a reputation for burying evidence.'

Kitty thought she was going to vomit. Her stomach contracted violently and a hotness flushed down her neck.

'Breathe, Cleo. You don't need to hear this.'

'Yeh, I think I do.' Kitty forced open the window, welcoming the freezing draft on her dampening forehead.

'He talked about it once. In all the years I knew him. One time. The day he made me your guardian.'

'Go on,' Kitty encouraged - Burt had stopped again.

'Claudius was working on a case. A stabbing. Gang related. He had the guy but—'

'Something didn't add up?'

Burt ignored Kitty's presumption, instead continuing with his memory of events, 'The guy Claudius had, had previous convictions. He wasn't a good man.'

There is was again, "*good*". Kitty felt her stomach contract once more, 'But what? The evidence suggested otherwise on this occasion?'

'It was the witness testimony of a druggie—'

'And he buried it?'

'Nope. Not that case. The guy got off. But the next time Claudius saw him, he got him for the murder of a young woman. She had a one week old baby.'

Burt's eyes seemed to glisten, as though he was going to cry and so Kitty pressed on faster - Burt never cried.

'So what? After that he just started making up his own rules?' she asked.

'Cleo, the criminals he put away maybe didn't do the things he locked them up for, but London was a safer place without them wandering about.'

Kitty couldn't hear anymore. Raphael had been right. 'He was no better than they were.'

'He made a choice.'

'He lied.' Her voice had fallen to a pained whisper.

'He made a choice, Cleo, and he had to live by it. But he didn't want you anything to do with it.'

'Hence you and Truro and…' Kitty let the words fail, finally understanding why Claudius had sent her so far away from everything she had ever known.

'Your father loved you very much. He believed in the "*greater good.*" The end justifying the means.' Burt couldn't justify the facts anymore, but he knew it wasn't his place to judge.

'He was a liar.' Kitty felt her eyes hot and wet.

'Unfortunately life isn't that black and white.'

Kitty grappled with the buttons on her coat. Despite the draft coming through the open window she was still heating up. Throwing the coat loose on the bed, her phone flew out of the pocket and hit the floor. The screen lit up on impact. She had five new missed calls.

'Well that answers that,' she mumbled to herself, noting the caller. She tried to steady her breathing, but it was too late. Kitty had just enough time to reach the sink in the kitchen before her stomach contracted violently again and she vomited. She retched again and again until only clear liquid was coming up and her stomach was as empty as a newborn.

THIRTY-FOUR

Kitty stared at Raphael as he opened the large black door to the Italianate villa and a confused sadness filled her. After all this time, here they stood, more like strangers than friends. She looked at him and all she saw was a stream of unanswered, perhaps unanswerable questions. Either way, they would not be silenced this time. He would answer her or she would leave, and there would be no going back.

Having accompanied Burt to Waterloo Station an hour before, Kitty felt as shaky as the foundations that had carried her her entire life as she crossed the stone-tiled hall into the living room beyond. The revelations about her father had taken away the one thing she had ever believed in. Burt, for all his failings, had shown a wisdom befitting his age and as much as she hated it, he was right, the world wasn't black and white. So if Kitty couldn't get an explanation from her father why he had done what he had, then she sure as hell was going to get one from Raphael. It was this promise, that she had made herself on seeing his missed calls, that now bolstered her resolve.

Having answered Raphael on his sixth attempt at contacting her, Kitty had asked to see him. She wasn't sure why he had phoned so many times, and hadn't waited long enough to find out, although the sternness of his features since the moment she had arrived suggested he hadn't been about to ask her round himself. On reflection, Kitty realised she had given him no choice but to accept her request.

Kitty sat on the L-shaped sofa. Sinking into its cushioned embrace, no longer delivering her the comfort it once had, she pushed the memories of the last time she had sat there from her mind.

'Do you want a drink?' Raphael broke the silence. His tone was impassively polite. Cold.

Kitty swallowed. 'No.'

'What do you want, Kiti?'

'I want you to be honest with me.'

'Why?' Raphael asked. Still cold.

'Don't be like that.'

'Like what?'

'Like that. Cold. Rude. Don't you care at all?'

Raphael set his jaw.

Ignoring the hurt left by the first unanswered question, she swallowed again, reminding herself of her promise, 'I want to know why Elliot is so convinced you're breaking the law?'

'I told you he—'

'No you didn't. You said it was personal for him. That doesn't count as an explanation.'

Raphael stood up and made his way over to the fireplace. Stroking the cool marble mantle he sighed.

'Raphael,' Kitty pressed. 'Just tell me.'

Raphael eyed her warily before turning away. He looked as worn down as she felt, but Kitty was not certain if this wasn't just her own projections - or desires. Maybe the idea he felt anything for her at all was the grand delusion she had constructed after all.

'There was an assault case,' Raphael began, catching Kitty off-guard. He was still staring at the marble, tracing the lines in the stone with his index finger. 'Grievous bodily harm. The victim had suffered three fractured ribs, a punctured lung and a serious concussion after a fight outside a pub in London. It should have been an open and shut case. Easy for the CPS. There was a witness, CCTV footage further down the street showing the accused had been in the area and of course the victim's own statement.'

'So what happened?' Kitty asked, keeping her eyes firmly fixed on Raphael as he continued.

'Case got dismissed before trial. The judge threw it out.'

'Why? That doesn't make sense.'

'There was a contradictory witness and the video footage that had been captured was inadmissible.'

'How so?'

Raphael looked up briefly, 'Because it had been filmed on a domestic surveillance camera. There'd been no signs saying there was one in operation and the storage of the footage was, questionable to say the least.' He remembered

407

the expensive lawyer lecturing wearing an Italian suit the colour of freshly dug truffles - his tricks had been about as dirty.

'But with the other evidence surely it still could have made it to trial?'

'The second witness hadn't been disclosed correctly. So the case was dismissed as the defendant could no longer have a fair trial.' Raphael looked away again.

'How does Elliot fit in?'

Raphael paused, 'He was the prosecutor. First big case. It nearly ruined his whole career.'

'And you fit in how?'

Raphael now looked at Kitty directly. He held her attention, the answer to her question despairingly written all over his face.

'So why didn't he disclose the witness?' she continued, ignoring the pull of his cerulean stare.

Raphael set his jaw.

'Raphael?'

'He didn't know about it.' Raphael sighed.

'So it was the police's fault then instead of the prosecution?'

'Not exactly.'

'But you made it look like it was Elliot's own incompetence.' Kitty finally understood.

'It was much more believable that a young, eager prosecutor had withheld a piece of evidence that undermined his entire case.'

'And the police?'

'The investigating officer had… some problems.'

'Which got sorted on the completion of his compliance no doubt.'

Raphael nodded. He turned away from Kitty, placing both hands on the mantlepiece as though for support. She saw his shoulder blades tense under his shirt.

'What was the fight about?' she asked.

Raphael hung his head, his voice, quiet now, filled with emotion as he spoke, 'I don't even remember.'

Kitty sat still for a moment before another question came to her, 'When?'

'Sorry?'

'When did this happen? The fight.'

'Oh,' Raphael nodded. 'A few months before I did the Army Officer Selection Board.'

As the evening closed in around them, Raphael, still refraining from joining Kitty on the sofa, explained his reasons for joining the Army. The purpose. The structure. Something to believe in. A value system. Kitty, although she didn't say this to him, understood all too well how that must have felt. The wanting to be better. To have someone affirm your worth, but there was still something she didn't understand, 'So why though, if your family means so much to you and they were so against the Army, did you join anyway?'

Raphael stopped.

'Please?' Kitty implored.

'Kiti—'

'Please just tell me whatever it is.'

Raphael, succumbing to some unspoken desire, closed the gap between them. He sat for the first time that evening. 'You'll leave.'

'What?'

'If I tell you this, you'll never see me how you used too.'

A memory resurfaced in Kitty's mind, 'That's why you came inside?' She shook her head, 'That night at Jaz's student house. When we met'

'You saw me as the soldier.' He smiled weakly, shaking his head as though he had just shown himself to be some artless fool.

Kitty felt a pang of sadness, 'And who were you before that?'

'Someone else.' His smile vanished instantly.

'Who?'

'Kiti, please…' Raphael began, his eyes widening.

'Raphael, what we have or don't have doesn't matter. It's nothing anyway if it's all built on a lie. So you can either tell me now and I might stay. Or you won't and I'll definitely leave.'

Raphael watched Kitty, trying to ascertain if she was really going to follow through with her threat. She remained still, sitting with her arms crossed over her chest, waiting for him to explain. After a few minutes of silence, she made a move to leave.

'Fine,' Raphael sighed.

Kitty sat back down on the sofa as Raphael began to talk.

'My family has a home in Tuscany. We spent our summers there as far back as I can remember. The main house formed part of a monastery in the fifteenth century and then later became a Medicean villa. It's beautiful, Kiti. It has gardens filled with frangipani and orchards and we used to… yeh. Anyway…'

* * *

'Raphael, you piece of shit!' Martina yelled from the driveway.

We could hear her screaming from the Kitchen and God knows where else. She had always been wildly over-dramatic. Understated was still proving to be an alien concept to her.

'She noticed then,' Luca chuckled darkly from his seat opposite me at the kitchen table. His eyes sparkled like a feral beast. He knew what was coming.

Our cook, Giulia, had just finished a batch of fresh cannoli shells and I was desperate to have a few with Nutella before she filled them with ricotta cream. It always tasted better here than the crap English alternative we were palmed off with at school. I had tried to take some proper Italian stuff back with me at the beginning of the school year, but some meathead pricks in the year above had stolen it on the second day of term. Spouting some hierarchical bollocks. It was hard to fit in to a place you simply didn't belong.

Less than a minute had passed by the time Martina found me. I didn't bother looking at her until she smacked me so hard on the back I thought I was going to choke. She had beat the wind right out of me, and a piece of cannoli shell that I had not quite swallowed in time flew across the table. Stupid girl. It wasn't my fault that she had left the keys to her new car so easily accessible. A gift from our uncle for her seventeenth birthday - I had not been given the same.

'You aren't going to say anything?' she spat acidly.

I watched out the corner of my eye as Luca tried to swallow his smile. He had started forcing Nutella-smothered cannoli shells into his face at top speed now. He was a piece of shit. It had been his idea, but clearly he was not about to leap to my defence. Damn siblings.

'Nothing?' Martina growled.

Only when she smacked me around the ears did I stand up. Giulia wisely left the room.

'I needed a car,' I stated, forcing my voice to stay casual. That would piss her off even more and besides, it was the truth.

'Get your own.'

'He can't,' Luca interrupted, grinning again. 'He failed his driving test!' he added doubling over in fits of laughter like it was the most hilarious thing I had ever done. It had been the bloody instructor's fault. Grumpy old coglione.

Martina took a moment to lift her jaw off the floor. She had obviously not heard about my recent failure. Why she had thought Nero hadn't given me the same birthday present as her escaped me.

'It's just a scratch,' I offered. As soon as I had said it I knew I had made a grave mistake.

'Vaffanculo! Go fuc—'

'Grazie tesora. Thank you darling.' My mother swept into the kitchen. Her clean fresh smell filled the room.

I sat down picking up another cannoli shell. *Thank god for Giulia,* I thought, having just noticed Martina's close proximity to a stack of carving knives. Covering the sweet pastry in chocolate I almost had it in my mouth when my mother smacked it out of my hand.

'What happened?' she breathed.

'You knocked it out my hand,' I gestured to the chocolate mess on the tablecloth.

'To the car?' Mother growled. She could be scarier than Martina when she wanted to be. Under the perfume and finely pressed linen she was the fiercest woman I had ever met - perhaps that ever existed.

Luca had stopped smiling. I swallowed, 'I…' I paused to allow Luca to join in. He remained silent. I rolled my eyes. 'I borrowed the car.'

'You don't have a license?' she queried.

Luca snorted, before he started coughing violently, trying to cover for his amusement. He wouldn't be winning an Oscar anytime soon.

'Yeh that's basically where the problems began.'

'It's missing a door,' Martina protested emphatically.

'And that's where they ended,' I added getting up from the table.

That afternoon I was made to take the car, despite my last efforts at driving, down to the local garage in town. The repairman was nursing an impressive headache from his previous evening at the dog fight. Notte, one of Nano's pups, a jet black, furious beast of a creature had torn the competition apart. Thanks to this, I was up on my personal finances and thanks to the fact I knew the repairman was also up, due to some insider information I had provided him with, I planned to keep it that way.

Martina had been exaggerating that the door was missing. I had the door. It just was no longer attached. Some fool drunk, who had lost a lot on the fights, had bust it off. Luca, another fool drunk, had been taunting the poor sod and mid insult he had opened the door and the madman had driven right into it. Fortunately we had recovered the door before leaving.

I was still at the garage, having agreed with the repairman that I could have this job on the house, when one of Nero's men came to find me. They didn't explain much as they hauled me into the back of a large tinted Range Rover. Nero was sat in the adjacent seat.

'I've sorted Martina's car,' I began on seeing Nero's expression. He looked furious. His forehead deeply creased. 'I'm sorry I left the villa last night,' I tried again. Nero had told all of us to stay inside all evening. I had been surprised that I had been allowed to head to the garage in town that afternoon. Apparently there had been some death threats made. Not that that was particularly uncommon, but Nero seemed to be taking these seriously. Something was strange.

Nero raised his hand and I knew to be silent, 'Your stupid sister went out earlier,' he growled, lighting a cigarette.

'What?'

'She went out because you pissed her off,' he yelled.

'Where did she go?'

'We don't know, because she hasn't come back and we can't find her.'

'What do you want me to do?' I asked. It wasn't so much what he had said that unnerved me, it was the edge of apprehension in his voice. I had never seen Nero like this.

'You are a man are you not?'

'Yes,' I answered. I was seventeen.

'Then this is your mess and you will sort it out when we find her.'

'Fine,' I hissed back, full of young male-pride.

Nero slapped me hard across the cheek. I clenched my jaw, trying to ignore the stinging pain. His rings had done the most damage and I could feel a cut below my right eye.

I restrained from wiping it, just letting the blood slowly trickle down my cheek.

We didn't talk the whole way back to the villa. Nor did we talk as we waited to hear about Martina. Pulce was kept in her room with our mother, but Luca was forced to wait with me in the hall. Looking at the state of his face, he had been given the same telling off. He must have confessed to his part in the crime. I stared hard at the ground. Counting stone tiles, trying to breath through the frustration. Martina could never just do what she was told.

It was just after eleven o'clock in the evening when Nero got a call from one of his contacts. They had found her. She had been taken by some man and he had kept her hostage or something. Nero was not forthcoming with any of the facts. He kept leaving the hall, before returning, shouting at Luca and then leaving again. Luca really had confessed.

By half past, the three of us, accompanied by one of Nero's drivers, were back on the road heading to collect Martina. The sun had set on a cloudless day and the perfect inky sky was glistening with stars. A large moon illuminated the cypress-studded hills as we drove for about an hour, progressively getting more and more remote. None of us spoke. We all knew what was about to happen. The man, if they had him, was about to be given the beating of a lifetime and Luca was going to be the one to give it to him. *Stupid Martina, stupid Martina,* played on a loop in my brain. Over and over I kept thinking it. Cursing her. She never listened. I balled my fists then un-balled them. Then began repeating that too, until Nero smacked me around the head for fidgeting - I was so angry I hadn't even seen him reach for me from the front seat.

'Your mess,' he kept saying to Luca. Taunting.

Luca said nothing.

Obviously my part in yesterday's escapades had been excused.

After navigating a winding road that was little more than a dirt track, the car finally stopped outside an old, fairly dilapidated church surrounded by a parched graveyard that seemed almost as forgotten as the building itself. The only sign of life was a tall rosemary bush, with an abundance of sky-blue flowers, that cloaked the eastern wall of the bell tower. Another SUV with private plates, and a rust-riddled transit van were parked by the edge of the graveyard, where three men hovered. One was smoking heavily. We watched as he finished one cigarette then loaded another into his eager mouth - a clearly practiced exchange.

Luca and I waited by the car as Nero disappeared inside. The night was warm and the distinctive smell of the summer Rosmary hung in the dry air. Luca was unusually quiet. I didn't ask him why. A while later we were told by one of Nero's men, the one who had been smoking by the SUV, to go inside.

As I approached the Church's ancient wooden door I saw Martina briefly as she was escorted past me and taken straight to the car we had just left. Her face was bruised and she was crying. She gave me a look, but I couldn't tell what she had meant by it. It was intense, I supposed. Then again, my sister was always intense.

Inside the church was simple but surprisingly well-kept. There was no doubt that it was still in regular use by someone. The crisp alter-cloth was entirely creaseless and

416

the air inside was tinctured with the scent of incense and regularly lit candles.

As I made my way up the aisle I found myself making the sign of the cross. Luca, unsurprisingly, did not.

As we walked up the nave Nero came into view. He was standing over the body of a man not much older than us. The man was bent over as though in prayer and where the moonlight was pouring through a stained glass window behind him, his skin was tinted an unnaturally dark red. As we neared, Nero began shouting about the man's crimes. I was not sure who it was he was shouting to, but it was loud enough that everyone in the vicinity would be able to hear. Number one on the list was the kidnapping of Martina - that point he hammered home louder than the rest.

Luca was readying for a fight beside me. I could feel his energy change. Intensify. He was practically lunging at the man by the time we made it to the alter, his muscles coiled tense.

Up close the man's eyes were bloodshot, his lip was badly split and his right ear was bleeding. Blood, as dark as the stained glass, coloured his ripped shirt and lay in pools covering the stone floor around him. Intermittently, his head bobbed and eyes rolled in his skull. There was not much left for Luca to do. That was when Nero pulled a pistol from his jacket.

Luca stopped still. The tension in his muscles vanished instantly, any plan he had harboured entirely forgotten.

I watched disbelieving as Nero handed the weapon to my brother.

'Tidy your mess,' was all Nero said. His words now not much louder than a whisper.

Luca finally took the gun from our Uncle, but over the sound of the kneeling man's sobs, I could hear he was murmuring his disbelief. He was as lost as I had ever seen him.

I watched as the pistol wobbled back and forth in his trembling hands.

'Now,' Nero growled, growing impatient.

I didn't know what to do. I still didn't know what I was doing when I started yelling at Nero. 'We're in a church,' was the best I could manage and once I had let it out I stood by the fact like a guardsman to his post, unsure of whether it would help, but determined to try.

Nero looked at me with steely cold eyes.

'This is consecrated ground,' I added, trying to sound defiant and ignore the shivers of adrenaline that were running up and down my spine. Luca would be damned. What was Nero thinking? He had gone insane.

We stared at one another for what felt like a long while before Nero grabbed the half dead man by the shoulder and wrenched him up onto his feet. A frail scream gurgled from his limp jaw - I thought it was broken.

Shoving passed us, Nero began to walk the man toward the doors. 'Still consecrated?' he jeered back at me every few steps. 'Now?' He took another few steps further back. 'Now?' He was blind with rage.

Nero's men, who had been skulking in the shadows by the door, dragged Luca and I outside after them, making light work of my protestations. Luca did not look well. The pistol still shaking at his side, his cheeks had gone as grey as the tombstones that surrounded us. The Range Rover had vanished along with Martina.

'Where's the priest?' Nero shouted to the burly man whose hand was clamped like a vice around my shoulder. 'Where is he?' he bellowed.

It was not long before the priest was located. Just long enough for the blood to return to my shoulder where I had been restrained. I rotated it slowly.

'Is this consecrated ground?' Nero asked the priest.

The man nodded calmly. He was a man of God alright. I could tell by the way he looked at us - more in sorrow than judgement.

'Here?' Nero hollered.

The priest nodded again.

'Here?' Nero dragged the body further from the church.

The priest shook his head. They had apparently made it beyond the reaches of God's protection.

Bile rose in my throat. 'Uncle! Stop.'

Nero dropped the half dead man in the dirt and walked up to me. He back handed me so hard across the face, cutting my lip in the process, that I fell to the floor.

'Luca. Sort your mess. Now,' he growled.

Luca started to cry and Nero began to beat him for it. He hit him until Luca pissed himself and, standing in his own urine, the pistol fell to the floor. Thankfully, due to its internal safety, it didn't go off. Instead the gun just skittered along the faded, thirsty grass toward me and stopped centimetres from my hands.

They all stopped when the gun went off.

The shouting. The beating. The crying.

It all went away as the sound of the shot echoed around the hillside.

'Finally, someone with balls,' was all Nero said as he climbed into the SUV. The two heavies dragged the corpse to the transit van.

I didn't move. I couldn't move. My body had become heavy, my muscles refusing to respond to even the simplest of commands. I thought maybe I would piss myself like Luca had. I didn't.

I don't remember going into the church. But that's where my mother found me. Kneeling before the alter. The cloth clenched in my hands. Tears streaming down my face.

'You did well Raphael. You are a man now.' Was all she said before she kissed me.

I still didn't move.

It had been my idea to go to the dog fight.

* * *

'She kissed me like it was ok. Like...' Raphael's voice trailed off.

'And that's why you and Martina don't get along?'

'She should never have left the villa.'

'Mmm,' Kitty mumbled lost for words. She was not sure how long she remained silent. Her mind racing through endless questions. Unanswerable dilemmas.

'Say something,' Raphael whispered.

Kitty remained quiet. Sitting completely motionless.

'Kiti?' he pressed. But she was unable to summon any response.

'I'll call Wilson to take you home.' Raphael stood to leave the room. His voice hollow.

'Wait.'

420

Raphael turned back to face Kitty.

'You were a child,' she began.

'I was seventeen.'

'You didn't have a choice, you—'

'Kiti, you don't need to try and defend what I did. I killed that boy. That's who I am.'

'Who you *were*.'

'*Am,* Kiti,' he frowned.

Kitty stood. She closed the distance between them and took Raphael's hands in hers. They were cold. 'Thank you,' she whispered, ignoring the bruises.

'For what?'

'Telling me.'

'Why?' his frown deepened.

'Honesty.'

Raphael looked away, 'I'll get Wilson.'

Kitty caught his arm. 'I don't want to leave.'

Raphael could hide many things, but his eyes couldn't mask the shock her words had caused.

'You may have done those things, but I can't imagine the situation you were in and your family and...' Kitty continued talking, rambling as she tried to make sense of what she knew. She was no longer certain who it was she was talking too, the broken man before her, or the one who had died when she was seven. She knew she had to believe in one of them. She knew there was only one of them left to believe in. 'But—'

'There are no buts. That's me. I did it and I can't undo what I've done and I've done it so many times—'

'Look at me.' Kitty placed her hands on either side of Raphael's face. 'Look at me.' He reluctantly obliged her as she pulled his face so he met her gaze. 'That's not the man I see.'

Kitty felt Raphael's muscles relax under her fingertips. An element of relief in his expression and underneath that something much more profound. Intense. They stared, holding each others attention until they found themselves kissing. Softly at first but with a need so strong Kitty thought it would break her. They kissed again, Raphael gently holding her to his chest, his hands resting on the small of her back.

Then he pulled away, 'Kiti, are you sure you want this?'

His concern touched her. He asked so little of her yet so much of himself, 'Yes.' She answered.

Kitty didn't remember much of their journey to his bedroom. Just his lips. His face on hers. Hands on her. He was being more restrained than the last time. Cautious. Delicate. As though she could change her mind at any moment and he would simply walk away.

Kitty clung to him. Tangling her hands in his hair she held him to her. Minimising the distance between their entangled bodies. She didn't want him to leave. She didn't want him to walk away. Kitty knew inside that she hadn't processed anything of what he had told her. Not really. But right now none of that seemed to matter. He hadn't lied. He had been honest, the first man in her life to show himself to her, fully and without restraint and that was all she cared about. Kissing him, she let him back into her life.

Kitty could feel the warmth of Raphael's body beside her as she lay cocooned in the silk sheets of his bed. His breathing was shallow and regular, and she wasn't sure if he was still awake.

'You were right by the way,' she said quietly to the ceiling. She was not sure if she wanted him to be asleep or not. Kitty felt Raphael shift.

'About what?' he murmured.

'My father.'

'Kiti,' Raphael rolled onto his side and looked down at her. She was not looking at him as he spoke. 'I should never have said—'

'Well it's true,' she answered quickly. Flatly. She didn't want to talk about it, she knew well enough processing happened with time and nothing could circumvent that journey. She just needed to hear herself say it.

'Can I ask you something?'

'Seems fair,' Kitty answered, her eyes still fixed on the ceiling.

'Why do you hate your name?'

Kitty turned to Raphael, thrown by his question. 'What?'

'Cleopatra. Why don't you like it when people call you that?'

Kitty stifled a humourless laugh. It all seemed painfully ironic now, 'My father was born into a very poor family. His parents tried their best but they *"couldn't manage"* was all he used to say about it. He was taken by social services and grew up in various foster homes around the city. He'd been too old to win the hearts of another family and so'd never been adopted. When he turned sixteen he changed his name legally to Claudius.'

'What was his name before?' Raphael asked.

Kitty looked away, 'I don't know. He would never tell me.'

'So why Claudius?'

Kitty scratched at her palm, 'Claudius was the name of the first Roman Emperor to be born outside of Italy. Due to illness as a child he had a limp and a speech impediment. Because of this he was ostracised and never seen as a threat or contender for any real leadership position. But he succeeded anyway. When he was the last man of his family left alive, on his own, he rose to Emperor and triumphed where everyone thought he couldn't. He's responsible for the conquest of Britain, among other things. He—'

'He became something great.'

'Quite.' Kitty moved to sit up. Pressing her back against the headboard she continued, 'My father had a belief that a name meant everything. It was your declaration to the word that you meant business and were going to make something of yourself. So when I came along—'

'He named you Cleopatra.'

'Yeh.' She smiled, 'The world's last Pharaoh, and arguably the first woman to rule alone for more than a decade. In his eyes she was greatness personified.'

'So why do you hate the name?' Raphael moved to sit up too. He was staring at her intently, showing he didn't understand. His eyes scanned her expression.

Kitty stared hard into his questions, 'Because I never did any of the great things we talked about.'

'That's not the woman I see,' he breathed.

Kitty put her hands on Raphael's shoulders, 'Tell me you had nothing to do with Haye's murder.'

Raphael opened his mouth, but before he could answer, Kitty placed a silencing finger over his lips, 'As in *you* Raphael. Were *you* personally, not your bastard uncle or anyone else in your family or Daring or… just you. Were you involved in the events that led to that happening?'

'No.'

As his answer hit her, she fell into him, pressing against his chest. This time there was no caution. No delicacy from either of them. They made love as though they would never get the chance again.

Kitty woke to the sound of her phone buzzing. Her limbs still heavy with sleep, she made her way unsteadily towards the garment slung over the back of a nearby armchair, that would have looked perfectly at ease in a European palace. Memories of the night before came back to her, slowly drifting in and out of focus, as she picked a path through the discarded clothes that littered the bedroom floor.

She looked back to the bed. Raphael's face looked more peaceful than she had ever seen it, meandering soundlessly through the unencumbered oblivion of sleep. She wondered if she would ever tire of seeing him like this. Whatever they had wasn't perfect. How could it be? In her way she knew she was as broken as he was, but there was a solace in that, in not being alone. A tiny smile flicked at the corner of her mouth. She had always defined her loneliness as coming from her lack of family. To have found a kindred spirit from the biggest family she had ever seen seemed oddly amusing.

She was not so naive to assume that it would ever be simple, but for now she would enjoy the feeling of the soft stiffness in her muscles from her sleepless night. The warmth from his body. His touch. She didn't know how she felt about what she had been told - about her father and about the boy Raphael had killed outside the lonely church. There was no guarantee that she would ever know. Then there was Vasili and the containers and...

Kitty's phone buzzed again and she refocussed. Reaching into the pocket of her jacket she removed the thin black device. The illuminated message consisted of only three small words. Three words that seemed to laugh in the face of everything she had just thought. Every hope.

Reading the screen, Kitty's vision blurred and she had to put her hand against the chair to steady herself. She looked to the window. It had started to rain outside and she couldn't tell whether it was that, or her own tears that were clouding her vision.

She blinked back at the screen. At Elliot's three small words.

We got him.

Kitty felt a weakness at her knees and the room seemed to spin. A soft whimper burst unexpectedly from her lips and Raphael's hands were suddenly on her. Steadying her.

'What's wrong? Hey, Kiti. Stop,' he said, his peaceful face now anxious and confused.

'I'm so sorry,' she whispered, unable to meet his eyes. There was nothing else she could say.

'Why? Kiti? Hey, stop.' He wiped an errant tear from her cheek.

'I'm so sorry. I—'

'What have you done?'

She looked up at him for the first time, staring into his confused frown, 'I don't know.'

THIRTY-FIVE

Fourteen hulking floors of British brutalism overlooking the Georgian houses of Queen Anne's gate and St Jame's Park beyond, the concrete edifice of 102 Petty France (the headquarters of the Crown Prosecution Service), was as uncompromising inside as it appeared from the street below. Despite her father having never actually worked in the building, Kitty feared his presence, his dirty legacy embroidered into every suit that passed her, in every fibre of the unyielding cord carpet beneath her boots and in every passing sign that bore the word upon which the entire system professed to be built - justice.

'He didn't do it!' Kitty shouted at Elliot's withdrawing figure.

Elliot turned toward her protestation, the fifth of the morning, and led her from the worryingly populated, seemingly endless, strip-lit corridor and into a sparsely furnished meeting room.

'Bullshit,' he countered as soon as the door was closed to curious ears. He was running out of patience.

'He didn't do it,' Kitty protested.

Number six, Elliot counted as he crossed his arms in frustration, 'Alright, Kitty. Enlighten me. How are you so sure?'

'I just know.' Kitty knew it sounded ridiculous, but what else could she say?

'You know. Right. That'll work in court.' He turned to make his exit.

'You're wrong about him.'

Elliot sighed, but his voice dropped a fraction, losing its bluster, 'Please, Kitty. Let it go. We got him. The evidence is all there.' He moved again toward the door.

Kitty cut in front of him, blocking his escape from the room. 'That's a lie.'

'A lie?' Elliot growled, his chest rising with umbrage. 'A lie?' His face contorted in anger.

'Like the fact you said this wasn't personal,' Kitty spat. She was no better prepared to keep the conversation civil than Elliot was proving to be.

'So he told you then?' Elliot snorted. 'He told you he set me up.'

'And now you're setting him up.'

'No. There's solid evidence.'

'Then tell me what it is?'

Elliot took a step away from the door, 'The containers you found tested positive for drugs. Cocaine to be exact.

429

The building you lead us to, also positive for drugs, at least what was left of it. The pricks tried to burn it down. The shipping numbers you found that found the whole trail you discovered in the Daring accounts—'

'You can't link any of that specifically to Raphael,' Kitty stated, confident in her assessment of the facts.

'We'll see what a jury think.'

'Elliot. It's all circumstantial,' she pressed. 'The judge'll laugh you out of the courtroom before you get anywhere near a jury.'

'See, Kitty, you're wrong.'

Kitty thought she saw a smile tug at the corner of Elliot's mouth.

'How?' she asked, the uneasy feeling that had settled in her stomach, finally registered in her voice.

Elliot smiled brazenly now. 'They *are* linked to Raphael,' he continued.

Kitty waited, folding her arms. She wouldn't indulge him with another question.

'Linked through you.'

Kitty's mouth dropped open as she watched Elliot swagger to the table in the middle of the room. She followed, dodging the two chairs he pushed out of his path.

As he spoke, he began to place a series of photographs, previously concealed in the deep pockets of his trench coat, on the table. Kitty braced herself for the sight of Hayes' gruesome corpse, but it did not appear. What did was much more concerning. Each picture was a surveillance shot. Each one taken from afar, using long range lenses. Each one was her.

'You work at Daring. You're dating the CEO, or at least sleeping with him…' Elliot continued to lay the photos out on the table. 'You've been photographed at all the locations. Your name is listed on the accounts the money is being paid through, and we've watched you coming and going from Raphael's private residence.'

'You had me followed?' Kitty did little to remove the disgust in her voice, hoping it would mask some of her escalating panic.

'I told you that you weren't our only person at Daring,' Elliot replied matter-of-factly.

'So what about Hayes? What about—'

'There was cocaine in the house where he was murdered and flights booked through the Daring servers *that* weekend to BVI.'

'Raphael wasn't there that weekend.' Kitty felt a spike of hope. 'He was with me.'

'For all of it?'

She remained silent.

'I didn't think so,' Elliot breathed, wearing his self-satisfaction like an Olympic medal.

'Elliot. Stop. You have too—'

'Calm down,' he cut her off. 'All you have to do is testify and we can remove you from any repercussions.'

Kitty felt her knees go weak for the second time that morning, but this time a growing rage held her up instead of a chair. Claudius's legacy was clearly alive and well. She steadied herself on the table, 'I don't care about… I won't—'

Elliot cut her off again, launching into a cockeyed ramble about legal precedents and how well she had done.

431

How it would all be fine and how she would get over her crush or whatever it was. She didn't hear the rest.

Kitty let the words wash over her. She just tried to breath, focus on what she had seen. The handcuffs. The containers. Vasili. Nero. Hayes. There was something she had missed. Something she wasn't seeing. The thought danced around the outer corners of her mind. Vanishing before anything could fully form, allowing Elliot's rambles to fight their way back in.

'Just stop!' she yelled. She couldn't hear anymore. He was wrong.

'What's your problem?' Elliot spat, scowling darkly again.

'Just take your head out of your arse for one second and listen. There's more going on here.'

Elliot began collecting the photographs on the table. Apparently he had heard enough.

'Why would he do this for a bit of cocaine? All this fuss? I saw the containers. I saw the building. There were handcuffs. There's Vasili and it's got to be more than—'

'We have him, Kitty. And you can help or go down with him.' Elliot made his way to the door.

'Elliot.'

'Stop.' He raised a warning hand.

'Why did you ask me to help you if, when I'm telling you you're wrong, you won't listen?'

'I asked you to help because I thought you'd understand that sometimes the law's what protects these bastards. What d'you think your old man was doing all those years? He saw the bigger picture.'

'What happened to Blackstone's ratio?'

Elliot laughed disbelieving.

Kitty continued undeterred. She had to get him to stop. 'Isn't that what you lawyers all learn? Isn't that the foundation of our entire justice system?' The merry St Bernard from her childhood gambled into the centre of her mind. She squished the paradoxical irony of his name considering Burt's recent admission, 'Better ten guilty persons escape than—'

'Than one innocent suffer,' Elliot finished. 'I know what it is. But he's not innocent, Kitty. He's not innocent of shit.'

'You couldn't have known from the beginning that I would end up with Raphael or even find anything?'

'I had no idea how it would work out. But I trusted as Claudius' daughter you'd find something if there was anything to be found, and then you'd do the *right* thing.'

"*Right*" - the word unchained a host of emotions in Kitty. 'You mean lie for you.'

'I don't need you to lie for me, Kitty. It's up to you if you're gonna lie now to protect yourself.'

'Where is he?'

Elliot looked back at Kitty, '*So* disappointing.' He shook his head before he spoke, 'Don't worry, the son-of-a-bitch'll get bail. But whether you testify or not, he's going away for a long fucking time.' Elliot opened the door, but, with his hand still on the knob, turned back unexpectedly. 'Don't throw your life away.'

'Don't throw his,' Kitty replied evenly.

Elliot sighed as he disappeared into the corridor.

433

THIRTY-SIX

Kitty sat on the steps outside Raphael's house. She felt the cold of the stone seeping through her clothes, chilling the backs of her thighs and wondered how long she would have to wait. There was no guarantee he would return. No guarantee he would come back here once he was granted bail. She had tried to get hold of him but he was not answering her calls. Thankfully, having recognised her from before, the security had let her in and so far she hadn't come up with a better strategy than waiting.

The memory of Raphael's arrest played over and over in her head. The police had arrived moments after Elliot's text had buzzed her into consciousness. Raphael had gone willingly but they had still handcuffed him. Elliot, who arrived in a separate vehicle, had watched on with a smug pleasure as Raphael had been locked in the back of one of the police cars. The whole ordeal had been way over the top. Like a scene from a poorly made crime film. Too many people. All amped up. She had been spared the ordeal of being arrested herself, instead being ushered into Elliot's car and taken to his offices where she had spent the rest of the morning lobbying on Raphael's behalf. But between the blue flashing lights (another ludicrous addition) she hadn't seen anything beyond Raphael's face on hers. His expression caught somewhere between shock and disappointment. On reflection she understood it now. It was betrayal. A hotness pricked in her eyes and she blinked them hard. She would not cry.

The highly tuned roar of an engine was followed swiftly by the sight of the dark Range Rover spinning round into the driveway. Wilson was nowhere to be seen, instead Raphael was driving. He must have seen her on the steps as he pulled the vehicle to a stop, but his expression gave nothing away. As soon as the engine noise fell quiet, Raphael was out the car and striding purposefully toward the house. He didn't look at Kitty, passing her as though she were unknown to him, or worse invisible - a snub she felt more keenly than she would ever admit.

'Nothing?' she called after him, allowing her voice to saturate with incredulity.

Raphael paused momentarily with his hand on the door but offered nothing.

'Fine. I'll start,' Kitty began. 'I need your help, and you need mine too, for what it's worth. There's something else going on here. I don't know what but it's bigger than drugs and I saw a—'

'Kiti. Stop.' Raphael did not turn around.

435

'So you won't even try and prove your innocence?'

'Not with you.'

'What?' Kitty waited for an answer that never came, 'Why "*not with me?*" What did Elliot say?'

Raphael turned, 'This isn't about Elliot.'

'No then—'

'You set me up. *You* did. Why would I trust you?'

'I didn't… I—'

'Just leave,' his voice cooled to stone as he disappeared through the door.

Kitty threw herself against it before it closed. She would not be ordered away like some Jehovah's Witness evangelising on Christmas Day. Forcing her way into the villa, she walked fast to keep up with Raphael's pace as he marched across the hall.

'I'm the one being set up here,' she called.

Raphael ignored her.

Kitty stopped walking, rooting herself in the centre of the hall. She wondered how long she had before she was physically escorted off the premises. She assumed security could do that for him. Just as Raphael reached a doorway on the far side of the hall, she spoke again, 'Jesus, Raphael, you can't have it both ways! You can't profess to be trying to change then when the time comes do nothing about it.'

'Neither can you,' he snarled spinning on his heel.

'What does that even mean?'

'You can't have me when you want and then switch sides when you don't like what you're getting. I warned you who I was. You said you were fine with it and then you chose Elliot and all the shit he represents. I told you it

436

wasn't me. I was honest. Where was your honesty last night?'

'I didn't, and this isn't about *us*.'

'Get out of my house.'

Kitty ignored the order. He was being ridiculous. Male pride never ceased to amaze her, 'He has photos of me at the containers. At the building where one of them was moved too. Leaving your house. Vasili's Daring account is in my name, and he has flight bookings the weekend Hayes was killed booked through Daring. I don't know if there's anything else. I don't know what's connected or how, but we can at least start—'

'Get out, Kiti,' he spoke clearly and without emotion. They were strangers again.

Something Kitty had always been good at spotting was a lost cause - she just wasn't good at acknowledging when to let go. However, on this occasion, knowing Raphael wasn't going to hear anything she had to say, and with the unsettling worry that time was somehow running out, mixed with the sick knowledge that no-one was looking at whatever the hell was really going on with Vasili and the containers, Kitty retreated from the villa.

It was a long way back to Brixton. With storm clouds coming and the smell of rain she should have started her return immediately. But she didn't. She didn't head for the tube. She just began to walk. Walk wherever her senses drew her. She didn't see what was in front of her as she moved. She was vaguely aware of crossings and traffic lights, with the odd car horn reminding her to go more cautiously at the next road. As she wandered, she played over everything she thought she knew.

437

She couldn't explain to herself why she had walked to the Mission but somehow, in crisscrossing the London streets it had drawn her in like the tide and she found herself discarded on its shores. Exhausted and footsore.

Inside the lights were on and the refugees were settling down for the approaching evening. Food had already been served and only the leftovers now lay, cold and unappetizing, on the side by the servery. A few children were helping themselves to seconds or perhaps thirds. When you had travelled how they had, come as far, you always ate when there was food and ate as much as possible, however cold and unappetizing, for the promise of the next meal was not one you could rely on. Checking her watch, she realised the sunset prayers, Salat al-maghrib, would be starting soon.

Scanning the room, Kitty noticed the friendly, elderly man from her last visit, the one whose family she had delivered food to in the corner of the room. Their group had been too frightened to approach the servery, but on this occasion she found him alone. A worried feeling settled in her stomach which deepened when he spotted her.

The man began to yell at Kitty across the room. The local imam, wearing a traditional white thobe was standing beside him, his body language giving the impression that he was trying, with little success, to calm the old man. Kitty crossed the room. Pairs of eyes, brimming with anxiety, removed their gaze from her as she caught each one. Once she was a couple of feet away, the old man switched to English and began shouting again. His voice found a strength which his body appeared incapable of supporting.

'Where Layal?' he repeated again and again.

'I'm sorry?' Kitty asked, confused.

'Where La—' he started but broke down in tears before he could finish the question.

The imam gestured for Kitty to move to one side and she obliged him.

'Where is his family?' she asked quietly.

A sadness crossed the imam's face, 'The children are with their mothers and aunts. We set up a wash house and they are cleaning. But the eldest, Layal, she has gone missing.'

'What? How is that possible?'

'It happens more than you know.'

'So have you phoned the police?'

The imam shook his head.

'With respect you have too—'

The imam raised his palm, 'I know you were here the other day, and this community needs all the help it can get, but you have to understand not all these refugees arrived here by legal means.'

'But—'

'So they're not protected by the law. With respect,' the imam nodded, 'calling the police won't help this man. He got so irate when you arrived I was hoping you may know where Layal had gone too.'

'Can I talk to him?'

'I don't think… He is very upset.' The imam delivered Kitty a kind smile. He gestured toward the door, but she ignored him.

The old man looked so broken. To have travelled so far, then to lose one when you were supposed to be safe - she had to at least try to understand. Maybe she could help.

'Please translate for me so he understands.' Kitty asked as she returned to the elderly man.

The imam nodded. He would not cause a scene, and although he was not certain, perhaps she could help. He began translating as she spoke.

'My name is Kitty and we met the other day.'

The old man nodded launching into Arabic.

'Rifaat remembers you. He says you brought them food,' the imam translated.

'Yes. Rifaat? Is that your name?' Kitty asked.

'Yes,' the imam replied.

The man nodded in agreement, clearly recognising his name. His eyes burned with a fierce determination. 'Where Layal? She has no English. No speak here,' Rifaat started to wail again.

'I don't know where she is. Can you tell me anything about where she might have gone? I can look there for you or…' Kitty ran out of suggestions. She waited in silence before Rifaat's response was translated.

The imam looked uncomfortably at Kitty and then back at Rifaat, asking him something in Arabic. By the tone of the imam's apparent questions, Kitty sensed he was asking for some sort of clarification.

'This shelter relies on donations,' the imam began after a wary pause.

He was not translating.

'What did he say?' Kitty asked.

'Without the donations these people would be out on the street.'

'I understand.'

'Are you sure?' the imam pressed.

'Yes,' Kitty replied sternly.

440

'Rifaat,' he nodded once more to the man, 'seems to think that Layal was taken by the men who work for your friend.'

'My friend?' Kitty was lost again.

The imam started speaking hurriedly to Rifaat again. He turned back to Kitty, 'The woman. With the jewels he said. Do you know her?'

Rifaat started nodding despite not having been asked himself.

'Yes I do. But Irina wouldn't—' Kitty stopped, she didn't know what she was saying. She didn't know Irina. Irina was married to Vasili after all.

'That's all he said.' The imam raised his hands in apology. 'Please don't—'

'I'm sorry.' Kitty began to retreat across the hall.

Reaching the street she took a series of deep breaths, large gulps to try and fend off the maelstrom of ideas crowding her head, all jostling for centre-stage. She began to pace, pausing briefly to stabilise herself on a nearby wall before pressing on. That was a mistake.

Her dizziness having not yet subsided, Kitty crashed into one of the newspaper stands outside the independent corner shop. The shopkeeper hurried out as she began scooping up the newspapers which had fallen onto the pavement. Flung open, their grim contents did little to calm the chill which had begun in the base of her spine. Photographs...Syria... drowned children... more bodies. She stuffed the pages back onto the stand and began to put as much distance between herself and the shelter as possible. Layal had taken centre-stage. Or a dark-eyed figure representing her. Young. Full of potential. Kitty couldn't be certain she could remember exactly what the

441

girl looked like, but she didn't need to. She could imagine and that was proving to be a whole lot worse

'Irına, hi...' Kitty began, switching to Russian to finish her greeting. In the maelstrom she had somehow answered her phone. An automatic response she wished had not occurred.

The connection wasn't good, and twice Kitty checked to see how strong her signal was as Irina whispered down the line. Kitty strained to hear the woman in between her coughing, which was protracted and affected, her voice unaffected by any ailment in between the fits. The woman was seeming to be trying to apologise for something, and it took Kitty a minute to remember that the event, the rooftop extravaganza over looking St Paul's, was supposed to be starting in less than half an hour. Apparently Irina had been taken ill and wouldn't be attending. Having shown no great interest in the event previously, it would not have been, in the normal order of things particularly surprising that she was clearly bailing, feigning an illness to cover for her bad manners. But there was something else. Something in her voice.

'Is there anything else?' Kitty asked. 'Just tell me. You can trust me Irina.'

There was a pause on the line.

'Irina?' Kitty pushed. She thought she heard Vasili's voice in the background before the connection went dead. Kitty checked her phone again - full signal.

Less than a minute later the phone began ringing and Kitty answered in record time.

'Don't go tonight,' was all she caught from Irina, whispering even softer than before, before the woman hung up.

Kitty tried Irina five times. Three times in two minutes. Then a fourth and fifth attempt spaced five minutes apart, just incase Irina had lost signal, or battery power. In her heart, the chill now spreading to all corners of her body, Kitty knew that neither poor signal, nor low power, was why Irina was now uncontactable.

Everything she had learned in the last few weeks about organised crime flooded her head. The newspapers. The Syrian crisis. Russia's loud support for aggressive intervention. Policy change. Professor Betzalel's prophecy he had made all that time ago at Cambridge about mindsets. Perspective. Perspective.

'Perspective.' Kitty froze, and despite how crazy, how unimaginable and surely impossible her conclusion, as soon as the word was out of her mouth, everything in her told her she was right, and something else was terribly, terribly wrong.

THIRTY-SEVEN

Kitty stuffed her phone into her pocket. Raphael wasn't answering - again. She cursed herself. Him. Her father. Vasili. The whole damned world.

Kitty had guessed, considering her dismissal earlier, that Raphael wouldn't be back at the villa and even if he was, she was not as confidant about navigating her way past security as she had been earlier in the day. This left only two other alternatives, and so, as the Uber tore along the darkening London streets, she prayed she was right about her first choice. If she had taken a minute to check her watch, it would have told her to change direction.

Passing under Janus, his unnatural double-face illuminated by the glowing copper letters below, Kitty raced into the entrance lobby of the Daring headquarters.

The hour was late and the lobby was deserted as she made a beeline for the lifts. Once inside she held her ID pass against the scanner and waited for the numbers to light up, activating the elevator.

She held the pass closer when nothing happened. Then removed it and tried again. Disembarking the lift and entering an adjacent silver box, she tried twice more before giving up. Cursing Kitty ran back under the spectral installations toward the front reception.

Approaching the desk, Kitty heard the distinct click of high heels on a hard floor, glimpsed a sleek brunette bun and silently gave thanks that one of the receptionists hadn't gone home for the evening. It was a stroke of luck. Raphael could often be found staying long after business hours had ended, but these girls usually clocked off with military precision as soon as their shifts were over.

When the brunette bun heard Kitty calling to her across the lobby, she turned and switched on the requisite Daring smile. As soon as she saw Kitty, she switched it off.

'Hi,' Kitty started, unperturbed by the bun's attitude. A tiny voice in her head told Kitty that she didn't recognise this receptionist, but it was squashed under the more pressing matter at hand.

The bun looked away and continued to tidy her belongings into her handbag - an imitation Louis Vuitton embellished with a chain too flashy for any respectable fashion house.

'Hey, my pass isn't working and I really need—' Kitty tried again.

The receptionist finally looked up with an expression that implied it had pained her. 'I'm sorry it's employees

445

only past the lobby. You'll need to be accompanied by someone who works here'

'I *um* an employee. I pass here every morning. If you could just—'

'I'm sorry.' The brunette bun, heels clicking on the marble, began moving in the direction of the exit.

Kitty stood in front of her, 'If you just check your database.'

The bun pushed Kitty aside, moving her with surprising strength.

'Hey!' Kitty grabbed the woman's arm.

In that moment a voice rang out across the lobby and Kitty didn't need to read on the receptionist's face who had spoken. It was as though someone had poured a barrel of gasoline on the spark of fear in her stomach and her entire system had ignited.

'Do we have a problem?' the voice called.

Kitty removed her hand from the receptionist's arm and turned to see Nero standing under one of the large rotating installations. She had never realised how strong the similarity was between him and the floating wraiths. In her momentary distraction, while her limbic system was struggling to decide between flight, fright or freeze (and had apparently become stuck on the third), the brunette bun snuck out of the building and Kitty found herself alone with a man who frightened her more than anyone else she had ever met.

Nero slowly began to close the distance between them. Instinctively, Kitty took a couple of steps backward, lessening the distance between her and the doors the receptionist had just bolted through. Freeze was thawing swiftly to flight.

446

'Mr Ossani,' Kitty spoke with as much calm as she could muster. 'No problem.'

'So why are you here?'

'I was just leaving. I forgot... it really doesn't matter.' Kitty took another few steps toward the doors.

Nero held her gaze, 'Shouldn't you be heading to Mr Nechayev's event? You put so much work into organising it.' His crocodile grin returned to his ugly face.

'Yes. I was just picking up a few things.' Two more steps back. Three. Four.

Nero's smile widened with each step, stretching further than she had ever seen it and in that moment, if it hadn't been clear before, she knew he was aware she was lying. Flight became run.

Turning for the doors, Kitty bolted toward the exit. Throwing her weight against the glass she slammed hard against it. It was locked.

Scrambling to find where the lock was, her mind struggled to understand what had happened and assess what was happening. Kicking at the glass to no avail, Kitty turned and to her horror, saw Nero, his face unsettlingly calm, still slowly closing the distance between them. She felt the blood drain from her face - she hadn't recognised the receptionist and whoever she was, she had locked Kitty in.

Keeping Nero in her sights, Kitty pulled the phone from her pocket and called the last number saved on her phone. This time, there wasn't even a ring, instead Kitty was delivered straight to a pre-recorded answerphone message, and with Nero only a few feet away, she began yelling into the handset, 'It's Vasili. It's the event. Something's wrong. Call me back now!'

447

Nero slipped his hands into his pockets and Kitty momentarily stopped breathing.

'Just a key,' he smiled grimly, withdrawing his hand from his pocket. 'Calm down.'

Thrown, her heart beat out a fast rhythm that thumped in her ears. Transfixed on the key in Nero's hand, Kitty did not hear the door open behind her.

The first thing that alerted her to the change was the cold air that rushed up her back. Biting her neck and ruffling her hair. She spun around just in time to see a swathe of dark material coming for her face. Then everything was obscured.

THIRTY-EIGHT

Across town, gazing out over the illuminated, lead-clad dome of St Paul's cathedral, Raphael fiddled with his cufflinks. Solid eighteen carat gold, they seemed as unnecessary as the event he was now attending. He had yet to witness one where more money went to the actual charity rather than the exorbitantly lavish dinner designed to stroke the ego of whichever lollipop-headed social skeleton was hosting. So far, this one was proving to be no different.

Inconsequential polite conversation, black truffles, caviar entrées, blue lobster, ubiquitous penguin suits and champagne so expensive it was a marvel the host couldn't single-handedly end world hunger - or whatever it was they were raising money for.

'Raphael, is that you? What a treat,' a woman called across the balcony.

Turning to face the woman, Raphael forced a polite smile, greeting her with a well practiced enthusiasm. In truth, the evening had just become a whole heap worse.

'Lady Crapstone,' Raphael nodded, kissing her outstretched hand as was expected of him. He had gotten better at this part of the job, and his mother would have been proud of his charming performance he had acted so far this evening. Charming despite his brother and his uncle's unexplained absences.

'Lady Crapstone!' the woman howled in mock disgust, 'Oh please, dear boy, you make me sound so old. Augusta please. Just Augusta.' She laughed in her characteristically brittle manner, a sound reminiscent of breaking porcelain. The woman continued to prattle on about their acquaintance, something she was apparently rather proud of, followed up with customary introductions to the fellow cronies who surrounded her. And so, as was the way at these gatherings, they each took their turn to ogle and judge the young billionaire as though he were some prized bull at a farmers' market.

Augusta Gillian Crapstone, thrice divorced widow of the late Earl Crapstone, had florid pampered skin and an unfortunate penchant for sandalwood perfume and was, by Raphael's estimation, the biggest of all the big-name society hags.

Having approached her late sixties with a level of defiance only afforded by lashings of plastic surgery, it was well known that she was in search of a husband for her daughter, Euphemia Horatia Crapstone. Tonight, upon being informed that the elusive Raphael Daring was in

450

attendance, she had found herself re-invigorated in her hunting efforts - of course she had secured her invitation under a different guise. Instead by discussing - at length with whomever it was required - the "*abject horror*" of the Syrian Refugee crisis. For Augusta this had in fact been quite a challenge, for her idea of abject horror began and ended with an empty bank balance, and to her, Raphael was indeed a piece of prime breeding-stock - a bull for all intended purposes.

The small talk continued in circles. Business. Martial status. Previous holidays. Tan lines. The healing properties of organic, cold-pressed aloe vera. Future holiday plans. Future marital plans and then back to business. Augusta herself only interest in the future marital plans she hoped for Raphael.

Eventually, having gone around the ring for the fourth time, remaining sufficiently coy about his marital desires, did Raphael find an opportunity to excuse himself.

'Walk me inside darling, there's someone I want you to see,' Augusta crooned, the free-flowing champagne having instilled in her a schmaltzy affectation.

Raphael had already spotted her daughter, Euphemia, one of a few one-night mistakes from his youth that he'd rather not re-live, standing just inside with her back to them. Her attempt at understated sophistication was ruined by a platinum Rolex the size of a dinner plate fixed to her skeletally thin wrist.

'Mi dispiace, signora. Forgive me but I must make a call.' He held up his phone implying he had just received a message of paramount importance - the Italian was merely for the sake of charm. Raphael did not wait for a response,

451

instead slipping out of the woman's bejewelled clutches, and beating a hasty retreat toward the balcony doors.

Augusta was not used to being denied and unfortunately, judging by the following conspiratorial smirk pulled across her tight skin, he worried vaguely that he had only encouraged her pursuit.

Pushing that nightmare from his mind, Raphael swiftly crossed the main reception room. He slipped unseen past Euphemia and, keeping his head down to avoid being stopped, followed one of the waiters into the kitchen. Just for good measure, he held his phone to his ear the entire way, as though listening intently to an urgent message.

He was not. The bloody phone was dead and had been for some time - a problem he was looking to remedy. He may have been a free man this evening, but Raphael knew, clear as the diamonds on Augusta Gillian Crapstone's boney fingers, that with everything his lawyers and those at the CPS had told him, he was in a whole world of trouble, and if Kitty had been telling the truth earlier, then so was she.

The waiters and kitchen staff looked a little startled at Raphael's appearance. It was not often that one of the penguins sullied their experience by spending time behind-the-scenes. However, they did not put up much of a fuss, instead distracted, not by the langoustine which was to be served five different ways in under five minutes time, but by another intruder. This one having entered at the opposite end of the kitchen, through the fire escape.

Raphael, enjoying a moment of relief in the smalltalk free zone that was the kitchen, watched, at first with only tepid curiosity, as the chefs started trying to escort the intruder out.

The intruder, drowning in an oversized padded coat, seemed not to hear their shouts. Their increasingly agitated insistences that she leave at once. She was a young woman or maybe a teenage girl - it was hard to tell. Despite her clothing being more akin to that of a homeless person, she had somehow managed to possess more grace than any of the individuals Raphael had just left on the balcony, bestowing her with a level of sophistication not often found in the young. Her wide almond eyes were fixed on some distant point and Raphael wondered if she was even seeing the room before her. As she came further into the light, much to the exasperation of the event manager who had been called in to assist, Raphael saw that she was wearing a headscarf and that, almost hidden under the enormous coat, her legs were shaking so much they looked like they were about to give way.

The reason the event was being held suddenly came back to him. They were feasting to raise funds for Syrian refugees. For charities who housed the lost souls in London and kept these half-starved travellers fed and warm while people far off, grey politicians dispersed throughout the governments of Europe, argued about immigration laws and the national debt and somewhere in all that, what to do with them. Yet here was someone, young, potentially homeless and in need, who was being shooed from the premises like a stray dog, for fear she may spoil the langoustine, or worse, the frivolity going on the other side of the wall. He took a step toward the terrified girl and she fixed him with her wide almond eyes. That was all she was, just a girl.

He didn't make it two feet before the improvised explosive device detonated and the almond eyes disappeared in a blinding flash like sheet-lightning which then engulfed the entire kitchen.

Blindness followed by pain. Pain followed by panic and then Raphael found himself once more in the desert. His calloused feet assaulted by sand. An RWMIK Land Rover in mangled pieces behind him and he heard the same words he had spoken a thousand times over. *To everything there is a season...*

THIRTY-NINE

Silvertown, as if in defiance of its name, was situated in one of the most deprived local authorities in London. Despite a three billion pound development program, much of the area surrounding the Royal Docks was still as uninhabitable as it had been since the end of de-industrialisation, an enduring symbol of London's decline and the slow death of British manufacturing.

It was here, in a decaying hotel whose threshold was these days only crossed by the disenfranchised, the mentally lost and the odd vagrant who had collected or stolen just enough for a night's stay, that Vasili waited.

'It's a funny thing life,' he mused, moving into the centre of what was supposed to be a living room. A Body from MOYNA had arranged for the suite as a suitable stopping point before the plane, his reward, was ready for departure. The term *suite*, even hotel for that matter, was a stretch - there was more asbestos than furniture, the numbers on the doors the only resemblance to the Four Seasons where Irina was waiting with Sofia before her own flight to Moscow.

The voice, the familiar inflection to it, pulled Kitty back into the living world. Her vision took a moment to stabilise. Having been hooded and at some point battered hard over the head as a reward for a well timed kick, her eyes struggled to focus as the figure kept talking, the thumping pain returning with each speck of definition.

'What it rewards. What it ignores. In this country there seems to be this belief that the truth will out. Ha. The nativity of the children of a nation that has long enjoyed the benefits of security bought by the lives of those with less. It's easy to have morals when you are rich. And you are all rich. You get sick, NHS takes you in. You lose your house, your government gives you one. It allows you to speak freely. Learn freely. Think freely. Yet no one does.' Vasili started laughing.

His yellow veneers came into sharp relief and despite the pain, Kitty realised who was talking and then, feeling the ache of her shoulders and the biting sensation around her wrists, realised she was imprisoned. Trapped. Tied with her arms behind a chair that, although perhaps had been cushioned at one time, was now a hard metal skeleton, with only a few sorry drapes left of its former self. Nicotine and the stench of something stronger was seared into every last fibre.

'My country has faults. But at least we don't pretend to be better,' Vasili continued. In his delirium, he wasn't particularly aware of the direction his ramblings were taking him. He just couldn't stop himself. It had worked. He had won and with every passing jet engine roaring overheard, the giddy sensation was building momentum like a runaway train. He was no longer looking at the reeking cesspit of the suite. He was on The Summer Terrace at Café Pushkin, indulging in the large buttery pearls of caviar at Novikov, his heart beating to the relentless flow of the Moskva river. He would be like Maxim Gorky, returned from exile, to be given his just reward. Everything was about to begin and the excitement was almost too much to bear.

'You're wrong. The truth always has its day.' Kitty didn't know for whose ears she had said that. A cut she had sustained whilst inside the hood was leaking around her teeth, leaving a nauseating metallic taste. She spat onto the floor, a spatter of congealing blood laced the globule of saliva.

'You disappoint me.' Vasili walked toward her, 'What has life taught you? It is usually the orphans who realise first that all it does is take. It takes until there is nothing left.'

Whilst Vasili spoke, Kitty tried to focus on her hands, on discovering whatever was binding them. In their haste, or perhaps their underestimation of her, her captors had not tied her feet and so she knew she had two jobs. Free herself, but first, keep the madman talking. Focussing on this was the only thing keeping her mind from falling into the beckoning well of hopelessness and panic. She prayed her spiking adrenaline would be enough to keep her mind from derailing, and listened hard as it shouted its one clear instruction - survive.

457

'There's always something,' she spat again. It was rope - that was good.

'Your... urgh... boyfriend perhaps?' Vasili's face contorted. 'I must admit I didn't see that.' Vasili knelt in front of Kitty and placed a hand on each of her thighs. She tried to shake him off but he held firm and with her hands still fixed behind her back, and the throbbing pain in her skull, she couldn't muster the strength nor coordination. She had been immobilised better than she had first thought.

'Where is he?' Kitty asked, finally registering Vasili's comment, trying to keep him talking.

'He's dead.'

In between her waning strength and the panic threatening to overrun her body, the two short words did not hit at first. Did not register. Instead she felt a detachment, a welcome numbness wash into her veins and then, just as she thought she had hit the bottom, it all disappeared. The words smashed into her so hard it was like she had been thrown against a brick wall and panic submerged her in a way that felt like she might have actually been drowning.

'He's dead,' Vasili repeated.

'You're lying,' she found the coordination to speak. Resurfacing above the panic she breathed hard and fast.

'Im not,' Vasili wagged his head. 'Your actions forced me to speed up the timeline. The stupid bitch hadn't made it out of the kitchen, so the damage of the bomb was smaller than I'd hoped. But for some reason he was there. A prince in the kitchen with the workers. Ha! Life.'

Kitty felt another surge of fear and was submerged again. Her head, too heavy to support bobbed. She struggled to breath, 'You staged a suicide attack?' Her worst fears, the seemingly impossible conclusion she had come to outside the newsstand, had come to pass.

'The best part,' Vasili moved his hands from Kitty's thighs and held her dropped head, forcing it back. Forcing her to look at him. 'They blame Raphael for the cocaine, but the irony...' he smacked his lips together. 'He was the one member of the whole thing, linked only by the randomness of birth, who knew nothing about any of it until it was too late. That's the problem at the top.' Vasili let go of Kitty's head, 'You start to feel in control. Relax. Then those below get to work without you.'

'They'll work out it was you,' her voice came out like a whisper.

'I doubt that. He's a real killer. Woah, the stories. And anyway, even if they do, I will be *long* gone, and Russia won't extradite one of their own for a drugs offence.'

'Why Layal?'

'Was that her name? Huh.'

'Why?'

'Some people feel perspective needs to change in this country, Kitty. It needs to wake up.'

If he hadn't already decided her fate, if his own muscle-laden bodyguards weren't just outside the door, if Nikolay wasn't already lost in a drunken stupor in the adjacent room and if Pavel was not already preparing a bath of sulphuric acid, by far the largest single product of the chemical industry and commonly found in drain cleaner, mere feet away, Vasili would not have obliged Kitty's next questions.

'Why the drugs?'

'The Italians think they're so smart. Something had to be transported in those containers to convince them to do it, and then we needed to test the route, see if it worked.' Vasili slipped into Russian, 'Не зна́я бро́ду, не су́йся в во́ду'

He did not translate the proverb, but Kitty knew its meaning, 'Don't wade into a river without knowing a ford.' Or in other words, *see which way the cat jumps.*

She stared and a terrible thought struck her, if Raphael was dead, no one would come for her, they wouldn't even know to start looking.

Vasili continued, unaware of the newfound ferocity with which Kitty was struggling with the rope around her wrists.

'Islam is a threat to our way of life,' he said.

'It doesn't have to be,' she countered, desperate to hold his attention. Keep him talking. Keep his attention on her face.

'But humans have never been very good at sharing.'

'Why you?'

'I'll admit it's not my usual sort of thing, but I wanted to go home and this was the deal I was offered. Терпи каза́к – атаманом будешь.' This time Vasili translated, 'Be patient Cossack, you will some day become an ataman.'

Kitty couldn't stop herself from translating in her head. *No pain no gain.* The English equivalent seemed sickeningly flippant and Kitty couldn't believe what she was hearing, 'Who offered the deal?'

Vasili smiled, shaking his head, 'Even you don't want that knowledge.'

'You're insane.' Kitty turned her face away, trying to forget the smiling yellow veneers burning into her memory. The rope wasn't budging.

'I learned that to stop life taking from you, you have to start taking yourself. Perhaps with all your brains, if you had learned that, you would not be sitting here.'

Kitty, not expecting an answer, did not turn back while she spoke, 'Where's here?'

Vasili took hold of her head once again, 'Your final resting place.'

She kicked out as hard as possible into Vasili's chest. He flew backward onto the floor and she knew as soon as she saw the anger ignite in his eyes, that his retaliation would be much worse.

FORTY

Of the five known domestic intelligence agencies operating within the United Kingdom, the National Crime Agency, NCA, is the largest and arguably most daedalian of them all. A delicate amalgamation of specialist bureaus and units from a myriad of institutions: Interpol, Europol, the police force and the Serious Fraud Office, to name but a few. They transcend, like the organisations and individuals they hunt, regional and international borders, fronting the crusade against organised crime, human trafficking, drug smuggling, gun-running, as well as economic and cyber crimes.

In the back of a large SUV, fitted with blackened windows, doubtless bulletproof, and missing both sets of rear internal door handles. Ears ringing and a nasty wound gushing steadily down the right side of his face, Raphael knew they had come for him with everything they had and that, considering the gear they were packing, this was no ordinary unit. This was one of the outlier cells he had heard about during his time with the SAS. The teams who operated within their own parameters, answered only to the very top and were assigned to the NCA solely in order to capitalise on the anonymity provided by such a large organisation.

The beam of a medical grade penlight was directed into his eyes, first the right then the left and back again until his pupils began to respond as desired to the fluctuating conditions. Still in darkness, he felt a pressure on his right temple as someone tried to stem the flow of blood and later was aware of a bandage steadily encasing his right arm and shoulder.

With his eyes shut to the world, the almond-eyed girl was there, shaking in her padded coat, and his gut told him she would be there, along with all the other horrors he had witnessed throughout his life, for a long time to come.

'He's bloody lucky to be alive,' Raphael heard a voice calling, followed by a sharp sting - they had put a cannula in his arm and he briefly wondered how the hell he was alive. The voice eventually answered that too, 'Everyone the right side of the main kitchen area survived, you know the prep area in the middle, big metal section, made a sort of mini blast shelter they reckon. Incredible.'

A low humming started and the corresponding tightness on his left arm told him his blood pressure was being taken.

'Burns, cuts... can't see much else.'

Having not heard a question, Raphael wasn't sure if the voice was still talking about him.

They drove quickly, without leaving the confines of the city, until at last the SUV pulled to a stop outside an unmarked tower-block. The road was deserted, those out for the evening having returned to their homes as the first reports of a suicide bomb detonating in the heart of the City had starting appearing across the main news channels.

There was always silence before hysteria. Before they learned she had been just a girl. Before they learned she had detonated at an event being held to support her own people. Before they internalised how it could have been them. *Seven people*, Raphael thought. *Two more than the last attack in London. Fifteen less than Manchester. But it would be enough.*

His hands restrained in cuffs, Raphael was pleased when his limbs responded reassuringly to orders. Once he had disembarked the vehicle, more coordination returned and escorted, he made his way into a service lift. Having travelled up four floors, he was deposited in a small, windowless isolation room, where he remained alone within the four block walls, for the next few minutes.

The voice, which as it turned out belonged to a powerfully-built woman, stocky like a boxer, with steel-rimmed glasses, hair salted with the first signs of age and apparently some medical training, visited him first.

'Where am I?' Raphael asked.

The woman remained silent as he'd expected, removing the cannula.

He winced at the sting of the exiting needle. 'Not God's waiting room then?' he quipped.

The woman smiled in an amusingly irreverent way, before she began to check Raphael's vital signs. Blood pressure, body temperature, pulse rate, breathing rate. Then she beamed her penlight back into his eyes, checked the bandages on his right arm and the wounds on his head - which had finally stopped bleeding - and left the room and Raphael, now handcuffed to the table.

'He'll live,' he heard her say to someone moments before the door closed.

His next visitor was not as friendly.

Raphael had encountered a good proportion of finalists vying for the nastiest individual in the world title by the time most people were beginning to obsess over secondary school romances and university applications. This meant he had learned, among other things, that often the most dangerous individuals were not those who drove motorbikes, were smothered in tattoos or swore like sailors. The most dangerous were the ones like the middle-aged woman, with her sharp suit and black ball-bearing eyes, who had just taken the seat opposite him in the isolation room. Intelligent, overconfident and a devout believer in one thing above all else - the power of leverage. They were dangerous because, from personal experience, they never seemed to give up until they had found something on you, and, when they had what they were seeking, you were finished. He had seen this trait in the bleak hallways of government, the deserts of Syria, Yemen and Iraq, in the jungles of Colombia and most of all, where he had first learned of its existence, on the terraced lawns of a villa in Tuscany. He recognised it now.

Raphael leant back in his chair, utilising the full extension of the chain he was attached too. The bite of the handcuffs was more than unpleasant, but he would not sit up like a well trained dog. Their eyes locked in silent combat, Raphael waited for the woman to speak.

The woman waited too, enjoying the silence. She did not stop her wordless evaluation even when they were interrupted by a third party. Badly limping, carrying dark bags of sleeplessness, Alec took his position in the remaining seat positioned to the right of his boss. He looked between the two frozen faces.

'Raphael this is—' Alec began, trying to diffuse the tension - he was not so naive to think it possible.

'I had nothing to do with anything,' Raphael started.

Alec tried again, 'Raphael, this is Rosa Amiton. She will be—'

'Am I under arrest? Well?'

'Raphael.'

'Alec?' Raphael growled.

Rosa started to laugh quietly, drawing the attention of both the men. The noise was unnervingly sinister. 'Thank you children. Now, I'm not here for a cock fight,' she said.

Her voice was as Raphael had expected. Emotionless.

'Where's here?' he asked.

Rosa looked as thought she might smile, 'Mr Daring. Tell me about this evening.'

'I have nothing to tell you.'

'If you're waiting for a lawyer then please give up. One isn't coming for you.'

'I have nothing to tell you because I don't know what happened.'

Rosa's eyebrows flicked up, 'Ok. Let's start with Inveniam Viam then.'

Raphael's face remained impassive.

466

She continued undeterred, 'From the Latin phrase inveniam viam aut faciam. "*I shall either find a way or make one.*" How poetic. Did the nuns insist on Latin at school?'

Raphael continued to stare, forcing his features to not respond to his mounting frustration.

'I'll make this easy for you. You can nod if you like. I know you set up the consortium. I know who you set it up for. IV. The Roman numeral for four. There are four Daring siblings aren't there?' She turned to her right, 'Alec?'

Pained, Alec briefly looked to Raphael before answering, 'Yes there are four.'

'Lovely. But I wonder, do they all know about the cocaine shipments?'

'I had nothing to do with those.'

'Really. Well then, the CPS have done a fine job of setting you right up.'

Raphael continued to stare, inside feeling the flames of frustration beginning to rise. He knew letting them out would be a huge mistake.

'So you know nothing about the consortium?' Rosa queried.

'Correct.'

'Had nothing to do with Andre Hayes' murder?'

'Correct.'

'So you didn't go to the location of his death in an old Hyundai?'

'Correct,' Raphael answered without hesitation - apparently someone had not been paid enough.

'That's not what the taxi-driver said,' Rosa stated nonchalantly, qualifying Raphael's unspoken assumption.

467

She continued keeping up the brisk pace, 'And you know nothing about the bombing that just killed seven people?'

'Correct.'

'See, I find that very hard to believe.'

'That's not my problem.'

'Actually yes is is.' Removing a small remote previously tucked inside her jacket pocket, Rosa aimed it in the direction of a large LED screen bracketed to the wall. The dark box flickered to life, the empty grey rectangle replaced by a grainy picture of a man, a headshot, taken long ago for a passport. There was nothing remarkable about the face, male, dark haired, liver spot on his forehead, blue collar shirt.

'Do you recognise this man?' she asked.

'No,' Raphael answered honestly.

'Movlid Varayev. In Russia they call him d'yavol'skiy portnoy. It means the Devil's tailor. Varayev was a Chechen separatist who conveniently disappeared after the second Chechen War. It's believed Mr Daring, that Varayev has kitted out more female suicide bombers than anyone else in the last two decades. The Black Widows as they have become known. He is a wanted man to say the least.'

'Then you should get on and find him,' Raphael maintained the calm in his voice, although the almond eyed girl was threatening to break his resolve.

'We have. Thanks to you.'

Raphael looked shocked, unable to keep the confusion from his face.

Noticing, Rosa clicked a button on the remote and the screen changed to show an image of a building Raphael had never seen before. Industrial, some kind of factory.

The left wing burned to the ground. She continued to flick through various images of charred rubble, a pile of metal hooks that had survived the inferno, and then stopped on the image of a body. Blackened beyond recognition, its torso almost entirely devoid of skin. The face mutilated by something much more aggressive than fire.

'Here he is,' she commented pleasantly, as though having found the correct address in a phonebook. 'He was dead before the fire. Two bullets. Close range. Something go wrong?'

Raphael remained silent but before Rosa could continue, Alec's phone began to vibrate loudly. She gave him a withering look as he hurried for the door.

Alone Rosa continued and Raphael knew the psychological manipulation would begin shortly. She started slow.

'The buildings here were the listed address for the delivery of one of the consortium's containers. One of three that carried the cocaine and, new evidence suggests, this man. Your man?'

Raphael looked back to the burned corpse.

'Tell me about Vasili Nechayev?'

'I don't know him,' he answered.

'I have it on good authority that his event meant a great deal to you, *personally*.' Rosa silently thanked the agent who had tracked down the preppy American, it was exactly the kind of intel she liked, Raphael didn't flinch so she continued, 'But he is a Daring client no?'

'I wouldn't know.'

'Mr Daring. Ignorance is not a defence.'

Raphael held firm. He would not be forced into a confession, nor offer some conciliatory gesture. Not this easily.

'I can make this all go away. I just need a little compliance.'

Raphael sat up, leaning forward he spoke low and quiet, annunciating each word, 'Go to hell.'

Outside in the corridor, Rosa stood as still as a statue. She was in no rush and had faced more formidable opponents than a young billionaire ex-soldier who thought he was untouchable. She would enjoy this one.

Appearing around the corner, hobbling toward her, Alec began to speak in a hushed, hurried tone, 'I told you this wouldn't work. Raphael won't be bullied, Rosa.'

'Remember who you're talking to, Alec,' she hissed.

'We can't find Kitty.'

'And I care why?'

Alec held out his phone, a small video played in a loop. There was no sound.

'CCTV?' Rosa queried.

'Outside Daring head offices.'

'Well that's a shame, but the catch is in there, Alec. Not some second rate secretary who decided to get down in the ring with the scumbags and lost.'

'Rosa, you know as well as I do that that isn't the case. Elliot—'

'Elliot can never see the bigger picture.'

'But Kitty—'

'But what, Alec? Do your job and remove the personal.'

Alec returned the phone to his pocket. He knew he could regret saying it for the rest of his life, but he had run out of options, 'He's in love with her.' The words tumbled from his mouth.

Rosa's own parted and shut so quickly it went unnoticed. Then she smiled, for the first time that evening, with genuine emotion, 'That'll work.'

Alone in the cell, Raphael turned away from the LCD screen, a reminder of his failings. Kitty had been right and he hadn't listened.

Rosa returned, and he braced for phase two.

'Smart girl your Kitty,' she offered. 'So you care about something? Huh? She must be very special to have interested something as cold-hearted as you.'

Alec entered the room sheepishly, remaining in the corner. Raphael glowered at him. Rosa had obviously found her leverage and he knew he was looking at the source. He waited for her to go on.

'But I'm afraid curiosity has finally killed the cat.' She laid a small black box on the table, no bigger than a matchbox. 'She phoned you. Just before the explosion actually. We've been recording her calls. You'll like this one.' Hitting the switch on the side, Kitty's voice filled the small room. Screaming about Vasili. The event. Then it went dead, before starting all over again.

Rosa, encouraged by the pallor of Raphael's face, continued, 'From that I'm guessing, Mr Nechayev is in a bit over his head. Then again, it's amazing what you'll do to get home.'

'Do you know where she is?'

'Yes,' Rosa nodded.

'Then do your fucking job and go and get her,' Raphael growled.

'That's not my job.'

'Then your duty.'

'There it is… *duty*. It's always the same with you military lot. How about we start by talking about how you can do yours?'

Rosa Amiton was not a woman who minced her words and so for the next five minutes, uninterrupted, she meticulously outlined everything she wanted from him. It was exactly what he had suspected since Alec had appeared in his office wanting information on Hayes. The entire Daring/Ossani "*Little Black Book*" as she called it. All their contacts. Information. Account numbers. Enough to lock up some very bad and very dangerous clients. A treasure trove of subterranean activity. A discovery that would make her career. More, it would make her a legend. Raphael heard her terms - it was an impossible request.

'What you're asking for will get me killed.'

'No one likes a rat. Especially one masquerading as a king I suppose,' she said, offering no alternative.

'Three.' Raphael knew time was not something he had on his side - or Kitty's.

'I'm sorry?'

'I'll give you three,' he spoke with a finality which, although Rosa didn't respect, responded too. In thirty years it would be more than any of her colleagues had managed to get and they both knew it.

'I'm not talking names, Mr Daring. I need everything on those bastards for watertight convictions.'

'I'll get you everything you need.'

She smiled extending her hand, 'And then I want you.'

Raphael stared at her, his hands still bolted to the table, he made no move to take hers. Alec opened his mouth to object but Rosa silenced him. 'You, or your Kitty doesn't get her rescue party.'

Raphael set his jaw, 'You'll get me. None of my siblings. But I get Kitty myself. I lead the team that gets her back.'

'I love it when everyone starts playing nicely.'

Rosa unlocked the handcuffs and Raphael, ignoring her still outstretched hand stood up, 'But if we don't get her. If we're too late, you get nothing.' Then he made one final condition. A condition that was more important to him than dying whilst providing the details of some drug baron in Bogota or whichever objectionable character she wanted.

Rosa narrowed her ball-bearing eyes, but took the deal and with that, and no handshake, left the room.

Alec started up as soon as they were alone, 'I'm sorry I —'

'Where is she?'

Alec swallowed, the damage was done. 'Rosa uses private hires. She prefers it that way. But they run on similar principles to the military guys we both worked with.'

'The NCA huh?'

'A division of,' Alec muttered, leading Raphael from the isolation room and into the labyrinth of corridors.

'Where are they?'

'Downstairs. Second floor. There's an ops room. I sent the call out as soon as I knew she'd been taken.'

Raphael remained silent, his mind racing through his memories of the SAS led extractions he'd been involved with, as he followed his limping friend. They had once been on the same team and, if he was right, he knew this would be the last time they were even close.

FORTY-ONE

Pavel entered as Vasili delivered another blow to Kitty's stomach, ramming his boot hard into the soft flesh beneath her ribs. She screamed in pain.

'Босс. Boss,' he called.

Vasili turned, sweating. The vein on his forehead protruded like a broken bone as he followed Pavel across the small internal corridor, through a cramped unfurnished space and into the largest of the two bedrooms. Nikolay lay semi-conscious on the bed, his arms outstretched and enough fluid in his system to pass as a beached sea creature. Vasili shut the door on the wails of the screaming girl who sat two rooms behind him.

The Embraer Legacy 600 jet was ready for them.

'It is time,' Pavel said. 'Everyone is talking about what happened and we need to leave.'

Vasili flicked on the television, an old Toshiba that had somehow survived the hotel's miserable decline. Every channel was showing the suspected suicide attack, and already the BBC was leading the charge with discussions about what this could mean for the escalating Syrian crisis. An old Cambridge professor was explaining the politics behind the current, more liberal approach and then proceeded to weigh it against the cost of aggressive intervention. His time was cut short as he started an impassioned spiel concerning the role of perspective. He would no doubt be back when the recordings they had made of Layal were released. With no English, the girl had had no idea what she had even been reading.

'And this,' Pavel held up his phone.

Despite no official statements having been released from Westminster, the President of the United States had been commenting extravagantly online since the first reports had begun circulating the faster regions of the internet. Vasili laughed, a full jocular rumble. He had always liked the man.

The two men turned at the sound of one of Vasili's bodyguards entering the bedroom, a big, beefy man with hardly any neck.

'These just arrived,' he said, handing over a neat stack of brand new passports.

Bright red and stamped with a golden, twice imperially crowned double-headed Eagle. Vasili held them to his face and inhaled deeply. The books were symbolic rather than necessary, but the message was clear. He could go home.

Tucking the passports into his pocket, Vasili ordered the bodyguard to begin transporting his brother to the car waiting in the street outside. There was no way Nikolay was going to be able to make the walk unaided, and Vasili would not be made to stoop under the weight of his drunken brother in his moment of triumph.

Once Nikolay had been removed, Vasili unzipped his fly and began to urinate in the corner of the room. Pavel had finished the bath of sulphuric acid in the loosely termed "*en-suite*" and now all that was missing was its occupant. The fumes emanating off the pool of chemicals were beginning to reach the bedroom and Vasili did not fancy the irritation that would be caused by standing anywhere near it - besides, from the look of the room, he was not the first to use its soft furnishings for the excretion of bodily fluid.

Two rooms away, Kitty continued striving to loosen the rope around her hands, twisting and contorting as far as her screaming muscles allowed to achieve the correct angle. After having to almost dislocate her shoulder, finally, with a gasp of relief, Kitty managed to slip one hand free. The second followed almost as soon as the first was out.

She rubbed at her arms. Two raw red bands ringed the swollen flesh at her wrists and she shook them, willing the circulation back into them. She almost cried out with the pain, instead biting hard on her tongue to keep silent. Vasili had disappeared and only one thing seemed important, she needed to leave. Now.

Catching sight of a heavily muscled, bullet-headed man dragging a semi-conscious figure down the corridor, and assuming the man was not alone, Kitty instead raced in the opposite direction, toward the window, in search of escape. Guarded by a pair of stained polyester curtains, she threw back the fabric, praying she was near the ground. Praying she could jump. She couldn't remember travelling in a lift or being carried up a set of stairs. Wiping the condensation from the panes, her spirits plummeted when she looked through the glass. She estimated she was at least six storeys high.

Before Kitty could arrange her thoughts, her mind becoming an increasingly tangled jumble, she heard a door slam on its hinges. The noise was close. Too close. Not entirely sure she could manage the first idea that broke through her panic, Kitty forced herself back to the chair she had just escaped. Grabbing hold of the decaying frame, she positioned herself behind the door. Vasili would have to come all the way into the room before he would see she was no longer held captive in the corner, and his confusion could provide her only chance at escape.

Kitty waited behind the door, keeping her breath as shallow and quiet as possible. One second passed. Then two. Three. Four. She counted to twenty before she saw his shadow cross the carpet. Then waited two more until the back of his head was visible.

Using all the strength she could muster, her reluctance driven out by the will to survive, Kitty brought the metal frame down hard toward his exposed scalp.

Having sensed a movement behind him, Vasili turned just in time for a chair leg to take him square across the bridge of his nose. It smashed his septum, spraying blood and sending him half diving to the floor. A savage pain ripped across his face, shock stifling his initial screams.

Without looking back, Kitty stumbled into the corridor and was taking the first door at a run by the time she heard Vasili's shouting start. Passing through a narrow room she kept going until she had made it into the next. A bedroom. Kitty stopped almost as soon as her back foot had crossed the threshold - there was no exit here. A large double bed dominated the space. A gun and an empty vodka bottle furnished the side table, beside which two eyes glared in her direction.

A breath later Kitty began to retreat, as Pavel, exiting the bathroom, started to run toward her with a resentful determination. Kitty had only managed two steps before she slammed backwards into something despairingly immovable. She knew even before she saw the blood-stained body, what she had hit.

Swiping wildly at Vasili's smashed face, throwing him off balance, Kitty managed to evade his flailing arms and bolted down the corridor. She didn't know what she was going to do if the neckless man was there, or anyone else, but her hopes grew with every step toward the door.

Kitty never found out what was on the other side. Pavel, uninjured and fast, caught up with her long before she even reached the handle.

Clamping his arms around Kitty, digging his nails into her skin, he dragged her screaming back into the bedroom. Vasili was waiting by the door. His expression wired. Livid. Blood still pouring from his broken nose.

'Put her on the bed,' he snarled. 'And hold her.'

Pavel looked set to object, they had diverted from the plan so much already. 'The jet—' he began, using all his strength to hold the flailing girl, but Vasili's answering expression was enough to silence him.

Kitty kept trying to free herself, twisting and kicking, like a fox in a snare. But Pavel was strong and she found herself pinned to the bed, despite her best efforts, her arms fixed to her sides. Immobilised and overpowered, Kitty watched with wide eyes as Vasili walked to the countertop by the television. She hadn't noticed the grey box before and now saw that it was on.

News images, early press footage of the bomb's aftermath played in a loop on the screen. Then the police cordon came into view, behind which a puddle of terrified faces wrapped in aluminium blankets stood huddled together. A comment about islamic terrorism flashed up followed by a face from her past. Kitty started screaming at the screen.

'You ever tried drugs?' Vasili spoke as Kitty's screams cracked and faded, 'No?' He didn't wait for an answer, instead he continued, his anger audible in every word, 'I was taught when I was young. They are like women my father used to say. Tina makes you horny. Molly makes you hyper. Then the new shit came along, GHB… makes you easy.' He flashed his yellow veneers, now smeared with crimson, 'And then there's this.' Vasili held up a small white packet, before he turned back to the counter. 'Good, old-fashioned cocaine. People want so much more now. They want something synthetic. Something crazy. But I still see nothing wrong with the classics. Well, nothing wrong if you take them like this.' He dropped the powder into a glass. 'Some is soluble. Did you know that?' he continued, his back still turned.

After a moment, Vasili turned to face Kitty and a deep horror consumed her. A fine pointed syringe lay balanced between his fingers.

Kitty thrashed hard against Pavel, freeing an arm she buried it into his side, trying to free the other. He grunted with discomfort before smashing his own fist against her ribcage with such ferocity Kitty thought she actually heard her own bones crack. The pain almost swamped her.

'You worked out almost everything, the whole plan, but still never actually found this stuff. This is probably a bit much,' Vasili flicked the syringe, a spout of fluid leapt out of the top, 'but consider it a gift.' He smiled as he buried the needle into the crook of her arm. A searing point of heat followed the sharp sting.

Within seconds Kitty could feel the cocaine polluting her bloodstream. Pulsating. Racing through her veins. Wiring her senses. Her body began to tremble as the room around her fell out of focus. A pain in her chest was matched by a steady thumping in her temples.

'We need to go,' Pavel stood, picking up his pistol from the beside table as Kitty succumbed to the first seizure.

Vasili placed his hand on the barrel, 'Leave her. Trust me that was enough for her to enter psychosis. It's beautiful,' he smiled, entranced by Kitty's writhing body. 'And it will be worse.'

'The acid?'

'Surplus to requirement.'

Kitty was no longer sure where she was. The walls around her fell away to nothing leaving a vast, swirling blackness which flowed out before her in all directions, twisting infinitely like the Milky Way. She felt a moment of weightlessness before a shooting pain spiralled up her spine. Her back collided with something hard. With the carpet against her cheek, Kitty realised she was on a floor and suddenly the room was back. Four bleak walls.

481

Cramped. Polyester curtains. It was smaller than she remembered. She had fallen from the bed.

Two warped faces leered down at her. One grew fatter, rounder like a clown, the other's face was being torn apart by a set of enormous teeth, stretching into long, citrine daggers. Kitty screamed as the clown fell away, exploding into a thousand red shards. The citrine daggers ran from the shards, fading to a minuscule distant point and then vanishing completely.

Alone, Kitty began to scramble along the carpet. Drawn by the lure of a cave, Kitty huddled in to the shadows, folding herself into the compact space. It was small for a cave. She thought as she pulled the darkness in around her, whimpering, she squeezed her eyes tight shut. Trying to forget the faces.

There, in the bottom of an empty cupboard, hunted by death and blinded by fear, Kitty slipped into a painful, psychotic subconsciousness.

FORTY-TWO

The team was as good as Alec had promised. Six in-out guys. Well-trained, disciplined, not looking for some glorifying showdown, dying like martyrs in a hail of gunfire - it was amazing what this kind of work could attract and Raphael was pleased with what he saw. It would give them a chance at least.

Rosa had made her expectations clear - Vasili had to survive. Privately, Raphael was not sure that he was going to be able to deliver on that, but the team had planned for it all the same. At any rate, something Raphael had learned a long time ago in the desert, on a road that was supposed to have been cleared, plans usually went out the window.

Vasili had been tracked to a rundown hotel on the fringe of Silvertown. Ops had counted two bodyguards, a brother Nikolay Nechayev and another, currently unidentified, white male. However, on arrival it was clear Raphael's team was the second to visit the hotel that evening and the first had seemingly been operating under different expectations.

The engine of a parked car was running, its steady humming mumbling into the night, as Raphael, flanked by two other members of his team, Mac, a red-headed mammoth and Viper, whose nose had been broken so many times it appeared to be a miracle that he could even breath, made their way to the front of the hotel. Thirty feet from the door they found the first sign something was wrong.

Nikolay Nechayev, reeking of alcohol, lay slumped over one of the men identified as hired help. Two bullets had smashed through each of their spines. The bodyguard had also been gifted one to the chest which, looking at the angle, had likely burrowed deep into the lower chamber of his heart. It was undoubtedly the work of a sniper - a good one at that. Whoever had arrived first knew exactly what they were doing.

Raphael dropped low and, alongside Mac and Viper, slipped into the hotel. The three men used whatever cover they could find, trying to make themselves harder to target. Ops hadn't spotted a sniper anywhere, but the threat of one had just forced the timeline to speed up exponentially.

Raphael cursed silently as they entered the building. The reception was deserted, the manager, if one existed considering the state of the building, most likely had been paid to disappear for the evening - or a few.

The first of the hotel's clientele were found, half-dazed, shooting up in the stairwell as the three men began climbing the stairs. They knew from intel that Vasili was meant to be on the sixth floor, and with the remaining three members of the six-man team guarding the other exits and elevators, if there was anyone left to find, they wouldn't be leaving.

The bodyguard who had been stationed outside the front of the suite hadn't been as lucky as the poor bastards in the street. Shot with some kind of handgun, at exceptionally close range, the man had had no chance against professionals. He had probably only heard the sound of bone braking as his skull had shattered. The walls were spattered with the evidence of his messy demise.

Viper signalled for Raphael to stand back in order for Mac to have a clear shot at the door, but Raphael was tired of waiting, they were taking too long and clearly they had been beaten to the hotel. If Kitty was there he had to find her and the chances of her being alive were disappearing rapidly.

Protocol falling by the wayside, becoming the kind of soldier he hated, one whose emotions ruled their actions, Raphael kicked hard into the door. It swung open instantly, the lock having already been broken by the first intruder. He saw the unidentified male splayed out on the ground at the end of the corridor, shot in the skull, leaving his clothes as the only indication that it wasn't Vasili.

Mac and Viper hurried to cover Raphael's back, cursing into their radios, as he tore through each room.

They found Vasili next. His eyes, still open, fixed Raphael with a glassy stare as he searched the room. Despite the blood which covered his front, Vasili had no bullet wounds. Instead the Russian hung suspended from a light fitting, fixed crudely by the neck with what appeared to be his own belt, his feet stretched toward a floor they could not reach. A stack of Russian passports lay discarded at Vasili's feet and Raphael knew then, if it hadn't been obvious before, that whoever had hired the Russian, had clearly never intended to allow the man to go home.

Returning to the corridor, Raphael caught sight of what appeared to be the remnants of a chair. The frame was bloodied and a rope lay tangled around one of the legs. He felt his heart rate increase as he inspected the tattered seat. It was different. It didn't fit the professionalism they had witnessed on the way in. Everything indicated it had been used during a different part of the evening and the fear seemed to cripple him. He froze.

'Clear!' Mac, who had been checking the smaller of the two bedrooms, called as he returned to the corridor.

Raphael felt winded, as though the air had been punched out of his lungs, as Viper shouted the same from another part of the suite.

Forcing himself to keep going, Raphael ran into the final remaining room. A cesspit of a bedroom. Seeing nothing, he breathed deeply, steadying himself. The air was stuffy, reeking like a public toilet, but after a minute in the room, breathing in the rank air, Raphael realised it was contaminated by something much worse. Crossing the room he braced as he opened the bathroom door. At that range, the acid scratched at his eyes and they began to water. His knees almost buckled on seeing the empty tub.

'Boss.' Viper shouted from the other side of the bedroom, his head bent over his lapel, speaking quickly into his radio.

Closing the bathroom door on the pool of bleach, Raphael turned to see Mac emptying the drawers of the unit below the television and, beyond him, Viper stood by an open floor-to-ceiling wardrobe. A few remaining shards of a broken mirror hung on the inside of the door. In them, Raphael saw his worst fears reflected.

Raphael threw himself to the floor beside Kitty's crumpled body. Supporting her head, he stroked her cheeks, tapping gently as he spoke. 'Kiti, hey Kiti,' he started, willing her to respond. 'Kiti.'

With one hand on her chest, he could feel her breathing shallow and ragged and saw her chest rising in faltering waves. 'Kiti,' he tried again. This time her eyes flickered open. Fully dilated, her pupils engulfed her once shining irises, blotting out all the colour.

'Hey—'

'Raf,' Kitty mumbled no louder than a whisper. Her hand reached for his face frail but tender, 'You're alive?'

'In over your head yet?' Raphael smiled, catching hold of her hand. The relief was flooding his system. She was in shock. She had been hurt. But she was alive. She was alive and she was here. With her resting against him, his army training began to kick in and he spoke soft and certain, 'Stay with me, Kiti. You're going to be fine. It's shock, it's —'

'Boss,' Mac called, drawing Raphael's attention. He unwillingly turned away from Kitty.

A syringe rested on Mac's gloved palm.

Raphael grabbed Kitty's outstretched arm. Turning it over, he saw with horror a small puncture wound, almost invisible, except the area around was already purpling, bruised because whichever arsehole had injected her had done it so hard. He felt the tiniest pressure on his hand and looked back to Kitty's face just in time to see her eyes roll back. 'Where's the fucking ambulance?' he growled.

FORTY-THREE

A fiery smell, antiseptic and institutional assaulted Kitty's nostrils. In an instant she was awake again. Screaming. Twisting. She knew she was being taken to the bathroom. It would be over soon. All her hopes and ambitions erased like they had never existed, like she had never existed. The stinging odour continued its assault, overwhelming her other senses. Blinding her. She opened her mouth to scream, to shout one last time but instead was drowned in darkness. Her words swallowed by the shadows.

Raphael appeared in the lightless gloom, but she could not get to him. He remained just out of reach. A sadness etched into his beautiful face, his eyes bluer than she had ever seen them. She began to thrash, a last fight to survive, but Kitty felt her limbs failing her. This was it. A cool numbness encased her like a tomb.

'Sir, you need to leave,' the nurse said, directing Raphael to the door.

The noise of the ventilators, heaving and sighing like great robotic organs, surrounded Kitty's limp figure, rapidly trying to cool her soaring body temperature, stabilise her breathing and oxygenate her poisoned blood. Monitors beeped incessantly, lights flickering in rows like tiny runways to death, sounding out warnings of her racing heart. She had vomited and the bleach that had been used to clear the floor still hung in the stagnant air, polluting the space with memories of the hotel. Reminding him of the horror he had seen in the bathroom. There was no pill, no magic antidote to cocaine poisoning.

'She'll be experiencing hallucinations. A cocaine psychosis. She's delusional and you're not doing anyone any favours by standing there. Least of all her. Now sir, please,' The nurse waved again toward the door. This time, she placed a firm hand on Raphael's shoulder, her brow set in frustration. Around her, the team whirled like well-choreographed dancers, dealing with the present but preparing for the worst. The doctors appeared every few minutes to read charts, debate their course or try a different approach - nothing was working.

Kitty had fallen still again, her face serene once more as though in sleep. A new dose of heavy sedatives had started to take affect. It would slow her down for a while. Raphael didn't need to be a doctor to know her heart rate could not continue at its current speed for long.

Raphael walked slowly from the room. The nurse shut the door softly behind him, cutting off the sounds of the machines.

Outside the corridor was quiet, the stillness of anxious relatives standing guard by adjacent bays, was punctuated only by the occasional rattle of a passing trolley, or the hushed, hurried whispers of doctors coming and going from patient to patient.

Alec leaned against the wall, watching Kitty through the square glass observation window as the medical team tried to save her. 'She'll be fine, mate,' he said with a grave ambivalence, as Raphael stopped beside him. The silence between them was unbearable.

'You don't know that.'

'You found her. She's here. This isn't your fault, Raf.'

'I'm the reason she's in fucking intensive care in the first place,' Raphael glared at Alec.

The doors at the end of the corridor opened, filling the ward with a snatch of the Accident and Emergency department beyond. Raphael turned to see Rosa, striding toward him, her shoes clapping purposefully on the linoleum. She was pissed about the mission and had already made her views abundantly clear. He moved to leave. It would be a bad idea to be anywhere near her at this point.

'If she dies at this point, our deal's still on,' Rosa called after Raphael's retreating back.

Raphael spun around to face her, 'If she dies you have nothing,' he snarled.

'We still have an unexplained murder in Tortola and you're the prime suspect. I have enough.'

'I wasn't in Tortola when Hayes died.'

491

'Flights from the Daring system say otherwise,' Rosa's mouth twitched. After everything, she was smug.

Alec stepped in between the two adults, sensing Raphael was about to snap. Instead he surprised him.

Raphael's anger had brought with it a memory. Dredged from a moment he had tried to forget. When Kitty had come to the villa - when he hadn't listened - she had warned him about the so-called evidence Elliot had collected. She had said that there were flights to the British Virgin Islands booked through the Daring computer system. But he hadn't been stupid enough to book flights through Daring. He had gone private. Totally off-record. Not even as himself.

'Get a team to Daring,' Raphael shouted already ten paces nearer the exit.

'Why?' Alec called after him.

'I can't do it from here,' Raphael answered, already working out which files he needed to access.

FORTY-FOUR

It was gone midnight when Raphael arrived at the Daring offices. On route he had sent a message to his entire team, a high-priority email containing a load of bollocks about an investigation requiring full access to their personal accounts and that he would be handing over the files in the morning. Some wouldn't see it, but if he was right, the correct person would no doubt be watching for exactly that sort of thing.

Installed behind his desk, furiously typing, Raphael hoped he had done enough to encourage Hayes' killer from the shadows. He hoped whoever it was, they would want to come and clear up their trail and, thanks to a security program employed four years back, all personal files, including personal expenses found on the Daring servers, could only be accessed though each employee's assigned desktop computer within the building. Then everything was encrypted. No doubt a hacker could bypass the system, but Raphael doubted that whoever in his team had disfigured Hayes possessed the patience for those types of skills.

Scrolling through the server's files on his entire team, Raphael narrowed his search to include travel expenses only. They were organised in named groups for accounts. So any one of Raphael's wider team could book those flights and it would come under his team name. Someone looking from the outside, or someone in a junior position, could infer whatever they wanted, they could even assume it had been him specifically. On closer inspection the facts would be revealed, but it would be enough, with everything else Elliot had, to get him before a jury and that was all Elliot wanted. The killer wouldn't have known about Elliot's investigation so they wouldn't have thought twice about using the Daring servers to book flights, especially if they were senior enough to get away with expensing it - with a company as big as Daring, despite the Accounts team's insistence to the contrary, it was surprising how much people got away with.

Raphael had never thought to even check. He would never have believed someone would have had the balls to expense the flight. He couldn't believe the killer was from within his own team. Although the more he thought about it, the more it made sense that some disgruntled parties had decided to keep a closer watch on the decisions of the new Daring CEO, or at least be in a position to have access should their concerns need addressing. He knew Nero had placed people in all sorts of triads and gangs around the globe for years.

The search results pinged onto the screen. One name appeared and everything finally made sense. Raphael cursed his own stupidity, or perhaps, naivety.

A shadow moved in the doorway and Raphael realised, in his rush, he had left himself completely unarmed. He looked up to where the shadow had solidified. 'It was you,' he said, slowly moving back from the desk. Caneel had been right. The killer had had an unusual voice, but it wasn't an accent she had heard, it was a lisp.

Hugo stood in the door, feet set wide apart, arms folded behind his back. 'You bastard,' he spat, 'You thought you could ship cocaine from a rival and what, nothing? We wouldn't find out. We have people everywhere.'

Raphael's fears that Nero hadn't bothered to check the origin of Vasili's cocaine were coming to fruition. He clenched his fist, 'Which cartel, Hugo?'

Hugo glared. He was in no mood for conversation. Instead he pulled the Beretta from behind his back and fired. He missed.

'Better with a knife?' Raphael yelled back as he scrambled behind the desk, making himself a smaller target. He doubted Hugo would miss again.

Hugo fired again and the bullet grazed Raphael's shoulder. He bit his lip hard to stop himself from crying out. Raphael listened carefully as Hugo crossed the office floor. Stone. Rug. Then back onto stone. His heels once more clicked tellingly. Taking a best guess as to where Hugo was, Raphael launched out from behind the desk and slammed into him. He had been closer than he'd expected.

The Beretta fired off again with a deafening bang, missing its intended target, instead the bullet burst through one of the huge window panes behind Raphael. The glass shattered loudly on impact, fracturing into hundreds of knife-like pieces. Through the hole, a torrent of icy wind rushed into the office, whistling and shooting the smaller shards toward the two wrestling men.

Hooking his right leg behind one of Hugo's, Raphael forced the man off-balance and they tumbled to the ground. Tiny splinters of glass stuck into both of their bodies, tearing at their arms and spiking into their backs as they rolled across the floor. They stopped dangerously close to the gaping hole where the window had been. Out of the corner of his eye, Raphael saw the street below, without the safety of the glass barrier, it seemed much further away than usual. The streetlamps stood like tiny matchsticks.

Stabilising himself, Raphael stabbed his elbow into Hugo's upper arm, then slammed his hand into his exposed wrist. Screaming Hugo spasmed and lost his grip on the weapon. The gun flew across the carpet of broken shards, coming to a stop beside a sofa leg.

Enraged, Hugo swung wildly at Raphael, knocking him hard in the throat. Freeing himself from under Raphael's body, he made a manic lunge for the gun.

Raphael caught him by the ankles and dragged Hugo back toward him and the drop to the street below. The second he was close enough, Raphael released Hugo's ankles and threw his hands around his neck. He watched as the man's eyes bulged under the pressure, and the panic began to dilate his irises, as the air began to leave his body.

With the noise of the wind and the image of Kitty in the hospital tormenting his mind, Raphael no longer saw the man dying beneath his hands. Nor did he hear the person entering the room behind him.

'Stop,' Raphael heard Alec's voice and felt his hands on his shoulders. 'Stop, Raf.'

Raphael released Hugo, who lay choking and spluttering on the ground. The man stared aghast as Rosa's team entered the office. 'You are everything we hate. You betray your own kind,' he spat hoarsely at Raphael.

Raphael kicked him satisfyingly hard in the stomach.

After the woman with the steel-rimmed glasses had cleared them both, the room emptied and Raphael found himself alone. He stood staring out the remaining glass windows into the night, wondering why he had been given this life.

Down on the street below, Hugo, incarcerated in a high security van, was disappearing and with him the secrets of whoever he had been working for. Hugo would never cut a deal. He wasn't a stupid man. It was a death sentence from both sides of the war he had been fighting in. Raphael wasn't sure if the cartel would stop at this. There was no way of knowing, but he was pretty certain Nero would have some idea. Not that he could tell Nero about Rosa Amiton and that whole tangled mess he was now embroiled in. Hugo's words played over in his mind. Who even was his "*kind*" these days?

As though fate was answering, Rosa entered with Alec limping behind her. For the first time he wondered if she had something on his old comrade.

'You cut it fine,' Raphael said without turning.

Rosa didn't answer as expected. They all knew she had been hoping to see Raphael in all his killing glory. Then she could have held that over him. More leverage. More power. Insurance incase Kitty didn't last the night. After all, with Hugo's arrest for Hayes' death, that chip had been played and spent.

'You think Nechayev was working for the same cartel as Hugo?' Alec asked.

Rosa cut in, 'No, this is something far bigger. The drugs just funded the operation. A sideshow. What do you think, Mr Daring? Isn't this your area of expertise?'

Raphael shrugged, unwilling to speculate. He had his suspicions and he knew Amiton did as well, but they also knew, with their only credible source hanging from a light fitting, there was no way to find out. Nero wasn't much of a talker and besides, Daring's involvement had been placed as an unfortunate misunderstanding, a sorry coincidence that Vasili had been a client - for now at least.

'I reckon Vasili was never making it home,' Raphael offered for Alec's sake.

Rosa shrugged, 'Perhaps.' She headed for the door. 'We'll be in touch Mr Daring.'

Raphael turned, 'Remember my conditions. Three contacts. No family and Kitty is nothing to do with any of this anymore. Absolutely none of it. I mean it, this isn't the life she's going to lead.'

Rosa smiled, 'I know your conditions. You just focus on remembering mine.'

FORTY-FIVE

'He's spent the last three days here. Three,' The nurse rolled her eyes holding up the corresponding number of fingers. Removing the blood pressure cuff from Kitty's arm she continued, 'You want me to let him in sweetheart?'

Kitty smiled.

'Don't tire yourself though. Ok?' The nurse called over her shoulder as she left the room, shaking her head with amusement as she jotted down Kitty's heart scores.

'I'm so sorry,' Raphael began as soon as the door clicked shut behind him and they were alone. 'I—'

'I heard you've been waiting a while,' Kitty croaked. She didn't even recognise her own voice. It was cracked and shallow and she was caught for a second by the half-strangled sound.

Raphael perched on the side of the bed, staring hard at Kitty's bruises, lost for words that expressed what they did to him. She took his hand, drawing his gaze upward and privately, checking he was really there. The hallucinations had been exceedingly vivid.

'I hate to say I told you so, Mr Daring,' she smirked.

Raphael raised his eyebrows, momentarily stumped by her humour. 'What happened to let every fox take care of its own tail?' he replied after a moment.

Kitty started to laugh, but the answering pain in her ribs forced her to stop. She squeezed her eyes tight shut and focused on her breathing. She counted to eight before the pain began to subside.

'Let me get the nurse,' Raphael said, leaning to stand.

'No,' Kitty grabbed his arm, holding him with everything she had. 'Dear God, she'll never let you in again.' She flashed a smile before resting her head back on the pillow. Her eyelids felt heavy but she didn't want them to close. Not yet. She struggled to remain alert, the strain was visible.

'Kiti—'

'Stop.' She knew Raphael was only about to apologise, or call the nurse, and she didn't want to hear either. 'Just tell me about Vasili. Did you nail the bastard?' she let her eyes close, instead holding onto Raphael's hand for reassurance that he couldn't move without her knowing.

Raphael sighed, 'Someone got there first.'

'What?' Kitty's eyes opened. 'Who?' She heard a dark pain colour his words.

'They don't know and they won't find them.'

'Who's *they*?'

Raphael paused, 'The authorities.'

'The authorities?' Kitty repeated, awash with scepticism.

'I'm not sure what *they* want to be called,' he offered.

'But you were there. In the hotel room. You—'

'It was a one time thing.'

Kitty sat up again. Using her arms to support herself, she winced at the sting as the cannula snagged in her arm, 'So no more SAS-ing for you?' she joked trying to distract the pain which had returned to Raphael's expression.

'No. I think I prefer the suit.'

'But surely whoever *they* are, they can find who Vasili was working for? Whoever used Layal and—'

'No. Not these guys.'

Kitty registered the finality in Raphael's voice - he was certain.

'You know who they are?' she asked.

'I have my suspicions.'

'Who?' she pressed.

'Please don't let these facts become a part of your world.'

Kitty lay back, welcoming the support provided by the mound of carefully arranged pillows. 'They already are don't you think?' she mumbled.

Raphael broke free from Kitty's grasp. He stood and moved to the corner of the room. Kitty could hear him breathing deeply, the sound caught somewhere between frustration and exasperation, she couldn't tell. He didn't answer her question.

'So what about Hayes?' Kitty changed tack.

'He was a revenge killing I suppose.'

'For what?'

'A deal was made with the wrong people and he paid for it '

'Who killed him?'

'Kiti,' Raphael turned with a beseeching glance.

'Well do they know it wasn't you?'

He frowned, 'Yeh, they know.'

'So what about the charges?'

'They've been dropped. Hayes' killer was found and Vasili was shipping in the cocaine which financed the bomb. Layal appears to be a tragic victim. The trail ends there, but it doesn't stop at my door, and they have nothing to suggest it does.'

Kitty smiled encouragingly, willing Raphael back within touching distance, 'So you are an innocent man once again.'

Raphael visibly recoiled at her words and Kitty caught a look of utter bewilderment as he turned away again.

'I need to make a few calls... find my uncle,' he said as he made for the door.

'Ok. You're coming back though aren't you?' Kitty asked, but Raphael was already gone and did not hear the catch in her voice. Alone, Kitty felt her lip tremble.

Two hours had passed, dominated by a restless sleep when, on waking, Kitty heard the creak of the door opening. She smiled in anticipation, but it faded as soon as her eyes had fully opened. She placed a hand on the red emergency button that called the nurses' station.

'That won't be necessary,' a suited woman said with calm conviction.

'Who are you?' Kitty asked trying to sound strong, all the while keeping her hand hovering over the button beside the bed.

'My name is Rosa Amiton. I'm with the National Crime Agency.'

Kitty did not reposition her hand.

Rosa smiled, 'We have taken over Elliot's case. Investigating it properly this time.'

'So you know it wasn't Raphael?'

'Yes.'

Kitty relaxed a little, 'So what do you want with me?'

Rosa came to stand beside the bed, 'Officially I'm here to debrief you. You may have noticed that neither your guardian nor any of your friends have been here. We need to discuss your *car accident* and what you are going to tell them.'

Kitty hauled in the information. She had wondered what, if any, of her ordeal was going to become classified. 'And unofficially?'

Rosa smiled again, 'Unofficially, I would like to offer you a job.'

'At the NCA?' Kitty frowned.

'We investigate—'

'I know what you do, I just don't…' Kitty cut her off. She hadn't even begun to process the past let alone consider her future. Not regarding the graduate scheme nor Elliot's CPS law scheme offer, which now seemed much less appealing and had probably been rescinded anyway.

'You don't need to make any decisions right now, but a woman with your talents, that investigative drive could make a real difference in the world.'

'I tried that. No one listens.'

'I would,' Rosa replied, her tone forcefully assertive, 'Kitty. I'm a woman who has been investigating criminal activity for over thirty years. I understand how tough it is to be taken seriously.'

'Sorry,' Kitty croaked apologetically.

'No offence taken. Being honest with you, my team has a much wider remit than most. I think you might be quite impressed. Think about it.' Rosa turned for the door.

'I assume I can't tell anyone about this?' Kitty called.

Rosa laughed softly, 'See you're perfect. You look tired honey. I'll be in touch soon. Just rest up. You were so unbelievably brave.' With a wave, she disappeared.

It was dark when Raphael finally reappeared. The overhead lights had been switched off throughout the ward and visiting hours were long since over. The corridor was deserted, vacated of grieving relatives, and the patients, resting in darkened bays, lay for the most part quiet, exhausted from their days of procedures and pain. Under the wan glow of the LED nightlights, nurses occasionally could be heard at their station, responding to alarms which fired off periodically, signals from the restless machines which heaved and sighed as before.

Kitty was not sure how much time had passed. She had fallen asleep again after Rosa's visit, but remembered the nurses delivering her supper and evening painkillers. With four fractured ribs, a mass of heavy bruising in her abdomen and a concussion from where she had been beaten, the morphine was still a welcome addition to the other treatments the doctors were trying to repair the havoc Vasili's cocaine had wreaked.

Seeing him in the shadow of the doorway, no more than a familiar silhouette, all the descriptions he had ever been given seemed to roll from her subconscious.

Killer.

Criminal.

Brother.

Lover.

Soldier.

Saviour.

He had saved her life had he not?

Kitty watched as Raphael approached the bed, cautious as if he no longer trusted the ground he walked on.

Rosa's offer invaded her thoughts as he sat once more beside her. He stroked the back of her hand, and Kitty felt the enormity of what had happened and worse, what could happen. She knew that tomorrow, or the next day, or weeks from now she could make a decision that would see them on two diametrically opposed paths. With effort, Kitty forced the worries from her mind. For now, maybe for the first time, they were on the same one. He was there. He was alive, and so was she.

With silent tears spilling down her cheeks, Kitty pulled back the duvet and Raphael, understanding, lay next to her. She felt the warmth of his body and huddled against him, ignoring the dull ache it caused in her chest and the strain of the wires that were still attached to her.

'Quite some adventure,' she whispered, the words half lost to the encroaching sleep and the hum of the machines.

'Well you said you wanted one, Sherlock.' Raphael kissed the top of her head. Burying his face in Kitty's hair, he paused for a long second before returning his head to the pillows. He felt her smile into his shoulder, her tears dampening his shirt and he held her tighter.

Outside the temperature was falling swiftly with each passing hour. Across London tiny flakes of snow had begun to cascade down onto the empty, moonlit streets. By the time the first rays of the morning burned red across the city, the capital would be encased in a blanket of white.

Acknowledgements

Bonnie, I will be forever grateful for the hours you spent pouring over these words, questioning them, encouraging me throughout my recovery and, of course, for all of our debates about grammar! Thank you for all your help.

Thank you to all the beta readers who read Daring in all its forms — especially those who tackled it when it was still an unwieldy stack of A4 paper.

Thank you Brooke for making my soul smile throughout my illness and reminding me that big books are beautiful.

Finally, a special thank you is reserved for the readers of this novel. I hope you have enjoyed many hours of escapism and, if not, at least feel very pleased that you donated to a fabulous cause!

Printed in Great Britain
by Amazon